L.A EGERBLADH

Dream of the Dead

Even the dead can dream of living.

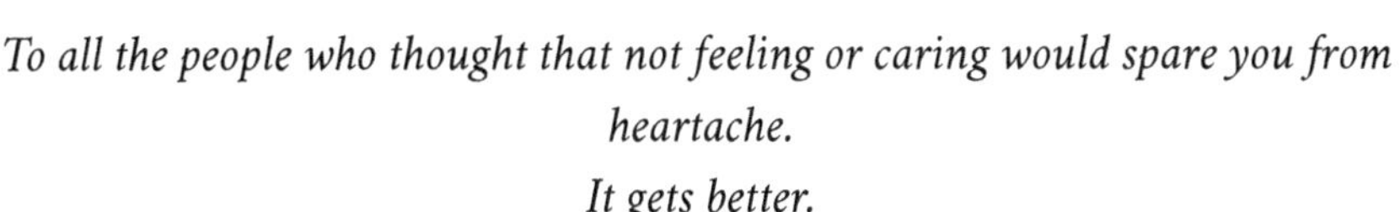

To all the people who thought that not feeling or caring would spare you from heartache.
It gets better.

Contents

Acknowledgement

Thank you to my friends, who have so kindly lend their names and likeness to some of these characters while also helping me develop this book to be the best it could be. This book would not have been possible without you. Thank you to my mother who has to constantly put up with me rambling about my newest story ideas.

Thank you to ANKBookdesigns for providing me with the gorgeous cover for my book.

And thank you to everyone who is currently reading this, you are making my dream come true.

Chapter 1

The sky was dark, the sun had been concealed by large and ominous clouds. Despite the gloom, the Town was alive with people, all going about their business, buying groceries for the evening meal or indulging in shopping for clothes most of them had no need of. Nothing was out of place, the houses were well maintained and painted in bright, vibrant colors, no trash could be seen laying around and music was softly playing, only adding to the quaint Town.

The only thing that stuck out like a sore thumb at the moment was a young looking girl. Her short dark hair was in stark contrast to her pale complexion. Her arms and chest were completely covered with tattoos, some of them looked pale and old while some of them were as alive and vibrant as the Town around her. Though, the tattoo that was most prominent was a thick line going around her throat like a necklace, it was impossible to miss. She was chubby and wore a knee length pale pink lace dress that looked older than herself, it was torn and faded at places and had dark stains that had been washed and washed but would never go away. She wore old leather boots that stopped just beneath her knees. Her almost golden eyes looked around, scanning the Town. If some townie came too close to her, they took a step back, almost like the girl sent out electric shocks, keeping people at bay. It was the tattoo on her throat that made everyone keep their distance, everyone knew what it meant. That she was not one of them. The only people that didn't seem openly frightened by her were the two women escorting her towards the large wall at the east side of

Town.

Liz scratched her neck and sighed, it was strange being back yet it almost seemed as if she'd never been away in the first place. Nothing seemed to have changed over the five months she'd been gone, the Town was as obnoxiously lively as before and the wall towered in the distance like a ugly landmark. The large wall was hard to miss but she knew most people tried to pretend it didn't exist. For them it was only a reminder of the stain on their society. For people like Liz, it was home.

The wall was at least fifty meters in height and impossible to climb. Liz knew because she'd tried more than once. Just to see if it was possible or not, she hadn't actually been trying to escape, there was nowhere to go anyway these days. As they came closer to the wall Liz could see at least twenty guards by the gate, it had more than doubled since she was here last. Something must have happened, even if it didn't look like it at first glance.

Just above the large gate leading into the Sanctuary was the number three. The amount of Sanctuaries across the globe was considerable at this point and according to the few news they received inside, they were increasing in number by the year.

Liz picked at the skin on her fingers by habit as they walked. When Liz and her escorts finally came to the entrance they were stopped as they saw Liz tattoo on her throat.

"Papers," one of the guards said with a rough voice.

Liz pulled out a crunched together piece of paper from her bra and gave it to the guard. He looked a little shocked but didn't say anything. Anyone could enter the Sanctuary if they wished, the paper was to make sure that Liz had the right to be in Town.

"Elizabeth Frost: Vampire. Can cause trouble but is a minimal danger to humans. This paper allows the owner the right to be in Town for two hours per day." The guard read it out loud.

Pause.

"This was issued a long time ago," the guard said slowly.

"I've been away," Liz said.

The guard's gaze narrowed and he exchanged glances with the man next to him.

"Everything's in order," one of the women behind Liz said. "She's been on official business."

The guard nodded quickly and gave Liz back her piece of paper.

"Just get a new one as soon as possible," the guard said. "The rules have changed."

Liz grabbed the piece of paper but didn't say anything as she shoved it down her bra again.

"Get going, it's full moon tonight and all residents in the Sanctuary must be inside by then," the guard said.

"It's only three p.m," Liz said, confused as she looked at the large clock in the middle of Town.

"Rules have changed," the guard repeated. "No residents of the Sanctuary are allowed outside after five p.m on the night of a full moon. No exceptions."

"Right," Liz muttered.

Before Liz was pushed through the large gate to the other side of the wall, the two women took her by the arm. Liz could feel their warmth and swallowed. She hadn't fed in a while.

"Lady Morgana appreciates your work," one of them said. "And we will make sure your paper is updated."

"Thanks," Liz said slowly but without much gratitude in her voice.

"And Lady Morgana would like to remind you that she might call on your favor again," the other one said.

"Yeah, yeah I know," Liz said. "You told me before."

"We wanted to make sure everything was crystal clear," the first one said.

"It is, don't worry," Liz said, annoyed. "I'm neither stupid nor forgetful."

They both nodded and then let go of Liz, and as they did so she could feel herself relaxing as well. She hadn't even noticed tensing up. Maybe it was the hunger growing steadily in her stomach or maybe it was the fact that those two women had always made her a little uneasy. The guards at the wall directed Liz through the entrance and pointed their guns at her but she knew they kept an eye out for anyone lurking on the direct other side of the gate as well. There had been more than one escape attempt when someone else was entering, but no one had ever succeeded. Most were shot instantly and even though a bullet wouldn't kill a vampire, a bullet filled with holy water would take it down long enough for back-up to arrive. But other creatures that lived inside the Sanctuary were mortal and one gunshot and they were dead.

The guards left Liz on the other side of the wall, retreated and closed the large gate behind them. Liz glanced behind her, the tall wall looming over her, making her feel impossibly small and insignificant.

The difference between the Town and the Sanctuary was palpable. No music could be heard, except from the vague tunes coming from the so-called Fun House; it had never looked fun to Liz. The streets were covered in litter, holes in the ground and stains that could be anything from blood to other bodily fluids. Most houses looked old and close to decrepit and had at least a few flaws, and that was just on the outside.

The only luxury place was the Fun House with its big neon signs and the scantily dressed people standing outside the building. The Fun House was nearest to the wall's entrance and for a good reason. Anyone visiting it from Town didn't want to go deep inside The Sanctuary to get to it. Even though the Sanctuary was despised in Town and no one would ever admit to ever having visited the Fun House, Liz knew that before she'd gone away, they'd had a steady stream of visitors and by the look of things, business was still good. Visitors usually had some form of bodyguards, just to be on the safe side. Even though most people inside the Sanctuary would never be stupid enough to attack a townie, people could do stupid things when desperate.

And things could get really desperate, really fast inside the Sanctuary.

But at this very moment, Liz could see no townie and she knew none would come tonight. Because as the guard had said, tonight was full moon night. The one night each month no townie dared step inside the Sanctuary. It could be dangerous any other night, but on the full moon night, it was practically suicide. But Liz knew she had a few hours left until nightfall, even though the sky was dark, the hour was not late.

Winter was coming and Liz loved that time of year. The sun rarely came out and if it did it was only out a few hours at the most. Which meant Liz could go out a lot more than in the summer and as she didn't sleep, those summer days locked away in a room with no windows became very long. Days like these were her favorite, the only thing that could make it better was if it started to rain and by the look of things, it wasn't impossible.

Liz walked with determined steps, even after five months away, walking towards the only bar in the Sanctuary felt as natural as ever. It wasn't just a bar, it was a meeting place, open at all hours, except of course on the full moon night. No one was open on the night of the full moon. The owner of the Bar was a friend of Liz, she'd been here even longer than she had and they'd known each other from before the Sanctuaries were put up.

Vendela had spent all her earnings over a lot of years to buy the Bar from some townies, and it was a rare thing to actually own something inside the Sanctuary. But even though Vendela technically owned the Bar, she was still supervised by some official townies, which Liz knew that Vendela loathed. Liz also knew that the Bar was one of the few good things about the Sanctuary and without it, it would be much harder for the townies to keep the peace inside the walls. The Bar offered free alcohol and blood, keeping the inhabitants of the Sanctuary drunk enough was a good way of keeping everyone calm and complacent. They kept the Sanctuary just miserable enough and just tolerable enough that not a lot of creatures had the strength to complain. And there weren't many that would listen to their complaints to begin with.

Liz passed the large Fun House and she could swear it looked even bigger and more extravagant than before. Or maybe she'd just been away too long, even if it felt like she'd been here yesterday. As she passed it she heard whistling and then a voice speaking to her.

"Hello there beautiful," a woman's voice spoke. "There's a 50% full moon discount tonight, why don't you join me up in one of the rooms where it's safe and warm?"

Liz turned her head towards the voice and what she saw actually surprised her. It was an unusually tall and chubby woman with dark skin. She was scantily clad with long, curly black hair and dark seductive eyes.

"Ami?" Liz asked low.

Ami was silent for a moment.

"Do I know you darling?" She asked slowly with uncertainty clear in her voice but trying to keep the light attitude.

Liz took a step forward.

"It's me, Liz," she said.

The act Ami was putting up was immediately dropped and Liz could see her face soften as a frown grew on her face.

"Liz?" Ami said, confused. "But you're dead."

"Says who?" Liz asked jokingly. "I feel pretty alive. Well, I mean… I'm dead alright, but I've been dead for a very long time so that's not exactly news."

Ami was silent for a moment.

"You've been gone for five months," Ami said, shocked.

"Someone's been keeping track of time," Liz said.

"Well, that happens when your friend goes missing," Ami said, and Liz could hear that Ami was getting upset. "And no one's been gone that long from The Sanctuary unless they're dead."

"Well, I'm not dead… Deader," Liz said.

Ami stared at her in disbelief.

"I'm not a shapeshifter," Liz said. "I promise. It's just little old me."

"Where have you been?" Ami finally asked.

Liz shrugged.

"Just… a little all over the place," Liz said evadingly.

Ami glanced behind herself at the Fun House and then walked closer to Liz. At a closer look Liz could see that Ami's face was caked in make-up, it was so thick that it almost looked like a second layer of skin but Liz could still see how tired she looked. It was a strange sight as she'd never worn make-up as long as Liz had known her. Maybe because it was impossible to get a hold of it inside the Sanctuary and it was ridiculously expensive if you got a hold of it in Town. It just wasn't worth it for creatures like themselves. Ami looked at her, suspicion still clear in her eyes.

"No one leaves the Sanctuary for that long, even less to just walk around all over the place," Ami said. "No one leaves the Sanctuary… Alive."

Liz rubbed her eyes. She was tired and not really in the mood to have this conversation.

"When did you start working in the Fun House?" Liz asked, changing the subject.

Ami rubbed her neck.

"It's not that bad," Ami said, evading the actual question. "I get food, a roof over my head and I get some spare change. I even got a pass to go into Town!"

"How long?" Liz asked again.

"Three months or so," Ami said and shrugged.

"Three months or so" Liz thought. Ami knew exactly how long Liz had been gone but apparently had only an idea of how long she'd been working in the Fun House. Liz found that interesting.

"Don't judge me," Ami said.

"I'm not," Liz said.

"Yes you are," Ami said. "I know how much you hate the Fun House but you've been away and things have changed!"

"I have only been gone for five months," Liz said.

Ami scoffed.

"Right… You never had any concept of time," Ami said.

"That happens when you're immortal," Liz said. "Time becomes kind of irrelevant."

"Yeah well many of us aren't immortal," Ami said. "And time still passes and for most of us, five months is a lot."

"Okay," Liz said. "I didn't think the first thing to happen when I got back would be that I got scolded."

Ami looked down and Liz could see that her words had hit their mark.

"I'm sorry," Ami said. "I am happy to see you alive but…"

"Things have changed," Liz said with a sigh. "Everyone keeps saying that."

Ami looked over her shoulder, a flash of worry on her face.

"I have to get back to work," Ami said low.

"There aren't many customers tonight," Liz said.

"More than you'd think," Ami said. "The Fun House is protected, it's a safe place during the full moon. A lot of creatures seek refuge here."

"For a price," Liz said.

There was a split second of silence before Ami spoke again.

"Of course," Ami said, with a tinge of sadness in her voice. "Nothing is free."

Liz didn't say anything in response, simply turned around and left Ami outside the Fun House.

"Don't judge me Liz!" Ami shouted after her.

"I'm not," Liz muttered to herself. "I've sold my body in more ways than one."

Chapter 2

Liz walked into an alley, the Sanctuary had many of them and it was easy to get lost between the buildings, alleys and narrow streets. But Liz had had years learning this place from the inside out and even though the Bar was in the heart of all the alleys, she had no problem finding it. But as Liz made her way down the streets she noticed how few creatures were out, in fact, she hadn't seen anyone except Ami. Which was strange, even if it was a full moon night. The moon wouldn't rise for another couple of hours and creatures should still be everywhere. How much had actually changed?

When Liz finally came to the Bar she stopped in her tracks, what she saw actually shocked her. The Bar, which had stood there for years, was now nothing more than ashes on the ground. It had burnt down entirely and by the looks of it, it had happened some time ago.

Liz looked closely at her surroundings, if she hadn't been so sure this was the place, she would have thought she'd taken a wrong turn somewhere. Liz was hit with a sudden and overwhelming feeling that everyone else was gone, that she was the only one left in here. But she reminded herself she'd just met Ami and she would have told her if anything of that magnitude had happened. But where were they all? And what had happened to the Bar?

Someone suddenly put a hand on Liz's shoulder and she reacted instinctively, she was perhaps more surprised than anything else that someone had managed to sneak up on her without being heard but with the many smells and sudden screams in the Sanctuary, it was sometimes hard to distinguish how far away someone was.

Liz gripped the hand on her shoulder and twisted it around and shoved the person into the wall. The person yelled out in pain as Liz wasn't very careful and didn't care that she was much stronger than mortal creatures. This person was at least a head taller than Liz but she had them pinned to the wall in an iron grip.

"P-Please let me go," they whimpered.

Liz was so close to them that she could smell them, and they smelt of blood and sweat. They were so alive. They must have scraped their face as she'd pushed them against the wall because the fragrance of blood was in the air. For a second she forgot her surroundings and all she could hear was the beating of their heart. It was irregular and quickened, they were afraid.

"I wasn't… Gonna hurt you," they stammered. "Please."

Liz blinked as the pounding of their heart stopped echoing in her ears and she loosened her grip of them a little, but only a little.

"Who are you?" Liz asked seriously.

"J-Just wanted to know if you were alright," they said.

Liz took a closer look and she didn't recognize them, which made her suspicious.

"I haven't seen you here before," Liz said.

"I'm a new resident," they said. "I… I thought you were new as well… I saw you enter and talk to that prost-…"

"That girl is my friend," Liz said and put a little more pressure on their arm. "And I'm not new here. I've just been away."

A small yelp escaped their lips before they were silent for a moment, like they were shocked hearing that.

"Okay, I'm sorry alright," they said. "Please."

Liz narrowed her eyes but she finally let go of them and backed away a little. They sighed in relief and turned around, rubbing the part of their wrist where Liz's iron grip had been. There was already a bruise forming and she could also see small drops of blood from the scratches on their face from the impact with the wall.

The person was older than Liz, or well, they looked older than her. Mid thirties with brown hair and soft caramel eyes. They were tall and muscular with dark skin and they towered over Liz, but their large eyes made them look harmless and kind. But Liz knew looks were deceiving.

"I'm Gray," they said slowly.

"I don't care," Liz said bluntly.

"I don't get an 'I'm sorry?,'" Gray asked low.

"I have nothing to say sorry for," Liz said, her tone of voice not changing.

Gray looked a little confused.

"Okay," they said slowly. "Well, if you're wondering what happened to the Bar, apparently it burned down a couple of months ago."

"I can see that," Liz said.

"They built a new one," Gray said. "Did you know that?"

Liz was silent for a moment.

"Where?" Liz asked.

Gray raised an eyebrow.

"Why should I tell you?" Gray asked. "You're not very nice."

"What are you, five years old?" Liz scoffed. "I have no obligation to be nice. Especially not to people creeping up on me."

"I have no obligations to be nice to people attacking me," Gray replied.

"Then why are you still here? Why are you still talking to me?" Liz said.

"You're just a kid," Gray said carefully.

Liz couldn't stop herself from laughing and Gray looked startled at her sudden outburst.

"That's funny," Liz said, still snickering.

"What is?" Gray asked carefully.

"You think I'm alive?" Liz asked. "You think I'm human?"

Gray swallowed.

"But you look-…" they started.

"Ever heard of vampires?" Liz asked.

"Yeah but…" Gray said.

"But?" Liz asked.

"They don't usually look like you do," Gray said low.

"Oh, I'm sorry, should I be wearing all black with a cape? Should I stink of decay and blood?" Liz asked, slightly annoyed. "I didn't know there was a dress code I had to follow."

Gray looked slightly embarrassed and Liz sighed.

"I'm going to leave now," Liz said. "Don't follow me."

Liz turned around and started walking, to where she wasn't entirely sure. Gray had said they had built a new Bar, she just had to find it. It couldn't be too hard, the Sanctuary wasn't endless and exploring the whole place didn't take more than a day or two and that was if you were slow.

"The Bar is to the right," Gray shouted after her. "You can't miss it."

Liz stopped as she heard their voice and came to the crossing, where she could either turn left or right and she almost wanted to turn left out of spite. Besides, who was to say that they were even telling the truth? Maybe they were leading her into some sort of danger, not that Liz ever was in much danger because of what she was. Maybe they were just pretending to be kind and acting weak, it wouldn't have been the first time someone had done that.

But in the end, Liz turned right. Not because she trusted them or thought they were telling the truth, but because she had nothing to lose. And if they were leading her into danger, at least she would have something to do.

This part of the Sanctuary was probably the one Liz knew the least. There were only residential apartments in this area and most of them were unlivable by now and Liz's apartment was on the other side of the Sanctuary, so she'd had very little reason to go here before. But she soon heard loud voices talking and it sounded like she got closer to the source with each step. Finally she saw a building that stood out from all the others, simply because it was clean and whole. The sign above the building said "Bar" and it reminded Liz of the Fun House, which gave her an uneasy feeling. It looked quite similar to the old one, except it lacked the rustic feeling and had a touch of extravagance. Even if it had changed she almost felt something in her chest, something reminding her of warmth. An echo or shadow perhaps of a feeling she remembered from long ago.

She'd spend most of her time in the Sanctuary in the Bar, it was the true sanctuary in this place. And seeing that it wasn't gone completely made her… Happy.

Liz walked towards it and entered, she was met by strong lights, laughter and a pungent smell of alcohol. No one seemed to care that Liz had entered and as she looked around she saw many faces she recognized but quite a few new ones as well. The Bar seemed more crowded than usual, almost every table was occupied, so this was where everyone was hiding. Then Liz saw Vendela standing behind the bar table and a faint smile spread across her lips.

Vendela was a young looking woman with short light brown hair and bangs. She was tall and slender but very muscular, not someone you wanted to get into a fight with. She had small gray eyes and a structural face which made her look a little harsh in certain lights. She was wearing a black tank top and had an old dirty apron wrapped around her waist. She looked exactly how Liz had remembered her, and Liz had thought about her more than once when she'd been gone.

Vendela was busy cleaning glasses as Liz walked up to the bar and leaned against the table, trying to conceal the smile on her face but Vendela still hadn't even looked at her. She probably was so used to all of these people walking in here that she barely took notice of them anymore.

"I'll take the usual," Liz said, trying to contain a smirk.

"The usua-…?" Vendela said but stopped mid sentence.

When Vendela looked up she gasped in surprise and dropped the glass she was holding. It fell to the floor and shattered into a million little pieces. The sound of the glass breaking caught everyone's attention and for a moment everyone was staring towards the bar in silence. But as nothing else happened and Liz kept her back to the rest of the room, soon everyone continued their conversations and everything went back to how it had been moments before.

"You look like you've seen a ghost," Liz said jokingly.

"I am seeing one," Vendela whispered, staring at Liz with large eyes.

Liz smiled weakly.

"Shouldn't you take care of the glass?" Liz asked.

Vendela ignored her and leaned against the table, making the space between the two almost non-existent. It took all of Liz's self restraint to not close the gap entirely, five months wasn't a long time but it was a long time away from Vendela. The change from Gray to Vendela was extreme, while Gray had been alive with pheromones and warm blood, Vendela was as cold as Liz was. Vendela looked angry, which wasn't what Liz had expected.

"Where the hell have you been?" Vendela whispered.

"I thought you'd be happy to see me," Liz said in a normal tone of voice.

Vendela shook her head in disbelief.

"You disappeared," Vendela said. "I thought you were dead."

"Okay, I understand that-…" Liz started but was interrupted.

"No, you don't understand," Vendela said seriously. "Where have you been?"

Liz shrugged.

"Just-…" Liz said.

"Don't lie," Vendela said. "I've known you long enough to know when you're about to lie."

Liz scoffed.

"You don't get to act like nothing after being away for five months," Vendela said.

"How come everyone knows exactly how long I've been gone?" Liz asked exasperated.

"What do you mean?" Vendela asked, confused.

"I met Ami on the way here," Liz said.

Vendela was silent and looked away.

"What? Liz asked. "Why'd you make that face?"

"Nothing," Vendela said quickly. "Just haven't seen her in a while, that's all."

Vendela looked back and stared right into Liz's eyes.

"Don't change the subject," Vendela said. "You always do that when you don't want to talk about something."

Liz looked away and sighed. Vendela made a short pause before she started to speak again.

"Did they take you?" Vendela asked, her voice now as low as a whisper.

Liz frowned and turned back.

"What?" Liz asked. "Who are they?"

Vendela was about to open her mouth to answer when they heard voices from the corner of the room.

"My wife's cheating on me?!" An upset voice spoke. "I don't have a wife! You're a fake, I want my money back!"

A table was flipped and slammed into the floor with a thud, alongside smaller things clattering onto the wooden surface. Liz and Vendela looked over at the spectacle and Liz saw that the subject of this man's anger was a girl, perhaps twenty years old with long blond hair but with dark roots, it was obviously colored. Her green eyes had speckles of yellow in them and she was tall and very skinny, she almost looked like a gust of air would carry her away. As the man had knocked over her table, she didn't look scared or shocked, just a veil of confusion over her face. The man raised his hand, ready to strike the girl. Liz sighed, almost regretting what she was about to do even before she'd done it.

"Don't," was all Vendela said and shook her head.

But Liz had already moved and before the man could strike the girl, Liz gripped his wrist. She could feel the warmth seeping through his skin into her and he turned, a look of shock on his face. First the shock was because someone with hands cold as the dead had gripped him but then when he recognized her, his eyes widened even more and it went from shock to fear.

"L-Liz," he stammered. "I-It can't be."

Liz didn't answer him, just stared at him with cold eyes.

"It's not possible, y-you're dead," he continued, clearly in shock.

Liz tightened her grip on his wrist and he winced in pain. Silence had fallen in the Bar and now all eyes were on her.

"Don't you all have anything better to do than stare?!" Liz yelled at them.

Everyone looked away and started whispering instead. Liz turned back to the man who's name she knew was Dan, she'd seen him from time to time in the Bar, picking fights with whoever he could.

"S-She tricked me!" Dan yelled in pain.

Liz looked to the girl who was now staring at her with fascination, not fear, in her eyes. Liz frowned slightly but turned her attention back to Dan who by now was down on his knees. Liz could see the vein in his neck and for a few seconds all she did was stare at it, because she knew a tiny little cut would expose the warm red blood within. Liz shook it off, making herself concentrate again.

"You're new," Liz said towards the girl.

She nodded excitedly.

"My name is-..." she started.

"Don't care," Liz said. "Did you trick him?"

"No, no, I didn't!" The girl said. "I just... get it mixed up sometimes."

"Get what mixed up?" Liz asked, confused.

"Present, future and past of course," the girl said and smiled. "It's very tricky sometimes, I confuse them all the time."

Liz frowned.

"What are you?" Liz asked.

"Future seer and I dabble in witchcraft," the girl said.

"I want my money back!" Dan complained.

Liz tightened her grip until she felt his bones break in her hand. Dan screamed an ear piercingly loud scream and finally Liz let go of him completely.

"No one likes a crybaby," Liz said. "Don't touch her again. Don't touch anyone again or I'll come for the rest of your bones."

Liz had no intention of making sure Dan never touched anyone again, people fought and died in here all the time. Liz just knew that the threat, the promise of pain, would keep him from hurting someone that wouldn't or couldn't defend themselves, at least for a time.

Not that she cared if people got hurt, Liz told herself. She'd only acted and stopped him because... Because she felt like it. Because her interference might have started a bigger fight and she had some anger she needed to let out.

As soon as Dan fell to the ground, screaming like he was being murdered, Liz knew there would be no fight. Some of Dan's friends quickly ran up to his side and dragged him out of the Bar, none of them seemed to want anything to do with Liz.

"That wasn't very nice," Vendela said from behind the bar. "And not good for business."

"Thank you," the girl said.

"Don't want your thanks," Liz muttered.

The girl reached out her right hand towards Liz, but Liz hesitated. She saw that the girl was wearing a glove on her left and the other glove was laying on the ground.

"How exactly do you see people's future?" Liz asked suspiciously.

The girl smiled lightly before she picked up her glove from the floor and put it on.

"It doesn't hurt," the girl said. "You pick up faster than most."

"Yeah, I've been around for a while," Liz said.

Liz then turned her back on the girl and went back to the bar where Vendela was shaking her head.

"Since when do you care about 'good business'?" Liz asked. "And would you rather I just stand and watch as he hurt her? Isn't it you who always says I should do something?"

"No, but knowing you, I knew you wouldn't just stop him, the few times you actually do something you always go too far," Vendela said. "And I care since I have to care nowadays."

"What do you mean?" Liz asked.

"You couldn't have chosen a worse five months to be gone," Vendela said with a deep sigh.

"What happened to the Bar?" Liz asked. "I saw the remains."

"No, no, no, no," Vendela repeated. "You don't get to ask the questions."

"Come on," Liz said. "Are you really gonna stay mad at me?"

"You have been gone for five months and for all I know you just left," Vendela said, her voice cold. "Don't know how you'd escape from here, but I don't really care either. You just disappeared, not a single word from you."

"I didn't exactly leave," Liz said low.

"Tell me what happened," Vendela said.

"It's not important," Liz said and shrugged.

Vendela laughed out of frustration.

"It's like talking to a brick wall," Vendela said more to herself than to Liz.

"Where I've been isn't important," Liz said. "What's happened here is."

Vendela was silent for a moment, contemplating what Liz just had said.

"You should find a place to hide," Vendela said. "I'm going to close up soon."

"Fine," Liz said. "I'll come back tomorrow when you've hopefully calmed down a little. For being dead you're awfully emotional."

"For being dead you're awfully frustrating," Vendela said in response.

Liz couldn't help but smile at her comment and as she looked around the Bar she hadn't noticed that almost everyone else had already left. Liz stretched her back slightly and made herself ready to leave but before she'd gotten far Vendela spoke.

"You're an idiot," Vendela said. "But don't get yourself killed."

"You too," Liz said with a faint smile as she exited the bar.

Chapter 3

Liz came out into the empty alley, looked up into the sky and found it empty of any stars. The only thing worse than a full moon night, was a cloudy full moon night. Not seeing the werewolves clearly roaming the streets was not optimal for survival, even from indoors.

"Do you have a place to stay during the full moon?"

Turning around, Liz saw the girl from before. It didn't happen often that people sneaked up on her or surprised her but now it had happened twice within a few hours. The girl looked at her calmly, her hands behind her back and a strangely neutral facial expression.

"'I'm not a fool," Liz said with a sigh. "I have an apartment here."

"Oh, that's nice," the girl simply said.

The girl did not make any signs of walking away, she just stared at Liz.

"Do you want something?" Liz asked, trying not to sound too harsh.

"Not really," the girl said with a shrug. "I have space in my apartment if you don't have anywhere to go."

"I just said I do," Liz said.

"Yes, you did," the girl agreed.

"You're strange, you know that right?" Liz said.

"Yes," the girl said. "And my name is Katarina."

"Didn't ask," Liz said dismissively.

"Do you mind if I walk with you?" Katarina asked. "I'm still learning how to make my way through this place."

Liz was silent for a moment and she was a little surprised how calm this girl was, after all it was soon night and the moon would rise and she was all alone in an empty alley with a vampire. The girl looked like the type of creature that didn't last very long in the Sanctuary. They were taken advantage of. The stronger, often vampires, took advantage of weaker creatures. The craving for blood was a strong force and vampires who were usually kind and gentle could in a second turn into something unrecognizable from the person they were before. Then there were of course the sadistic vampires and creatures in general that just relished in hurting others, but Katarina looked untouched.

Though Liz had no idea how long she'd been in here, maybe it was only her first week or so? But the tattoo around Katarina's neck was smooth and healed, which told her that she'd been here at least for a few weeks. Perhaps the reason Katarina had asked to walk with Liz was because she thought Liz would protect her, because of what she'd done inside the Bar. Which wouldn't be the case, Liz wouldn't fight a horde of werewolves or creatures for this girl. But Katarina had said nothing about protection, only that she didn't know her way around here yet. The question then was if she was stupid or simply naive? But she was no threat to Liz, so walking beside her didn't bother her and could maybe even benefit her.

"Fine, join me," Liz said. "Then maybe you can tell me what the hell's been happening here."

Katarina nodded and they started walking.

"Where is your apartment then?" Liz asked.

"It's quite close to the gate," Katarina said.

"Good, means it's not a big detour for me," Liz said and glanced around.

"Would you mind if I touched you?" Katarina asked. "I find it easiest to get to know a person that way."

"Don't touch me," Liz said bluntly.

"Do you have something to hide?" Katarina asked with a vague smile on her lips. "Most people do."

"Yeah, no surprise there," Liz said sarcastically. "People don't like sharing their deepest darkest secrets, shocking. "

"And you being an immortal vampire, I suppose you have more than a few dark secrets," Katarina said calmly.

Liz laughed low.

"You're not scared little miss human?" Liz asked, Katarina's heart was beating steadily and calmly, not even a touch of fear strangely enough. "Being all alone on full moon night with a vampire?"

"Not really," Katarina said. "Even if I don't touch people I can feel their energy. You're not going to hurt me."

Liz didn't say anything, those words had actually left her speechless. Liz cleared her throat before she spoke again.

"So tell me, what's been happening?" Liz asked.

"I've only been here for little over a month," Katarina said.

A month. Katarina had been here a month but seemed unharmed and unbothered by the circumstance she'd found herself in, which unnerved Liz a little even if she would never admit it.

"But you seem bright enough to notice things," Liz said and cleared her voice.

"A compliment," Katarina said. "How nice."

"Just tell me what you know," Liz said and rolled her eyes.

"I know creatures have been disappearing," Katarina said. "Not a lot of them. But a few here and there. I also know there was an escape attempt, though that was before I got here so I don't know much about that. No one talks about it."

"An escape attempt?" Liz asked.

Katarina nodded.

"It failed," Katarina said. "That's all I know. They don't like to talk about it."

"*Obviously it failed,*" Liz thought.

"What about the disappearances?" Liz asked.

"So few and so far apart no one noticed it at first," Katarina said. "But they don't come back. Some say it's the resistance getting creatures out of here, a few at a time. Others say it's townies coming in and taking them, for what purpose I don't know."

"Wait what, what resistance?" Liz asked, stopping them both in their tracks.

"It's not public or anything," Katarina said. "But there are whispers of a rebellion and that the escape attempt was just the beginning."

Liz shook her head in disbelief but Katarina just smiled lightly.

"Ah, there is my apartment," Katarina said and pointed towards it. "You're welcome to visit me if you wish."

"Yeah, sure," Liz said as if the thought in itself was ridiculous, she had no intention of seeing this girl again except maybe passing her on the street.

Katarina ran towards the apartment, it was small and looked strangely newly renovated. Liz wondered how Katarina had afforded to do that.

Liz followed the girl with her gaze for a few seconds, then walked down the street, towards her own apartment thinking that it would be nice with some peace and quiet. Not that full moon night ever was quiet.

It was starting to get late and Liz did not want to be caught outside when the full moon rose. It wasn't a pleasant experience.

Her apartment had been a single room but she didn't really need more, just a place to sit, a roof over her head and she was satisfied. As she passed houses she noticed some of them looked worse than when she'd left, whole walls and roofs were missing. Liz knew that the werewolves were one of the biggest reasons why the Sanctuary was in the state it was in, they tore down doors and even walls. Inside was safer than outside, but it was by no means safe.

Liz came to the building where her apartment was and she sighed deeply. Her apartment had been on the top floor and she could see that the whole roof was gone and the wall facing the street was completely missing. It was just her luck. Liz looked around, her dark vision helping her see because there were no street lights to guide her way. With the roof and wall gone, it was not safe to spend the night there anymore. Even if it was on the top floor, werewolves had no problem climbing.

Liz scoffed and turned her gaze down the streets towards Katarina's apartment. She had known. Liz had no idea how, but Katarina had known that her apartment was in ruins. It explained her strange behavior, but Liz had made sure that Katarina had not touched her. Who knew what would happen if she actually did. Not to speak of the fact that Katarina would never invite Liz into her apartment if she knew of some of the things Liz had done.

Liz reminded herself that she was on a tight time schedule and that she had to move unless she wanted to get in the way of the werewolves. Liz contemplated whether she should go up to her apartment or deal with that in the morning. She had no idea how long ago it had been destroyed so she didn't know if any of her things would still be there. It had to have been looted as soon as someone noticed no one lived there anymore. Liz decided against her better judgment and quickly ran up all the stairs to her apartment.

As soon as she came to the top floor she noticed an odor in the air, one of decay. The smell became stronger the closer Liz came to her apartment door. Her door was ajar and Liz stopped and just stood outside for a moment. She hadn't seen anyone in there from below but she hadn't had a good look of the whole apartment from down there, she'd just seen that it looked fairly destroyed.

Liz slowly pushed open the door with her foot and the smell of death hit her like a wall. Inside her tiny apartment she saw four dead bodies, all of them laid on their stomach and their clothes were covered in dry blood. From where Liz was standing, their skin looked paper thin and almost like someone had poured acid over them. If Liz had been human, she would probably have been standing in the corridor, throwing up at this moment. Instead, now Liz just frowned in disgust.

Liz walked up to one of the corpses, they were laying very close to one another, almost like they'd been clinging to the others in their last moments of life. With her foot she slipped the corpse around so she could see its face. It was not someone Liz recognized but she recognized what had happened to her. She had seen it once or twice before and it was always this messy. The skin around the corpse's mouth had been pulled back, showing two rows of razor sharp teeth. The vampire's mouth and neck was also covered in old blood.

"Disgusting," Liz said low to herself.

Liz saw the many bite marks on the vampire's neck and she didn't need to inspect any of the other vampires, she knew what had occurred.

Drinking the blood of another vampire in small doses was like a drug. There was something sexual and addictive about it, it brought a high of joy like nothing else, but in large doses, it was lethal. It was dead blood after all.

More than two teaspoons and it would render a vampire incapacitated for at least a few hours. Though, sometimes that was the point.

Liz walked past the dead vampires and as she'd thought, the whole apartment was ransacked, nothing was left. But the floor was fairly intact which gave Liz some hope. She walked up to the right corner and lifted one of the floorboards. Liz sighed in relief, it was still there. A small and extremely old wooden box laid beneath the floor, just waiting to be picked up.

Liz grasped it with her right hand and opened it with her left, everything was still inside as well. Liz looked at all the small jewelry pieces, and the pieces of paper laying safely inside the box and the shadow of a smile crossed her lips. She knew she was being silly and sentimental and she would probably rather die than let anyone see this box. She had to keep reminding herself to be cold and to not care, her life was too long to be seen as weak by others. They would take advantage of that.

Liz quickly closed the box and she cursed herself for not having anywhere to put it. She loved this dress but it was annoying that it didn't have any pockets. Liz looked over at the corpses and saw that one of them had a bag laying beside them. It looked looted as well, she was not the first one here since those vampires had died. But the bag could still serve its purpose, and besides, a dead vampire had no use of it. Liz picked it up and tipped it over, just to be on the safe side and the only thing that fell out was a picture of a pretty young lady with golden hair. For a split second, Liz was overwhelmed with sadness. Was this picture of one of the dead vampires or of a loved one? Then she reminded herself that she didn't care. She reminded herself that she could physically not feel sadness anymore or anything else for that matter. She was just remembering those feelings from when she'd been alive. That was all.

Liz shoved her box inside the bag and then left her apartment.

Chapter 4

As Liz once again entered the streets, she knew it was getting dangerously late. And even though Liz wasn't scared she ran all the way to Katarina's apartment, she had no intentions of fighting werewolves tonight. When Liz came to what she assumed was Katarina's residence, it looked more like a shop than an apartment. There was a sign above the door saying "Magical and Mystery Stuff – I can tell your future". It was not the greatest sign Liz had ever seen but it got the message across at least.

Liz stood outside the door for a few seconds, almost laughing at herself. Not long ago when she'd parted with Katarina, she'd thought she'd never speak with her again, certainly not asking to stay in her apartment for protection.

Liz raised her hand and only hesitated for a split second and before she even touched it, the door opened, almost like Katarina had been waiting for her.

"Hello again," Katarina said and smiled.

Liz just stared for a moment, her hand still raised as if she was going to knock on the door any second.

"You knew," Liz finally said, lowering her hand.

"Knew what?" Katarina said, a smirk lingering on her lips. "That you were outside my door?"

"My apartment is destroyed." Liz said, a hint of annoyance.

Katarina had known that her apartment was destroyed so she had just been waiting for Liz to come and beg for a safe place. It infuriated her.

"Oh really? I am sorry to hear that," Katarina said, her voice still as flat as before.

Katarina's eyes drifted to the bag around Liz's shoulder. It was hard to miss, it didn't fit in with the rest of her clothes at all and it was obvious that she'd picked it up somewhere along the way as she hadn't had it when they'd parted ways. But Liz had no intent on mentioning it and if Katarina asked, she'd just lie.

"Does your offer still stand?" Liz asked slowly.

"I almost thought you'd be too proud to come," Katarina admitted.

"You don't know anything about me," Liz said.

"Yet," Katarina said with a shadow of a smile on her lips.

Liz was silent and didn't move.

"You have to invite me in," Liz said and looked at the threshold. "Curses are sticklers for rules you know."

Katarina looked her up and down and Liz almost thought for a moment that she wasn't going to allow her inside, that she had just been toying with her.

"Please come inside," Katarina said and stepped aside. "And does being a vampire really count as a curse? Some call it a kind of disease."

Liz walked inside the shop and was met by quite a large room filled with strange things, some looked like plants while others were clearly none organic. Liz had always stayed away from witches and magic, and for very good reasons. So she did not recognize much.

In the left upper corner was a small kitchen and a large dinner table standing to the right side of the room with a few chairs around it. A small and uncomfortable looking sofa was crammed into the bottom left corner and a bookshelf filled to the brink with old looking books. Liz also noticed two doors leading into other rooms, probably a bedroom and a bathroom.

"Oh no, it's a curse alright," Liz said, still letting her eyes wander around the room.

"Can you have more than one curse?" Katarina asked curiously and walked up to a shelf.

Liz froze in place for a split second, her eyes narrowing as her gaze followed Katarina closely. That comment made her shiver but she quickly tried to shake off.

"Well, you're the witch," Liz said slowly. "You tell me."

"I am not technically a witch," Katarina said and picked up two small jars from the shelf. "I only started with magic a year ago."

"Well, you have magic," Liz said. "That classifies as a witch to me."

Katarina put down the two jars on the table and brought forth a large bowl as well.

"I think most people have some magic in them," Katarina said, not glancing over at Liz once. "They just need to access it, that is all."

"If that's true, the Sanctuaries would be a lot more crowded," Liz said and picked at the skin around her finger nails lightly.

There was a short pause.

"Apparently since you've been gone, there has been an increase in inhabitants," Katarina said.

Liz sighed, she'd known it was only a matter of time before things escalated, and if she was being honest, it had taken longer than she'd expected. But it also meant it would be over soon.

"What are you doing?" Liz asked instead.

"I am making a protective seal to put on the door and windows," Katarina said. "It keeps the werewolves away."

"How old are you?" Liz asked.

"Nineteen," Katarina said and started mixing the ingredients together.

Nineteen. The number spun on repeat in Liz's head and it wasn't until she noticed that Katarina had stopped what she'd been doing and was watching her intently that she managed to clear her throat and speak again.

"Did you spend time in another Sanctuary before this one?" Liz asked, trying to keep her voice steady.

"Does the number nineteen mean anything to you?" Katarina asked curiously instead of answering.

"No." Liz said a little too fast. "Answer my question."

Katarina shrugged lightly and turned her attention back to the protective seal.

"No," Katarina simply said. "I lived in Town before this."

"You're very calm about all of this for someone who's spent their entire life with humans," Liz said slowly.

"I don't see any point in panicking," Katarina said. "And besides, in here I don't have to hide."

"You don't miss it?" Liz asked.

"Oh, of course I do," Katarina said. "I miss my parents more than anything really."

"Did they turn you in?" Liz asked.

Katarina was quiet for a moment.

"How hungry are you?" Katarina asked, ignoring Liz's question.

"What?" Liz said, confused.

Katarina turned to Liz.

"I need blood for the protective seal," Katarina said. "So how hungry are you?"

"I'm fine," Liz said.

"Please don't lie to me," Katarina said calmly. "It will make things… complicated."

"I can control myself," Liz said.

"Now you can, yes," Katarina said. "But can you if you smell my fresh blood?"

"Whatever you've read or heard," Liz said annoyed. "Most vampires aren't completely without restraint."

"Okay," Katarina said. "I trust you."

"Well, I wouldn't go that far really," Liz said almost a little too quickly. "I haven't fed in two days, another day and perhaps then… Perhaps then I couldn't control myself."

Katarina nodded in understanding.

"You can put down your bag if you want to," Katarina said. "And feel free to sit down wherever you want."

Liz sat down on a chair around the table that Katarina was mixing the protective seal on, but she kept the bag still on her shoulder. Katarina picked up a thin needle and quickly pricked the skin on her pointer finger, she winched low in pain from the sting. A few drops of blood fell from Katarina's finger into the bowl. Liz looked at the bright red liquid and it felt as if her whole inside was on fire with hunger. Time seemed to slow down as she watched the drops of blood fall into the bowl with the other ingredients.

"Done," Katarina said and wrapped her finger in some cloth.

Liz snapped out of the trance-like state at the sound of Katarina's voice but it felt like someone had just snatched away a large hot meal from a starving person.

"Are you okay?" Katarina asked.

"I said I was fine," Liz said low.

"You look pale," Katarina said and mixed all the ingredients together.

"Well, I am dead after all," Liz said. "Not much blood circulating in my body, especially when I haven't fed in a while."

Katarina spoke some words which Liz didn't recognize, as she stirred in the bowl. The whole magic thing made Liz feel uncomfortable but she tried not to show it, though she knew she was hiding it badly.

"You don't like magic?" Katarina asked calmly but didn't look up at Liz.

"Who said that?" Liz asked nonchalantly.

"You did," Katarina said. "I can feel it. I told you that even when I'm not touching-…"

"Yeah right," Liz said, interrupting her. "Could you do me a favor?"

"What?" Katarina asked.

"Stop doing it," Liz said coldly.

"I can control my future seeing to an extent by wearing gloves and clothes that cover my skin and not touch people, but this I cannot control," Katarina said. "It happens automatically."

Liz didn't say anything else about it as she wasn't sure if Katarina was telling the truth or not and she didn't have the energy or curiosity to really push it. Katarina walked up to the door and dipped two fingers in the bowl and drew strange symbols, the blood dripping down ever so slightly. When Katarina had drawn the symbol on the door and all the windows they started to glow intensely before disappearing entirely.

"Is that it?" Liz asked skeptically. "That'll keep the werewolves at bay?"

"It has so far," Katarina said as she put down the bowl on the table and wiped her fingers on a cloth. "And by so far, I mean last time."

Liz quickly glanced over at the bowl before looking away, there was no point in tormenting herself by looking at it. By now with all the magic, it probably wasn't safe for her to eat but a part of her didn't care. Liz had been hungrier in her life, but seeing blood so close and still warm automatically made her stiffen. Katarina must have noticed that because she quickly took the bowl and poured the remains from it in the sink.

Liz walked up to the window facing the main street, wanting to take her mind off the blood and hunger, from where she was standing she could just make out the large gate. Then something strange happened, the giant gate slowly started to open. Something had to be wrong, there was no way they would open the gate, especially not on a full moon night.

"Ah, yes," Katarina said behind Liz's back. "You don't know about that either, I suppose."

"What?" Liz asked, confused. "They're opening the gate, why?"

"You'll see soon enough," Katarina said with a touch of melancholy.

"The werewolves will transform any second," Liz said, a hint of distress in her voice. "They'll either escape and kill people in Town or be shot dead on the spot."

Katarina backed away into the room but Liz continued to stare at the gate in bewilderment. The gate was opening so painfully slow but finally Liz could see some movement coming through the gate. Was this is? Was the thing Liz had feared would happen all along? But instead of an army of armed humans, there were only three silhouettes coming through the gate. Even from this distance Liz could see the fear in their eyes as they were forced inside The Sanctuary from what Liz assumed was the army men guarding the wall. As soon as the three humans were inside, the gate closed behind them.

All of them instantly started banging on the gate, screaming their lungs out, pleading for their lives, but it stayed shut.

"What the hell is happening?" Liz asked loudly.

Katarina had made herself a cup of tea and was sitting down by the table. The scent of ginseng filled the air.

"They're convicts," Katarina said. "Or that's what they say. It's their punishment, one full moon night in The Sanctuary, if they survive they are free to go. So far, no one has survived."

"No shit," Liz said. "They'll get torn to shreds."

"Yes," Katarina said calmly but Liz could see the tiniest tremor in Katarina's hands.

Then they heard it, everyone in The Sanctuary and perhaps even everyone in Town heard it. The howls from at least two dozen werewolves. Liz could see some color in Katarina's face disappear and there was a touch of panic in her eyes that quickly disappeared. She continued to drink her hot cup of tea and stared into the cup, almost like it could protect her from the horrors outside her apartment.

Even the three convicts had stopped banging on the giant gate as they'd heard the howls. They must have realized that the gate would not open and making noise would only make the werewolves find them faster. Two of them started running in opposite directions, tears streaming down their faces. The last one had fallen to their knees and by the look on their face, they were petrified with fear. And Liz heard them, she heard the heavy paws hit the ground and the rasping from the sharp claws ready to find their prey.

Liz couldn't take her eyes away from the last human at the gate, however much Liz tried to convince herself that she did not care about this one human's life, she couldn't look away. The humans' rapid breathing, bordering on hyperventilating and tears falling down their face like a waterfall.

Liz wasn't sure if she felt sorry for the humans or if she was jealous they could feel such intense feelings.

"You shouldn't look," Katarina said low.

"I've seen people die before," Liz said, her voice monotone. "Many times."

"Does it get easier?" Katarina asked.

"Yes," Liz lied. "You get used to it. You get used to everything eventually, no matter how horrific."

"Maybe there are some things we shouldn't get used to," Katarina said plainly.

Liz didn't say anything in response to her comment.

Liz could see things humans could not, a blessing and a curse depending on the situation. Her eyes could see further and see things moving too fast for humans. And right now she was seeing three werewolves scaling a building close to the human at the gate, just waiting to attack. But they were waiting, and Liz knew why. A sitting meal was not as fun as a running one, it was a cheap victory in hunting something that wouldn't defend itself. Werewolves were not alone in feeling that way.

Liz found herself reaching for the doorknob but quickly stopped herself. No, she wouldn't interfere. She'd said she wouldn't interfere, she said she didn't care and going out on full moon night and fighting all the werewolves for the lives of three humans, that was interfering something awfully. Liz had to stick to the rules she'd set up for herself, those were the only things that had kept her relatively sane all these years.

"You couldn't leave even if you wanted to," Katarina said.

Liz turned around, anger rising inside of her.

"I wasn't going to leave," Liz said as calmly as possible.

"I saw you reaching for the door," Katarina said. "You want to help the humans?"

"No, I don't give a shit about them," Liz said. "They die tonight instead of a year or forty, what does it matter?"

"To them it matters," Katarina said. "Would you like to die like that?"

"I can't die so the question is pointless," Liz said, crossed her arms and sat down.

Just as she sat down they heard multiple screeches, all in an almost supernatural unison, echo through the air.

"Banshee screams," Liz whispered.

"We'll hear two more tonight," Katarina said. "At least."

"You're almost as cheerful as me," Liz muttered.

She wondered who had died, if it was the human at the gate or one of the others. But she pushed those thoughts away, they didn't matter. In three hundred years they would be forgotten and no one would even know they'd ever lived.

"Did I ever thank you for saving me?" Katarina asked.

Liz rubbed her eyes and sighed in annoyance.

"I didn't save you," Liz said. "He wasn't going to kill you."

"He was going to hurt me," Katarina said.

"Well, you didn't look like you were going to defend yourself," Liz said.

"Is that also why you wanted to help the humans out there?" Katarina asked.

"I don't want to help them!" Liz said with a raised voice. "And I'm starting to regret helping you."

"Why? Katarina asked, tilting her head slightly to the side.

Liz opened her mouth to speak but chose to close it without saying anything. The night had just started but Liz had a feeling it would be a very long one.

Chapter 5

The night seemed to last forever and for once, Liz was looking out the window, hoping to see some rays of sun in the horizon. She was careful of course, the sun burnt her badly when it shone directly on her skin. If she wore a lot of clothes and an umbrella she could go out in the sun, but not for too long. Liz had been burnt multiple times by the sun and so far, it was one of the worst pains she'd felt. It didn't kill quickly, she hadn't burst into flames like in the movies of old. Liz thought it must be how insects felt like when being shone on with a magnifying glass, that intense and direct beam of sunlight frying their skin. It looked painful. It was painful.

Liz turned her head towards Katarina who was sleeping on the sofa in the corner. She'd fallen asleep a few hours ago, right after they'd heard the third banshee scream. Liz had no plan after this night, she'd thought she'd come back and everything would just continue as if she'd never left. But she was obviously wrong. And now, she had no home and the few friends she'd had were angry with her.

Liz sighed as she saw how peacefully Katarina was sleeping and couldn't help but to wonder why this girl had decided to trust her. Liz was a vampire, a monster to most people and Katarina was human after all. And Liz had confessed that she hadn't fed in days and yet Katarina had fallen asleep as if she was in the presence of an old friend, not an old monster.

Liz looked down at her hands who had started shaking and she tried to ignore the growing pit in her stomach, the beast inside her that craved blood. Liz looked up at Katarina again and the thought crossed her mind, how easy it would be. It would be over in a few seconds if she did it right, and she'd had plenty of practice in her long life.

Liz could make it painless, Katarina didn't even have to wake up; and the beast would be satisfied, if only for another few days.

Liz shook her head violently, she tried to push those thoughts away but they stayed in the back of her mind. She had to get out of here soon and feed. Liz sat down at the table and put the bag she'd stolen from the dead vampire on the table. Katarina made a sound and Liz looked over but Katarina just turned around and kept sleeping. With her eyes still fixated on Katarina, to make sure she didn't wake up, Liz opened the bag and took out her little wooden box.

When Liz was sure she was still asleep, she could hear her regular and calm heartbeat almost resonate inside her. Liz turned back to the box. She had to block out the fact that she was only a few meters from warm and alive blood. Liz traced her fingers over the crevices of the box, it had been through a lot. Liz had been afraid that it would have been gone when she came back but she'd known that if someone had stolen it, she would have gotten it back sooner or later. The Sanctuary was not a big place and there were not a lot of places to hide. She would have burnt the whole Sanctuary to the ground before giving up on her box.

Liz opened it and the first thing she did was look through the photos she'd saved through the years. Some of them were so old and fragile that it looked as if they would crumble if touched and on some of them, the faces were barely recognizable anymore. Others would see formless shapes but not Liz, because Liz remembered. She remembered everything.

Time passed quickly to Liz, people came and went in what seemed like the blink of an eye, but Liz remembered them all. Even if she wanted something forgotten, it was all etched into her mind.

One photo always caught her attention, and Liz stared at it for a few seconds before she went back to looking through the rest of the box content. The photo was simple, plain and almost looked like an old family photo. It was in black and white and torn at the edges. The photo was of three people, two women and one man.

As Liz looked at the photo, only one emotion surged through her body. Shame.

Finally she dragged her eyes away from the photo and put it back in its rightful place. Drawings and sketches also filled the inside of the box and she picked up her favorite one, it was of herself, still in the same pale pink lace dress, dancing happily with a less serious Vendela. This was quite some time before The Sanctuaries had existed but as Liz looked at the drawing it was like the memory came to life and she could hear laughter echoing in the apartment accompanied by music.

"Stupid," Liz said and shoved everything back into the box. "Meaningless."

Liz was just about to close the box when something shiny caught her eyes at the bottom of the box. Slowly, Liz reached for it and picked it up. It was a small silver ring, very plain and obviously old yet it had kept its shine by constant maintenance. Liz held it in her hand and just stared at it.

"I feel nothing," Liz muttered to herself.

Yet she didn't put it back into the box but instead she started to put it on. She stopped abruptly and threw it into the box and then shoved the box back into the bag as she heard Katarina waking up. Liz turned around and saw Katarina rubbing her eyes sleepily.

"Sleep well?" Liz asked, trying to sound calm.

"Yes," Katarina said and looked at Liz but her eyes were drawn towards the half open bag on the table. "What have you been doing?"

"Nothing really," Liz said quickly. "Thinking mostly."

"Not about eating me I hope," Katarina said and laughed.

Liz stared at Katarina with a restrained calmness.

"Of course not," Liz finally said.

Katarina stretched her arms into the air and took a deep breath before she looked out through the window.

"Is it over?" Katarina asked. "It's hard to know during the winter, some days it feels like the sun doesn't rise at all."

"If I were you I'd wait an hour before going out," Liz said.

Katarina looked at Liz but then quickly looked away.

"What?" Liz asked.

"Nothing," Katarina said. "I'm just tired."

Silence.

"Well, I'm going to leave," Liz said and threw the bag over her shoulder.

"Didn't you just say to wait an hour?" Katarina asked.

"That's for you," Liz said. "At this point they can't do anything to me."

"Where will you go?" Katarina asked.

"The Bar," Liz said and she felt her hands shaking slightly. "I need to feed, Vendela can help me with that."

The mere thought of feeding made Liz's whole body tense up and her hands formed fists to stop the shaking.

"Well Liz," Katarina said. "You're always welcome here."

Liz dropped her bag on the floor and clenched her jaw, the rage rushing over her like a sudden wave.

"Who are you?" Liz asked, her voice almost shaking with anger at this point.

"What?" Katarina asked, confused.

"How did you know my name?" Liz almost hissed.

"I-I..." Katarina stuttered.

Liz couldn't control herself and she rushed towards Katarina, her eyes dark with anger. Liz's hand was stretched out to grab her and push her into the wall but just as Liz was about to touch Katarina, something happened. A strong white light blinded Liz as she was pushed through the air by a shock wave and her body smashed into the wall opposite Katarina.

Liz groaned, there was a shooting pain in her back and both her chest and eyes felt like they were burning. Liz tried to open her eyes but she saw nothing but a veil of whiteness. She had never felt anything like it before and she was more shocked than anything else at first.

"I told you attacking me would have consequences," Katarina said low.

Liz felt around her with her hands and tried to lean on the now slightly broken wall behind her. She felt weak, her legs were shaking and something filled her; something she hadn't felt in a very long time.

Fear. She felt fear and she felt fragile, like she was made out of glass and if she fell to the floor, she would smash into a million pieces.

"W-What did you do?!" Liz screamed as her vision finally started to return to her.

It was blurry but she saw a figure standing at the other end of the room, it seemed like Katarina hadn't moved at all. It felt like every light in the room was blindingly strong and Liz tried to block it with one hand, while leaning her body weight on her other arm. Katarina didn't answer her and with Liz's vision returning, so did some of her strength.

Katarina became clear and Liz could see two symbols still glowing on her forearms, one on each arm. They almost looked like they were carved into her flesh and the glow coming from it was not natural. Liz frowned with a look of disgust on her face.

"Magic," Liz spat out. "You used magic on me."

"Well, you did try to attack me," Katarina said calmly. "I told you it was a bad idea."

Liz looked at the symbols again and even though she didn't know much about magic, she knew those were no normal protection symbols.

"That's no ordinary spell," Liz said.

"Who said it was?" Katarina said nonchalantly.

"You said, you dabbled in magic," Liz said suspiciously. "How could you even get a hold of a spell like that?"

"That's none of your business," Katarina said.

Finally, Liz felt like most of her powers had returned to her and she noticed that the symbols stopped glowing as well and they disappeared into the skin and there was no sign of them ever even existing. Liz took a step closer to Katarina but stopped.

"How'd you know my name?" Liz asked. "I didn't tell you."

Katarina didn't say anything. Liz suddenly laughed.

"It was Vendela wasn't it?" Liz said. "Did she tell you or did you touch her?"

Katarina still said nothing.

"Tell me!" Liz roared.

Katarina twitched slightly at Liz's sudden outburst but didn't look very frightened, which almost made Liz even more angry.

"You knew who I was long before I entered the Bar," Liz said. "What do you want with me?"

"Nothing," Katarina finally said.

"Don't lie to me," Liz hissed.

"I'm not," Katarina said calmly.

Liz was staring at Katarina with large and dark eyes, this was one of the few times violence wouldn't work, she couldn't even touch Katarina with malice intent.

"I'm only going to ask one more time," Liz said slowly. "How did you know my name?"

Katarina was silent for a moment, like she was thinking about her answer.

"Mostly because of Vendela," Katarina finally said. "But you are in the thoughts and memories of many people here."

"What do you know about me?" Liz asked, her anger a little less palpable.

Katarina shrugged.

"Not much," Katarina said.

"Why didn't you tell me?" Liz said.

"Because I wanted to see how you acted without that knowledge," Katarina said.

"Well, did I live up to your expectations?" Liz asked with spite.

Katarina smiled weakly.

"I'm not sure yet," Katarina said.

Liz was silent for a moment, still trying to calm down but finding it hard. The hunger made the anger worse, Liz knew that. Anger, hatred and aggression all got worse the hungrier she got until it was all she could feel.

"I'm going to leave," Liz said bluntly and reached for the door.

As she touched the door knob, she quickly let go of it as a shocking pain shot through her. Liz winced in surprise more than pain before she clenched her fists and closed her eyes. That damn magic spell Katarina had put up to keep the werewolves away, it kept Liz in here as well.

"Open the door," Liz almost growled, she'd grown tired of magic for one day.

Katarina muttered something low and the symbols she'd drawn on earlier lit up for a split second before they disappeared again. Liz grabbed the door knob again, though with some caution, she was sick of all this magic bullshit. This time she could touch it without problem and she opened the door. The sun was just about to rise so Liz had perhaps 30 minutes before it would burn her. Without looking back, Liz exited the house and slammed the door shut behind her.

Chapter 6

As soon as Liz exited Katarina's house she had to resist the urge to scream, why she wasn't entirely sure of. Maybe it was out of frustration as it seemed that she could not act kindly towards a single person. Katarina had done nothing wrong and yet Liz had shown her nothing but suspicion. Or maybe she wanted to scream out of the fact that she was so hungry and she'd just left an easy prey.

When Liz actually paid attention to her surroundings she saw the grim sight that was the main street. It was lucky Katarina had not gone out, this was a massacre. During all her time here she thought she'd never seen anything as bad. The street was littered with body parts, and the walls around had been painted red by the blood splatter. Liz saw a torso without a head with its chest ripped wide open and the heart missing. Even Liz, who'd seen some horrific things in her life had stopped in her tracks, shocked at what she saw.

There had been three convicts let in during the night, now they lay all over the streets in pieces. Not even their closest relatives would recognize them anymore.

The image of the human cowering at the gate flashed before Liz's eyes but she pushed it away. They were dead now, she knew they wouldn't survive the night. Though she couldn't help but to wonder what they had done to deserve this?

Liz heard low sounds of pain coming from further down the street. Liz looked down and saw a naked person, their body looked like it was breaking itself or rather putting itself back together. Liz had witnessed werewolf transformations before and they looked painful. Though Liz would trade for a curse that only lasted one night once a month, then hers that was eternal. When the werewolf laid their eyes on Liz there was almost a look of shame on their face. Liz could have sworn she recognized them but in mid transformation it was hard to tell, their facial features were still half animal. They quickly took off into a nearby alley and Liz paid no more attention to them. They were no threat to her anyway.

Liz walked across the street, watching her steps, making sure she didn't step in any of the pools of blood or on any of the body parts. They'd been dead for quite some time, she could smell it and the blood had started to dry and was cold. If it had been fresher she wasn't sure if she could have stopped herself from licking the street.

Pathetic.

Liz had wasted enough time staring at something that didn't matter anymore. Dead was dead, at least most of the time. Liz walked with quick steps, but the image of the carnage still lingered in her mind no matter how hard she tried not to think about it. The sun would be up in about twenty minutes which didn't give Liz much time to get to the Bar. She met no one else as she passed through the many alley ways, but that was not strange. Many didn't leave their houses until the next day, which was pointless, as soon as the moon disappeared the danger was over. But fear made people do strange things.

Liz tried to push the image of all the blood out of her mind but not because it was disturbing or disgusting, but because the hunger inside her only grew by thinking about it. She once again formed her hands into tight fists to stop them from shaking. Vendela would help her, she repeated to herself. Liz knew Vendela was angry with her and that she wanted answers, but she also knew that Vendela would help her nonetheless. Liz finally came to the new Bar, the sign was turned off and it looked closed. Liz walked up to the door and knocked hard three times.

"We're not open yet," Vendela's voice shouted from the other side. "Come back later."

"You said I was always welcome here," Liz said with a smirk on her lips.

Silence.

"We're closed," Vendela repeated. "Come ba-…"

"Open the door Vendela," Liz snapped. "The sun will be up any minute."

"Then maybe you should find some shelter," Vendela replied coldly.

"Vendela," Liz said more softly.

There was a short silence before the door was opened slightly and Liz slipped in through the crack.

"Thank you," Liz said.

Vendela slammed the door shut behind Liz. The windows were all closed and sealed shut, drenching the bar in darkness, but they didn't need light to see.

"What do you want?" Vendela asked and sat down.

"Are you still angry with me?" Liz asked.

Vendela stared at her in disbelief.

"Oh no," Vendela said sarcastically. "All my anger just went away during the night, like magic."

"Oh please, don't mention magic," Liz said tiredly and groaned. "I've had enough of that."

Silence.

"You talked more with Katarina then I assume?" Vendela asked.

"You could say that," Liz said. "And if anyone should be angry here, it should be me."

Vendela rose to her feet with cold eyes as she slowly approached Liz.

"You cannot be serious," Vendela said upset. "What do you have to be angry about?"

"Did you tell her about me?" Liz asked.

Vendela scoffed.

"That's what you're angry about?" Vendela said with disbelief. "Everyone in here knows who you are!"

"Yeah but they don't know me from before all of this," Liz said. "You have no right to-…"

"No right?" Vendela said and closed the gap between them so they almost touched. "My memories are my own and I can share them however I please."

"But why did you have to tell her about *me*?!" Liz yelled. "Of all the things in the world, why *me*?"

Vendela just stared at Liz, not taken aback by her anger at all.

"What did you tell her?" Liz asked when Vendela didn't answer.

"What does it matter?" Vendela asked and shook her head.

"It matters to me!" Liz said.

"I told her almost nothing," Vendela said. "You know why?"

Liz didn't answer.

"Because I realized I know very little about you, I don't know where you were born, where you died, when you died," Vendela continued. "Because *you* never told me."

"Good," Liz said low and took a few steps back and sunk down into a chair.

"Good? Good." Vendela repeated in frustration. "I can't-…"

But she stopped herself mid sentence.

"Did you only come here to argue with me?" Vendela asked. "Did you only come here to get some of that pent up rage out of your system?"

Liz was silent, her jaw clenched in anger and she tried her hardest to not let any hurtful words slip past her lips, it happened all too easily.

"No," Liz finally said. "No, I didn't."

Liz looked down at her hands, they were now shaking so badly that she could not stop them, no matter how hard she tried. And Vendela noticed it as well and she sighed deeply.

"How long has it been since you fed?" Vendela asked.

"Two days maybe," Liz said.

"And you're shaking that badly?" Vendela asked with a sudden worry in her voice.

Liz looked away.

"Have you been over feeding again?" Vendela asked seriously. "Where have you been-…"

"Stop," Liz said abruptly. "Please, just stop."

The worry vanished from Vendela's face and was replaced with contained anger.

"I don't need a lecture," Liz said. "I just need some blood."

"Of course," Vendela said. "All I've ever been to you is means to an end."

That struck a nerve in Liz and she gave Vendela a gaze warning her not to go there.

"That's unfair," Liz said.

"Unfair…" Vendela repeated. "You know what's really unfair? The way you're treating me. I might not know a lot *about* you Liz, but I know *you*. Don't forget that."

Liz took a deep breath and collected her thoughts. The hunger in her stomach, the growing pit that demanded blood, got worse and she was in no state for this kind of argument.

"Please, I just… I just need some blood," Liz said.

"Sorry," Vendela said with a flat voice. "I'm not allowed to serve blood to just anyone anymore."

"What the hell does that mean?" Liz said and it came out harsher than she'd meant it to.

Vendela slammed her hand on the table and laughed low.

"You're not stupid Liz," Vendela said. "You really think I could afford to build this place up again after it was burnt down? I almost lost everything in that fire."

"I don't know, I just…" Liz started but didn't finish.

She hadn't even thought about it, her mind had been too occupied with other things to even consider that Vendela didn't own the Bar anymore.

"Who built it up again?" Liz asked instead.

"The same man that owns the Fun House, Mr. Greenlund," Vendela said coldly. "He rebuilt it and said if I just followed some of his rules, I could still pretend to be the owner."

Liz could see the anger and disgust in Vendela's face as she was saying this. Vendela had never liked being controlled or told what to do, especially not by someone who thought they were better than her simply because they were human.

"And one of the rules-..." Liz started.

"No blood, no exception," Vendela said. "He was very, very strict on this rule."

"Why?" Liz asked.

Vendela sighed and shook her head.

"Things have changed-..." Vendela started.

"Goddammit," Liz said annoyed. "Stop saying that and just tell me what's happened instead!"

Vendela gave her an irritated gaze.

"What's happened is, that I'm not allowed to serve blood anymore, the blood supplied by the Town only comes every third day, if even that and when we get it its cold and nauseating. Which means there is only one place to get fresh and warm blood," Vendela said bluntly. "If you don't want to attack someone that is."

"The Fun House..." Liz said low.

"Exactly," Vendela said. "Vampires make the best workers for the Fun House after all, we don't age, don't run out of stamina and we're hard to kill. We're the perfect worker for him."

"What's that su-..." Liz started.

"So if you want blood, you'll have to wait two more days to get it from Town but it will be cold and sickening, or you can start working for the Fun House," Vendela said, interrupting her.

"I'd rather starve," Liz said angrily.

"Don't take out your anger on me Liz," Vendela said, the warning clear in her voice. "I can't help you."

"Can't, or won't?" Liz asked.

Vendela was silent for a moment.

"Can't," Vendela finally said. "I can't risk crossing Mr. Greenlund. Not even for you."

Liz looked away then rose from where she'd been sitting. Her mind was blank, she'd been sure Vendela would help her and now when reality hit her, she was left with nothing. She had no plan, no ideas. Just a hunger growing inside her, clouding her judgment. Liz was staring into a wall and just tried to collect some thoughts, form some plan but nothing came to mind. She had no home, no friends to help her and most importantly, she had no way of getting blood.

"Are you alright?" Vendela asked with a softer voice.

That snapped Liz out of her thoughts and she turned and faced Vendela. Vendela's face said it all and it actually made Liz feel ashamed. Liz had seen the same facial expression of worry on Vendela before, a long time ago and it just brought up memories of who Liz had been. What she had been.

"Don't look at me like that," Liz snapped.

Vendela sighed irritated.

"You're impossible," Vendela said.

Liz walked towards the door, she just wanted to get the hell out of here.

"Where are you gonna go?" Vendela asked. "The sun is up."

Liz stopped dead in her tracks, her hand on the door handle. Her head was so muddy that she'd forgotten about the sun, forgotten about the restrictions of her curse. A part of her just wanted to say to hell with it, and go out anyway, but it wouldn't solve anything.

"You should be able to leave in a couple of hours," Vendela said. "Thank God it's winter, right?"

Liz didn't move, her hand still on the door handle. She would be stuck in here for God knows how many more hours in here with no blood. She felt as if she would go insane, she couldn't wait much longer, especially not two whole days for cold blood. If nothing changed, she was afraid she'd attack someone and when she was this hungry, she wouldn't just settle for a mouthful of blood. She'd want it all, she would kill someone without hesitation.

Vendela put her hand on Liz's, which was still lingering on the door handle. Liz, out of pure reaction, pulled her hand away from the touch. There was a split second of hurt on Vendela's face when Liz looked at her, but it was gone as fast as it had arrived.

"Sit down," Vendela said. "It'll be fine. You'll be fine."

Liz looked at the door once more before she was led by Vendela to a chair. She sunk down in the chair and gripped it by the sides to lock herself into place. Liz knew that when she got to a certain point, she wouldn't be able to control herself.

Chapter 7

Liz stared into the wall, trying to concentrate on something simple and distracting. She found a spot on the wall that did the trick, so she just looked at it and nothing else. But it only worked for so long, as she could feel Vendela's intense gaze at the back of her head. Finally she couldn't stand it anymore. It was clear that it had been a mistake coming here.

"Stop looking at me," Liz said tiredly. "Don't you have anything better to do?"

Vendela was silent for a moment, it was obvious that there had been something on her mind ever since Liz had arrived.

"Where have you been?" Vendela asked after a few minutes of silence.

Liz sighed.

"I'm not in the mood," Liz said almost pleadingly. "I'm really not."

"And I'm not in the mood for games," Vendela said. "Where the hell have you been that makes it so hard to tell me?"

Not where I've been, Liz thought, *what I've done is what makes it hard.*

Liz didn't answer her.

"You've obviously been drinking blood regularly," Vendela said. "How often?"

"You're not my mom," Liz snapped.

"No, thank God for that," Vendela said. "I just happened to be a fool who for some strange reason, cares about you."

"Well, maybe you shouldn't," Liz hissed low.

Liz sighed deeply and closed her eyes, already regretting what had just slipped out of her mouth.

""I'm sorry. I'm fine," Liz lied.

"Yeah, clearly," Vendela said sarcastically.

"I know what you're imp-…" Liz said.

"No, I'm not implying anything," Vendela said. "I'm saying it straight out. How much blood did you drink when you were gone?"

Liz was silent for a moment, but she was just so tired.

"Too much," she finally answered. "Too often."

Blood wasn't just something they needed to survive, it was a drug. A dangerous drug. If not consumed often enough they would become weak and eventually die, but too much of it was an entirely different story. The more she fed, the more she needed it, until she couldn't go a day without it. Until she couldn't go hours without it. Until the only thing she saw were walking blood bags surrounding her.

"Where were you?" Vendela asked again.

Liz just shook her head as an answer.

"Why did you leave?" Vendela asked, her voice sounding a lot more fragile.

Liz looked up and stared into Vendela's eyes.

"I…" Liz started.

"You can't say it can you?" Vendela said. "You can't tell me the truth. After everything we've been through, after everything I've done for you."

"Don't," Liz said low. "Please. Don't."

"I shouldn't even care," Vendela said angrily. "I shouldn't care about you but I do and it makes me furious."

"I'm sorry," Liz said almost inaudibly.

"What?" Vendela said surprised.

"Nothing," Liz said a little louder. "Scream at me, yell, punch, do whatever you want if it makes you feel better."

"What I want is for you to let me help you," Vendela said almost desperately.

"Then give me some blood," Liz said harshly.

Vendela scoffed.

"See, you don't want to help me," Liz said. "I don't know what you want, but it's not to help me."

"Go to hell," Vendela said. "Just because I'm not willing to risk everything for someone who only lies to me, doesn't mean I don't want to help you. It might sound incredible to you, but there are things more important in this world than you and me."

Liz had to resist the temptation to burst out laughing; out of important things, Liz was at the bottom of the list even to herself. Vendela on the other hand was infinitely higher up on the list.

Liz didn't say anything else. The bag Liz had kept securely on her shoulder shifted slightly and slid down her arm which caught Vendela's attention.

"Whose bag is that?" Vendela asked with a frown.

"Mine," Liz lied.

"One more lie Liz and I'll throw you out myself," Vendela said threateningly. "I won't care that the sun is up."

Liz looked at Vendela with dark eyes.

"We both know that's a lie," Liz said.

"You want to test that?" Vendela asked, her voice steady and cold.

Silence.

"I found it," Liz finally said and looked away from Vendela.

"You stole it," Vendela said as a statement of fact.

"The bag's owner was dead, so I don't think that counts as stealing," Liz said.

"Did you kill them?" Vendela asked.

"No," Liz said.

"Why'd you take it?" Vendela asked, confused.

"I don't have pockets on this dress," Liz said.

"Yeah but what do you need a bag for?" Vendela asked. "You barely own anything."

Liz shrugged.

"I thought it was pretty," Liz said sarcastically as it was torn and obviously quite used.

"Fine," Vendela said, she had grown irritated by Liz's tone. "Fine. Sulk, sit by yourself and tell yourself how bad you have it. Push away anyone trying to help you. If you want to talk like real adults, I'll be in the other room."

Vendela walked out of the room and slammed the door shut after her. Liz bit her lip and swallowed down the desire to call after her. She loosened her grip slightly off the chair and let her hand glide to her bag. She reached down and picked up the small box and laid it down in her lap. First she just stared at it but then she closed her eyes and leaned back in the chair. The box brought some tranquility and any other time perhaps it would even have drowned out the darkness inside of her but not this time.

Liz tried to tell herself that Vendela was wrong, she wanted help. She'd explicitly said to Vendela that she wanted her help. But they were talking about different things, Liz knew that. Liz wanted help with her hunger, a quite immediate problem but what Vendela was talking about. That was a much bigger and more complicated problem. The less Vendela knew, the better. Liz couldn't tell her where she'd been or what she'd been doing. Vendela was angry with her as it was and no matter what Liz said or how she acted, she didn't want to lose Vendela. She didn't want Vendela to look at her with disappointment or disgust; or worse, with hatred.

Even though Vendela and Liz were both vampires, they had quite the opposite view of the situation. Vendela had been turned into a vampire as she'd been dying, so this was her second chance at life. Liz on the other hand, had been robbed of her life and thrust into this hell.

Liz's fingers traced the cracks on the wooden box as it had a calming effect, how long had she been sitting here with her eyes closed? It both felt like seconds and hours at the same time. Liz wanted to leave even though she had nowhere to go and if she left she was afraid she'd do something stupid. Liz had killed a lot of people and creatures and most of the time she could justify it, if she was in control.

When the hunger got to bad, she had no control and the true monster was unleashed. Not being in control, there was no knowing what she might do and that terrified Liz.

A sudden bolt of pain surged through Liz's body and she yelled out in surprise. The pain was concentrated in her stomach and she fell out of the chair and the box she'd had in her lap also fell to the floor and everything inside spilled out. Another bolt of pain struck her and she screamed low, trying to contain it. It was like a fire inside her belly, a white searing pain that spread through her body with the intent to burn her up from the inside. Liz back arched in pain and she slammed her right hand into the floor and dug her fingers into the wood, leaving deep markings and weak traces of blood in it.

"Liz? Liz!"

It was Vendela's voice but it sounded like it was miles away, a simple echo trying to reach her. The pain was blinding and it felt as if her thoughts were in a haze. A strong hand pulled at Liz to try and bring her back but Liz didn't think, her body just reacted. Within seconds, Liz was at Vendela's throat. Liz's sharp teeth were out and she was almost growling as she clawed at Vendela in a blinding rage. The hunger was so bad that Liz could smell that Vendela had fed recently and even her dead blood was preferable to nothing at all. But Liz was weak from hunger and Vendela was strong and had no problem overpowering her. Liz's eyes had turned a solid black but that didn't seem to faze Vendela, she had seen it many times before.

Vendela gripped Liz by the throat and pushed her hard into the floor and pinned her there so she couldn't move away. Liz tried desperately to get loose but Vendela flashed her sharp teeth as well and that aggressive show of power made Liz calm down a little, but just a little.

"Sorry Liz," Vendela said.

Vendela raised her hand and with one hard punch, she knocked Liz unconscious.

Chapter 8

Being unconscious was a strange sensation, as Liz didn't sleep and her mind never really got a break to mend and take things in properly. Liz never got the chance to dream or just shut down for a few hours.

The closest she got to sleeping was when she entered the trance state, Liz guessed it was from that state that people had gotten the assumption that vampires slept during the day. Which was false, but the trance state could seem like sleeping from an outsider's perspective but it was just a way for the vampires to power down a little. Days trapped inside a room while the sun was shining outside could be very long otherwise. But the vampires were far from sleeping in the trance state, they were aware of everything going on around them and if someone tried to sneak up on them, they would immediately know it and kill the assailant. It wasn't like in the movies of old, where vampires slept in coffins and could easily be overpowered and stabbed during the day without any resistance from the vampire.

They were already dead, why would they need to sleep?

Liz woke up screaming in blind and wild panic, she was soaked in sweat and her whole body hurt. She could not remember anything from when she'd been unconscious or even what had led to her being unconscious. But all she felt was a dread and fear that seeped into her bones. She looked around, trying to move but found herself trapped. She was sitting in a chair and there were chains around her body making it impossible to get loose. If she hadn't been so weak from the hunger then maybe she could have broken free but at this point she wasn't sure if she could have escaped even if it had been a simple rope. There was nothing around her, just an empty and dark concrete room.

"No, no," Liz repeated to herself. "No… I'm dreaming."

But she wasn't even sure if she could dream anymore. She struggled with the chains but they didn't budge and the panic rose inside her again. This couldn't be real.

"Hello!" She screamed, not even trying to conceal the panic in her voice. "Get me the hell out of here! Hello!?"

She then heard something from above her, light steps walking slowly. Was she in a basement? The sound of the steps had quieted her down as she waited for what came next. Memories she'd long tried to forget came rushing back to her, but she refused to acknowledge them. Flashes of men in white coats and sharp knives came before her eyes so she shut them hard and tried to think of anything else as the footsteps came closer.

Her bag.

Was her bag here? Liz opened her eyes and looked around but there was no bag and there was no box. She could not for the life of her remember what had happened, the last thing she remembered was sitting in a chair in the Bar with the box laying securely in her lap. It was frustrating, Liz could remember things that had happened hundreds of years ago and yet the last moments before she'd become unconscious were dark for her.

It wasn't until a door opened behind her and light entered the room that she realized that she'd been sitting in total darkness. Liz tried to turn around to see who it was who'd opened the door when she smelled it. It was like a slap in the face, the scent of human blood and Liz could feel her eyes flicker shut and her sharp teeth come out.

"Liz?" A low voice spoke.

Liz could barely hear the voice, it sounded so far away and all she heard was the beating of the person's heart. It was beating steadily.

"Are you alright? I heard you screaming."

From what seemed like a haze, Liz could see Katarina stand in front of her. She was looking at Liz with cautious eyes but not with fear. Was this girl ever afraid? Liz found her whole body shaking and she closed her eyes and held her breath. She didn't really need to breathe but she usually did it out of reflex, now she tried hard to resist that reflex. She didn't want to smell Katarina's warm blood pumping through her body, but she could do nothing to stop it from beating like a drum in her ears.

"Leave," Liz managed to growl, showing Katarina her sharp white teeth.

"Vendela said she'd come by with blood when the Town supply comes in," Katarina said, almost ignoring Liz's warning. "Until then you'll stay down here."

"Leave! Get the hell away from me!" Liz roared, opening her eyes which once again had turned completely black.

Katarina took a step back in a mixture of surprise and horror at the sight of the black eyes. Perhaps that was the closest Liz would ever see Katarina scared. Liz had started to strain against the chains with force and she could feel them almost tightening the more she struggled, leaving red and irritated marks.

"T-The more you struggle-…" Katarina said slowly.

But Liz had already realized what she was going to say. Katarina had put a spell on the chains, which also made sense why she felt so trapped. There was no escaping them, even though Liz didn't really want to. She knew this was the best scenario if Vendela refused to give her blood. But the blood hungry beast inside her just wanted to be free.

Liz struggled so hard against the chains that the chair she was sitting on fell over and she hit the cold stone floor with a bang, her body almost felt like it was going to break into a thousand little pieces and she felt how the chains had teared at her skin leaving wound like marks beneath them and with a black liquid oozing out of them. When she was this weak her healing ability was next to none existent.

Katarina made a move towards Liz to help her up from the floor but when Katarina's warm hand reached out for her, Liz snapped her mouth towards her and almost snarled out of hunger. Katarina pulled back her hand and hesitantly left the basement.

The moment the door shut and Liz could hear it lock she sighed lightly in relief. Liz guessed Katarina was smart enough to put a spell on the door if by some chance Liz would get out of these chains, not that that was very likely. The smell of blood and the sound of the beating heart disappeared and Liz could feel her whole body relax. If she hadn't been dead, she knew she'd be out of breath at this moment, that was what it felt like.

Liz felt empty as she laid on the cold floor, not even the chains hurt anymore.

Two days, was that what Vendela had said the Town's supply of blood came in? Physically she knew she could survive two more days without blood, it wasn't that she was afraid of. Not that Liz ever was afraid of death, not anymore. It was not being in control of her thoughts, words or actions that frightened her. Liz could feel how she'd started to shake again, and her head was clouding over.

Her last clear thought before she started to scream was, she hoped that Katarina would keep that door shut, no matter what.

Chapter 9

Liz's time down in the basement felt like years passed by, the hunger pains came with such force that it left her unable to do anything else but scream. And when they left her, she felt unable to control herself and what words left her mouth. The hateful words and threats that spouted out of her mouth like acid towards Katarina and anyone who could hear her. Though as soon as they left her mouth she couldn't remember a single thing she'd said, except she had a dreadful feeling they were words she would never have uttered under any other circumstance. Which said a lot, considering some of the things Liz had said during her lifetime. She had strained so hard and often against the chains that her skin barely got a chance to start healing. Every time it did, the wounds were ripped open by another one of her fits. Black liquid had dried on her skin and it had stained her pink dress.

Once again, the pain passed and she felt the anger and hatred rise inside her. She had no control over her words but neither of her thoughts, it was like they belonged to someone else entirely.

Her vicious thoughts and words were interrupted by the door behind her opening. Liz who was still laying on the floor went completely quiet and still, her eyes dark as coal . There was no scent of blood in the air and no sound of any heart beat which made Liz cautious but she could clearly hear someone entering the basement.

"I've been hearing you haven't been acting very nice," a sweet voice said.

Liz closed her eyes and almost laughed. It was Vendela, she would recognize that voice anywhere.

"You alive Liz?" Vendela said carefully as Liz didn't move, said nothing and had her back towards the door which Vendela had entered.

Liz stayed silent, she was concentrating hard on every sound Vendela made. Vendela made her way around and with one quick motion, she picked up the chair still with Liz in it and placed it up right. Liz didn't have time to react and then she was staring into Vendela's cold gray eyes. Liz's first thought was that Vendela looked tired, her second, was that she wanted to rip her throat out with her teeth.

"You look like shit," Vendela said calmly.

"Well," Liz said with a hoarse voice. "I have you to thank for that."

Vendela scoffed.

"I'm guessing it was you who brought me here," Liz said with spite in her voice. "Left me to die, left me to suffer."

"I did bring you here," Vendela said, unmoved by Liz's words. "Because you attacked me. And I didn't leave you here to die, I left you here so you wouldn't hurt anyone. There's a difference, even if you can't see that right now."

"*I attacked you?*" was Liz's immediate reaction before her mind was clouded by hunger again. Liz laughed low to herself.

"You didn't do this for me," Liz said. "You put me here because you have a pathetic need to save everyone. Go find some other defenseless creature to protect so you can feel good about yourself instead of keeping me down here."

That seemed to strike a nerve in Vendela but she only swallowed and her face turned hard again.

"Talk about pathetic," Vendela said. "Look at you. You have been down here barely one day and you're acting like you're dying."

"I am in *pain!*" Liz roared viciously and tried to throw herself towards Vendela but failed miserably because of the chains.

Vendela didn't even flinch and there it was again, that look on Vendela's face. It tore through the hunger and the pain and Liz suddenly felt shame surge through her body instead. Liz averted her eyes and tried to swallow but her throat was so dry she suddenly felt unable to speak, yet words escaped her lips somehow.

"Why did you come here?" Liz asked slowly. "To gloat? To laugh at me?"

Vendela walked closer to Liz until she was just out of reach if Liz would launch herself towards her again. Liz looked back at Vendela and saw the sadness yet absolute resolution in her eyes. Before Liz could have said anything else, Vendela tipped her chair and Liz fell backwards. She hit her head against the hard floor and if she'd had a breath, it would have been knocked out of her. Pain shot through her body and she closed her eyes and growled low.

"Either try to kill me or release me," Liz said furiously.

But there was a third option that Liz had not thought of at this moment. Vendela knelt down beside Liz and grabbed her jaw with a firm hand. Liz stared at Vendela, her eyes burning but Vendela's was as cold as ice. With her free hand, Vendela picked up something from her pocket. Then Liz felt something being forcefully poured down her throat, at first Liz fought it like it was holy water before her body realized what it was.

It was blood, fresh, it couldn't be more than half an hour old. It was warm and silky and Liz felt her whole body relax as her eyes rolled back into the back of her head. Her black eyes vanished and her almost golden eyes returned, it was like the haze clouding her mind disappeared and the chill that had gripped her body was replaced with wonderful warmth. It felt like she hadn't fed in years.

The blood poured into her mouth and she swallowed as quick as she could, but she could feel it spilling out of her mouth and running down her face but she didn't care. Finally it stopped and Liz licked her blood stained lips and then bit her lower lip softly, she was just staring into the ceiling, a feeling close to euphoria running through her body. Being starved of blood was painful but there was nothing like the first drop of blood afterwards, it was like drinking water after having walked in the desert for days. There was nothing compared to the feeling.

"Come see me when you're ready," Vendela said softly and started to leave the basement.

"Vendela," Liz said, her voice thick and hoarse.

Vendela turned around and their eyes met.

"Thank you," Liz said almost as low as a whisper before she closed her eyes.

Vendela looked away before quickly leaving.

As Vendela left, Liz heard new footsteps entering the basement and there it was again, the now very subtle beating of a heart, not like the drumming she'd heard before. Katarina came into her eyesight and Liz, who now realized what she looked like, sighed deeply.

"Are you alright?" Katarina asked.

Liz looked at her, she looked exhausted and pale and there was caution in her eyes.

"Yeah," Liz said. "Just… This isn't exactly an ideal situation I'm in."

"Why"? Katarina asked and cocked her head.

"Well, firstly, I'm laying on the ground, chained, and covered in blood," Liz said. "Not exactly dignified. Secondly…"

Liz looked away from Katarina and didn't finish her sentence.

"You have nothing to be ashamed about," Katarina said.

"Could you please just… Release me?" Liz asked.

Katarina snapped her fingers and the chains fell off her with ease. Liz rose with some difficulty, her body felt stiff and it ached slightly. Even with the fresh blood in her body, she didn't feel totally restored yet. Liz looked at the stains of black on her dress and sighed, that stuff was impossible to wash off. Liz could feel the still liquid blood that had run down her face and she quickly tried to wipe away as much she could with her hands and arms, staining them light red instead. She then looked over at Katarina again, who was gazing at her with tired, yet steady eyes.

"I'm… gonna go," Liz said.

"Are you sure?" Katarina asked. "You can stay until you feel fully restored."

"I'm fine," Liz muttered. "And I think I've outstayed my welcome anyway."

"No, you haven't," Katarina simply said.

Liz muttered something beneath her breath but said nothing more about it. Liz started to walk up the stairs and out of the basement and she entered

Katarina's living room, where she had been not long ago. But she hadn't even realized this door existed, which was strange as it was large, heavy and made out of metal.

"I didn't notice this door last time I was here," Liz said slowly and touched the metal.

"There's a spell on it," Katarina said. "To keep it hidden."

Liz quickly pulled her hand away from the door, like it had given her an electric shock.

"Why?" Liz asked, trying to hide her disgust for the magic spell.

"If by some chance someone would break down my front door, they would not find my safe room immediately," Katarina said. "It increases my chances of survival."

"Was this here when you moved in?" Liz asked, slightly confused.

"To some extent," Katarina said. "Apparently quite a lot of the single apartments have these types of rooms, they were built to hold the werewolves I think. But as no one fixes things when they break-…"

"They stay broken," Liz said.

"Obviously," Katarina said. "So my parents had this house renovated for me as I was moving in."

Liz turned towards Katarina with disbelief in her eyes.

"Your parents… Renovated this house for you?" Liz asked.

"Yes," Katarina said. "They are quite influential in Town and have no shortage of money."

"And yet you are here," Liz said.

"What do you mean?" Katarina asked, slightly confused.

"You said they were rich and influential and still you're in the Sanctuary, like the rest of us who no one cares about," Liz said. "How's that?"

Katarina smiled gently.

"I am what I am," Katarina said and shrugged. "And according to the law, I belong here."

The law, Liz had to stop herself from laughing. The law that was made up out of fear and ignorance and had turned the whole world into a literal witch hunt for anyone different. Liz wondered how far it would go this time around, would humans start to end up in The Sanctuaries if they spoke up? The line between monster and human seemed to become blurrier by the day, how different was different enough to justify imprisonment?

There would come a point of no return, a point where all hell broke loose; but by then it would be too late for a lot of the inhabitants of The Sanctuaries.

Liz shook off those thoughts, what did she care about other inhabitants of Sanctuaries. She wouldn't die in here, it would disappear as everything else had done and the world would move on to its next fear and hatred; never learning from its past. Liz would just follow along, as she always had, a watcher from the shadows; rarely a participant.

"You were born with your gift right?" Liz asked after a short pause. "So how come you managed to escape the Sanctuaries and the authorities for so long? Did your parents find out and turn you in?"

The smile was wiped off Katarina's face.

"No," Katarina said.

"So how-…" Liz asked.

"How did you end up here?" Katarina asked instead.

Liz laughed low and took a pause before she spoke.

"I've been here a long time," Liz said slowly. "I was here when the place was new and full of promises. Promises of safety and a place to live. Though I never believed a word they said, I came forward and freely entered the Sanctuary."

"Why?" Katarina asked, frowning slightly.

Liz sighed.

"Because I knew the hunt for creatures would begin, and it did shortly after, and I was tired of running and hiding," Liz said. "So I accepted the course of history."

"You knew this would happen and still you did nothing to stop it?" Katarina asked, confused.

"Know is a strong word," Liz said hesitantly. "Let's just say… I've seen it before, I've lived it before. And the best thing for someone immortal like me, is just to wait it out. This will be gone in 100 years, and a 100 years is not a lot in my eyes. Nothing lasts forever…. At least almost nothing."

Katarina stared at Liz, still with that frown on her face. Liz looked away, feeling that she had said too much.

She knew people didn't understand and she couldn't blame them, mortals had no idea of the struggles of the immortals. Liz had only lasted this long with a somewhat stable mental health because of the rules she'd set for herself.

Liz had seen many, too many, immortals like herself gone mad at the thought of eternity.

Liz didn't say anything else and quickly left the apartment before Katarina could say anything to stop her. Liz hadn't meant to tell Katarina all that but with the warm blood rushing through her body she felt oddly sentimental. It happened from time to time, especially when the blood was at its freshest. It was like life hadn't left the blood yet and it transferred into the vampire, making them… Almost feel alive for just a short time. Making them feel vulnerable. So Liz had to get away from Katarina's piercing and curious eyes before she let something worse slip past her lips.

Vendela had wanted to meet her and luckily, if anyone understood Liz and what she was going through, it was Vendela.

Chapter 10

As Liz came out into the large street again, she was shocked at what she saw. Nothing had changed, the body parts still laid around and the blood had dried into the street and onto the walls.

A quite pungent smell of decay and death lingered in the air. Liz almost felt nauseous by the smell and swallowed, telling herself that it was just the fresh blood running through her body making her react this way. Why had no one come and cleaned this up, taken the bodies back to their families to bury? By the look of the sky, even with the sun behind clouds, it seemed to be close to midday and Liz wasn't sure how long she had been down in the basement but it had at least been 24 hours. Before she'd left if someone died during the full moon, or at all, a few people from Town would come in and clean up and burn the bodies, at least if the bodies were visible and a disturbance. The smell of decaying bodies could probably be smelt even in Town. Everyone who'd died when Liz had been here had been creatures. Why didn't they do anything when their own kind was killed in here? Even if they were convicts.

Liz saw a few creatures make their way down the street further away and they seemed quite unaffected by the fact that there were body parts rotting on the main street of The Sanctuary. Liz guessed this wasn't the first time this had happened since she'd been gone.

Liz licked her lips and tasted copper, some blood must still be on her face. Then she walked with quick steps towards the Bar, which was closed, strangely enough. The Bar was almost never closed, perhaps only during the full moon. Liz walked up to it and knocked three times. The door opened on the second knock, as if the person on the other side had expected her.

Liz walked inside and Vendela closed it behind her.

"I hope you feel better than you look," Vendela said. "You look awful."

"Well, I'm sorry I don't look like royalty, one rarely does when one has been starved and kept locked in a cellar," Liz said sarcastically.

Vendela didn't say anything in response and the silence was killing her, so Liz spoke once again.

"Why'd you want to see me?" Liz asked carefully.

Vendela sighed, walked past Liz and stood in front one of the many doors in the Bar.

"Take off your dress," Vendela said.

"What?" Liz said with a weak smile on her lips. "If I knew me covered in blood turned you on I would ha-..."

"Your dress is dirty," Vendela said, interrupting her. "I thought I'd be nice and wash it for you, you can take a shower in the meanwhile and borrow some of my clothes."

Liz looked down at her plump body and then looked over at Vendela's thin and muscular body.

"I don't think much you have will fit me," Liz said. "And I'm fine."

"When was the last time you washed that dress?" Vendela asked. "Was it a year ago when I did it?"

"Maybe," Liz said slowly. "What? Do I smell?"

"It's dirty, look at it," Vendela said.

Liz didn't need to look at it, she knew it was dirty and old.

"Why are you doing this?" Liz asked, confused.

"What do you mean?" Vendela asked.

"Give me blood, offer to wash my clothes and so on," Liz said. "Last thing I remember before this was that you were quite upset with me."

"Don't think that has changed," Vendela said. "I'm still upset with you."

"So why-..." Liz started.

"Take a shower while I look for clothes for you," Vendela said. "The shower is through that door and then the second door to the right."

"Okay," Liz said and gave in, she guessed this conversation would continue later.

Vendela smiled faintly towards Liz before she disappeared behind the door she'd stood in front of. Liz smiled back but something didn't feel right. There wasn't anything strange with Vendela helping her, she'd done that more than probably anyone else but this sudden change of heart was something else. Vendela had been adamant on the fact that she would not give Liz any blood and yet, a mere day later she'd done just that. Vendela wasn't usually someone that changed her mind like that but Liz had to admit, she preferred when Vendela wasn't yelling at her. Vendela had said she was still upset with her but there was not the same kind of coldness in her eyes as before.

Liz made her way over to the door Vendela had pointed to, it was directly to the right of the bar table. As Liz opened it she was met by a long corridor, this place was obviously much larger than she'd first thought. The last Bar had only one extra room for Vendela to "sleep" in when the Bar was closed. Liz guessed it was a gift of some sort to Vendela from the man that owned the Fun House, not that Vendela needed much, Liz guessed she only used one or two rooms here.

An involuntary chill went down her spine as she thought about the Fun House and her mind drifted towards Ami who was working there. Liz didn't blame Ami for taking the job, she really didn't. Whatever they said, she understood the reasons to start working there. Liz shook her head and made her way into the bathroom and when she found it she was a little shocked. It was all white, a marble floor with a shower that looked brand new and in the corner there was even a large bathtub, large enough for two people to fit comfortably. Liz just stared at it for a few seconds, it was years since she'd seen anything like this, anything this clean and fresh.

There was a large mirror opposite her and her eyes passed over it, almost expecting to see a reflection but of course there was nothing there except her dress, seemingly floating in the air. It really looked dirty and Liz also saw that she'd ripped a hole in the lace on the right side. Liz sat down on the edge of the bathtub, turned the handle and heard the water starting to fill it up, and slowly started to take of her large boots and dropped them to the floor, as she put down her feet once again on the marble floor she felt heat coming from it, warming her cold skin.

"Nice touch," Liz muttered to herself.

She quickly undressed, throwing the dress and her underwear on the floor and then stepped into the half full bathtub. As soon as her body hit the water it turned from clear to a dirty reddish, brown color. Liz took some of the water in her hands and splashed it on her face, she saw that it quickly turned light red. Liz drew her hand through her short hair and closed her eyes as she leaned back into the bathtub.

When Liz had cleaned herself properly and the water had started to look too grimy for comfort, she got out of the bathtub, emptied it and wrapped a towel around her to dry herself. She put on her underwear and thought about putting on her dress again but she stopped herself and opened the bathroom door instead. And just as she'd suspected, Vendela had left some clothes neatly folded for her laying in the corridor. Liz smiled weakly and picked it up before dressing. She had been skeptical if Vendela really had anything that would fit her as their body sizes were clearly very different. But as she put on the large sweatpants and a shirt that was almost too large for Liz something struck her. She had seen this shirt before. It was a simple black t-shirt with green and purple roses spread all over it. Liz touched it carefully with her hands.

"Is this my shirt?" Liz whispered low to herself.

Not that anyone could have answered her and for some reason Liz didn't know, she smelt it. It smelt of Vendela, of roses and something sweet but also with a hint of smoke and ashes. Perhaps she was wrong, maybe it wasn't her shirt. Liz shook off the feeling of sentimentality, what did it matter if this had been Liz's shirt? That was many, many years ago. It was only the fresh blood in her veins making her feel this way, she told herself.

Liz pulled the shirt over her head, picked up her dress and walked out of the bathroom. Liz walked out of the corridor and entered the bar area again but there was no Vendela in sight, she was just about to go and look for her when there was a low knock on the front door of the Bar. It was a very distinctive knock which peaked her interest.

For a few seconds, Liz stood absolutely still and just stared at the door but then there was that knocking again. The exact same knock. Vendela didn't seem to hear it or she was ignoring it but it did intrigue Liz. Everyone knew not to knock when the Bar was closed, well except Liz but that was different.

Liz threw her dress onto a table and walked over to the door and opened it.

"Thank God Vendela I need to ta-…"

The young girl that stood in front of Liz was even shorter than herself, which didn't happen often. She had short, bright red hair with bangs and she was staring at Liz with large clear blue eyes. There was a look of shock on her face, she had obviously not expected Liz to open the door.

"Why do you need to talk to Vendela?" Liz asked with a raised eyebrow. "I don't think I've seen you around before."

The shock had now changed into panic, though it was obvious that the girl was trying to remain calm.

"I… I just… Ehm…" She stammered. "I was just wondering… If that Bar was open?"

"Bad lie," Liz said and crossed her arms. "The windows are dark, the sign is off. Everyone knows that means it's close. You want to try again?"

The girl was silent for a short moment, clearly trying to think of something.

"I… Who are you?" She asked instead.

"A friend," Liz said. "Now your turn."

The girl swallowed and smiled a forced smile.

"I'm just… Gonna go," she said.

Liz grabbed her by the fabric of her shirt arm.

"What's your name?" Liz asked calmly. "What are you?"

The girl looked down at Liz's iron grip of her shirt before answering.

"It's Tess," she said. "Banshee."

"Now what does a banshee want from my friend?" Liz said, her gaze steady.

"What the hell is happening?"

It was Vendela's voice coming from behind Liz and she quickly let go of Tess who took a step back. When Vendela saw Tess there was a half second of anger in her eyes before it disappeared, if Liz didn't know her as well as she did she would have probably missed it. For a moment there was total silence, like Vendela was contemplating what she was going to say.

"Haven't I told you before not to open the door when the Bar is closed?" Vendela said towards Liz.

"A long time ago," Liz said. "I thought, new bar, new rules."

Vendela shot her a gaze of warning.

"I'm gonna go," Tess said and laughed nervously. "I'll come back later."

Vendela nodded and then closed the door before Liz could stop her.

"Who was that?" Liz asked.

"Don't," Vendela said seriously.

"She was obviously in a hurry to talk to you," Liz said. "I haven't seen her before so she must be new here. You got a girlfriend while I was gone?"

"Are you jealous?" Vendela asked with a tinge of malice.

Liz laughed, but it rang false.

"Me? Jealous?" Liz said. "Don't be ridiculous."

"Then why'd you ask?" Vendela asked.

"B-Because…" Liz started. "As I said she looked in a rush to speak with you and I've never seen her before."

"Well, you're in no position to ask questions," Vendela hissed at her. "Not about her, me or us."

"So you can ask questions but I can't?" Liz asked. "And there's an 'us' is there between you two?"

"You'll start getting answers when I get some," Vendela said. "I don't have to tell you anything."

"What are you, three?" Liz said.

Vendela took a deep breath and looked away from Liz.

"Fine," Liz said. "Fine. I guess I should thank you instead of fighting with you."

Vendela slowly turned her gaze back to Liz, with a slight frown, like she wasn't sure of what she had just heard.

"You have a nice bathroom as well," Liz said when Vendela remained silent. "This place is way bigger than the last."

Vendela scoffed and she almost looked disgusted.

"Not my idea," Vendela said.

"I guessed as much," Liz said. "I didn't think you'd ask to live like this while the rest out there live in filth. "

Vendela looked straight into Liz eyes and her gaze had softened, but still with that suspicious frown.

"I'll chuck this dress in the washer," Vendela said instead of saying anything about Liz's comment.

"You have a washer?" Liz asked.

"Yet again, not my idea," Vendela said, slightly irritated but it was obvious that this time it wasn't directed towards Liz.

Vendela picked up Liz's dress from the table but before she could leave, Liz grabbed her arm to stop her.

"Why did you help me? Why are you helping me?" Liz asked.

Vendela opened her mouth and closed it twice before she actually spoke.

"I didn't do it for you," Vendela said and pushed away Liz's hand. "I did it because Katarina asked me."

"What?" Liz said, confused.

"You were screaming, constantly," Vendela said. "Either in agony or you were shouting how you were going to rip out her heart, making her watch it happen."

Liz took a step back, trying to keep her face neutral but she was afraid there were cracks in her facade.

"Apparently you screamed things about me as well," Vendela continued.

"I don't remember it," Liz said plainly and with as steady a voice as she could manage.

"How convenient for your conscience," Vendela said. "I bet Katarina won't forget it though."

"She didn't say anything about it," Liz said slowly.

But as she said that she remembered the caution in Katarina's eyes that had not been there before she had been in the basement.

"Katarina's a good person," Vendela said. "Perhaps a little naive and inexperienced. But she… I don't know if like is the right word but you have her interest anyway."

Liz had nothing else to say, she certainly had nothing to say in her defense. Vendela sighed softly.

"I'm sorry," Vendela said tiredly. "I didn't mean to be so harsh. I know it wasn't you that yelled those things."

"Don't defend me, I don't deserve it" was Liz's immediate thought, but she said nothing, just averted her eyes.

"You can be harsh and even mean at times," Vendela said. "But you're not cruel."

Liz's lips separated slightly out of shock but the rest of her face remained neutral.

"You give me too much credit," Liz said and tried to laugh but it sounded fake even in her ears.

The corner of Vendela's mouth twitched almost into a smile, but it quickly disappeared as she probably reminded herself that she was still cross with Liz.

"I'll put your dress in the washer," Vendela said. "Make yourself at home."

Liz nodded lightly and just before Vendela disappeared behind one of the doors, she stopped and paused.

"Right, Ami came by a while ago," Vendela said, her voice cold. "She wanted to talk with you."

"What did she want?" Liz asked.

"She wouldn't say," Vendela said.

Short pause of silence.

"Did something happen between you?" Liz asked, surprised by the tone in Vendela's voice.

Vendela gave Liz a glance before turning away again.

"I told her to come by at nightfall," Vendela said.

"Vendela," Liz said and took a step towards her but Vendela had already disappeared behind the door and slammed it shut behind her.

Liz sighed and clenched her jaw in irritation. She had been the one to keep secrets and speak vaguely, she wasn't used to Vendela doing the same and it drove her crazy not getting any proper answers. She knew it was hypocritical of her but it was as if she couldn't help herself. If she hadn't been fed so recently, she probably wouldn't have been able to keep her temperament in check.

Liz sunk down into one of the many chairs in the Bar and put her face in her hands. She was annoyed with Vendela that she wouldn't talk to her, that she obviously didn't trust her enough to tell her anything of importance. But Liz knew she had done nothing to earn that trust and she had done everything, though unintentionally, to make Vendela lose it. Vendela was kind, but she was not soft or weak and her patience with Liz had started to run dry.

Liz slammed her hand on to the table next to her out of frustration and bit her lower lip. Perhaps she was mostly mad at herself and she took it out on Vendela. It was the blood that made her feel this way, she had built a wall around her dead heart that had to hold no matter what.

It was at this point, when everything had settled properly and the warm blood rushing through her body wasn't all she could feel, that she realized she still did not have her bag or her box. Liz shot up from the seat she'd been sitting in, her eyes wide open. Vendela must have it, there was no other explanation. Liz didn't remember anything from before she fell unconscious, she only remembered holding her box in her hands, and as it was Vendela who had taken Liz to the basement she must be the one to have it. A feeling of dread washed over her, threatening to drown her, what if Vendela had looked inside the box? Seeing all of that pathetic sentimental crap, Liz could barely stand to think about it. That box was one of her greatest shames, and she carried it with her everywhere. That box was evidence that Liz wasn't just a cold and relentless creature, that she was more than the facade she put up for others to see.

The things inside that box personalized her, and told a story about her. And she wasn't ready for anyone to know her story, not even Vendela.

Liz looked over to the door Liz had seen Vendela enter before she'd gone to the bathroom, which had to be her bedroom. Liz tried to listen closely if she could hear Vendela come back this way but everything was perfectly quiet. With soundless steps Liz walked up to the door and put her hand on the door knob. Was this a violation of Vendela's personal space? The thought crossed Liz's mind but the idea of Vendela looking through her box was of a bigger concern to her. But Vendela was already angry with her, this would make things worse. If Liz was found out that was. Liz would just go in, take her bag with the box and then walk out, like it had never happened. But then when Vendela came back she would see the bag on Liz's shoulder and she would instantly realize what Liz had done. Liz glanced over at the door Vendela had disappeared through, her hand still on the door knob.

Liz swallowed, and felt her grip around the door knob tighten and she had the urge to just rip the door off its hinges but decided against it. She couldn't ask Vendela about it, she just couldn't, it would kill her. Before Liz could stop herself she kicked the door in anger and gave out a low yell. The door shook but stayed intact.

"Damn it," Liz said and was just about to turn the door knob when she heard a low sound coming from the front door.

It sounded like paper sliding through the crack of the door, Liz had heard that sound countless of times and knew it without fault. Liz turned her head towards the door and could see a white envelope laying on the floor. Liz froze where she stood and just stared at the letter, it was most likely meant for Vendela. Maybe it was that girl Tess that had left it.

Liz was now faced with two options. One, enter Vendela's room and hope that for some reason she wouldn't realize Liz had taken back her bag or two, she could take a closer look at that letter and maybe shed some light on what Vendela was up to. Both were invasive and would do nothing to gain Vendela's trust. Liz glanced over at the door to her right to make sure Vendela wasn't coming back yet and she bit her lower lip before she slowly let go of the door knob. She would have other opportunities to find her bag, but she was sure this would be her only chance of seeing what was in that letter. With quick steps she went over to the front door and slowly lifted the letter and turned it over to see if it said anything on the outside. When she saw what was written on the front side, she felt as if the fresh blood inside her turned cold.

There was just one thing written on the front of the letter and it was written in an obnoxiously pretty and professional handwriting. "Liz."

For a moment she just stared at it with confused eyes and almost thought she was reading it wrong, but there was no mistake, her name was written on that letter. Without thinking Liz tore open the door and was blinded by the light but she managed to close it again before she got burned. The sun must have suddenly poked through some of the clouds as it had been cloudy just a few minutes ago.

"Shit," Liz said and blinked fervently.

No way of finding out who had left the letter and how the hell they'd known to find her here. Liz tore open the envelope and picked out the things inside. It was a letter and another smaller laminated piece of paper. With a frown she first looked at the smaller piece of paper.

"Name: Elizabeth Frost. Species: Vampire. Age: ????

Minimal danger to humans.

She is allowed two hours in Town every wednesday."

It was her updated papers, just like they had promised. Which meant she knew who the letter was from. Liz glanced over to the door. It would be bad if Vendela came back at this moment and saw the letter. Vendela had to be back any moment, it didn't take that long to put a dress in the washer. Liz pushed her luck and started to read the letter instead of putting it away and reading it later.

"Liz.

Meet us in Town tomorrow, we have some things to discuss. Meet us at Café La Rouge at midday, the weather forecast says it will rain so you should be in no danger. If it is sunny then we will contact you for a new time."

It wasn't signed but there was no need for it, Liz had been right about who it was from. Without her noticing it, her hands had started to shake slightly and she closed her eyes before she tore it in multiple pieces and shoved what was left in her left bra cup and put her updated paper in the other cup.

Chapter 11

Liz reminded herself that she had to get rid of the remainder of that letter as soon as she could, preferably burning it so no one could ever read it again. Not that it was that incriminating but it would absolutely lead to more questions.

"What are you doing?"

Liz turned around a little too quickly at the sound of Vendela's voice.

"Nothing," she said as innocently as she possibly could.

Vendela frowned slightly, like she didn't entirely believe that.

"You're shaking," Vendela said instead.

Liz looked at her hands and indeed, they were shaking ever so slightly. Vendela walked behind the bar and pulled up two glasses and then a large bottle filled with something that looked similar to red wine. She poured the blood into both the glasses and picked up one and took a sip, color immediately flushing into her pale face.

"Drink," Vendela said.

Liz walked up to the bar and stared at the glass, hesitating slightly. Vendela must think the shaking was because Liz was still hungry, which wasn't entirely true. She could surely go for some more blood, she almost always could. Liz would let Vendela believe she was shaking from hunger and not the real reason.

"You didn't have that much before, it's fine," Vendela said. "I've broken the rule once today, I might as well break it twice."

Liz picked up the glass and took a small sip. It was warm and fresh. It was almost as if the blood had come directly from a body which surprised Liz. She'd half closed her eyes without noticing it and when she looked over at Vendela she could just see a smile on her lips before it disappeared.

"How fresh is this?" Liz asked.

"I got it yesterday I think," Vendela said and shrugged.

"That's not possible," Liz said. "It tastes as if it's straight from a body."

"A spell," Vendela said. "On the bottle."

Liz immediately put down the glass and let go of it.

"It keeps the blood fresh," Vendela said. "It's a good thing."

"You could have told me that before I drank it," Liz muttered angrily.

"The blood is fine," Vendela said. "Don't be a baby. It's the bottle that has the spell on it."

"You know how I feel about magic," Liz said.

"Yeah and the Fun House," Vendela said. "But guess what, the blood I gave you in the basement, that bottle had a spell on it and it came from the Fun House, same as this."

Liz's hands formed into fists and she could feel her fingernails dig into her palm. Vendela calmly took another sip of the blood.

"Are you really angry?" Vendela asked and looked at Liz fists. "Should I have continued to let you starve and then give you the cold blood provided from the Town that comes in tomorrow, at best?"

Liz looked away but she relaxed her hands slightly.

"In times like these," Vendela said. "We sometimes have to stretch our principles."

"Like you working for the Fun House?" Liz asked.

Vendela licked her lip and put down her glass.

"I'm not working for the Fun House, I'm working for Mr. Greenlund," Vendela said. "You weren't here. You have no right to say anything about it. You're the one who left, remember?"

"I didn't leave exactly," Liz muttered.

"Then what happened?" Vendela asked with force.

Liz laughed but it was an empty laugh with a sharp edge in it.

"I'm not doing this," Liz said and turned around.

She could hear Vendela move and in the blink of an eye, Vendela was standing in front of her, her gray eyes cold and focused. For a brief second Liz just stared at her, at all her features, and she remembered why she'd always been reminded of the moon when she looked at her. Cold, beautiful, dependable but hard to reach. Liz herself was the sun, intense and if you got too close you'd get hurt.

"And I'm not doing this again Liz," she said, her voice shaking with anger and she almost seemed out of breath.

"What are you talking about?" Liz said confusedly and took a step back.

"You left me Liz – Again! Without a single word – Again!" Vendela yelled, her eyes cold and steady but her voice gave her away with the raw emotion in it.

Liz was taken aback by her words and her mouth fell open slightly but she tried to keep her face neutral, like Vendela's words hadn't penetrated every wall she'd built inside.

"So that's what this is really about," Liz said as a statement. "You don't really care what I've been up to or where I've been, you're just upset I left *you.*"

As the words left Liz's mouth she was almost shocked herself; had she really said that? How had those words possibly slipped past her lips? But they had, there was no denying it and Liz knew with great certainty that she had royally screwed up. Vendela looked like someone had just slapped her and she swallowed hard.

"I…" Liz started but couldn't finish.

"Maybe I was wrong," Vendela said, her voice thick. "Maybe you are cruel Liz."

Vendela turned around and all Liz wanted to do was to grab her and hold her and whisper how sorry she was, how sorry she was for everything she'd done and how she'd never do anything like it ever again. But it would only be lies and Liz had lied to her enough. Vendela deserved better, which was ultimately why Liz didn't move.

"Did you ever love me Liz?" Vendela asked, her voice now very low. "At any point? Or was that another one of your lies?"

Liz felt as if someone had kicked her in her stomach and her throat closed itself so she could barely make a sound.

"Yes. Yes." Liz thought. "*If my heart could beat it would beat only for you.*"

But it was like the words reached her tongue and then dissolved into nothing. Leaving Liz quiet in a time where a few simple words would have been sufficient.

Vendela waited, but not another sound escaped Liz's lips.

"Okay," Vendela said coldly. "Good to know."

"Vendela," Liz said and she was surprised by the softness and pleading tone in her voice.

Vendela said nothing else and marched into her room, slamming the door behind her. Leaving Liz in complete silence.

Liz stood as still as a statue, if anyone had seen her at this moment they would most likely not have thought she was a real person. Her golden eyes were shiny and she stared at Vendela's bedroom door with her mouth slightly open. It was like she was not entirely sure of what just had happened, it all had happened so quickly and it felt as if she had witnessed it from afar, unable to do anything to change the outcome.

Then Vendela's bedroom door opened slightly and Liz moved for the first time in minutes, even though it felt like hours for her. Maybe Vendela had changed her mind and wanted to talk things over.

"Vende-…" Was all Liz could get out.

"Take your damn bag, leave and don't come back," Vendela yelled from the inside and her bag was thrown out of the room towards Liz, and then the door was shut firmly again.

Liz moved quickly and managed to catch it before it hit the floor and she could feel the weight of her box in it and it sent a feeling of calm through her body, though it only lasted for a split second. Then the shock settled and the numbness overtook her once again. She walked out of the Bar in a haze, not thinking about the danger of the sun but it must have been cloudy once again as she was walking unharmed. Her feet walked without purpose, her mind blank and just replaying the last conversation with Vendela over and over again in her mind. All the things she should have said, all the things she could have said, they would haunt her forever. Finally she was stopped by a brick wall at the end of an alley and with a single sob escaping her lips, she leaned against the wall and slid down until she was sitting on the ground, her face in her hands, unable to make another sound.

Chapter 12

Liz sat in that alley as the sky got darker and darker until she could barely be seen, it was almost like she didn't exist at all. Liz didn't understand what was happening to her, this fight with Vendela had made her think of their time together, of every lie Liz had told her. Thinking it was for the best, when in reality, if Liz was honest with herself, she'd only lied because she was afraid, afraid of what Vendela would think of her if she knew all the things she'd done. Afraid she would look at her in a different way. And that started a chain reaction, making her think about all the things she had done during her long lifetime.

Liz closed her eyes and put her hands over her ears, as if that would help keep out the voices inside her head. *"Don't think about the things you've done." "I did what I had to do."* Liz repeated those two sentences in her mind like a mantra, trying to kill any other voices in her head. Any voice of conscience, any voice of the people she'd done wrong.

"Liz, is that you?" A soft voice spoke.

Liz shot up to her feet and she saw a body belonging to the voice standing at the opening of the alley but she couldn't make out the person's face for some reason, her eyes just wouldn't focus properly. The face, the body, the voice, it all sounded so foreign, so strange. Was she hallucinating? It wouldn't have been the first time.

"What the hell do you want from me?" Liz asked, her voice shaking.

"Liz, I've been looking for you for hours," the voice said and walked closer.

Finally Liz could see the soft and kind features of Ami but her beautiful face had an expression of worry on it. Liz exhaled in relief at the fact she wasn't hallucinating before she instantly put up her walls and her neutral face.

"Ami?" Liz said, trying to avoid her voice from shaking. "What are you doing here?"

Ami stopped in front of Liz and gently grasped her hands. Ami's hands were so warm and soft and she held Liz with such care that it almost hurt more than if she had been rough.

"What happened?" Ami asked.

Liz couldn't bear Ami's gentle touch, she couldn't bear the worry in her voice or face. Liz snatched back her hands and she saw the surprise in Ami's face.

"I'm fine," Liz said, her voice had an edge.

"What are you doing here?" Ami asked. "I came to the Bar but Vendela only said you weren't there anymore. I have *never* seen her like that, did you two fi-…"

"I'm not in the mood Ami," Liz said harshly. "You really do not want to be near me right now."

Ami frowned slightly but she looked over at Liz as if she was seeing if she was serious or not, if this was the right time to push Liz or let her be.

"I really need to talk to you," Ami said. "I need your help."

"Ask Vendela," Liz said with spite.

Liz swallowed and she felt disgusted with herself. Ami had been nothing but kind to her during their friendship, always caring and always ready to help. But that was Liz's problem, she couldn't stand people being too nice to her, because she simply didn't believe she deserved it. People that were kind to her obviously didn't know her very well and as Liz didn't want to share her stories, her only way of separating herself from others was to be someone she absolutely loathed. It was ultimately, for their sake rather than hers. They would all be better off without her.

"I can't," Ami said, ignoring the spite in Liz 's voice. "I can't trust her."

Liz frowned slightly, feeling some of her defense failing at those words.

"What do you mean?" Liz asked, confused.

"I know how close you two a-…" Ami started.

"Ami," Liz said impatiently and interrupted her. "Just get to the point."

"She's working for the same man I do," Ami said. "Mr. Greenlund."

"So?" Liz said. "She hates it."

Ami swallowed and it looked like she was choosing her words with care. She glanced behind her before she started talking again.

"You've seen the Bar," Ami said low. "At all the things she's gotten, you don't think there is a catch?"

"She's working for him," Liz said. "Isn't that bad enough?"

Ami laughed low.

"In that case, that is not a very high price to pay," Ami said. "Most pay a lot more for a lot less."

"Ami," Liz said. "Just tell me what the hell this is about."

"I can't tell her about my problem because I think she's spying for Mr. Greenlund," Ami said low yet very quickly, like she wanted to just have it said. "That's why I've been avoiding her ever since we both started working for him."

Liz shook her head.

"No," Liz said. "You're wrong. She wouldn't do that."

"She works at the Bar, the meeting place of all the creatures," Ami said. "She hears everything. You really think he built up the Bar and let her act like she owns it without anything in return? That he did it out of the goodness of his heart?"

"I don't know why he did it," Liz said. "I wasn't here."

"Right," Ami said. "You weren't here."

"But I know Vendela would never spy for the Fun House," Liz said. "She would never spy and betray her friends."

But as Liz was talking, she could hear Vendela's voice echo in her head: *"We sometimes have to stretch our principles."* and a chill went down her spine.

Ami didn't look convinced.

"I know you though," Ami said with a soft smile. "You've been away so you can't be working for him and I know how much you hate the Fun House. I know I can trust you on this Liz."

Liz frowned and was quite astonished by the trust in Ami's eyes. Liz closed her eyes and swallowed. There were two choices she could make at this point. One, push away Ami and tell her that whatever it was Liz couldn't help her. Or two, swallow some of that goddamn fear and pride and help her friend.

Liz had already made one person hate her tonight, perhaps she didn't need to make that two.

"What's wrong?" Liz asked almost against her better judgment.

Ami smiled and it was a genuine and heart warming smile that almost made Liz feel it twitch in the corner of her mouth. Ami had always had that effect, the aura around her made everyone close to her feel that things would be alright.

"Okay," Ami said and took a deep breath. "There are four floors to the Fun House, we who work there live on the bottom floor and the second and third floor is where we... work."

"And on the fourth floor?" Liz asked.

"Mr. Greenlund's office is there," Ami said. "But that is one room of maybe a dozen."

"What's in them?" Liz asked carefully.

"I don't know," Ami said and bit her lower lip. "They say it's for workers who... are stressed or worn out, a place for them to take a few days off. But the thing is... Not a lot of people actually return from there. I'm not sure if anyone has actually returned."

Liz didn't say anything, she just let Ami continue talking but the more she talked the less Liz was liking what she was hearing.

"And I... I had a little breakdown the other day," Ami said and pushed some of her black hair behind her ear. "I was just so tired and... Anyway, Mr. Greenlund wanted to speak with me and he asked how I was and if I needed a few days off, on the fourth floor. I lied, immediately and said I was fine. But I am so afraid Liz, so afraid they'll force me there."

"Maybe you're overreacting?" Liz said, but she didn't believe her own words at all, it was just a futile attempt to try and calm Ami down a little.

Ami shook her head.

"I don't know what to do Liz," Ami said.

Liz looked away.

"Let me talk with Vendela," Liz said, ignoring the fact they'd fought only hours ago, Vendela wouldn't turn down helping a friend; at least Liz didn't think so. "I'm sure she can help you."

"No!" Ami said with panic and gripped Liz's arm. "Please don't."

Liz sighed and she didn't entirely know why, but she felt a need to protect Ami. Maybe because unlike herself and Vendela, Ami was very much mortal. Soft and warm and very easily killed.

"What do you want me to do?" Liz asked hesitantly.

"Just… Keep an eye out for me?" Ami said. "Like if you don't hear from me in a while…"

"And if I don't hear from you, then what do you want me to do?" Liz asked carefully.

"I don't know…" Ami said, as if she hadn't exactly thought that far. "Find me?"

Liz frowned slightly and swallowed. If Ami did disappear as she feared, finding her meant Liz had to get involved with the Fun House, which also meant getting involved with the humans. Liz might not like the Fun House but she had sworn to stay out of anything that had to do with the humans or anything really that had severe consequences. Like going into the Fun House with the intent of stripping the walls bare to find her friend. That would not only draw attention to her from the humans, but in a worst case scenario not only she but others could be punished for it. But as Liz looked into Ami's eyes once again, she couldn't help the words slip past her lips.

"Of course," Liz said. "If that calms you down."

She almost regretted it the moment she'd said it and she hoped with all of her dead heart that Ami was just being paranoid. Ami smiled and showed two rows of white teeth and it was almost like she was shining in this dark alley.

"Thank you Liz, I knew I could count on you," Ami said and leaned over and kissed her gently on the cheek.

Liz bit her lower lip before smiling lightly back at her.

"No problem," Liz said low.

Ami looked behind her and then up at the sky.

"I should get back," Ami said. "I've been gone for too long really."

"You're not allowed to leave?" Liz asked with a touch of worry in her voice.

"Oh, of course we are allowed to leave," Ami said. "We just have to… To account where we're going and how long we estimate to be gone… And we have a curfew I am quite certain I've broken at this point."

"Let me walk you back okay?" Liz said.

"You don't have to Liz," Ami said.

It wasn't as much for Ami's sake Liz wanted to accompany her, but for her own. Ami was like a ray of sunshine on a rainy day and just her presence had made Liz calm down and gotten her mind on something else. That was the one good part about helping others, it was a distraction. And as Liz didn't really have a place to go to, she might as well walk with Ami. Liz might be able to talk with Vendela in a few days when she's calmed down, but right now going back to the Bar would be like walking into a storm. The only other person she really knew well enough or liked well enough to go to was strangely enough Katarina. But she couldn't impose on her all the time, it wasn't like Liz was great company and even though Katarina didn't say anything about it she must be getting tired of Liz showing up at her doorstep all the time. Even if it had only happened twice… It felt like a lot more.

So she might as well walk the short road to the Fun House with Ami and to make sure nothing happened to her on the way back at least, but it did trouble Liz a little that she could practically do nothing for her on the inside. Liz shook off that feeling, she was acting like Ami was a child who couldn't take care of herself which wasn't true at all. Even though compared to Liz, Ami might as well be a child when it comes to age. Ami wasn't unable to take care of herself but she wasn't stupid either, she knew she was more fragile than a lot of other creatures in here. A shapeshifter didn't have much to their advantage except that they could disappear into a crowd easily. No extra strength, no super speed, no immortality.

Ami knew that Liz was pretty much made out of steel compared to her.

"Just humor me," Liz said.

Ami took Liz by the arm and smiled gently. Liz could instantly feel the warmth coming from Ami and she could also feel the slow and steady pulse coming from her wrist. As Liz felt Ami's warmth, she must have felt how cold Liz was and yet she acted like she didn't notice it. They were quite a strange pair when they stood directly next to one another, they looked like complete opposites in more than one sense. Ami was tall with dark skin and long black hair and almost always with a smile on her lips. Liz was short and she was as pale as a ghost, her whole arms and legs covered in tattoos and with her short cropped hair.

And perhaps the most important difference, Ami was very much alive while Liz was very much dead.

"Lead the way," Ami said.

They started walking and if Liz hadn't been a vampire, she would never have been able to keep up with Ami, as one of her steps were two or three of Liz's steps.

"Not that I want to seem like a nosy nancy," Ami said. "But what were you doing in that alley?"

To lie or not to lie, that was always the question for Liz. She was quiet for a moment before she sighed and spoke.

"I had a fight with Vendela and I… Kinda of just wandered in there," Liz said with as much humor in her voice as she could muster.

"What happened?" Ami asked with genuine concern.

Liz chuckled low.

"Me," Liz said. "If you haven't noticed I'm kind of an asshole."

"Liz," Ami said.

"It's okay," Liz said. "Really. I know what I am, it's okay."

Liz took a second's pause before she continued.

"I said… or rather did not say some things and now she hates me," Liz said, still the humor in her voice, like it wasn't bothering her at all.

They came out of the alleys and entered the main road again and Liz could now see the bright lights coming from the Fun House. Ami stopped them both in their tracks.

"I might not have talked with Vendela for a while," Ami said. "And I don't entirely trust her anymore but… She can't hate you, she just can't."

"Well, no offense but you weren't there," Liz said.

"No, but I was here when you were gone," Ami said. "And before the Bar burnt down and she started working for Mr. Greenlund she walked to your apartment every day for weeks, seeing if you'd come back. It was only when the Bar burnt down that she stopped or at least that's when we lost contact, so I don't know if she continued for another while."

Liz took a step back and she frowned in confusion.

"She told me," Ami said. "I even walked with her a couple times."

"W-Why would she do that?" Liz asked.

Ami laughed but there was no malice in it.

"Liz really?" Ami said. "You disappeared without a trace. One day you were here, the next you were gone. She hoped you'd come back of course."

Liz laughed without really knowing why and shook her head.

"Even though anyone else disappearing never showed up again?" Liz asked in disbelief. "You'd have to be-…"

"In love?" Ami filled in.

Liz was completely silent for what felt like an eternity.

"I was gonna say insane," Liz said with a melancholy smile.

"Whatever you did Liz," Ami said. "Give her some time and then talk to her."

"She pretty much made it clear that she doesn't want to see me again," Liz said quietly. "I don't think a few days will solve that."

"She's angry," Ami said. "Just give her a reason to listen to you, I know you're not as bad as some might think Liz. I mean you're doing this favor for me right?"

A favor that might involve me doing nothing" Liz thought but didn't say anything. Ami looked behind her towards the Fun House and a flash of worry came across her face.

"I really have to go," Ami said. "But I'll contact you tomorrow, okay?"

Liz nodded and Ami gracefully ran off towards the Fun House and quickly disappeared inside.

Chapter 13

As Ami disappeared into the Fun House, Liz sighed, rubbed her eyes and couldn't help but wonder what she'd gotten herself into. Liz said both to others and herself, that she would not interfere and that she did not care, but for someone who said that, Liz often found herself in situations that meant she had to interfere. Which in itself, showed that she at least to some extent cared.

Liz stared up at the dark sky, there were quite a few hours until dawn and if it was going to rain all day tomorrow as the letter had said she would be fine out on the street. But if the sun rose and the rain came in the afternoon, she would be in a little more trouble. Liz turned around and thought that there was no point in thinking about what's and if's, she couldn't change the weather even if she wanted to. She would just have to wait and see and if the sun did indeed rise she'd have to find a place to hide, there had to be somewhere unoccupied and whole enough to protect her.

As Liz turned around her eyes glanced over Katarina's apartment and to her surprise she saw that the door was wide open. Liz frowned, that was strange, everyone locked or barricaded their doors at night especially when it was this late. There was light coming from inside the house but Liz couldn't see any movement from the place she was standing.

With slow and careful steps she walked towards the apartment and all she could think about was what Katarina had said. *"Creatures have been disappearing, but so few and so far apart no one noticed at first."* There was a lump in Liz's stomach, she didn't know Katarina that well and she was more than a little strange. But Katarina had helped Liz more times than most, with the exception of Vendela, without asking for anything in return and when she knew nothing about Liz. The least Liz could do was check out her place to see if she was alright, but as Liz came closer and closer to Katarina's apartment she wasn't exactly sure what she would do if she indeed found the place empty.

If Katarina was gone, could Liz just walk away pretending she hadn't seen anything? Pretending Katarina hadn't given her shelter during the full moon and helped keep her and others safe when she was starving? Liz honestly didn't know, it was one of the things she found most frightening about herself. Until the moment arrived, she never knew how she would react. If she would just shrug and move on or if she would rip the world apart.

As she came closer, she still saw no movement from inside but the little she did see through the open door was that everything looked fine, nothing looked out of place or destroyed. That was comforting, if only a little. If they'd come to take Katarina or if someone had attacked her, Liz knew that she would have put up a fight. Liz involuntarily shivered at the thought of the protection spell that was carved into Katarina's skin and what it had done to Liz. But then again, maybe they'd taken her by surprise? Or maybe they'd come and Katarina had hidden in the basement and when they couldn't find her they just left? Though that didn't seem very likely to Liz.

"Katarina?" Liz said carefully and finally peeked through the door, expecting to either see no one or a lot of armed humans jump out.

Instead what Liz saw perplexed her. It was Katarina, standing at the stove and it looked like she was making tea. Katarina's back was turned to Liz as she poured the liquid into a cup for herself and the aroma of ginseng filled the air.

"I would ask you if you wanted a cup but I feel that would be unnecessary," Katarina said, turning around to face Liz, taking a sip of her tea.

Liz just stood dumbfounded and stared at Katarina for entirely too long.

"I-I… I was just gonna check if you were… Alright…" Liz stammered uncertainly.

A small smirk came across Katarina's face but she covered her lower face with the tea cup as she took another sip.

"Would you kindly shut the door behind you?" Katarina asked and sat down at the table. "It is getting a little chilly."

For a moment, Liz wasn't entirely sure on whether Katarina meant to shut the door behind her as she left the apartment or when she entered. But as Katarina was sitting and almost waiting, it would seem that she wanted Liz to enter. So that's what she did, and she closed the door behind her as Katarina had told her.

"Thank you," Katarina said and put down her cup.

"I don't understand," Liz said finally, still standing by the door.

Katarina looked over to her, tilting her head slightly. Katarina's eyes looked wide awake but the bags under her eyes told another story.

"What do you mean?" Katarina asked.

"Your door was open," Liz said. "I thought-…"

"I was in danger?" Katarina asked, almost amused.

Liz shut her mouth and clenched her jaw.

"You wanted to help me," Katarina stated and took a large sip of her warm tea.

Liz chuckled lightly and bit her lip.

"I've had a long day," Liz said. "I'm not really in the mood for… Whatever you're doing."

"Sit, please," Katarina said and gestured to a chair opposite herself.

Hesitantly Liz sat down and let her bag fall to the floor.

"Why was your door open?" Liz asked.

"Because I felt your energy out there and thought I'd invite you in," Katarina said simply. "It is quite late."

"You could feel me out there, from here?" Liz asked with hidden amazement.

Katarina nodded.

"When people are experiencing intense emotions, it is much easier for me to pick up on them," Katarina said. "And as everyone has different energies, if you learn them, it is quite easy to distinguish one person from another."

"Intense emotions," Liz muttered.

"You're wearing different clothes," Katarina said, changing the conversation entirely.

"Great deduction skills you have there," Liz said sarcastically.

"I guess you got them from Vendela," Katarina said calmly.

Liz bit her lower lip.

"And as you are out this late roaming the streets, with… intense emotions, I assumed you'd had a fight with Vendela and needed a place to stay," Katarina said. "So I opened my door for you as I also assumed you would be too stubborn to come here by yourself."

"You deduced that from… My energy?" Liz asked skeptically.

"Am I wrong?" Katarina asked, as if she wasn't at all embarrassed if that was the case.

Liz stared at Katarina, her eyes narrow but there was no anger or irritation in them.

"No," Liz finally said. "Are you sure you're only… That you're not even twenty?"

Liz stumbled on the word nineteen again, the number tasting like acid in her mouth and she avoided it if possible.

"Yes," Katarina said with a low laugh. "Quite sure. How old are you?"

"How old am I?" Liz repeated with amusement. "Older than you."

There was something with Katarina that fascinated her. She was powerful, both in her future seeing and her magic. More powerful than any teenager who'd only lived with their parents and started magic a year ago should be. Liz wondered if even Katarina knew her true potential, how could she if she had never had a teacher? She must have learned things somehow, if not from someone, then from somewhere. A spell book perhaps?

"You want to take a guess?" Liz asked. "At my age?"

There was almost a look of surprise on Katarina's face.

"Do I get something if I'm right?" Katarina asked.

Liz picked at the skin around her nails, contemplating what to say next but then she thought what the hell? As Katarina had never touched her and no one in the Sanctuary, not even Vendela, knew how old she truly was, it was a gamble worth taking.

"Okay," Liz said. "If you guess correctly, I'll tell you something about me. Whatever you want."

"And if I get it wrong?" Katarina asked.

"I get to ask you something," Liz said much more seriously.

Katarina tilted her head slightly and her eyes almost shone from excitement or curiosity, Liz wasn't sure which one it was.

"Are there any rules?" Katarina asked.

"What do you mean?" Liz asked.

"Am I allowed to touch you first?" Katarina asked.

"That'd be cheating," Liz said.

"I might just see your future," Katarina said. "Or a point in your past. I cannot decide what I see."

"Then it doesn't matter now does it?" Liz said.

"It would give me a hunch," Katarina said slowly. "Of your age. It isn't as hard to tell if someone is very old or young when I've touched them."

"Well, I can tell you this," Liz said and leaned forward. "I'm old. Now guess."

"Do I have to get it exactly right?" Katarina asked.

"If you're within fifty years," Liz said. "I'll give it to you."

Katarina stared directly at Liz and her face expression hadn't changed at all but there was something much more serious about her now that made Liz a little uncomfortable. The way Katarina was staring at her, barely blinking and Liz struggled to keep eye contact with her. Liz felt as if Katarina could read her mind and even if people said that the eyes were the window to the soul, one Liz didn't believe in that or that Katarina could read minds; and secondly she wasn't so sure she had a soul anymore. Katarina finally sighed, looked away and drank up the last bit of her tea.

"I'd say… Around 195 years old," Katarina said slowly.

Liz leaned back in her chair and crossed her arms as a smile came across her lips, showing a row of white teeth.

"Wrong," Liz said. "I win."

Katarina didn't really look bothered that she'd lost, but then again Katarina always had a very neutral look on her face.

"So how old are you?" Katarina asked.

"I won," Liz said. "I get to ask the question."

Katarina frowned slightly.

"You're not going to tell me?" Katarina said.

Liz bit her lower lip and was quiet for a moment.

"Do you feel it reveals too much about you?" Katarina asked curiously.

Liz laughed but mostly to conceal the truth, that Katarina was completely right.

"It's just a number," Liz lied.

"Then what is the problem?" Katarina asked.

"The problem is that you lost," Liz said and she felt like she was repeating herself. "So you don't get to know shit."

Katarina only stared at Liz with her green and yellow speckled eyes.

"So what is your question?" Katarina asked as she rose from her chair.

Liz watched as Katarina walked over to the pot of tea she had made earlier and she realized how late it was for Katarina. It was well past midnight and yet Katarina was awake and she was making herself a second cup of tea. Was she trying to stay awake for Liz or was there another reason?

As Katarina poured her second cup of tea Liz spoke.

"What book did you get that protection spell from?" Liz finally asked with a dead serious tone.

As the words left Liz's mouth, Katarina almost slammed the pot with the remaining tea onto the stove and she stood still with her back turned towards Liz. Liz arched an eyebrow, she hadn't expected that reaction. She wasn't sure what she'd expected really, but it hadn't been that.

"Who said anything about a book?" Katarina finally said.

"I guessed," Liz said and shrugged. "You said you'd lived with your parents and as they aren't here with you I assume they're just ordinary humans. So I also assumed you didn't have a teacher but you'd have to learn magic somewhere and that spell you have on your arms isn't something for beginners. It had to come from a powerful spell book."

Katarina finally turned and faced Liz, her cup of tea still in her hands. Katarina licked her lips before taking a sip again.

"For someone that supposedly hates magic, you seem to know quite a lot about it," Katarina said.

"Yeah well sometimes the more you know about something, the more you hate it," Liz said.

"And why does someone who hates magic want to know about a spell book?" Katarina asked with caution in her voice. "As far as I know you don't possess any magic powers."

"I don't, thankfully," Liz said. "I don't need another curse."

Katarina didn't say anything else but her eyes had become slivers as she looked at Liz. Obviously she was suspicious and Liz didn't really blame her, this question must seem strange.

"Are you gonna answer my question or not?" Liz said. "We had a deal."

Katarina sighed lightly, put down her cup of tea and walked over to her book shelf. She let her hands glide over the backs of the many books on the shelf until she reached a certain one in the middle of the top row. Then, if Liz hadn't known Katarina had magic, she would have thought her eyes were deceiving her. Katarina reached *into* the book as if it didn't exist and her hand disappeared before it reappeared again, now holding a very large and old looking tome. Katarina must have put some kind of spell on the shelf to hide it, which meant it must be important to her.

Katarina took the tome in both of her hands and her fingers traced over the golden details on the front of it. Katarina then shot Liz a quick look before she went and sat beside her and laid down the tome carefully on the table. There were no letters on the front or any indications at all that this was a spell book or any special book at all. It looked completely ordinary, one that you'd use for writing a diary or something. It was beautiful and the gold that went around the front almost looked like live snakes, slithering all over the place. Liz raised an eyebrow and looked at Katarina who was staring intently at the tome.

"This is it?" Liz asked skeptically.

"Yes," Katarina said.

Liz hesitantly reached to open the tome but found herself stopped by Katarina. She had put her hand on the front side of it, stopping Liz from even touching it. And Liz found herself grateful that Katarina hadn't gripped her as Liz was wearing a short sleeve shirt and Katarina wasn't wearing her gloves. But Liz was sure that Katarina had thought of that, she had lived with that ability her whole life. By now she must be very aware of her every movement, and as Liz had said quite a few times that she didn't want Katarina to touch her, it would seem that Katarina respected that more than most would have by now.

"You won't be able to read it," Katarina said. "You said you wanted to know what book it was, this is it, now we are done."

"Why won't I be able to read it?" Liz asked, ignoring the fact that Katarina obviously wanted to end this discussion.

A sigh escaped from Katarina before she slowly removed her hand from the tome.

"Okay," she said. "Open it and look for yourself."

Katarina leaned back in her chair and shifted her gaze from the tome to Liz, which made Liz hesitate a little. Would it hurt her if she touched it? The thought crossed her mind and as she didn't trust magic, it wouldn't surprise her.

"It's not going to hurt you," Katarina said calmly.

"Are you lying to me?" Liz asked half as a joke.

"I don't lie," Katarina said plainly.

Hesitantly and only with a little trust in that Katarina wasn't lying to her, she reached for the tome and when her fingers brushed over the hard front she felt something. Liz wasn't sure on what, but it was something. Like a soft heat emanating especially from the thin gold parts that slithered around the cover. Katarina must have noticed the fact that Liz was just keeping her hand on the cover and not actually opening the tome.

"It's testing you," Katarina finally said.

"Testing me?" Liz said and couldn't help but laugh a little.

"It's testing to see if you have magic," Katarina said and her eyes were focused on Liz with curiosity written all over her face.

Liz finally lifted her hand from the cover and opened the tome and she frowned deeply when she saw the content. She flipped through all the pages and found herself feeling both fooled and irritated. All the pages were blank, it was just a plain writing book.

"What the hell is this?" Liz said irritated. "You said this was the spell book."

"It is," Katarina said.

"So where are the spells?" Liz asked with force.

"I told you, you wouldn't be able to read it," Katarina said. "The words only show themselves for those who possess magic. A way to hide the powerful content within."

"I thought you said everyone had a little magic in them," Liz said sarcastically.

Katarina smiled weakly.

"The magic has to be accessed before you can use it," Katarina said. "I've had the tome for years but it wasn't until a year ago that the words appeared for me."

"So it's useless for me, is what you're saying?" Liz asked.

"What do you want with it anyway?" Katarina asked. "I can't imagine any spells would interest you."

Liz slammed it shut and rose from the chair.

"Forget it," Liz said. "It doesn't matter."

Katarina rose and as she walked up to Liz, she let her hand glide over the cover of the tome and it almost looked like the gold was glowing this time. Katarina looked at Liz, her gaze quite soft while Liz had hardened.

"If you want something done with magic," Katarina said. "You could just ask."

Liz, who'd half had her back towards Katarina, turned and she tried to mask her surprise.

"What?" Liz said.

"I don't think I can make it much clearer," Katarina said. "All you have to do is *ask.*"

Liz scratched her neck, desperately feeling the need to put up all her walls, as if she'd lowered her defense in Katarina's company without barely noticing it. Making herself vulnerable.

"Why?" Liz finally said, because that question had been eating at her for almost as long as she'd known Katarina.

"Why what?" Katarina said.

"Why are you helping me?" Liz asked. "Why did you give me shelter during the full moon? Why did you help me when I was blood deprived? Why are you trying to help me now?"

Katarina shrugged.

"I find you fascinating," Katarina said with a neutral voice.

"I'm not a lab rat," Liz said with a harsher tone than she'd intended.

"I know that," Katarina said. "I never said you were."

"And you don't do all of that just because you find someone fascinating," Liz said. "You have to want something from me."

"I don't," Katarina said. "Why have you taken my help? Come into a stranger's house twice from your free will to seek shelter?"

"B-Because… I had no choice," Liz stammered, not expecting the question.

"Okay," Katarina simply said.

Silence.

"You don't want anything from me?" Liz asked slowly.

"Nothing," Katarina said. "Except perhaps your company from time to time."

"My… Company?" Liz said in disbelief. "You know who you're talking to right?"

"I know," Katarina said.

"Do you have a fever? Are you sick?" Liz asked. "I'm not exactly good company."

"Perhaps you don't enjoy your own company Liz," Katarina said. "But I do. As I said, you fascinate me."

Liz let out a half pathetic laugh.

"You can't have had much company throughout your life if you enjoy mine," Liz said.

There was a flash of something so desperately sad in Katarina's eyes, making her look like a small child, but it was gone in an instant. Liz frowned, that flash of emotion was the closest to vulnerable or sadness that Liz had seen in Katarina.

"Perhaps you are right," Katarina said with a vague smile. "Perhaps if I'd had more company earlier in my life, I wouldn't enjoy your company as I do now."

Liz wanted to ask, but what she wanted to ask she wasn't entirely sure. Perhaps, why hadn't she had much company? And it was like Katarina read her mind.

"My parents love me," Katarina said. "Which is why, when I at the age of four started to show signs of my future seeing, they locked me in my room. They told everyone I was very, very sick. So I never talked to anyone other than my mother and father and I didn't leave that room for fifteen years. They wanted to protect me."

"I'm sorry," Liz said low and sincerely.

"Why?" Katarina asked. "They did it because they loved me."

"But they isolated you, locked you up," Liz said a little more harshly.

Now when Katarina had told her this, her personality did make a little more sense, except the fact that Liz was surprised that someone who'd spent their entire life in one room wasn't more scared of the outside or its people. Katarina seemed almost fearless, but it wasn't entirely like she was brave, more like she didn't fear things that perhaps should be feared. Like Liz. But that didn't mean she was stupid of course, the protection spell she'd put on herself proved that.

"Yes, but they fed me, gave me anything I asked for," Katarina said. "They home schooled me and read books for me. They loved me, they still do."

"Then how did you end up here?" Liz asked instead.

Katarina was silent for a moment.

"When the escape attempt happened I still lived in my room," Katarina said. "And I told you I didn't know a lot about it and that was true. But what I do know, is that the ones who tried to escape were executed in the square of the Town to set an example. I could just see it from the one window in my room. The Mayor had a long and dramatic speech about how they would not tolerate creatures rebelling and that anyone hiding a creature would be severely punished. So I turned myself in and because I did it out of my free will and because my parents were so influential it was kept quiet and I was moved into this apartment."

Liz was silent for a few seconds, trying to take in everything that Katarina had said.

"You… Gave yourself up…" Liz said with a slight frown. "For your parents?"

"If I'd been discovered then things might not have been kept under the rug," Katarina said. "They would have been punished. I couldn't live with that."

"So instead you get to suffer?" Liz said. "You went from being locked in a room your entire life to go into a new prison? Why didn't you just run away, try to get as far away as you could?"

"And go where?" Katarina said. "I know very little about the real world, only what I've read in books. And Sanctuaries exist all over the world, there wouldn't have been a place for me to hide."

Liz took a few steps back away from Katarina.

"Why are you telling me this?" Liz asked instead.

"Because you have trouble trusting people," Katarina said.

"Is it that obvious?" Liz said sarcastically.

"And I thought if you knew a little more about me," Katarina continued. "If I opened up, you might trust me a little more. At least to know that I do not want anything in return for the help I give."

Liz bit her lower lip.

"You're strange," Liz said.

Katarina smiled.

"You've said that before," Katarina said.

Liz's gaze went from Katarina, to the spell book on the table and to the window before she spoke again.

"You should probably get some sleep," Liz said. "It's late."

"I'm not tired," Katarina said.

Liz stared at Katarina and even though her eyes looked sharp, there were dark bags under her eyes and she looked pale.

"I thought you said you didn't lie," Liz said.

Katarina chuckled low.

"A white lie," Katarina said.

Liz couldn't take her eyes off Katarina and she remembered when she'd first seen her, she had looked carefree and well rested. But since Liz had been in the cellar, Katarina had had this exhausted look on her face no matter how much she tried to conceal it. Was it that Katarina found it hard to sleep or was it that she simply didn't want to sleep? Was that what the tea was for? And the worst thought, was it Liz's fault? Shame surged through Liz's body and even though she didn't remember anything she'd said, her whole time down in the basement was a haze, but she knew, she felt it in her whole body; the things she'd screamed were probably things that could keep someone up at night.

"I'm sorry," Liz said almost inaudibly.

"Excuse me?" Katarina said, confused.

Liz cleared her throat and looked away from Katarina, her eyes lingering on her bag that was laying on the floor by the table.

"It's my fault isn't it?" Liz said. "You don't want to sleep around me since… It's okay. I can leave and let you sleep, I'm sure there are oth-…"

"What are you talking about?" Katarina asked, still that confused look on her face.

Liz bit her lower lip and tried to drown out the irritation she felt, the irritation at herself for always causing hurt, worry and problems no matter where she went.

"You've looked tired ever since I stayed in your basement," Liz said." I know I must have said some *horrific* things and I don't blame you for not wanting to sleep when I'm here but-…"

Liz kinda stopped herself from finishing that sentence as she didn't really know what more to say, and she was still avidly trying to avoid eye contact with Katarina.

"I didn't hear anything you said during that time," Katarina said.

"What?" Liz said confused.

"Once you started screaming I put up a muffling spell, I could hear you but not anything you said." Katarina said.

"But... Vendela said..." Liz said low. "She said you asked her to give me blood because of the things I said..."

"I didn't ask her," Katarina said. "She just showed up."

Liz tried to make sense of what she was hearing. Vendela had said that Katarina had begged her to give Liz blood, and that was the only reason but according to Katarina it wasn't true? Had Vendela lied to her and in that case why? Why had she changed her mind if it wasn't because of Katarina?

"Me not sleeping has nothing to do with you," Katarina said after a few moments of silence. "I don't think you'd hurt me in my sleep and even if you would, I still have my protection spell."

Pause.

"Then why-...?" Liz asked low. "If not because of me?"

"Nightmares," Katarina said. "They come and go. Sometimes they come every night for weeks, other times they don't come for months. I've had them for as long as I can remember."

"Oh..." Liz said and she suddenly felt very silly for making this about herself. "So... The nightmares and me staying in your basement were just... A coincidence that they happened at the same time?"

"Yes," Katarina said plainly.

Katarina then walked back to the table and picked up the spell book and Liz saw the way she was holding it, like it was part of her.

"If you change your mind about wanting my help," Katarina said. "Just ask."

Liz opened and closed her mouth, almost letting the words escape but stopping them at the last second.

"Whatever," Liz said and sat down at the table as Katarina was putting away the book again.

"But you are right," Katarina said and rubbed her eyes. "I should try to get at least a few hours of sleep."

Katarina was making her way towards the door beside the book shelf but stopped and turned and looked at Liz before she went inside.

"I would advise you," Katarina said slowly. "Not to enter my room when I'm asleep."

"Why would I?" Liz asked carefully.

"If you hear anything," Katarina said. "Just ignore it."

"Will I be hearing anything?" Liz said cautiously.

"You might," Katarina said and then opened the door and disappeared from Liz's sight.

Liz swallowed and was looking at the closed door with a frown. She didn't like the sound of what Katarina had said but she would take her advice. Liz knew better than to go against it now.

There were still plenty of hours left of the night and quite a few more until Liz was going to the meeting in Town. Liz scratched her neck and then rubbed her eyes. What the hell was she doing? First the fight with Vendela that could have easily been avoided if Liz hadn't been so emotionally stunted or if she at least could have lied, then the impossible promise she'd made to Ami, just because she didn't want to disappoint another person within hours of each other. And now this with Katarina, she was letting her guard down and she was afraid that it was all because of the fight with Vendela.

The only person who had truly ever been able to make it past Liz's walls was Vendela and even though she had rebuilt them, they could never be as sturdy as they once were before she'd met her.

Liz didn't want to be the person that hurt everyone, which is why she often pushed people away, but by doing so she was hurting them anyway. But Liz knew that the closer she let someone, the more they trusted her and liked her, the more she could disappoint and *really* hurt them. That was why she'd pushed Vendela away, because she was getting too close to her once again, she'd been an asshole because she felt that even if she hurt them now, in the future they would be happier. But hurting people took its toll on Liz, pushing them away took its toll and she was weak to kindness.

Liz took up her box from the bag and she was horrified when she saw it.

When she opened it she felt that the lid was loose and the wood around the hinges were slightly broken. What had happened to it? But that thought was quickly replaced with her making sure that everything was inside, at first she felt relief in the fact that it looked like everything was in there when she noticed that wasn't the case. The drawing of her and Vendela dancing was gone and no matter how much Liz looked, even if she emptied all of the box contents, she could not find it. Panic spread through her as she was scrambling through her old things, looking for a simple drawing and finally Liz just leaned back in her chair, a feeling of dread in her stomach. Because there were only two possibilities, either the drawing was gone, where it had gone, Liz had no idea. Or Vendela had it. Liz wasn't sure which possibility she preferred. That drawing was the only thing she owned that reminded her of Vendela, she'd had it for years, she'd had it when they'd been together and she'd had it when she'd lost her.

Liz had to get it back, even if it meant asking Vendela about it.

Hours passed in silence and Liz had closed her eyes, and entered the trance state. It usually had a calming effect on her but it also meant she was completely alone with her thoughts and Liz and the voices in her head weren't always on the same side. But they were strangely silent at this point, maybe it was because the box she held in her hands kept them at bay. Even the panic about the drawing had passed a little, she was trying to tell herself that there was nothing she could do about it at this point but that after the meeting in Town she would go and see Vendela. Vendela could yell all she wanted, she could even punch Liz, she wouldn't care. She probably would deserve it after all.

Chapter 14

As if from nowhere Liz was disturbed from her trance and her eyes shot open when she heard a sudden sound. It was a mix of a low scream and what almost sounded like vague explosions coming from Katarina's room.

"Katarina?" Liz said low in surprise.

More screams, not in pain but in fear and mumbles of words Liz couldn't make out filled the apartment and then there was a sound almost like thunder that even made Liz jump. It made Liz uneasy but still she made her way over to Katarina's door with weightless steps. Then she just heard one word, repeated over and over.

"No, no, no, no, no," Katarina was saying quite loudly and with some force.

Without thinking about Katarina's earlier warning, Liz opened the door and she immediately regretted it. Katarina was laying in a small bed, still dressed in the same clothes as she'd worn during the day, but it looked like she was hovering over the bed slightly. There was a soft light emanating from her body, her face was covered in sweat and strands of her blond hair had stuck to her face.

Even though she was hovering above the bed she was writhing as if she was trying to look away from something or even get away from something. Katarina screamed out in fear and there was a loud bang and a bolt of what looked like lightning struck out towards the room and it hit the wall. Liz immediately dropped to the ground, her hands covering her head.

"Holy shit," Liz said with large eyes as she laid on the floor.

A part of Liz just wanted to run out of the room and close the door behind her and pretend she hadn't seen anything, but the look of terror on Katarina's face and the way she was moving her body, like she desperately wanted to wake up but just couldn't, made it impossible for Liz to just walk away. Another bolt of lightning shot out into the room and without thinking, Liz moved as fast as she could, she really didn't want to get hit by whatever magic Katarina was projecting.

Liz ran up to Katarina and grabbed her shoulders, shaking her and trying to wake her up.

"Katarina, wake up, come on," Liz said impatiently.

"No, no, no, please," Katarina muttered and she recoiled at Liz's touch.

"Wake up!" Liz said with force.

Then, before Liz could react, Katarina screamed and multiple bolts of lightning shot from her and one of them hit Liz straight in her chest. Liz was knocked back into the wall and fell to the floor with a hard thud. Liz moaned in pain as it felt as if her chest was on fire and there was a slight ringing in her ears. She tried to open her eyes but everything was just a blur. She could barely hear Katarina anymore, every sound was muffled and distorted. Liz shook her head, trying to shake away the blurry vision and the ringing in her ears. Her vision slowly returned and she managed to get on all four at first.

Liz looked down at her chest, there was a large burnt hole in the shirt and her skin beneath looked black and crackled. Liz cleared her throat, bit her lower lip and then even though her chest hurt like hell, she stood up and leaned on the wall she'd been knocked into. Once again, Liz shook her head and blinked a few times because when she looked over at Katarina, she saw two of her; which obviously wasn't normal. When she opened her eyes again and looked over at Katarina, Liz saw that she was still fast asleep in this nightmare state, still muttering words Liz couldn't make out. Liz sighed deeply and cursed herself for ever caring.

"This is why I hate magic," Liz said bitterly.

Liz didn't know what she was most upset about, the shocking pain in her chest or the fact that the mark the magic had left, had messed up the tattoos there.

Obviously, just shaking Katarina wouldn't work to wake her up and Liz didn't want to get that close to her again without a plan. The closer she was to Katarina, the less time she had to evade her magic. Liz made her way out of the bedroom, now with a lot less hurry in her step and leaning against the walls at all times; she was grabbing at her chest which was still aching something terribly and what worried Liz a little was that it wasn't getting better. Other injuries often healed within a few seconds, the only other kind of damage that took real time to heal was sun burns.

Liz walked up to the small kitchen area and took out a glass from the cabinet and filled it to the brim with cold water from the tap. She was a little surprised, even if she had seen Katarina make tea plenty of times before, a lot of the houses here didn't have running water anymore, except the Bar and the Fun House.

It was a tall glass and there was a moderate amount of water in it, it should be enough to wake her up, at least Liz hoped so. With slow steps she walked back into the bedroom and just saw another bolt of lightning hit the opposite end of the room and that was when Liz took her chance. With as quick steps as she could manage, the pain in her chest was only increasing, she walked up to Katarina and she emptied the water over her face.

A thought had crossed Liz's mind, as Katarina was almost glowing and sending out what looked and honestly felt like lightning bolts, she wondered what would happen if she poured water on her. But there was a part of her at this point that didn't care, it probably wouldn't kill her at least.

As the cold water hit Katarina's face, her body slammed down into the bed and she opened her eyes and for a split second it looked like they were completely white, but quickly it was her normal green and yellow speckled eyes looking back at Liz. Katarina was pale yet her cheeks were red, it almost looked like she had a fever. Katarina frowned deeply and looked around the room as if she wasn't sure where she was.

"Liz?" She said uncertainly. "I thought I told you not to come in here while I-…"

"Yeah, well I've never been a great listener," Liz said and she almost felt out of breath.

Liz sank down at the edge of the bed beside Katarina and she sighed deeply, trying to hide the fact that she was in pain.

"You alright?" Liz asked and looked at Katarina. "That didn't look like some ordinary nightmare. What was it about?"

Katarina swallowed and she rubbed her eyes and shook her head slightly.

"I'm fine," Katarina said. "I can never remember them. It's all a haze… Like I can almost remember it but then it slips through my fingers…"

"Alright," Liz said and tried to stand up but she quickly sunk down into the bed again and groaned and clenched her jaw.

Was she imagining it or was the pain getting worse?

"Are you okay?" Katarina asked and got up from the bed.

"I'm fine," Liz said with some force. "Make yourself some tea or something."

Liz was still holding her hand over the wound on her chest and Katarina moved her hand to touch Liz but stopped herself at the last moment. Liz sighed and let her hand slip from her chest to her lap. Katarina barely reacted when she saw it, there was perhaps a split second of surprise in her eyes but it was quickly gone.

"I did that?" Katarina asked carefully.

"I was the idiot who didn't listen to your warning," Liz said and tried to laugh but found it too painful so she stopped. "This one is on me."

"It's not healing?" Katarina asked, raising an eyebrow slightly.

Liz looked down at her chest again and she could see no change, there hadn't been any healing at all so far as she could tell. And the pain wasn't getting better either, it actually felt as if it was draining her of power. Liz shook her head at Katarina's question.

"Lie down," Katarina said. "Let me see if I can find something to help you."

Before Katarina could even move Liz spoke.

"Stop," Liz said. "I'm fine. Really. Just give it some time. I'm an incredibly old monster, you don't think I've been through worse?"

Liz once again tried to stand up but found the whole room spinning and she reached out her arms in an attempt to find anything to hold on to, if she didn't find something solid it felt as if she would float away. Instead of a wall or anything else sturdy, she felt something soft and warm catch her. When everything had stopped spinning a little Liz could see that it was Katarina that had caught her and if Liz hadn't felt as if she'd been shot in her chest and was simultaneously going on a roller coaster, she would have been horrified because Katarina was touching her skin directly. But at this point, that thought didn't even cross her mind and she swallowed hard before she felt herself almost falling back into the bed, so she was now laying with her face staring directly at the roof.

"I'm fine," Liz muttered, more to herself than to anyone else.

Pause.

"I'm fine," Liz continued to mutter even though Katarina had left the room a couple of minutes ago without her really noticing. "I'm fine."

Even though she was laying down, it felt as if she was on a boat in the middle of a storm, and her eyes had trouble concentrating on anything concrete. Everything looked hazy and Liz squinted her eyes in an attempt to see anything clearly. But it just caused a headache and Liz let out something close to a chuckle, she hadn't felt this bad since she had died. In fact it literally felt like she was dying, but there was no fear, she knew she wouldn't die here and the thought of death hadn't frightened her in centuries. Liz closed her eyes as the vague light in the room was almost blinding at this point.

"Liz?" Katarina had entered the room again but to Liz it sounded like she was miles away. "Stay awake."

"I'm fine," Liz said low.

"You need to tell me what happened," Katarina said with a commanding voice. "I don't know what spell hit you and I don't recognize the symptoms."

Liz licked her lips.

"I-I'm fine," Liz stammered.

"Liz," Katarina said with force. "Tell me what happened."

Liz was so tired, she felt as if there was acid on her chest that was trying to burn its way through her whole body and all she wanted to do was to sleep it away.

"I-It was like… Like lightning," Liz said, trying to remember. "Bolts of lightning."

Liz could hear someone fervently flipping through pages and Liz tried to open her eyes and lift her head to see what was happening but it was pointless, her head was heavy as concrete.

"Okay, I know what it is," Katarina said almost triumphantly. "I've been trying to master this spell for a month but I've never been able to do it, but it must be what hit you."

"Congrats," Liz said sarcastically.

"It's amazing the shock itself didn't kill you," Katarina said. "Must be because you're already technically dead."

"Good for me," Liz said low.

Liz closed her eyes again and she could almost feel herself slip into unconsciousness.

"Liz, stay awake," Katarina said.

"I'm fine," Liz said. "I'll… I'll just sleep it off."

"You don't sleep," Katarina said seriously.

"Oh, right," Liz said.

Silence.

"I'll be fine," Liz finally added after a few seconds of silence.

Liz almost felt like a broken record, saying *"I'm fine"* over and over again.

"It's going to get worse," Katarina said. "I'm going to have to see if there is some kind of counter spell."

"No more magic," Liz said trying to sound awake. "Don't you… Don't you dare use more magic on me."

"It will kill you Liz," Katarina said. "If I don't do anything it will kill you."

Liz chuckled but that sent shocks of pain through her body, so she ended up grinding her teeth instead.

"I'll be fine," Liz said. "A little… magic won't kill me."

"I'm going to get Vendela," Katarina said. "Maybe she can talk some sense into you."

There was a surge of power through Liz and she threw herself at Katarina and grabbed her shirt with her hand and held it as hard as she could. Katarina stared at her, her eyes slightly bigger than usual, but otherwise her face was neutral. Liz had to close her eyes and she could feel her body shaking from the pain.

"Don't," was all she could manage to say. "Don't. Please."

Then Liz's grip of Katarina's shirt loosened and Liz collapsed and fell unconscious, part of her body dangling outside the bed.

Chapter 15

Liz slowly opened her eyes and stared into the ceiling, she felt… Strange. Had she been unconscious again? That would make it two times within a few days, which was probably a new record for her. The soft light in the room hurt her eyes and she strangely felt as if she was hungover, even if the last time she'd been hungover was centuries ago, she was pretty sure this was close to how it had felt. Liz almost felt nauseous, her whole body hurt and she felt weak as a toddler. What had happened before she fell unconscious felt like a dream or a memory from a long time ago. Though she remembered the pain and it had been worse than starving.

Liz managed to sit up in the bed and she realized that she was still in Katarina's room and when she turned her head a little to the right, she saw Katarina sleeping in a chair in the corner. Liz was so weak that she hadn't even heard her steady breathing. Liz groaned slightly and looked down at her chest, the hole in the shirt was still there and there was still a pretty nasty mark where the lightning bolt had hit her. It wasn't as black and cracked as it had been before, but in the cracks that were left Liz could see red peeking through. It seemed to have healed a little at least and as she was feeling better than before, she assumed she was only going to get stronger from now on.

How long had she been unconscious? It had probably been a few hours, she just hoped she hadn't overslept her meeting. Liz picked at the skin around her nails out of habit before she slowly swung her legs off the side of the bed and placed them on the floor. With shaky legs she rose, the pain in her chest wasn't as intense as before but it did feel as if she was carrying around a large boulder on her chest.

"Just get it together," Liz whispered low to herself. "You've been through worse."

Katarina moved slightly and Liz wondered if she had woken her up but she kept sleeping soundly. Liz wasn't planning on waking Katarina up, she would just leave and let her rest. At least it was looking like Katarina wasn't having nightmares anymore, which was good.

Liz took one step but felt her legs fold on themselves and she fell clumsily to the floor with a hard thud. Liz swore to herself, gripped her chest and she immediately knew she had woken Katarina.

"Liz? Liz, you're awake!" Katarina said sleepily.

Katarina walked up to Liz and Liz noticed that she was wearing gloves, which was a little strange. Katarina gripped Liz by the arm and helped her stand up, and Liz for once accepted the help. Then when Liz was standing she snatched back her arm from Katarina.

"I'm fine," Liz said and tried to smile. "Told you I'd be fine."

Katarina was looking at Liz with large eyes and there was almost disbelief in them.

"What's with the face?" Liz asked. "I'm fine, I promise."

"Liz, you've been unconscious for a week," Katarina said seriously.

Liz took a small step backwards.

"I'm sorry, what?" Liz said. "That's impossible."

Liz touched the dark mark on her chest lightly.

"I didn't think you'd wake up," Katarina said. "And honestly, it was a little hard to know if you even were alive when you are still technically… Dead."

"A week?" Liz said, not listening to a thing Katarina had said.

"Yes," Katarina said. "A week. It is Wednesday morning today."

Liz rubbed her eyes and slightly shook her head.

"You should sit down," Katarina said. "You're still weak-…"

"I'm fine," Liz snapped. "What's happened? When I was unconscious I mean."

Katarina sighed.

"Sit down and I'll tell you," Katarina said.

Reluctantly, Liz sat back down on the bed but her legs were thanking her. Then it hit her, she was weak, but she wasn't hungry. If it really had been a week, Liz would be starving but she felt as full as before.

"I'm not hungry," Liz said slowly.

"Vendela came by," Katarina said. "When you passed out I fetched her."

"I told you not to do that," Liz said irritated. "I specifically told you not-…"

"Don't be a child," Katarina said.

Liz almost looked offended by that comment.

"Vendela brought blood every few days and fed it to you," Katarina said. "We thought that if you would have any chance of waking up, you'd need to feed."

"She did that?" Liz asked low.

"She didn't hesitate," Katarina said. "When I told her what had happened that was."

Liz was speechless for a second, then she quickly spoke, not wanting Katarina to know how much that knowledge had affected her.

"Anything else?" Liz asked and cleared her throat.

"You've got a letter," Katarina said.

Liz tensed up but tried to relax.

"A letter?" Liz asked, trying to sound like she had no idea what it was about. "From who?"

"It doesn't say," Katarina said. "It was apparently delivered to The Bar so Vendela brought it here."

"Can I see it?" Liz asked, trying not to sound too pushy.

"I'll get it for you in a minute," Katarina said.

Liz sighed and bit her lip, she knew that if she pushed it too much it would be more suspicious than if she just waited a little while.

"Alright," Liz said.

"And Ami came by," Katarina said. "She's very lovely. She asked for you but I of course told her you were… Incapacitated."

Liz looked at Katarina, a flash of worry in her eyes.

"When did she come by?" Liz asked.

Katarina was quiet for a short while, obviously thinking her answer through carefully.

"Last time was… Two days ago, I think," Katarina said. "Why?"

"Nothing," Liz said.

Liz rose again.

"I need to leave," Liz said. "Can I have my letter?"

"You're really going to leave in your state?" Katarina asked skeptically.

"I'm fine," Liz repeated. "The letter?"

Katarina sighed but didn't argue with Liz and walked out of the bedroom and Liz slowly followed her. As Liz entered the main area of the house she saw that her box was still laying on the table next to her bag, she had totally forgotten that she'd just put it down when she'd heard Katarina scream. Liz clenched her jaw and her eyes darted to Katarina who was standing by the book shelf. With as quick steps as Liz could manage she walked up to her box and shoved it down the bag again, hoping that for some strange reason Katarina hadn't seen it. Though that was stupid to think, Liz had been unconscious for a week, of course Katarina had seen it. Liz just hoped that she hadn't opened and looked through it, the mere thought was mortifying.

"Here," Katarina said from behind Liz.

Liz almost jumped, she hadn't heard Katarina at all. Katarina was holding an envelope in her hand and Liz snatched it from her.

Liz glanced from the envelope to out the window and saw that it was raining heavily.

"What time is it?" Liz asked.

"It's 11 a.m," Katarina said. "Why?"

Liz managed to stand up again, she was holding the envelope in an iron grip. Liz flung her bag over her shoulder but it felt heavy on her back and it hurt her chest.

"Just wondering," Liz said.

Katarina glanced down at the envelope.

"Aren't you going to read it?" Katarina asked. "You won't be able to read it out in the rain without destroying it."

Liz shot her a quick glance.

"I'll give you some space," Katarina said calmly and went over to her stove and started making herself some tea.

Liz didn't sit down again, even if her legs were shaking. Her eyes were focused on Katarina, who by now wasn't paying attention to Liz at all. But Liz felt paranoid and she almost thought that even though Katarina wasn't looking at her, if Liz opened the letter, she would know what it said. But Katarina was right, she wouldn't be able to read it out in the rain. Liz opened the envelope, and took out the letter. There wasn't much written on it, just a few lines.

"You did not come as decided. Meet us at the same time and same place next wednesday. Show up this time."

No signature this time either but that didn't matter. *"Shit"* was Liz's only thought as she read the letter.

"It wasn't good news?" Katarina asked calmly as the kettle started to boil.

Liz quickly crunched the letter in her hand and shoved it in her pants pocket.

"Stop reading me," Liz snapped.

Now there was anger and irritation inside Liz, more than the pain she was feeling and she welcomed it. Anger she was used to, not this feeling of weakness and pain. And right now she felt she needed to take out her aggression or she felt like she would explode.

"Did you use magic on me to heal me?" Liz asked, the anger poorly hidden in her voice.

Katarina stopped everything she did and kept her back to Liz.

"I take that as a yes," Liz hissed. "You did *everything* I asked you not to do!"

"I'm not going to apologize for saving your life," Katarina said calmly and turned around.

"I wouldn't have died!" Liz yelled with anger. "You should have just done what I asked!"

"Just because you're a vampire doesn't mean that you can't die," Katarina said.

Liz opened her mouth then quickly closed it and felt the anger run off her like water and she just felt tired from the pain again. She felt pathetic as she stared at Katarina who hadn't even raised her voice, who hadn't matched her energy and anger in the slightest. Liz was picking a fight with someone who was simply trying to help and she hated herself for it.

"I'm sorry," Liz muttered almost inaudibly. "I'm sorry."

Katarina raised an eyebrow, she must have been confused at Liz's sudden burst of anger and then the sudden lack of the same. Liz was confused by herself at times so she couldn't imagine how others saw her; she honestly must seem insane at times from an outside perspective.

"Thanks for helping me," Liz said a little more loudly and gripped her chest. "I'll repay you by not coming back again."

"Liz," Katarina said. "I don't mind helping you."

"Whenever I'm here something bad happens," Liz said. "I am bad luck. And maybe right now most of that bad luck has happened to me, but believe me, it will happen to you. I don't bring good luck, happiness or anything pleasant. I bring death and destruction."

Katarina didn't say anything.

"Find someone else to be your friend," Liz said harshly.

Liz then walked out the door and slammed it behind her.

Chapter 16

Liz entered the main street and within a few seconds she was soaking wet. She closed her eyes and turned her head up to the sky and just let the rain pour down on her. It was cold and Liz almost felt chilly which was a strange sensation, the temperature in the air never mattered, she couldn't feel it anyway. It didn't matter if it was 100- degrees or 100+ degrees. So feeling chilly for the first time in centuries and not because she was starving, was a feeling she could barely explain.

Liz didn't move, she just had to take a few seconds to clear her head.

Liz appreciated what Katarina had done for her, but she was young and didn't realize what a train wreck Liz really was. And sooner or later Katarina would get hurt because of her, and this was Liz's way of repaying her. Katarina would find someone else to help, someone else to keep her company, someone a lot better than Liz. Liz sighed and opened her eyes and looked around, the smell of decay and death was gone and so were the bodies. Someone must have finally done something about it but Liz wasn't sure if it was someone in The Sanctuary or if it was the Townies.

As Liz scanned the street there wasn't a single person out and her eyes finally settled on the Fun House and Liz thought to herself that after the meeting in Town, she'd go check on Ami to see how she was. And after that… Liz wasn't so sure, she would probably go and speak with Vendela. It might have been a week, but Liz hadn't forgotten about the drawing or their fight. Liz looked down at her shirt, which still had a hole in it and revealed the dark mark. Vendela would probably not be happy that she'd damaged her shirt, not that Vendela was happy with her otherwise.

Liz wondered what people's reactions would be to see the wound on her chest, the creatures inside The Sanctuary would probably not care all that much, they had other things to worry about. But the Townies, they'd probably think she was carrying some kind of disease. Liz just hoped they'd let her into Town, she couldn't miss the meeting again.

Liz walked up to the gate and then she waited, she knew that at around twelve the gate would open and a lot of people would point their weapons at her. And then if she had the right papers she was allowed into Town and Liz was a little surprised to see that she was apparently the only creature who planned on going into Town today. Maybe it was because of the rain.

Liz was drenched, she was glad that her new papers had been laminated or they would have been completely ruined by the rain. It wasn't like she had an umbrella or anything, and the rain had never really bothered her. Suddenly, the gate started to open slowly and Liz sighed. As she'd expected, though there were more than she'd thought, a lot of people were pointing their weapons at her.

"Creature, stand down!" One of them shouted.

Liz didn't move and through the soldiers came a man with an umbrella. He walked up to Liz with three, what looked like, personal body guards that stayed very close to him at all times. He seemed to scan the street around her before he actually looked at her.

"Papers," he said with a monotone voice.

Liz picked up her paper from her bra and there was a look of disgust on his face as she held it out for him to look at. He took the paper carefully between his thumb and index finger, acting as if he thought he could catch vampirism from this one touch. He slowly read it and then gave it back to Liz. As Liz shoved the paper back into her bra, he saw the hole in her shirt and the black mark beneath.

"What's that?" He asked and pointed at her chest.

Liz could hear, though very vaguely so she might have imagined it, guns cock behind the man.

"An old wound," Liz said, her voice equally as monotone as the mans. "Nothing serious."

The man narrowed his eyes slightly.

"Are you gonna let me through or what?" Liz said. "I've got some things to do."

"You have things to do?" The man asked, almost laughing. "What kind of business does a vampire have in Town?"

"None of your business is what it is," Liz hissed.

"You'll answer him you freak!" One of the bodyguards yelled.

Liz tilted her head slightly and shot the man a sharp glance, she could see him swallowing hard.

"Are my papers in order?" Liz asked.

"Yes b-..." The man started.

"Then let me through," Liz said, trying not to sound too angry. "I have the right to be in Town for two hours."

The man took a step closer to Liz and now every soldier and all the bodyguards were on high alert, like they expected Liz to attack the man any second.

"It's not a right," The man said low. "It's a privilege. That you can easily lose, vampire. So I suggest you learn to respect your betters."

It took almost all of Liz's strength to not punch the man straight in the face, because she told herself over and over what trouble it would cause and she really didn't need that right now.

"So, do you have anything else to say?" The man asked.

Liz said nothing, just stared at him with fire in her eyes.

"That's a good girl," he said with a smirk.

Liz grinned but there was no happiness in it. There was pure aggression and hatred in the smile as she flashed her sharp teeth. A reminder to him that she could tear him apart if she wished. The smirk was wiped off his face when he saw the sharp teeth.

"If you're not back at the gate at 2 p.m, you will be hunted down," the man said seriously. "If you do anything criminal, you will be put down. Do you understand?"

Liz nodded, still with her creepy smile on her face.

He looked at her with disgust and then turned around and went back into Town. Liz let him get a head start because otherwise the soldiers might think she planned on attacking him. Then Liz slowly walked through the many soldiers, their weapons steadily followed her and she heard the gate being closed behind her. Liz cleared her throat as she started to walk away from the large wall and even though Liz had been outside the Sanctuary not long ago, she was almost always surprised at how the outside world looked.

It was like she forgot, because the Sanctuary became her world and it was like nothing else existed.

The Town was so clean and colorful, even in the rain and Liz could smell something and if she wasn't mistaken it was cinnamon buns. A vague smile came across her lips, even though she couldn't eat them, the mere smell filled her with warmth. Liz looked at the large clock in the middle of the square and saw that it was 12.10, she was already late to the meeting, she hoped they had waited for her. Liz knew where the Café was but it had been quite some time since she had been here so it took her a little while until she found the right alley. There weren't many people outside, she only bumped into two people and as soon as they saw her, they kept their distance and tried their hardest not to look at her. Liz could almost feel their fear, sometimes that made her feel powerful and could put a smirk on her lips, today it just made her more irritated and angry.

When she found the Café she saw the two women who'd escorted her back to the Sanctuary little over a week ago. Liz quickly sunk down in the chair opposite them, this short walk had drained her of most of her powers, but she tried to not let it show. The two women looked very serious.

"You're late," said the first one.

"I had some problems at the gate," Liz said. "The guy was a dick."

"That 'guy' I assume you're talking about is head security chief for this Sanctuary," said the other woman. "Know your place and show some respect."

Liz leaned back in her seat and folded her arms over her chest and she felt the mark sting a little as she did so.

"Why didn't you come last week?" Said the first one. "Lady Morgana was very… Disappointed."

"Well," Liz said and looked down at the hole in her shirt. "You could say I got struck by lightning."

Both the women raised an eyebrow and looked at the mark on Liz's chest.

"I've been unconscious for a week," Liz said. "So I'm sorry I missed our little meeting, not much I could do about it."

Liz's eyes focused on a couple of waiters behind the two women, who were whispering to each other and staring at Liz. When they saw that she'd seen them, they stopped talking and quickly went inside the café.

"What happened?" The first woman asked.

"Nothing serious," Liz said and shrugged.

"Being unconscious for a week sounds serious," the other woman said.

"Aw, do you care about my well being that much?" Liz said sarcastically.

"You're an investment," the first woman said. "We wouldn't want an investment being hurt beyond repair."

Liz clenched her jaw and her hands formed fists, she hated when they talked about her like she was some kind of thing they owned. She wasn't.

"You know as well as I do, that I can't die," Liz said seriously and low. "So I'm fine. So what the hell did you want to talk with mc about?"

Just as they were about to answer, the owner of the café appeared behind them and he looked both scared and disgusted at the same time.

"Y-You have to leave," he said, trying to sound brave.

"Excuse me?" Liz said and leaned forward.

"You're scaring my customers and my staff," he said and quickly glanced behind himself. "P-Please leave."

"She's with us," the two women said at the same time.

"Still-…" The owner said.

They interrupted him by shoving a piece of paper each in his face. His face turned red as he read what was on the papers.

"I-I'm sorry… I didn't know…" He stammered.

"We're soon done here," said the first woman. "She'll leave then."

He nodded and quickly rushed back inside the café. The two women turned their attention back to Liz. Liz followed the man with her gaze until he disappeared inside and she had involuntarily started to grind her teeth in anger.

"We wanted to talk with you about your payment," the second woman said and reached inside her jacket. "And something else as well."

Liz's gaze shot back to the two women as soon as they spoke, though the anger diminished; it was right under the surface, ready to come back in full force.

The woman placed a purse filled with something heavy in it on the table, Liz guessed that it was money. Liz stared at the purse but didn't move to pick it up.

"And what about… The other thing?" Liz said and looked around. "Any progress on that?"

"No, unfortunately not," said the first woman. "But we're working on it."

Liz bit her lip and they must have seen the frustration in her face.

"We are working as fast and as hard as we can," the second woman said. "You'd think that someone as old as you would have more patience."

"I've actually gotten less patient with time," Liz said as a warning.

Liz finally snagged up the purse of money and held it in her hands before she looked over at the two women again.

"I want something else," Liz said and she then slowly put down the purse again.

The two women exchanged looks.

"I thought we had agreed on your pa-…" the first one started to say.

"Yeah, well, I don't really have any use for money," Liz said. "And you haven't delivered on the other part. So I want something else in the meanwhile."

The first woman sighed and they once again exchanged looks.

"What do you have in mind?" The second woman said.

"Blood," Liz said.

Both the women lost some color in their faces and the first woman cleared her throat.

"We-…" she started.

"I need it to survive or to stay functional at least," Liz said, interrupting her. "And if you don't 'want me hurt beyond repair' you'll give it to me."

"Mr. Greenlund would not be happy with Lady Morgana if she agreed," the second woman said bitterly. "He has worked hard to have a monopoly on fresh blood."

Liz was silent for a moment.

"Then ask yourselves this," Liz said low. "Who are you more afraid of? Him or me?"

Liz stared straight at them with her golden eyes.

"You hired me," Liz continued. "You know what I can do. What I'm willing to do. So I'd suggest you give me what I want."

"Lady Morgana doesn't like to be threatened," the first woman said seriously.

"No one likes to be threatened," Liz said. "I don't give a rat's ass about Mr. Greenlund and his blood empire. But I do care about surviving. You've supplied me with blood before, this is no different."

"The difference is that you are inside the Sanctuary now," the second woman said. "Where Lady Morgana technically has no jurisdiction. If Mr. Greenlund found out we'd been supplying you with blood, we would be in trouble."

"Make sure he doesn't find out then," Liz hissed.

They exchanged looks again and Liz sighed in frustration.

"Fine," the first woman said. "We will supply you with blood every other day."

"Good," Liz said and smiled vaguely.

"Where should we send it?" The second woman asked.

Liz opened her mouth but closed it. She didn't have a place to stay anymore. They couldn't send it to The Bar, that would be a very bad idea. They couldn't send it to Katarina, as Liz said she'd stay away from there. They could definitely not send it to Ami, as she actually worked in the Fun House.

"I..." Liz said slowly. "I don't exactly have a place to stay at right now."

"We can deliver it to the Bar, disguised of course," the first one said.

"Everyone knows about your… Relationship with Miss Amber."

Liz frowned slightly.

"Vendela?" Liz said. "What about our relationship?"

There was an edge in Liz's voice, warning them to choose their next words carefully.

"Well you've spent a lot of time with her have you not?" The second woman said. "And there are rumors you knew each other even before the Sanctuaries opened."

"So?" Liz said. "What are you trying to say?"

They exchanged glances and Liz wished they'd stop doing that every other minute, it was really starting to irritate her.

"You and her were-…" The first one said.

"Lovers?" Liz filled in. "Is that what you're trying to say?"

They nodded slowly.

"So?" Liz said with an edge. "What has that to do with *anything?*"

"Can you trust her?" The second woman asked. "And will your feelings for her compromise everything we've done?"

Liz clenched her jaw and thought about the fight.

"My *feelings?*" Liz asked. "I won't tell her about what I've done for you, if that's what you ask. That'd hurt me more than you."

The two women leaned forward.

"There have been… Whispers of a rebellion," the second woman said low. "Ever since the last escape attempt everyone has been on edge."

Liz swallowed and licked her lips.

"We want to know if a rebellion happened," the first woman said. "Your feelings for Miss Amber won't get in the way. We want to know that you'll be on our side, not on theirs."

Liz frowned and almost laughed, this was ridiculous. Finally she spoke.

"I don't take sides," Liz said. "I stay out of things."

"You stay out of things?" The second one said amused.

Liz shot her an angry gaze.

"As good as I can… But sometimes we have to stretch our principles," Liz muttered. "If there is a rebellion, you won't see me in the lead of it, of that you can be sure."

"Well I suppose that will have to do," the first woman said. "For now."

"So we'll send it to the Bar," the second one said. "You trust that Miss Amber won't open your packets and try to interfere? She does work for Mr. Greenlund."

Silence.

"Yeah, send it there," Liz said. "She won't cause trouble."

Liz had to go and speak with her anyway and now she had even more reason to try and patch things up with her. Not only because she wanted to, if she didn't, the blood sent there would cause even more questions. It would not be good in the slightest.

Chapter 17

They concluded their meeting and even if Liz had said that she didn't need the money, in the end she'd taken the purse anyway. The women didn't argue with her and who knew, maybe it would come in handy at some point? It wasn't like Lady Morgana couldn't afford it, she had plenty of money and this amount was small change to her. When Liz rose to leave the Café she could see both the owner and the staff sigh in relief.

Liz started to make her way back to the wall and she noticed that the rain had almost completely stopped. There was still no sign of the sun, which Liz was grateful for, she didn't want to have to run to take cover and in the worst case scenario she would have to hide away inside somewhere in Town, which no one would be happy with. As she reached the entrance to the Sanctuary the guards let her in without a word, without trouble and closed the large gate behind her.

As soon as Liz was once again inside the Sanctuary she made a sharp turn towards the Fun House. Liz had never set foot inside that building, she had refused and if she could avoid it, she would stay at least 10 meter from it but this one time, she made an exception. Liz had been unconscious for a week and she had promised to look after Ami, she had broken her promise even when she didn't mean to. And Liz just wanted to see Ami's smile and tell her why she'd been gone, even if Katarina perhaps had told her some of it when she'd come by.

Liz picked at the skin around her nails as she entered the Fun House.

It was even more extravagant than the outside, chandeliers were hanging from the ceiling and the room was decorated in red wall paper with golden details. The first thing Liz saw when she entered was a reception and then to the left was a door and to the right was a staircase that went up to the other floors. Something in there made Liz's skin crawl, no one else was there at the moment, no clients or workers. Just a woman that sat at the reception, who at this point wasn't paying attention to Liz at all.

Liz cleared her throat and walked up to the reception desk. The girl, because she looked very young, was almost unnervingly pretty with light brown skin, a prominent nose and small dark brown eyes that shone with life. She smiled pleasantly as she saw Liz and pushed some of her silky black hair behind her ears.

"Hello, what can I do for you?" She said.

"Eh…" Liz said slowly, not entirely sure on what to say. "I wanna see someone."

"Of course," the girl said.

Liz saw that she wore a name tag, it said Mona. Mona reached beneath the counter and picked up a folder and placed it in front of Liz.

"Here are all the workers," Mona said. "There is age, description of appearance and what type of creature they are and if you have any other questions don't be afraid to ask."

Liz stared at the folder for a moment before she looked up at Mona with a blank expression. Liz wondered if Mona was a creature or just a human working here, she was wearing a turtleneck shirt that covered her neck so Liz couldn't see if she had a tattoo or not. All Liz knew was that Mona had a steady heartbeat.

Mona smiled but it vanished slightly when she saw the black mark on Liz's chest.

"Are… Are you alright?" She asked carefully.

"I'm fine," Liz said quickly, her hand instinctively went up to cover the mark slightly. "And I… I don't…"

Liz didn't know why she was stammering exactly, she just couldn't find the right words at this moment. Perhaps it was the pain and the fatigue. Liz just wanted to sit or lie down but that had to wait. Or maybe it was that this whole place and situation made her uncomfortable, leaving her uncertain on how to act.

"When I said I wanted to see someone," Liz finally said. "I don't mean like that."

Liz pushed back the folder and Mona frowned slightly.

"I… I'm sorry," Mona said. "I don't understand."

"I just want to see a friend of mine who works here," Liz said. "That's all."

"I'm sorry, but the workers are not allowed company in their quarters," Mona said carefully. "You… You could see if they're working and book an appointment with them?"

Liz stared at Mona before sighing.

"Fine," Liz finally said. "I'll do that."

Liz took the folder and opened it, page after page was covered with information, names, appearance, height, weight, creature type, anything anyone could ever wish to know about someone's physical look. Above each description was a name, or at least the name they chose to use. Liz flipped through the pages, looking for Ami's name. As Liz went through page after page and didn't see Ami's name, a frown grew on her face and there was a seed of worry in her stomach. Finally, Liz closed the book after having looked through all the pages and just stared at the folder.

"Is everything okay?" Mona asked.

"I can't find them," Liz said. "Her name isn't in this folder."

Mona lost some color in her face but quickly put on a charming smile again.

"T-Then I'm sorry," Mona said. "They don't work here. Every worker is in this folder."

"I know she works here," Liz said and leaned forward.

Mona swallowed and at this point she must have been happy to be behind what Liz assumed was bullet proof glass.

"Her name is Ami," Liz said. "Ever heard it?"

Mona carefully shook her head.

"I-I don't know what to tell you," Mona said. "I… I just started this week, maybe she quit?"

Liz clenched her jaw and that seed of worry was now growing immensely with every second passing. Liz knew Ami hadn't quit, she just knew it. Ami had been taken to the fourth floor and now they pretended she didn't exist, just like she'd feared. Instead of starting a fight or making a scene, Liz tried to smile and pretend she wasn't panicking on the inside.

"Yeah, maybe," Liz said and shrugged. "I'm sure you're right."

Mona seemed to relax a little when Liz said that and she let out a sigh of relief.

"But if there is anything else," Mona said. "Don't hesitate to ask."

"Oh, I won't," Liz said. "I'm sure I'll be back soon."

Liz smiled at Mona, then turned her back and walked out the Fun House, the smile wiped off her face and replaced with a grim look.

Chapter 18

As soon as Liz had come out to the main street she started to run, her chest felt as if it was on fire and her legs threatened to buckle beneath her but she just continued to run. Liz's mind was almost blank, she didn't think about the fact that Vendela was angry with her, she didn't think about the meeting, she didn't even think about the drawing.

All Liz could think about was Ami.

As she ran, she hadn't forgotten Ami's words that she didn't trust Vendela anymore, but she simply didn't care. Liz knew Vendela would never be a spy for the Fun House, that she would never work against her friends and people who trusted her. Liz knew that when she told Vendela about Ami, she would help her, no matter how angry she was with Liz.

By some miracle, Liz managed to get to the Bar before she collapsed and for once she felt lucky she didn't have a reflection as she passed windows because she felt awful, so she guessed she looked worse. Liz slammed open the door to the Bar and she found it filled with creatures, Liz had almost forgotten about the fact that this was a meeting place and not just Vendela's personal space. As Liz entered a few of them glanced her way but most didn't even bother to look up and then Liz gaze landed on Vendela who stood behind the bar desk. Their eyes locked and Vendela looked like a statue, her face like marble as it stared at Liz with ice in her eyes, but Liz thought she saw cracks in that ice.

Liz could almost see the restraint it took for Vendela not to cause a scene.

Vendela shifted her eyes towards the door beside the bar disk, the door that led to the corridor with the bathroom. Liz understood and she saw that Vendela left her position behind the bar desk and walked towards the door and Liz moved slowly the same way. She put her hand over the mark on her chest as it was pounding and sending vague shocks of pain through her body, as she moved her legs it felt as if there were cement blocks attached to them.

She'd never felt this exhausted before without being on the brink of starvation.

Vendela had disappeared behind the door and Liz entered the same and the moment she closed the door behind her and opened her mouth to speak, she was interrupted by Vendela.

"So you lived," Vendela said coldly.

Liz chuckled weakly and leaned on the wall beside her.

"Barely," Liz said jokingly.

Vendela eyed her over.

"You look like you're dying," Vendela said, her voice a little softer.

"I feel like it," Liz said honestly. "But that's not why I'm here."

"You're here for your dress I assume?" Vendela said. "I'll get it, then you can go."

Vendela turned to leave but Liz made a leap to grab her arm and as she did it she almost tripped over her own feet, but she managed to regain her balance as she grabbed Vendela.

"Wait," Liz said low. "That's not why I'm here either."

Vendela looked at Liz hand on her arm and then looked up at Liz again.

"Then why are you here?" Vendela said. "I told you-…"

"Yeah, that you never wanted to see me again," Liz said and quickly let go of Vendela. "And I understand, okay, I do. You hate me and that's fine. You can scream at me, even punch me if you'd like. Thought I'm pretty sure if you punched me right now I'd faint again, but you know…"

Vendela stared at Liz like she was wondering if she was going anywhere with this or if Liz was just rambling at this point.

"I'm not here because of me," Liz continued. "Not about you, not even about us."

"There's an 'us' now is there?" Vendela asked almost mockingly.

Something close to a laugh escaped Liz's lips. There was a frown on Vendela's face, like she didn't understand why Liz was here or what she wanted.

"What's it about then?" She asked carefully.

Liz swallowed hard.

"I-I'm just gonna sit down a little first," Liz said and sank down onto the floor, her back leaning against the wall. "Sorry…"

Vendela's expression softened, but barely and she squatted down opposite Liz.

"I'm listening," Vendela said.

Liz looked up slightly surprised.

"I'm only staying and listening to you because you literally look like you'll fall down dead any minute," Vendela added quickly. "And even though… I don't want you dead."

"That's… Fair enough," Liz said. "I'm sorry about your shirt by the way."

Vendela looked at the hole in the shirt with a quick glance before her eyes returned to meet Liz's.

"Why are you here Liz?" Vendela asked and slightly shook her head.

"It's Ami," Liz finally said.

Vendela frowned.

"What about her?" She said.

"She's missing," Liz said.

"Are you sure?" Vendela asked.

"No, you know I didn't check or anything, I just went straight here, knowing you hate me, to tell you that *perhaps, maybe* she's missing," Liz said sarcastically and with some edge.

Vendela bit her lower lip.

"How do you know then?" Vendela asked.

"B-Because she came to me a week ago," Liz said. "Terrified about disappearing, and now she's gone."

Vendela drew her hand through her hair.

"She talked about the fourth floor in the Fun House," Liz said.

That seemed to catch Vendela's attention, there was a flash of something in her eyes that quickly disappeared. Liz frowned.

"Do you know about it?" Liz asked slowly.

Vendela shrugged.

"It's where workers are sent to relax," Vendela said. "So?"

"Except Ami said that almost no one returns," Liz said. "They just disappear. But I assume they're not counted among the ones you and Katarina said has disappeared, because hey, we creatures might be nothing but those Fun House workers, they're really nothing aren't they? Who cares about them?"

The last part was so filled with spite and it took most of her power to finish the sentence without stammering.

"Liz!" Vendela said outraged, her eyes large and unforgiving. "You're talking to me here! You've always been the one to hate the Fun House, not me!"

"The place!" Liz yelled. "The place and the scum that owns it and runs the whole industry! The ones who take advantage of the workers! Not the workers! I never blamed or hated the workers!"

Liz felt out of breath and she leaned her head against the wall and half closed her eyes. She couldn't even see Vendela's face, but Liz assumed she was fuming with anger by now.

"I'm sorry," Liz muttered. "I didn't mean to take it out on you… I'm just…"

"I still don't understand why you're here," Vendela finally said, her voice slightly thick.

Liz opened her eyes and looked directly at Vendela.

"I haven't seen Ami in months," Vendela said. "Doesn't mean she's missing."

"But you don't see me in one day and you panic?" Liz said.

Vendela opened her mouth but quickly closed it and looked away. Liz sighed and regretted what she'd said already.

"You haven't seen her because she's been avoiding you," Liz said honestly.

Vendela slowly turned her head back towards Liz, she was frowning slightly.

"What? Why?" Vendela asked low.

"Because she thinks you're spying for Mr. Greenlund," Liz said as if it was a joke. "That you couldn't have gotten all you got without paying a price. I, of course, said it was ridici-…"

But Liz didn't finish her sentence as Vendela's face went slack and her mouth dropped open slightly in shock. Liz knew what that meant but she didn't seem to be able to accept it. It didn't make sense in Liz's brain.

"Vendela?" Liz asked low.

Vendela swallowed and looked away before she quickly rose.

"You're kidding me," Liz said in shock. "Ami was right?"

And for the first time perhaps ever, the roles were reversed between the two. Vendela stayed quiet, seemingly unable to answer her.

"Vendela!" Liz said with more force. "Answer me!"

Liz managed to get on her feet so she was almost at eye level with Vendela. Liz's legs were shaking and her body felt as if it was made out of paper and would fly away in the wind, but at the same time she felt as heavy as if she was chained to boulders. Finally it was like Vendela regained her ability to speak.

"You don't understand," she said, still looking away.

"Oh, I understand alright," Liz said. "Yo-…"

"No, you don't," Vendela said angrily and interrupted her. "You weren't here! You have no idea what has happened or what I've been doing! Don't you *dare* to judge me Liz! You are no angel!"

"I might have done a lot of shitty things," Liz said. "But not this. I wouldn't do this."

Vendela shot her an angry gaze and took a few steps closer and Liz saw that behind the anger was something close to desperation.

"You don't understand," Vendela repeated.

"Then explain!" Liz said. "What the hell did he give you to betray your friends? Because I can't imagine you'd be bought with luxury items!"

Vendela closed her eyes and swallowed, she seemed to think about what to say next.

"Vendela, please," Liz said as gently as possible.

Liz had the impulse to reach out and touch Vendela, it took all her restraint to resist. Vendela bit her lower lip and the look in her eyes weren't filled with anger or frustration, it was just sadness.

"I lost everything Liz," Vendela finally said, her voice shaking ever so lightly. "First you disappeared and… And when I'd finally accepted that… My bar burned down and I had nothing. Everything I'd built up, everything I'd worked for, just gone. So I took his damn deal, to follow his rules and…. To give… Information if I heard something."

Vendela turned away, her eyes staring into a wall.

"But you have no right Liz, no right at all to judge me," Vendela said, her voice thick. "I did what I had to to get back on my feet. And it's not like I give him any vital information, just enough for him to trust me and not suspect me."

Liz frowned slightly.

"Suspect you?" Liz said. "Suspect you of what?"

Vendela glanced back over at her with caution, there was distrust in her eyes but Liz saw how badly Vendela wanted to tell her something.

"It doesn't matter," Vendela said and shook her head.

Vendela laughed low.

"You managed to turn this conversation against me," Vendela said, her voice thick.

"Vendela," Liz said gently and ignored what she'd just said. "What would he suspect you of?"

"No," Vendela said and shook her head again. "It doesn't matter. You wanted to talk about Ami, that was what this was about."

Liz opened her mouth to speak but no words came out, she felt conflicted. In one part she wanted to push Vendela for more answers because Liz didn't understand any of this, and on the other hand she had wasted enough time here arguing with Vendela when Ami was still missing.

"This conversation isn't over," Liz said. "I'll remember."

Vendela stared straight into Liz's eyes.

"Oh, don't worry," she finally said. "I have a few things to say to you too."

Liz swallowed and all she could think about was her box and the drawing.

But there was no turning back now.

"They took Ami to the fourth floor, I'm sure of it," Liz said. "I went inside the Fun House and asked to see her and they acted like she didn't exist."

A look of shock flashed across Vendela's face for a second as Liz spoke before she collected herself.

"She might come back," Vendela said. "You don't know she's missing for sure. Maybe she's really just relaxing on the fourth floor."

Liz shook her head.

"She was terrified, Vendela," Liz said. "And I... I promised that if she disappeared I'd..."

"You'd do what?" Vendela asked.

"That I'd find her," Liz said slowly.

Vendela had a look of disbelief on her face.

"You do realize what that means?" Vendela said.

"I do," Liz said bitterly.

"What happened to your never interfere policy?" Vendela asked. "The rules you fling around every time something happens?"

"What was I supposed to do?" Liz asked, trying to stop her voice from shaking. "Say no? Say that I didn't care if she disappeared? I'd already made you hate me, I-I... I couldn't make her hate me as well."

Vendela's face softened. Liz swallowed and leaned against the wall. Liz told herself over and over to calm down, to not get so emotional, it wouldn't help at all, in fact it would make things a thousand times worse.

"I promised her," Liz repeated. "And I am a lot of things. A killer, an asshole, a bystander. But if I make a damn promise, I try my hardest to keep that. Which is also why I rarely make them..."

"So..." Vendela finally said. "What do you want from me?"

"Help me," Liz said. "Help me find her. You work for the Fun House, you must kn-..."

"You want me to go against the Fun House?" Vendela asked with surprise. "To destroy everything I've worked to build up? If I do that I could lose everything all over again!"

"And if you don't, Ami might lose her life," Liz hissed.

"And I'm sorry about that," Vendela said with genuine regret in her voice. "But I have too much to lose. I lay low and don't draw attention to myself and I try to stay on Mr. Greenlund's good side. That's your problem Liz, you constantly draw attention to yourself and not the good kind. You're ruled by your heart, you do things by impulses. I am ruled by my head and I think before I act."

"You're afraid to lose the Bar so you'd let Ami die?" Liz said with utter disbelief in her voice. "Who are you?"

"Who am I?" Vendela shrieked. "Who are you?! Where has this compassion been for all these years? Why do you suddenly care about this one life so much when you're happy to watch hundreds of Sanctuary inhabitants die without doing anything?! I have more to lose than this damn bar, this is bigger than this!"

"I care!" Liz yelled before she could stop herself. "I care so much that it feels like it'll kill me! So I try not to care, with all my might! Because it's easier! But Ami… Ami is kind and nice and purehearted. She doesn't deserve to just disappear without a trace, like she never existed. She doesn't deserve that."

Liz's legs buckled under her weight and she half collapsed on the floor, Vendela instinctively reached for Liz and helped her sit up. It was now that the last part of what Vendela had said actually sunk in.

"Liz-…" Vendela said.

"Bigger than this…" Liz muttered weakly.

Liz looked at Vendela.

"What do you mean?" Liz asked.

"I can't help you," Vendela repeated.

Liz grabbed Vendela by the shirt.

"I know you said that," Liz said, almost out of breath. "So just answer my damn question and then I'll leave you with your conscience."

Vendela looked at the door to the side, like she was afraid someone was listening to them.

"When you were gone I…" Vendela started but her voice sounded uncertain and was as low as a whisper. "I joined the resistance. I'm helping them so believe me when I say that I can't attract attention to me, I mean it. And when I say I'm sorry I mean it b-…"

Liz let go of Vendela's shirt and stared at her with large eyes.

"Are you insane?" Liz asked.

Vendela stood up.

"I'm doing something," Vendela said and raised her chin. "For the greater good here. And I'm sorry but I can't let one life ruin that, not when all our lives are at stake. Even if that life is one of my friends."

Liz licked her lips and shook her head. Had Vendela gone mad? Joining the resistance would mean death if they were discovered and they would be discovered, it was just a matter of time. And if they were really unlucky, the humans would take that resistance as a chance to wipe them all out. To say that the creatures were too dangerous to be kept even in the Sanctuaries. That they had to be exterminated. They wouldn't start a revolution as Liz suspected they thought they would, they'd start a cleansing of all creatures.

Liz managed to stand up again, even though her legs heavily disagreed with her. Liz didn't even look at Vendela and without another word Liz started to move very slowly towards the door.

"Where are you going?" Vendela asked, her voice almost having a hint of desperation in it.

"Away from here," Liz muttered.

"If you're gonna storm the Fun House like that you're gonna get yourself killed," Vendela said, worry clear in her voice even though she was trying to hide it. "Hell, a gust of wind would kill you right now."

Liz turned around and looked at Vendela.

"Yeah, but hey, at least if I die that's just one life right?" Liz said bitterly. "And who cares about one life in the bigger picture? Apparently, one life means nothing."

Liz left Vendela with her mouth slightly open.

Chapter 19

Liz managed to get out of the Bar and into a nearby alley before she completely collapsed and fell to the cold and wet ground. She grunted in pain and her hand shook as she placed it over the mark in a pathetic attempt to make it hurt less. But at this point she didn't know what hurt more, the wound on her chest or the wound in her heart. Vendela had looked so cold as she'd spoken, so determined and so ready to let Ami suffer and die. As she'd watched Vendela she realized she didn't actually see Vendela, she saw a reflection of herself. After all, perhaps it was Liz who had made Vendela this cold.

Perhaps Liz would inevitably be Vendela's destruction, like she'd been so many others.

Liz closed her eyes, she just had to rest for a little while and clear her head. Then figure out what to actually do. It was also at this point that Liz realized that the people she worked for probably wouldn't be too happy with her if she got into a fight with the Fun House. Just as Vendela, Liz herself was also supposed to lay low and not bring attention to herself. But also, as Vendela had pointed out, Liz somehow always seemed to do the opposite.

The people she worked for wouldn't be happy, but she didn't feel like she owed them anything. She'd done everything they'd asked of her, she'd done things she bitterly regretted for them and for what? Something they might never deliver on. Something they might never be able to do. Liz owed more to Ami than to them.

She didn't know how long she'd sat in that alley, but it couldn't have been too long because she still felt drained when suddenly, out of nowhere, Liz heard a soft voice speak. Liz jumped as she hadn't heard any steps coming closer.

"I suggest you book an appointment with a worker," Vendela spoke low and softly. "See if you can convince them to help you. The guards rotate at 8 a.m, 6 p.m and midnight. The guards should be the most tired right before their shift ends, hopefully making them sloppy."

Liz stared at the shadow in the dark, she could just make out Vendela's silhouette. For the first seconds Liz thought she was hallucinating but when she realized she wasn't, she spoke.

"You changed your mind?" Liz said low.

"I can't do more," Vendela answered. "I can't. And I can't promise it will work."

"Why?" Liz asked, ignoring what Vendela just said. "Why did you change your mind?"

There was a pause before Vendela moved closer to Liz and she could see that she was holding something in her hands. At first, Liz couldn't distinguish exactly what it was but as Vendela came close enough, she saw that it was a piece of paper. Vendela looked at the paper with a frown before she reached it out for Liz. With a shaky hand Liz took the piece of paper from Vendela, and to her surprise it was the drawing missing from her box. Liz looked up at Vendela, uncertainty in her eyes.

"Because... One life does matter," Vendela said slowly and almost inaudibly. "And your care for Ami reminded me... Of how you used to be... Of who you can be when you want to..."

Vendela stopped herself and Liz felt as if there was something in her throat, making it impossible to speak.

"I wouldn't want you to lose the last of your compassion with Ami," Vendela finally said.

Vendela turned around and started to walk away.

"Vendela," Liz said, but it sounded more like a plea.

She stopped in her tracks but didn't turn around.

"Thank you," Liz said. "For everything you've done for me. Even though I don't deserve it."

"Yeah," Vendela said. "You always were my weak spot."

And you are mine. Liz thought but she couldn't make herself say it, no matter how much she wanted to.

"Just…" Vendela added quickly. "Don't disappear without a trace again. If you die that's… But don't just disappear."

She then left with quick steps, leaving Liz with the drawing held securely in her shaking hand.

Liz stared at the drawing in her hand and she couldn't help but to wonder why Vendela had taken it in the first place and left everything else in the box? She had to remind herself that that wasn't important at the moment, so she carefully picked up her box from the bag and folded the drawing once and put it back in its rightful place. As Liz was putting the box back into the bag her eyes glanced over where Vendela had stood not long ago and she felt an intense ache in her chest, but she tried to tell herself that it was just the wound making her feel strange. Liz regretted some of the things she'd said to Vendela, because she was right, Liz had no right to judge her.

What Liz had done while she'd been gone was far worse than what Vendela had done.

This whole rebellion thing made Liz feel sick, she knew Vendela's heart was in the right place and the others in the rebellion probably had pure motives but it wouldn't end well. Liz had seen it before but this time she was more afraid than ever because this time it looked like Vendela would be in the front line of it all, which meant she was in the most danger and if shit went down, then Katarina would be dragged into it as well. Young powerful Katarina who had parents she loved in Town, parents she'd turned herself in to protect. If a war broke out, which side would Katarina stand on? The side with her parents and the people who confined her, or creatures like herself fighting for freedom? With Katarina, Liz really didn't know. And if a war broke out because of this rebellion, would Liz be able to stand aside and do nothing as she'd done before?

Liz truly didn't know, she'd been able to do it many times before but Vendela had never been in any of those other situations. Vendela changed everything.

Liz shook away all these thoughts, there might not even be a rebellion. Sometimes it was just something people spoke about, in an attempt to keep some sense of hope but even if there was no rebellion and they were found out, Vendela would almost certainly be executed. That thought sent a chill down Liz's spine.

"Stop," she said to herself and closed her eyes. "Concentrate."

She had to get a hold of herself, none of this matter right now. Because there was no certainty, but what was certain was that Ami was gone and Liz had promised to find her. So when Liz finally had regained some of her strength, she stood up and made her way back to the Fun House. She had an appointment to make.

As she came close to the Fun House, she couldn't help but to glance over the street towards Katarina's house and in the window she could see a single shadow move inside, a strangely lonely sight.

Liz turned her attention back to the Fun House and walked inside, she had no idea what time it was but as she entered she saw a clock on the wall to the right. It was almost 4 p.m and according to Vendela they would switch guards at 6 p.m, making it closer to the end of their shift at least. Liz walked up to the reception, Mona was still sitting there and she smiled gently when she saw Liz.

"Back again already?" She asked.

"Yeah, couldn't stay away," Liz said and tried to smile. "I'd like-…"

But before Liz could say anything else Mona had picked up the folder from beneath the bench and laid it in front of Liz.

"Thanks," Liz said.

"No problem," Mona said. "I'm here to serve in any way possible."

Liz started to flip through the pages and she wondered if she should just pick someone on random or if she should try and have a strategy? Then she saw a name pop up, Nami, age: 24, Creature: Siren. If Liz wasn't mistaken, Ami had talked about them a long time ago, before she'd started to work for the Fun House. If Liz was right, they would be perfect.

"That one," Liz said and pointed to Nami's description box.

"Ah, good choice, siren," Mona said. "Some of our most popular workers."

Liz didn't say anything, simply trying to keep her face as neutral as possible. Mona flipped through some papers with what looked like a lot of different schedules.

"When would y-…" Mona started.

"As soon as possible?" Liz asked.

"Someone's impatient," Mona said and smiled lightly and looked through her papers once more. "They are available in half an hour. If you sit down someone will come and get you and escort you to the right room."

"What about payment?" Liz asked carefully.

"Oh, don't worry," Mona said. "You figure that out with the worker. They will explain how everything works if this is your first time."

"It certainly is," Liz muttered.

Mona smiled gently.

"Thanks," Liz said and forced a smile on her lips.

Liz was just about to turn around and sit down in one of the chairs lined up on the right side of the room when she stopped herself.

"Just one more question," Liz said. "Are you human or creature?"

Mona looked slightly surprised at the question but simply pulled down the collar that covered her throat and exposed the tattoo they all shared.

"Why?" Mona asked.

Liz shook her head.

"Nothing, sorry," Liz said. "Just curious."

"The only humans who work here are the guards and Mr. Greenlund himself," Mona said.

Liz said nothing more and sat down in one of the chairs and she felt her legs thanking her. Liz stared at the clock that hung beside her, it seemed to go unnaturally slow. Liz felt anxious, which wasn't a feeling she was entirely used to. To just sit and wait wasn't something Liz liked to do, she either decided to stay out of things completely or she rushed in head first. But she had to control her impulses and actually plan a little, as she was still very weak and she didn't want to drag too much attention to herself or actually start a fight. Liz could see the headline in front of her, war started between creatures and humans because of a terrorist attack towards the Fun House.

Liz wanted to avoid a war, or even a fight for once and yet she was in a situation that could start just that if she wasn't careful.

As Liz waited she saw people enter the Fun House, actual humans. It wasn't hard to tell if those people were human or creatures. Their clothes were clean and fancy, and they all had at least two personal bodyguards. Two humans entered and were escorted up the stairs before it was Liz's turn.

The guard that escorted Liz was a tall and extremely muscular man who looked a little intimidating, even for Liz, perhaps especially as she was so weak at the moment. He didn't say a single word to Liz as he walked up to her, but he made it quite clear that she should follow him. She glanced over at the reception and she saw that Mona gave her a careful smile as Liz started to climb the stairs.

They walked up to the third floor which made things a little easier for Liz and she managed to glance up towards the fourth floor before she was escorted further down the corridor on the third floor. The fourth floor was cut off with a door and in front of it stood two guards and Liz could just about make out the fact that they were carrying weapons.

Liz was escorted further down the corridor, far away from the stairway up to the fourth floor. The corridor seemed to go on forever until the guards finally stopped in front of a door. It had the number 333 on it. The guard still didn't say anything but Liz took it that this was the room with Nami in it. So she reached for the door knob and opened the door. The guard didn't stop her and she hoped he wasn't planning on standing outside the whole time, it would make things quite a lot harder.

As Liz entered the room she looked around, there wasn't too much inside. A large twin size bed with red and black covers, the walls were purple with silver details and to the right Liz saw a door that lead into a bathroom and right in front of her was a large window which oversaw the main street but Liz saw no one else in there and for a split second she thought this was some kind of trap. Then she heard a hoarse voice speak and it seemed to come from the bathroom. As Liz glanced over there again she saw a figure standing in the door opening.

Nami's thin and straight body was wrapped in a silky looking dress that was on the verge of see through. Their skin was even paler than Liz, an almost milky white shade. Their long silver colored hair covered one of their blue eyes and there was a smirk on their small lips.

"Hello," they said and smiled. "I'm Nami, what's your name?"

Chapter 20

"I'm Liz," she said slowly.

There was a flash of recognition in Nami's eyes and Liz couldn't help but to think about what Vendela had said before *"everyone knows who you are in here."* Perhaps she had more of a reputation than she'd thought. Liz saw that Nami's eyes glanced at the mark on her chest but it seemed like they ignored it, they'd probably seen a lot of things during their time here.

"I like it," Nami then quickly said. "So... Is this your first time here?"

Nami moved elegantly from the bathroom and their movement reminded Liz of a leopard.

"Yeah," Liz said and followed them with her eyes.

Nami sat down on the bed, which looked impossibly comfortable and crossed their legs. Liz had to resist the temptation to throw herself onto it and just rest.

"Then let me explain ho-..." Nami started.

"Let me interrupt you there," Liz said and slowly moved away from the door. "I'm not actually here for... That."

Nami's body tensed up and their pleasant looking features tightened. Liz once again looked behind herself at the door.

"Is the guard who escorted me here gonna stand outside the door the whole time?" Liz asked.

Nami shook their head slightly, and there was worry in their eyes.

"They patrol," they said low. "Why?"

Liz took a few steps closer to Nami but stopped when they moved away from her.

"I'm not going to hurt you," Liz said. "If that's what you think."

"Then why are you here?" Nami asked and swallowed. "If you're not here for s-…"

"I'm looking for a friend," Liz said.

Nami frowned deeply.

"I-I don't… Understand," Nami said slowly.

"Ami," Liz said. "You know her right? She spoke of you."

If there had been worry in Nami's eyes before, now there was full fledged panic. They'd lost the little color they'd had in their face and they seemed to struggle to say anything. Liz saw how they tried to regain some of their composure. They laughed, but it was quite obviously filled with worry and their eyes darted from Liz to the door behind her.

"Sorry," Nami said. "Never heard of her and if you're not here for business then-…"

Liz took another step forward and Nami twitched.

"Take one more step and I'll scream," Nami said seriously.

"I'm not going to hurt you," Liz said, trying not to sound annoyed.

Short pause.

"You're afraid," Liz said. "Just like Ami was when she came to me and asked for help."

Nami was quiet.

"They've taken her to the fourth floor haven't they?" Liz asked.

Nami didn't move, they barely breathed.

"I'm trying to help her," Liz tried to say as softly as she could. "Possibly help you all. You're afraid of the fourth floor as well aren't you?"

Possibly help you all. What she'd just said echoed in her head, had she completely lost it? She wasn't here for anyone else other than Ami, but it had slipped out of her before she'd even had time to think. It was a lie, a lie to try and convince Nami to help her and lies came all too easy for Liz. Scarily easy sometimes. Liz saw the fear in their eyes and she knew that the offer of help might be the best way to get through to them.

It was a cruel lie, maybe one of the cruelest she'd told in a long time. To dangle help and freedom in front of someone in need, only to snatch it away from them.

But Liz needed Nami to stay quiet for her, to not call the guards, otherwise there was no hope for her to find Ami. Nami still said nothing.

"Please," Liz said. "I need your help."

For a second Liz thought that Nami was going to scream for the guards but instead when they opened their mouth, they whispered.

"With what?" Nami said almost inaudibly.

A half smile spread across Liz's lips.

"Ami is on the fourth floor isn't she?" Liz asked again.

This time, Nami said nothing, but they nodded ever so slightly.

"Do you know what happens on the fourth floor?" Liz asked.

Nami shook their head.

"Okay," Liz said. "I'm going to try and get up on there."

"You're crazy," Nami said low. "You'll be killed…"

"Don't worry about me," Liz said and smirked lightly. "I might not look like much but I can take a beating."

Nami had a large frown on their face and their lips were as thin as a line.

"I'll have a bigger chance of success if you help me," Liz said as she just had gotten an idea.

Nami swallowed hard and Liz saw the doubt on their face and Liz understood their situation, why would they ever trust Liz? Nami licked their lips.

"If they find out I h-…" Nami started.

"If I'm discovered I won't say a thing," Liz said, that was not a lie at least. "I promise. I'm not trying to get anyone else into trouble, I just want to help my friend."

"She's my friend as well," Nami said almost inaudibly. "What do you need from me?"

Liz sighed in relief, even though the hard part was still left.

"All you need to do is scream," Liz said. "I'm guessing the guards patrolling the corridors are here for the workers as much as the clients?"

Nami nodded.

"Open the window and scream and when everyone comes in, say that I assaulted you and then jumped out the window without paying," Liz said. "Hopefully they'll buy that, I don't think they want to lose any money."

Nami bit their lower lip. Liz could see Nami's thin body shake ever so lightly, from nerves or fear Liz wasn't sure. Liz felt a tinge of shame, could she really ask this of someone in Nami's position? Nami was terrified of Mr. Greenlund, that much was clear.

"If you don't want to do it," Liz finally said with a sigh, she had grown soft hadn't she? "That's fine. I'll manage. Just… If they come to fetch me, don't tell them where I've gone okay?"

Nami swallowed hard and took a deep breath.

"I'll do it," Nami said with a shaky voice. "For Ami."

Now Liz just had to think about where she should be positioned when Nami screamed. She could of course not be in the room, she would either be discovered immediately or she wouldn't be able to get out without them seeing her. So her best bet would be to hide somewhere in the corridor, perhaps in the stairway going down?

Nami had walked over to the large window, they had already opened it and even though it wasn't very late, the room was filled with cool air from the wind outside. Liz could hear Nami take a deep breath.

Liz wasn't a hundred percent certain that Nami wouldn't betray her out of fear, but at this point she really didn't have a choice but to trust them on this.

"Where are you going to go when I distract the guards?" Nami asked quietly. "They'll rush here."

"I'll figure it out as I go," Liz said. "Get ready, I'm going to leave any second."

Liz started walking towards the door when Nami spoke again.

"Hey, wait," they said low. "Why are you doing this?"

"What?" Liz asked, confused. "I told you, Ami is m-…"

"She has many friends," Nami said. "No one else has come for her or even asked for her. We're all terrified, so… Why aren't you?"

A sad smile flashed over Liz's face.

"Let's just say that staying alive is a specialty of mine," Liz muttered. "I'm not afraid to die and I don't have a lot to lose."

Liz walked up to the door and she laid her ear against it to try and hear any footsteps or even a faint heartbeat that meant someone was right outside but she heard nothing, which for once wasn't very comforting. Her hearing had not been what it used to be since Katarina had struck her with that spell.

Liz hadn't been herself since it had happened.

Liz looked back at Nami, who was even paler than before and she tried to smile but it probably came off as forced.

"If you find Ami," Nami said just as Liz was about to open the door. "Tell her…"

Liz glanced back with a raised eyebrow.

"Tell her I'm sorry will you?" Nami muttered.

"You can tell her that yourself later," Liz said.

There was such sadness in Nami's face, mixed with fear but Liz barely noticed it.

Without saying anything else Liz slowly opened the door and looked down the hallway both ways, as far as she could see there was no one there, the guards patrolling must be on another floor.

"Scream in about ten seconds," Liz whispered to Nami behind her.

Nami nodded carefully and Liz slipped out of the room and moved as fast and as soundless as she could. She snuck down the staircase leading to the second floor and stood so that if all of the guards rushed past the staircase towards Nami's room they wouldn't see her, if they weren't looking for her, which they wouldn't be right away hopefully. And even if anyone would spot her in the staircase she could probably talk her way out of it and say that she was on her way out.

An ear piercingly loud scream filled the whole floor. She heard people shouting and could see one guard running down from the fourth floor but she only saw the one guard which meant they'd left the other one up there to secure the door.

But there was no turning back now.

Liz rushed as quickly as she could towards the fourth floor and she could see the lone guard standing there. As he saw Liz he opened his mouth to speak but before a single sound could escape his lips, Liz hit him as hard as she could at the temple of his head. The guard collapsed and Liz quickly caught his body so it wouldn't fall down the stairs and make too much noise. As she caught him, she almost fell alongside him down the stairs but managed to stay somewhat balanced.

Liz hadn't time to think about how her chest ached or how her head spun like she was on a carousel, she just had to move, she didn't have time to waste.

She saw a key hanging from his belt and she snatched it from him and unlocked the door. Liz opened the door and even though her chest burned she grabbed the heavy guard and dragged him into the hallway of the fourth floor. She then quickly closed the door and locked it, hoping that the others didn't have the keys on them or that it would take them a few minutes to get it open nonetheless.

Liz leaned against the door and took just a few seconds to calm down, but just a few. Liz's eyes glanced at the unconscious guard, and she saw that he was breathing. The question was to leave him alive or kill him? Leaving him alive meant that he could identify her but if she killed him, that could really start something bad, something she wouldn't be able to stop. She decided to let him live, not by the goodness of her heart but because it was probably the best option. If she was lucky, her hit to his head would cause amnesia, it wasn't likely but it wasn't impossible either.

Liz then looked down the long hallway on the fourth floor, it looked just the same as the second and third and it was as quiet as a grave. The first door, the one she stood in front of had the name Mr. Greenlund engraved on it but Liz quickly passed it, her business wasn't with him right now.

Liz walked with uncertain, yet quick steps down the hallway and when she came to the first room she grabbed the door knob and for a second she considered turning around and pretend none of this had happened. Pretend she hadn't broken her own rules about not interfering, pretend that Ami was fine and was just relaxing in one of these rooms.

Liz had done it many times before, if it was one thing she was good at, it was pretending.

But if she opened these doors in search of Ami and Liz didn't like what she saw, she wasn't sure on how she would react and there would be no turning back and pretending this had never happened. Some doors, once opened, could never be closed again.

Liz swallowed and against her better judgment, she opened the first door. As her eyes actually realized what she saw, she froze in place, her eyes big and her mouth fell open slightly. The room was small, around the size of a closet and there was basically nothing in it. Except for a young looking boy hanging upside down with a tube stuck to his arm and Liz could see red liquid running through the tube and into a container beside him that had strange markings on it, Liz recognized it immediately, a magical spell. Liz blinked a few times and took a step back as she tried to make sense of what she saw. The boy was obviously unconscious and he looked rough, pale beyond belief and she could barely hear his heart beating in his chest.

But as Liz stared at the boy, it started to make sense to her. Liz ran down the corridor, flinging up door after door trying to see if Ami's sweet face belonged to any of these bodies. Her mind raced, this was how Mr. Greenlund could have fresh blood to supply to whomever he wished, this was how he could have a monopoly on blood. Because no one cared if any of the workers disappeared and he scared the rest of the workers into silence.

This was why no one came back from here.

When Liz tore up the seventh door without seeing Ami, she started to panic. How long did they keep these people here? How long did they survive before they were thrown away like garbage? Liz ignored every warning her body gave her that she should slow down and rest, because there was no time.

At the tenth door Liz exclaimed in surprise. She saw Ami's tall body hanging in the same way all the others had and she looked ashy and her lips were chapped. Liz slowly walked up to her and saw that she had a bruise on her face that looked fairly new.

"Ami?" Liz said gently and touched her face. "It's me, Liz."

There was no response and Liz hadn't really expected one. She could hear Ami's heart beating, though very weakly. Liz guessed they were drugged before strung up. Liz looked at the rope around Ami's ankles and she saw how red and irritated her skin was beneath it. Liz clenched her jaw before slowly and carefully removing the tube from Ami's arm. Now she just had to get Ami down from there.

Liz would easily have been able to carry Ami before but she was uncertain of her strength at the moment, but she ignored it as much as she could, she couldn't doubt herself, not now. So Liz took a hold of Ami's upper body and turned her so she wasn't hanging upside down anymore, she held Ami under her arms with her right arm and with her other, Liz untied, or more tore off the rope from her feet. And then Liz caught her as if was holding a child, and Ami felt uncomfortably heavy and lifeless in her arms.

Liz's arms were shaking and the strain it took to hold Ami was taking its toll on her. Liz then came to the realization that she had no plan on getting out of here, especially not with an unconscious Ami in her arms. She'd been so focused on finding Ami that she hadn't thought at all about escaping.

Liz knew she probably didn't have much time until the guards returned and gathered that something was wrong, but Liz carefully laid Ami on the ground. She felt cold to the touch and some of her dark hair had stuck to her face, but Liz brushed it away.

"It's okay," Liz said. "It's okay."

She didn't even know if Ami could hear her. And as Liz was staring at Ami, the worry, the panic, all that started to fade. Ami was safe now, even if all the guards in the Fun House came after them, it wouldn't matter if Liz was hurt, she'd tear them apart before they took Ami back. Liz rose to her feet and she realized there was only one way to end this.

"I'll be back," Liz said coldly.

She had to pay Mr. Greenlund a visit and she walked towards his office with such anger inside that it was raging like a storm, just waiting to get out and cause destruction.

Chapter 21

As Liz walked with determined steps towards Mr. Greenlund's office she could hear voices speaking from behind the door leading to the third floor but she didn't care what they said. At least they hadn't started to bash the door open or even tried to open it, it seemed like. Liz glanced at the still unconscious guard and a flash of anger came over her and she deeply regretted she hadn't killed him. But no, she would save all her rage for Mr. Greenlund.

Liz didn't knock on the door, she just tore it open and slammed it close behind her. She could see who she assumed was Mr. Greenlund sitting behind a large desk at the far side of the room. The room was so big, it was like two of the bedrooms Liz had been in down on the third floor. Liz locked the door behind her, staring intensely at the man.

"Who are-…" Mr. Greenlund started.

Liz grabbed the bookshelf near the door and tipped it over so it blocked the entrance, the only way out now was the window behind him and Liz was quite sure he didn't want to jump out from the fourth floor. He was only human after all. Mr. Greenlund had risen from his seat, his face flushed red with anger. He didn't look entirely as Liz had expected. He was younger than she'd thought, and he had sand blond hair and vivid green eyes. He was tall and lean but there was something grim and cruel lurking in those large eyes.

"Now," Liz said, trying to contain her anger. "Let's talk."

"Who are you?" He yelled in a commanding voice. "What are you doing here?"

He then saw the tattoo around her neck.

"I suggest you leave before I have you executed, monster," Mr. Greenlund spat out.

Liz moved quickly, before he could yell or do anything really. She grabbed him by the jacket and flung him onto the floor. His body hit the wood with a hard thud and he gasped in surprise and pain.

"Bitch!" He yelled. "Do you know who I am?!"

Liz moved up to him and pinned him to the floor, she'd put one of her boots straight on his chest and no matter how much he struggled or wriggled, he was cemented to the floor.

"I know who you are," Liz said, her voice shaking with rage. "I guess you don't know who I am though. If you did, you wouldn't talk to me like that."

"Why would I know who you are? You are a sickness, a stain on this world, a disgusting mockery of humans! You are a monster!" He screamed with distaste. "My guards will be here any second a-…"

"You want to call me a monster," Liz said, challenging him, pushing down her boot on his chest. "I'll show you a monster."

He let out a yelp of pain.

"Did that hurt?" Liz asked without remorse. "Good."

She pushed down a little more and she thought she heard something crack, perhaps one of his ribs. He screamed, it was a high pitched sound that rang in her ears.

"What do you want?!" He yelled.

Liz took away her foot from his chest and instead she pulled him up to his feet and slammed him into a wall. Liz flashed him her sharp teeth and she could hear his heart beating faster and more irregular by the second.

"You thought you could string people up? Drain them of their blood? Kill them, so you could get fresh blood!?" Liz yelled. "You thought you could do that and no one would care?!"

He laughed low but she saw it pained him slightly, must be that broken rib.

"Almost three months I've been doing this," he said with a grin on his lips. "No one has noticed. No one *cares*. They're monsters. They're whor-…"

Liz slammed her fist into his face and she could feel his nose break beneath her knuckles. This time he didn't yell out in pain, he looked more shocked than anything else.

"Where did you think the blood came from?" He asked as blood had started dripping from his broken nose. "You thought people, real human people, would donate blood to *things* like you? So you disgusting creatures can go on, what you call, living?"

He laughed low.

"No," he continued. "You're a vampire, why do you care? Work for me and you'd get fresh blood regularly."

"I care since someone you strung up to die is my friend," Liz hissed. "And she matters."

His green eyes shifted to the blocked door and then back to Liz. Liz was burning up on the inside and she was surprised she'd been able to keep herself under this much control.

"So what now?" He asked. "If you kill me someone else will just take my place and you'll be branded a murderer, a terrorist and executed."

Liz clenched her jaw and her grip of his jacket tightened. He smiled a very unpleasant smile.

"You'll die either way, vampire," he laughed. "Abusing a human? Hurting me. I'll have you executed, I will watch you burn!"

Liz started to laugh and her grip of him loosened until she let go of him entirely. He had a look of shock on his face and placed a hand on his rib cage.

"I want to see that," Liz said.

He frowned. Liz looked around the room and saw a letter opener in metal, it wasn't very sharp but sharp enough for the purpose Liz had in mind. Liz picked it up and inspected the knife looking object.

"I told you if you ki-…" he said, a touch of fear in his voice.

"Oh, this isn't for you," Liz said and turned her gaze from the letter opener to him. "It's for me."

Now he looked properly frightened, but perhaps just because he wasn't understanding what she was saying. Liz walked up to him and shoved the letter opener in his hand. She then gripped his hand with her own and placed the point of the letter opener on her chest, right by her heart.

"Stake through the heart to kill a vampire right?" Liz said. "Do it. Kill me."

Mr. Greenlund had a look of mistrust and shock on his face, like he was thinking that she was tricking him somehow.

"Do it!" Liz yelled aggressively.

With one swift motion, he pushed the letter opener into Liz's chest with her help and she felt it piercing her heart. Liz gasped but there was no pain, it was more like a pleasant burning in her chest. She took a step back before her legs folded themselves beneath her and she fell to the floor. Mr. Greenlund looked at what was happening with confusion and fear, he didn't move for a while as if he was afraid she'd come back to life again. But Liz laid lifeless on the floor without moving, black blood sipping through the wound and staining the floor.

"Crazy bitch," Mr. Greenlund finally said and relaxed slightly, dusting off dirt from his jacket.

He walked up to her body and kicked it with some force but Liz didn't move, her eyes staring emptily into the ceiling. Mr. Greenlund spat at her before he pulled out his letter opener, it was covered in black blood and he watched it with disgust. He kicked Liz again and tried to stop the nose bleed.

"I liked this letter opener," he said and turned his back to Liz and started to walk up to the barricaded door.

He froze in fear as he heard something behind him. It was a low but intense laugh. His common sense told him he was hearing things, because she couldn't be alive. He'd pierced her heart and no vampire could survive that but he finally turned around and saw Liz standing up with a grin on her face and her eyes two pitch black holes. The black blood was still on the floor and it was stained where the knife had pierced her but there was no wound from it.

"Why aren't you dead?!" He yelled in panic.

Liz grabbed his shirt and slammed him hard into the wall again, he dropped the letter opener in the process and it clattered to the ground. She was so weak, she felt as if she was going to collapse any second. Healing that wound had taken practically all of her last powers, but she was running on anger fumes and spite at this point. She couldn't let him know how bad she felt. Liz smiled and showed off her sharp teeth again.

"I can't die," Liz said.

"W-What?" He said confused.

"I can't die," Liz repeated. "So listen closely. You can have me taken away. You can cut off my head. Put a stake through my heart. Leave me out for the sun. I will survive it all. Worse men than you have tried to kill me and all have failed, including myself."

"W-What are you?" He asked, his eyes almost tearing up.

"Your worst nightmare," Liz said. "I will survive everything you throw at me. So believe me when I say that I will come back and I will kill you if you *ever* touch someone I know or if you ever string someone up to die for blood. I will find you, I have an eternity to live, do not doubt I'd spend fifty years looking for and tormenting you.

Liz could feel him shaking and she smiled again.

"So I'm gonna let you live," Liz said. "Because you're right, someone else would just take your place. And now you know what I'm capable of and knowing how scared you are off me, gives me great satisfaction."

"I-I…" He stammered.

"I'm gonna take my friend," Liz said. "And leave. And if not the others strung up are let down and are free to go, I will come back."

Liz moved her face closer to him, so close she could smell his fear.

"And maybe, I won't kill you then," Liz said low and menacingly. "Maybe I'll just turn you into one of us, you're already a monster so it'd be fitting if you were branded as one as well."

Liz let go of him and he fell to the floor, his breathing shaky and irregular. It looked like he was trying to say something but couldn't, so Liz pushed away the bookshelf with some difficulty and then unlocked the door. As she opened the door, so did the door coming from the third floor. Shouting filled the corridor and suddenly Liz had four guns pointed at her. Liz put up her hands but glanced back at Mr. Greenlund who still sat in his room, pale as a ghost, with his broken nose and cracked ribs.

"Mr. Greenlund are you alright?" One of the guards yelled.

He didn't answer. But they could obviously see that he was hurt by the blood covering half his face from his broken nose and the fact that he looked like he'd seen death itself.

"You'll pay for what you've done, monster!" Another guard shouted.

"No!" Mr. Greenlund suddenly shouted with a shaky voice. "L-Let her go."

"But-..." One of the guards said but they all slowly lowered their weapons.

"I said let her go," Mr. Greenlund said, his voice spiking in anger. "A-And... And take down the blood bags."

"Are you su-..." The first guard said.

"Just do it!" Mr. Greenlund shouted.

Liz gave Mr. Greenlund a smile and flashed her sharp teeth before she walked past the very confused guards and went back to Ami.

Liz had to fight to walk in a straight line back to the room where Ami was, her vision was going blurry but she tried her best to shake it off. She still had to get Ami out of here, that was the priority, then she could collapse and faint as much as she wanted. Liz knew the guards were watching her as she walked down the corridor and she couldn't afford to let them see how weak she felt. If they knew how close she was to losing consciousness, they would attack her with all they got and Liz wasn't sure if she would be able to beat them; she was just so tired.

As she entered the small room she'd left Ami in, she knelt down beside her. It almost looked like some color had returned to her face, but the normal glow Ami possessed wasn't there and that worried Liz a little. Liz took a few seconds to recharge her batteries before she lifted Ami in her arms and made her way down the stairs. Liz was shaking pretty badly but all her concentration went to not dropping Ami and as Liz continued down the stairs she tried not to think about the fact that it felt like she was carrying a corpse. She had to remind herself that Ami was alive and would be fine.

They didn't meet anyone on the way down, she guessed all the guards were up with Mr. Greenlund at the moment. As she came to the bottom floor, she glanced over to the reception and she saw Mona gasping and putting her hands over her mouth as she saw Liz and the unconscious Ami.

"Oh my God," Mona whispered. "What happened?"

Liz looked away, she didn't even have the energy to answer her, she just had to keep moving one foot in front of the other, she just had to get Ami out of this place but Liz moved slow and before she realized it Mona had run up in front of Liz with a frown on her face.

"Ami," she said low. "Is she-…?"

"She'll be fine," Liz snapped tiredly. "Not thanks to you though."

Mona saw the simmering rage in Liz's eyes and stepped aside, and if Liz had actually paid attention to Mona, she would have seen the shame in her face.

Finally Liz exited the Fun House and was met with a cold and harsh wind. It didn't bother Liz but she looked at Ami who was only wearing a simple tank top and pajama shorts, and Ami was already cold as it was. Liz had once again no plan, she had to take Ami somewhere where she could rest and feel safe. Taking her to Vendela wasn't a good idea as Ami didn't trust her and she didn't want Ami to have another shock when she woke up.

Liz sighed deeply and cursed herself as her eyes glanced over at Katarina's apartment. Katarina had healed Liz, though against her wishes, perhaps she could help Ami mend a little quicker. Hopefully whatever kept Ami unconscious was just some drug that would pass in a couple of hours, but she couldn't know that for sure. There had been a magic spell on the blood container, who said they couldn't have put a spell on the workers as well? Katarina's apartment was cozy and warm and she made more tea than anyone should probably drink and Ami had met Katarina, which meant she didn't wake up at a total stranger's apartment.

But the only problem was that Liz really didn't want to go back there, she didn't want to burden Katarina anymore. Because every time she'd gone to Katarina it was because she wanted or needed something and it felt like

Liz was using her, and she hated that. Katarina had said that she didn't mind helping Liz, but she was young and naive and had seen nothing of the world. Liz hesitated but in the end felt as if she had no choice and this time it wasn't for her, it was for Ami's sake. Liz would just leave her there, then get out of Katarina's way and come back later to see if Ami had woken up.

It was a good thing that Katarina's apartment was just across the street because Liz would not have been able to go much further with Ami in her arms. She hated being this weak and there was a small part of her that blamed Katarina, but mostly she blamed herself for ever caring enough to get hurt in the first place. Every problem she'd gotten herself into was because she cared, and it was infuriating. Liz stopped in front of Katarina's door and was just about to kick it, because she couldn't let go of Ami at all to knock when the door flung open and there stood Katarina and stared at Liz with those green and yellow speckled eyes. Those eyes then shifted to the body in Liz's arms.

"This is a bit embarrassing," Liz said and tried to sound lighthearted. "But-..."

Liz didn't have the time to finish her sentence before she felt how she was falling forward, still with Ami in her arms. If Katarina hadn't been there to stabilize Liz, both Ami and herself would have crashed to the floor. Instead, Liz slowly sank to the floor until she was on her knees with Ami now laying on the floor inside the apartment in front of her. Liz closed her eyes in relief as the strain was lifted from her body.

"I'm sorry," Liz muttered.

Katarina still hadn't said anything but closed the door behind Liz and Ami and then went and fetched a pillow and blanket. She gently put the pillow beneath Ami's head and the blanket over her body. Liz had leaned against the closed door and she was finally ready to just lose consciousness.

"I'm sorry to come here..." Liz muttered low. "I'm sorry."

She then slipped into unconsciousness for the third time in little over a week.

Chapter 22

Liz woke up with a gasp and panic in her eyes as she scanned her surroundings. When she saw the familiarity of Katarina's living room she swallowed and her body relaxed a little. She hadn't moved from her sitting position by the door but she noticed a blanket had been put over her body. It was unnecessary, but a sweet gesture nonetheless. Liz looked around but saw neither Katarina nor Ami but just as she was about to open her mouth to speak, Katarina poked out her head from her bedroom. Liz averted her eyes and slowly rose, her body finally felt a little rested but not fully restored.

"You've been busy," Katarina said and closed the bedroom door behind her. "I didn't expect to have two unconscious people in my house today."

"Sorry," Liz said. "I didn't mean to… I mean…"

"Are you alright?" Katarina asked when she noticed how Liz couldn't form any coherent sentence.

Liz nodded quickly.

"I'm fine," she said. "How's Ami?"

Katarina glanced behind herself.

"Alive," Katarina said. "But still unconscious."

"How long was I…?" Liz asked.

"Three hours perhaps," Katarina said. "Not very long."

"Good," Liz said. "I've been sleeping more this past week than I've been doing for centuries."

Liz laughed low but Katarina just stared at her with her neutral face.

"I'm sorry for coming back," Liz said. "After what I said. I'm sorry for bothering you again."

Katarina shook her head lightly and walked over to her stove, she was probably going to make herself some more tea.

"You really don't understand do you?" Katarina said calmly.

"Understand what?" Liz asked carefully.

"I've been useless my entire life," Katarina said, filling her pot with water. "Locked away in a room where my powers were wasted."

Katarina put the pot to boil and turned back to Liz.

"And I thought that in here…" Katarina said. "I could find some purpose, to help people. But most seem to be… Afraid of me."

"Afraid of you?" Liz asked with a frown.

"I guess people don't like the idea of me finding out their darkest secrets," Katarina said and swallowed. "Or see what their future may hold. So even in here I'm…"

Katarina sighed lightly.

"You're not bothering me by asking for my help," Katarina said. "You're making me feel wanted. Like I matter, like I can make a difference."

Liz looked away and frowned slightly, she didn't know how to respond.

"Most people would see it as me taking advantage of you," Liz finally said. "Using you."

Katarina smiled gently and fixed the last part of her tea and the air was filled with the scent of ginseng.

"I could easily tell you no," Katarina said. "I could easily tell you to leave and that I would not help you."

Katarina turned back, with a cup in her hands.

"But I do want to help," Katarina said. "Isn't that what friends are for?"

Liz looked straight at Katarina, shock quite visible in her eyes. Had she just said friends? Katarina just calmly took a sip of her tea and sat down at the table.

"Friends…" Liz repeated low. "But I said-…"

"I know what you said," Katarina said with a soft voice. "Perhaps we have different expectations and ideas of friendship. If you do not want to be my friend, that is fine. I'll help you, but my help only goes so far until I feel what you fear. That you're using me."

"W-Why…" Liz stammered. "Why do you want to be friends with me?"

"You've asked that before," Katarina said. "And I'll give you the same answer. I find you interesting."

"Why then?" Liz asked with confusion. "Why the hell do you find me interesting?"

Katarina put down her cup and Liz could see steam rising from it. She tilted her head slightly before answering.

"You know that I knew about you, before we first met," Katarina said.

"Yeah, from Vendela and such," Liz said impatiently. "You saw people being afraid of me I guess? Does that say friendship material to you?"

Katarina nodded slowly.

"Quite a few remembered you with fear," Katarina said. "And I could feel them tense up by the mention of your name. But…"

"But what?" Liz asked.

"But then I saw you through Vendela's eyes," Katarina said and stared directly at Liz.

Liz frowned slightly.

"I saw glimpses of a past you shared together," Katarina said.

"And what? You saw how I broke her heart? How she hates me?" Liz asked, confused and with a mixture of anger and sadness in her voice.

"No," Katarina said carefully. "There was no fear, no tension or hatred in her memories. Just a tinge of sadness in the midst of a lot of happiness. She saw you in a gentler light, a more vulnerable state perhaps."

Liz tensed up by Katarina's words.

"That was what made you fascinating to me," Katarina said. "A person with such care and gentleness yet at the same time with such passiveness and anger. It's quite the contradiction."

Liz was silent for a moment.

"You saw how I once was," Liz said coldly. "At one point, years ago. That part of me you saw through Vendela's eyes is gone."

Katarina glanced over at her bedroom door, where Ami rested, a vague smile playing on her lips.

"If you say so," Katarina said.

Liz opened her mouth to protest but quickly closed it and looked away.

"I'm gonna leave," Liz said. "I'll check back on Ami in a while."

"You can't run forever Liz," Katarina said calmly. "Your past, your feelings, who you are. They will catch up with you."

Liz shot Katarina a glance, it was first filled with anger but it quickly softened. Liz knew Katarina meant no harm as she'd said that, and she also knew she was probably right. Liz tried to smile.

"I can try," Liz said. "I have forever to live, after all."

Katarina didn't smile at her words. Liz didn't say anything else, just reached for the door. If she'd only been unconscious for about three hours that meant there was still plenty of night time left for her to roam around. As she opened the door and was just about to exit, she did something, she was not quite sure why, but the words slipped past her well guarded lips.

"If you're still curious," Liz said low. "I'm… Around 600 years old. If you were still wondering."

Then Liz quickly exited the apartment before Katarina could say anything in response.

Chapter 23

The night sky was dark and filled with stars and Liz stopped right outside Katarina's house, picking at the skin around her nails. Why had she told Katarina her age? She hadn't asked since that conversation and why would it even be of interest to her? It was just a number, it didn't mean anything and yet it had been hard to say but she'd told Katarina anyway.

Every time Liz was with Katarina she had the urge to run away after a while, it wasn't reasonable and she couldn't explain it either. It felt as if the longer Liz spent time with Katarina the more she learned about her, without Liz telling her a thing. Liz knew Katarina couldn't read minds, she could just read emotions and if she didn't touch Liz, there was no way she could know about her past. Even though Liz knew all of this, Katarina seemed to always ask and say just the right thing to make Liz want to run away. It wasn't that Liz was afraid of Katarina, she was more afraid of what Katarina would find out if she spent too much time with her.

So perhaps to a certain extent, Liz understood what Katarina had meant when she'd said that the creatures in here were afraid of her. It wasn't her they were afraid of really, it was of not being in control and being completely open to someone. It was the fear of someone knowing every bad thing you've ever done, see things you'd rather forget ever happened or see a future you never wanted.

It could make you feel like an open wound.

Liz sighed deeply and there was as if a burden had lifted from her shoulders. Ami was safe and Liz doubted she would have to worry about the Fun House again, at least for a good while. Now she just had to deal with the fact that Vendela was part of a rebellion doomed to fail, Liz was still working for Lady Morgana and she was still feeling weak. Except for all of that, everything was peachy. Liz even thought that some of Vendela's anger had diminished from their last talk, and even though Liz felt that she deserved Vendela's wrath it was nice if she could talk to her without it being like walking on a road scattered with mines.

Though it always seemed that those mines were spread far apart and it was almost like Liz was trying to seek them out and trigger them. Unintentionally of course, but she did it nonetheless.

Liz started walking and she found her legs had taken her to the Bar. It looked closed, it seemed to be that a lot more than before. Liz raised her hand to knock on the door but hesitated slightly. Did she actually have anything to say to Vendela or did she just seek her way here because it was what she was used to? Because the sight of Vendela had once been the same thing as coming home?

"Old habits die hard," Liz thought.

Liz knocked and the door hastily opened and before Liz could react Vendela pulled her inside and closed the door behind them.

"You did it," Vendela said low. "You actually did it."

"Sorry?" Liz said, slightly confused and frowned. "I've done a lot of things you'll have to spe-…"

"I spoke with Mona," Vendela said. "And she said she saw you enter the Fun House and then shortly after, leaving it with Ami."

Liz swallowed as she thought about what she'd seen on the fourth floor, the bodies dangling from the ceiling and the containers with blood right next to them; it sent a shiver down her spine.

"You know Mona?" Liz asked instead.

"Just a little," Vendela said. "I didn't think you'd actually do it."

"Why not?" Liz asked.

Vendela laughed low.

"Because of your stupid rules!" Vendela said.

"So what, you thought I just came over here to ask for your help and then... Do nothing?" Liz asked with a frown.

"I don't know," Vendela said honestly. "It wouldn't have surprised me honestly."

"Then why did you help me?" Liz asked. "If you didn't think I'd try to find Ami."

Vendela sighed and looked away.

"I suppose... I hoped you'd do it," Vendela said. "That's what I always do, I hope."

Liz didn't say anything.

"But what happened? What did you do?" Vendela asked and took a few steps closer to Liz. "Basically everyone knows something went down in the Fun House earlier, but no one has any real information."

Liz rubbed her eyes, she was too tired for an interrogation.

"I talked to him," Liz said. "That's all."

"You talked to him? To Mr. Greenlund?" Vendela asked skeptically. "Just talked?"

"There might have been a fist or two involved," Liz said.

Then Vendela saw the small tear in the shirt and the now dried black blood stained on the fabric, that had been caused by the letter opener piercing Liz's heart. Vendela touched the shirt gently.

"Were you hurt?" She asked.

"I'm fine," Liz said and took a step back. "You should have seen him."

Vendela was still staring at Liz with such a look of disbelief in her face before she finally shook it off and regained some of her composure.

"How is Ami?" Vendela asked and sat down in a chair.

Liz sat down in a chair opposite Vendela.

"Unconscious," Liz said.

Pause.

"Did you know?" Liz finally asked.

"Know what?" Vendela asked carefully.

"What happened on the fourth floor?" Liz asked with a grim face.

"I told you-..." Vendela said.

"Yeah I know," Liz said. "But then I also remembered that you work for him."

Vendela's face turned to stone.

"I didn't know what happened on the fourth floor," Vendela said. "I still don't in fact".

"Did you really not know, or did you choose to look away?" Liz asked.

"Know what?" Vendela said annoyed.

"They strung them up," Liz said, her voice cold as ice. "Emptied them of blood for… For vampires like ourselves. Kept them alive until they discarded them like garbage."

Vendela's mouth fell open slightly in shock.

"You think I'd know that and do nothing?" Vendela asked. "That I would take the blood and turn a blind eye if I knew about it? You really think *I* would do that?"

"You almost did it with Ami," Liz snapped.

"I didn't know," Vendela repeated and Liz could see cracks in her facade. "I wouldn't have hesitated helping you if I'd kn-…"

"Really?" Liz asked. "Even if it would have seriously compromised your stupid rebellion? You would have helped?"

Vendela was deadly silent for a moment.

"Is Ami going to be okay?" Vendela asked low, not answering Liz's question.

Liz shrugged, she knew that it would be so easy to take it too far, to really say something hurtful to Vendela. To pierce her armor and let her bleed, but Liz had taken it far enough already; she didn't really want to hurt Vendela, she never did. The fact that it happened just showed how much easier it was to be hurtful than vulnerable.

"I don't know," Liz said, not pushing Vendela for an answer. "I left her at Katarina's place."

"Did you come here just to ask if I'm not only a traitor but heartless as well?" Vendela asked low.

Liz licked her lips and looked away before she sighed deeply.

"I'm sorry," Liz said low. "I'm tired and weak and… Still angry."

Vendela sighed.

"Angry with me?" Vendela asked and faced Liz.

"No," Liz said and shook her head. "At… Myself? I don't really know anymore. I'm just… Angry."

It was like no matter what, Liz had a storage of rage hidden inside of her; an unending supply always being refilled. Even when she felt empty and apathetic, there was always that anger hiding in the shadows. Ready to explode like a bomb and take out anyone happening to be close enough to her.

Vendela walked behind the bar, pulled out three bottles filled with blood and stared at them with serious eyes.

"I should get rid of them shouldn't I?" Vendela said.

"Why?" Liz asked. "It's not like you can put the blood back into their bodies. Give me one would you?"

Vendela stared at the bottles before she finally threw one across the bar and Liz easily caught it.

"How are you feeling by the way?" Vendela asked. "You look a little better."

"Being unconscious does wonders to you," Liz said sarcastically. "I'm fine."

Vendela took one bottle for herself and sat down in the same chair opposite Liz again. Liz opened hers and took a chug of the blood, for once she didn't care about the magic spell keeping it fresh or where it had come from. She deserved a treat after what had happened that afternoon. The blood was warm and it took away some of the pain from the scar on her chest and she felt a little of her strength return with it.

"I also wanted to thank you," Liz said low.

"For what?" Vendela said uncertainly.

"For giving me blood when I was starving," Liz said. "For giving me blood so I could heal when I was unconscious. For hearing me out even though you were mad as hell with me. For giving me tips with the guards."

"You've already thanked me for most of those things," Vendela said.

"Yeah, well, let's say I'm trying to make up for the past when I've lacked in the 'Thank you' and 'Sorry' departments," Liz said.

Vendela took a small sip of the blood.

"I'm still mad at you," she finally said softly.

Liz chuckled low.

"I know," she said. "And that's fine. I can leave if you want me to?"

"No, it's alright," Vendela said. "At least you're talking to me now."

Liz swallowed hard, she put the bottle down on the table and glanced over at Vendela. Liz knew what she meant, Vendela meant that it was impossible to talk to Liz at times. To get any answer out of her at all. That it would probably be easier to have the conversation without her there at all.

"I'll get your dress," Vendela said after a few moments of silence.

"Thanks," Liz said. "And once again, I'm sorry about your shirt."

Vendela looked at the hole in the shirt and the wound beneath.

"It's your shirt anyway," Vendela said. "You can do whatever you want with it."

Liz watched how Vendela walked through the door and she sank down in the same chair she'd sat in a while ago. Liz closed her eyes, took a few deep breathes and just relished in the calm silence that surrounded her for once. A few moments later, Vendela returned and threw the dress onto Liz.

Liz opened her eyes and looked at it quickly. It still had vague stains on it, those would never go away and there were still rips in the lace but it looked better than it had before at least. The dress was so old that it really needed a good repair but it had been impossible as long as Liz had been inside the Sanctuary, which was why it was practically falling apart at the seams.

"Thanks for washing it for me," Liz said.

"Maybe you should get some new clothes?" Vendela said. "I mean you've worn that for as long as I can remember."

"Yeah," Liz said. "I've got plenty of money to spare and lots of places to shop, I wonder why I haven't done it in years?"

"The sarcasm is not appreciated," Vendela said. "You had plenty of time before the Sanctuary to get some new clothes."

"I like this dress okay?" Liz said. "And as long as it keeps everything covered I'm good."

There was a moment of silence. Vendela was frowning slightly and had a look on her face which told Liz that she was contemplating something.

"What?" Liz said.

"What?" Vendela asked.

"What's with the face?" Liz said.

"It's just my face," Vendela said.

Liz raised an eyebrow, she was not buying it.

"Put on your dress," Vendela said, changing the subject. "You can use my room if you want to."

"I mean you've seen me naked be-…" Liz started but interrupted herself. "I'll use your room."

As Liz turned around and walked into Vendela's bedroom she could hear her sigh behind her. There was something on Vendela's mind, something she wasn't entirely sure on if she wanted to share with Liz and she saw it written all over her face. As Liz's defenses had weakened, so had Vendela's. It barely took Liz a minute from entering the bedroom to exiting in her dress.

"How do I look?" Liz asked and did a spin.

"Like you're homeless," Vendela said and tried not to smile.

"Well, I technically am so you're not entirely wrong," Liz said.

Vendela had started to fidget with her fingers and she bit her lower lip. For someone who didn't know Vendela they might not have noticed anything weird or strange; but Liz knew every mannerism and to her it was clear as day that there was something on Vendela's mind.

"Okay," Liz said carefully. "What's wrong?"

Vendela's face hardened slightly and Liz was almost afraid of what would come out of her mouth.

"I need you to be completely honest with me Liz," Vendela said.

That sent a shiver down Liz's spine.

"I'll know if you lie," Vendela said, still very serious. "And if you do, you'll have to leave. I can't take more lies, okay?"

The sudden change in atmosphere was palpable, Liz knew this was serious and she wasn't sure if she could agree to those terms. Liz couldn't tell the truth if the question was about where she'd been and what she'd been doing outside The Sanctuary. But there was no doubt that if a lie slipped from

Liz's lips and Vendela saw through it, that that would be it at this point. Vendela would not forgive that.

Liz was silent, contemplating her answer when Vendela spoke again.

"I'm serious Liz," Vendela said.

"I can see that," Liz said bitterly. "What if I just don't answer?"

"Not answering is still answering," Vendela said seriously. "You wanted to know what was on my mind."

"Yeah and I regret it already," Liz thought. She shouldn't have cared, she should have ignored the look on Vendela's face, but she just couldn't, she never could, especially not when it was Vendela.

"Alright," Liz said slowly and unsure. "What is it?"

Vendela almost looked a little surprised that Liz agreed and Liz was as well, but it wasn't the first thing she'd done to surprise herself in these past days.

"I know you won't tell me where you've been the past five months," Vendela said with bitterness in her voice.

"I'm not gonna-…" Liz started, her voice filled with caution.

"I'm not asking you to tell me where you've been," Vendela interrupted her. "Because I know you'll just shut down and freeze me out."

Liz looked down.

"But…" Vendela said, her voice was uncertain, almost like she didn't want to know the answer. "Were you taken and then brought back to spy on us for the Townies?"

Liz frowned deeply.

"You're asking me if I'm spying for the Townies?" Liz asked in disbelief. "*You* are asking me that?"

Vendela's eyes were ice cold, her lips were a thin line.

"What kind of bullshit is this?" Liz asked, her voice filled with agitation.

"Liz," Vendela said coldly.

"I'm not," Liz spit out. "Unlike you."

That seemed to strike a chord with Vendela but she quickly composed herself.

"I'm doing it to gain Mr. Greenlund's trust and get inf-…" Vendela said.

"I know what you've said," Liz said. "But I'm not spying for anyone."

Vendela stared into Liz almost golden eyes and she detected no lie, because for once Liz wasn't lying. The fact that Liz was upset wasn't an act.

"Well, what am I supposed to think?" Vendela finally answered. "You disappear for five months and then reappear? No one does that! All I've been able to think about is if you're betray-..."

"You've thought that ever since I returned?" Liz asked. "Then why the hell did you tell me about that idiotic rebellion you are a part of? Why have you helped me?"

Vendela frowned deeply and Liz could see her words had hit their mark.

"Because I wanted to give you the benefit of the doubt!" Vendela said. "Because I didn't want it to be true!"

"So why ask now?" Liz asked.

"Because..." Vendela said. "Someone wants to meet you."

There was caution in Liz's face.

"Someone wants to meet me?" Liz asked. "Who?"

"Her name is Josefine," Vendela said.

"Is that name supposed to mean anything to me?" Liz asked unimpressed.

Vendela looked behind her, almost to make sure that they were completely alone.

"She's the rebel leader," Vendela finally said.

Something close to a laugh escaped Liz's lips until she realized that Vendela wasn't joking.

"You're serious?" Liz asked. "Are you insane?"

Vendela didn't look amused in the slightest.

"She wants to meet you and I told her I'd convey that message to you," Vendela said and folded her arms, almost in defiance.

"Okay..." Liz said slowly. "Let's start with, why the hell does she want to meet me?"

"Mona didn't just tell me what she'd seen in the Fun House, she told Josefine as well," Vendela said.

"Hold up, Mona is in the resistance?" Liz asked, confused.

"Yes," Vendela said.

"She flat out lied to me and said she'd never heard of Ami when it was clear she knew her," Liz said, her voice filling with rage by the second. "She didn't help me at al-…"

"Are you stupid?" Vendela asked. "Most of us don't want to die and actually appreciate life. Mona had only heard about you, she's fairly new here, and your reputation isn't exactly great. What was she supposed to do? Tell you everything she knew, which wasn't a lot, and blow her cover and very likely get executed? I don't know what the hell you did Liz, but most of us would not have gotten out of there alive. We have to think about the long run and the consequences our actions have!"

Liz sighed and shook her head.

"And you say I don't do anything," Liz muttered.

Vendela's eyes flashed in anger and she closed the gap between them.

"I am doing something," Vendela said low and with a hidden fury. "Just because I'm not rushing into something head first without thinking and I don't see a result immediately doesn't mean I'm not doing anything. I am doing something to try and help *everyone* in here, for the long run."

"To get them killed?" Liz asked. "Because that's what your little rebellion will do."

"You don't know that," Vendela said coldly.

"I do," Liz said. "And you know it too, you just don't want to see the truth. You don't want to admit it, you never did."

"Admit what?" Vendela asked, annoyed. "I see the truth Liz, I see a corrupt system of oppression, murder and isolation and I'm trying to do something to change it!"

"No, the truth is that you see hope where there is none," Liz said. "You see hope and opportunity and freedom where there is just darkness and death."

"Why do you only want to see the worst in everyone and everything?" Vendela yelled, a hint of desperation in her voice. "There is so much beauty in this world! There are so many things to fight for! You don't want to admit that there is some goodness in this world! I am not a fool for clinging to hope! I am not an idiot for dreaming of a better world!"

Liz was silent for a moment.

"Cling to it all you want," Liz finally said. "But believe me, it'll hurt way more than if you let it go."

Vendela's eyes were burning ice cold as she stared at Liz and she bit her lower lip.

"So what? You want us to do nothing and sit on our asses?" Vendela asked, her tone of voice filling with more and more rage by the word. "Is that it?"

Liz shrugged.

"Nothing can last forever," Liz said. "We're immortal, we'll just wait it out."

Vendela took a few steps back, disbelief clear in her face.

"Can you hear yourself?" Vendela asked. "You think places like this will just disappear? That the humans will one day wake up and realize that ops, we've been a little mean, perhaps we shouldn't abuse creatures? Murder and imprison them? Are you honestly telling me, they will come to this conclusion before they have the idea to kill us all?"

Liz looked away.

"We have next to no allies among the humans," Vendela said. "And you've been away so maybe you haven't heard, but three of the biggest adversaries for creature rights were recently killed in 'accidents.'"

Liz's eyes shot back to Vendela.

"How do you know that?" Liz asked.

"Perks of being on Mr. Greenlund's side," Vendela said. "I hear things. But the point is, do you really think that this will disappear by itself? Who's refusing to see the truth now?"

Liz just carefully shook her head.

"There is only one certainty if we do nothing," Vendela said seriously. "They will tire of us. They will see us as too much of a burden. And they will find a reason to murder us all and call it justice and for everyone's safety."

Liz closed her eyes, that thought had passed her mind more than once before.

"And we might be immortal," Vendela said. "But we can still be killed."

"So instead of waiting for things to develop you're straight up gonna start a war and a massacre?" Liz asked. "Because that is what will happen. They'll take this as the opportunity to kill us all. Your rebellion will be the sign that we are too dangerous to be kept alive."

Vendela slammed her fist onto the table.

"I will not just stand around and do nothing and wait it out!" Vendela screamed. "Even if this by some goddamn miracle disappeared by itself, how long will we have to wait? Hmm? 10 years? 30 years? Longer? For us that might not be a lot, but for the mortals in here, that is a large chunk of their life time! For Ami, for Katarina, that is a large part of their life! Do you think they want to spend it in here? Too many creatures have already died here."

Liz clenched her jaw and her hands formed into fists. The anger diminished from Vendela's face a little and she was left with a sad frown on her face.

"You saved Ami's life because you thought one life mattered," Vendela said. "Then why doesn't all our lives matter? You'll interfere when one life is on the line but not hundreds?"

Liz closed her eyes hard and turned her back to Vendela.

"My rul-…" Liz started but was interrupted before she could finish.

"Your rules?" Vendela yelled in outrage. "You've broken them, more times than I can count! You can't pick and choose when you follow them Liz! Either you follow them absolutely or you don't follow them at all!"

"There is a gray zo-…" Liz said.

"No," Vendela said, interrupting Liz. "You can't choose to save your friends' lives when they're in danger and don't lift a finger when you see others being murdered. That's not how things work."

Liz clenched her hands and felt her nails pierce the skin of her palms.

"I don't want to meet your goddamn rebel leader," Liz said, annoyed. "I have nothing to offer her and she certainly has nothing to offer me."

"Liz please," Vendela pleaded. "Just talk to her."

Liz turned and faced Vendela.

"So I can tell it to her face that I think she will get you killed?" Liz said.

Vendela was silent for a second and frowned slightly.

"What?" Liz asked when she saw that expression on Vendela's face.

Vendela slowly shook her head.

"Please don't tell me you hate this rebellion just because you think it will get *me* killed," Vendela said and stared into Liz with her cold gray eyes. "Don't tell me you're that selfish."

"I am selfish," Liz spat out. "Why do you think I saved Ami? Pure selfish reasons."

"I don't believe you," Vendela said. "You're just trying to push me away again."

"Tell yourself whatever makes you feel better," Liz said. "But mark my words, this rebellion will get you killed, get you all killed."

"And you won't lift a finger to help stop that?" Vendela asked.

"I am one person!" Liz said angrily. "I can't d-…"

"You can move mountains when you want to Liz," Vendela said coldly. "It's just that you rarely want to."

Liz rubbed her eyes and sighed loudly.

"Just talk," Vendela said. "That's all I ask of you. And I am asking you to do this for me."

Liz was silent for a moment.

"You're asking me to break all my ru-…" Liz said.

"You've already done that yourself!" Vendela yelled.

"I can justify breaking my rules when it regards one person!" Liz yelled back. "Or perhaps two! When the consequences of that action aren't too high! When it doesn't make too much of a difference! But what you're asking me is to join in a rebellion that might shape the future!"

Liz almost felt out of breath as she finished talking and the wound on her chest was burning slightly again.

"Everything has consequences," Vendela said. "The smallest action can change everything. You don't think saving Ami will have any consequences? You think helping Katarina from getting beaten hasn't had any consequences? You think that leaving me twice hasn't had any consequences?"

"I don't-…" Liz started.

"You don't want to talk about this anymore, am I right?" Vendela interrupted. "I'm gonna ask you once more Liz. Please speak with Josefine.

There are no promises attached, you just have to talk to her."

Liz licked her lips and closed her eyes. Her mind felt muddled and it felt as if she was torn in two directions. One part of her wanted to agree and meet this leader, the other wanted to flat out refuse and for once, the two voices yelled and neither one of them out voiced the other. Liz could hear the women working for Lady Morgana in her head clear as a bell *"We want to know, that if a rebellion happened, your feelings for Miss Amber won't get in the way. We want to know that you'll be on our side, not on theirs."* Liz swallowed hard and there was a lump in her throat as big as a baseball.

"Fine," Liz almost whispered. "But I am not promising anything."

Chapter 24

"I'm gonna go and see how Ami is doing," Liz muttered unpleasantly. "You can come and get me later and then I'll meet this Josefine."

"Okay," Vendela said, ignoring the tone in Liz's voice. "If the weather allows it I'll be around at midday, otherwise I'll come at sundown."

Liz nodded slightly, her gaze lingered a little on Vendela before she turned around and walked out of the Bar. As soon as Liz exited she noticed that the there wasn't much time left until the sun rose but hopefully it would rain or be cloudy so she wouldn't be stuck at Katarina all day long. She wasn't happy with how all of that had developed. There was no way this was going to end well.

Liz picked at the skin around her nails as she tried not to think about the rebellion or how the conversation between Vendela and herself had changed so drastically. They simply didn't see these things the same way.

They never had.

Instead she tried to think about anything else but there was nothing that seemed to be able to calm her down, everything was spiraling out of her control. Liz's thoughts turned to the thing Lady Morgana had promised if she helped her and Liz felt cold inside. At that moment it had sounded like the best plan but at this point, five months later and they still hadn't delivered at all, made her think they never would. The mere thought of that made her angry, she wouldn't have done those things if she knew what she knew now. They wanted her to have patience and say that five months wasn't a lot to her and they were right to a certain extent. Five months wasn't a lot to Liz but her patience was running very thin.

Liz opened the door to Katarina's apartment without knocking and found her at the table, with a hot cup of tea in her hand. She didn't even glance over at Liz as she entered.

"How was Vendela?" Katarina asked and took a sip.

Liz clenched her jaw at that comment and slowly sunk down in the chair opposite Katarina.

"She's fine," Liz muttered.

"Hmm," Katarina said.

"What?" Liz said, slightly irritated.

"Sorry?" Katarina said and looked up.

Liz really wasn't in the mood for one of Katarina's games.

"Just say what you have to say," Liz said directly.

"You seem…" Katarina said slowly. "Conflicted, irritated even."

"Isn't that my usual state?" Liz asked with sarcasm.

Katarina smiled lightly.

"You've been gone for a while," Katarina said and glanced out the window. "What did you talk about?"

Liz was silent as her thoughts revolved around the talk about the rebellion.

"Not much," Liz said evadingly.

"Okay," Katarina said.

Liz saw in Katarina's eyes that she didn't believe her but Liz quickly looked away, she couldn't stand her scrutinizing gaze.

"How's Ami?" Liz asked instead.

"Still unconscious," Katarina said.

Liz looked back at her.

"Do you know what's wrong with her?" Liz asked.

"I'm not a doctor," Katarina said as a matter of fact. "I've never studied medicine or anything like that. So not except the fact that she's lost some blood."

"But you healed me," Liz said. "You must know something."

"I didn't heal you exactly," Katarina said. "You've still got a wound on your chest. I just… Helped the healing process a little and Ami doesn't even have a visible wound."

Liz bit her lip lightly.

"Is she unconscious by magic or drugs?" Liz asked.

"I don't know," Katarina said.

"Can't you feel if they've used magic on her?" Liz asked.

Katarina tilted her head slightly.

"I have told you, I am still very new to magi-…" Katarina said.

"But you can conjure a protection spell like the one on your arms?" Liz asked with a slightly raised voice. "You can shoot freaking lightning from your body? But you don't know if magic has been used on someone else?"

Katarina took another sip of her tea.

"I'm not lying to you, if that's what you think," Katarina said.

"I don't know what I think," Liz said. "But what you're telling me sounds like bullshit."

Katarina's green and yellow speckled eyes pierced into Liz golden.

"I am a natural at learning spells," Katarina said. "At potions and such. But I have very little knowledge of basic magic. And I have not met anyone else who has magic until a month ago. So no, I am not bullshitting you."

Liz sighed and closed her eyes and before she even opened her mouth Katarina interrupted her.

"Apology accepted," Katarina said calmly.

Liz opened her eyes and tried her hardest not to look too angry but she didn't know how well she succeeded.

"Is there anything you can do for her?" Liz asked, trying not to let the irritation seep through her voice.

Katarina sighed lightly and put down her cup of tea.

"I'm keeping her hydrated," Katarina said. "And warm. Some color has returned to her face and her breathing and pulse is stable."

"Is there anything magical you can do to help her?" Liz asked instead.

Katarina looked at Liz, with curiosity in her face.

"What?" Liz said irritated. "Stop staring at me like that."

"Nothing," Katarina said. "Just… You hate magic yet you're asking me to perform it on your friend?"

Liz licked her lips.

"I don't have a problem with witches and magic in general," Liz said. "I just don't like it when it's performed or used on me. "

"Why?" Katarina asked.

Liz opened her mouth but it fell shut before she answered.

"Lots of things happen when you live for hundreds of years, Liz muttered. "You learn to dislike things in such a long time."

"Okay," Katarina said calmly.

Liz didn't like it when Katarina did that. She didn't like it when she said *"Okay"* or *"Alright"* or *"If you say so"* because it was so obviously written in her face that she knew Liz wasn't telling the truth and that annoyed her immensely.

"I'm gonna go look at her," Liz said.

Katarina nodded lightly. Liz rose and walked up to Katarina's bedroom door and rested her hand on the door knob. If Ami was asleep in Katarina's bed, where had she been sleeping? Or had she slept at all? That thought made her think about when Liz had been unconscious for a week and woken up in Katarina's bed. Had Katarina slept in that uncomfortably looking couch all this time? And without a single word of complaint or objection? Liz had literally brought an unconscious person, basically a stranger, to Katarina's doorstep and then left and she hadn't said a single thing about it.

Liz's eyes drifted to Katarina sitting by the table, drinking her tea and at that moment there was something so lonely about that girl; drinking her tea as if it was her only company.

"Thank you," Liz said, almost surprised by her own words.

Katarina looked over at Liz with a slightly shocked face.

"What?" Katarina said.

"For everything you've done," Liz said and cleared her throat. "I know… You say you're happy to help but you don't have to. Most wouldn't have. And I'm not sure I can ever repay you."

Katarina smiled and her eyes had a shine in them that hadn't been there a few seconds ago.

"So if there's… Anything I can do for you," Liz said. "Just ask."

Pause.

"I mean I'm not saying I will do whatever," Liz added quickly and with a lighter tone in her voice. "But I'll consider it at least."

Katarina nodded happily and Liz then went inside the bedroom.

Ami was lying beneath one large cover and a blanket and Katarina had been right, Ami wasn't looking as ashy as before but there was still something very lifeless about her. Liz sat down on the bed and and just stared at her for a moment.

I don't care about this girl Liz tried to tell herself as she always told herself when she felt too vulnerable or emotional but it didn't work, she couldn't even convince herself this time. She did care and she hated it.

"Ami?" Liz said low.

There was no response and Liz hadn't expected it either if she was being honest. Liz bit her lower lip and looked behind herself at the closed door as if she suspected that Katarina was standing on the other side with her ear to the door. She then turned back to Ami and pulled a dark strand of hair away from her face. There was still a quite visible bruise on her face that sent pulses of anger through Liz every time she laid eyes on it.

"I found you," Liz said, almost inaudible. "As I promised. Just… Wake up please. Don't make me have done all that for nothing. Don't make me have cared just to…"

Liz couldn't finish that sentence, she cleared her throat and gently kissed Ami on the forehead before she exited the room again. If anyone else had been there, those words would probably never have slipped past her lips.

Chapter 25

Liz came back out into the living room and found Katarina with what looked like a newly filled cup of tea.

"You're gonna get poisoned if you keep drinking that much tea," Liz said.

Katarina didn't say anything, just took another sip. Liz sat down opposite Katarina again and looked at her, there were large, dark bags under her eyes. Liz guessed she hadn't gotten a lot of sleep lately.

"How's the nightmares?" Liz asked casually.

"Better," Katarina said. "They stopped a while ago."

"Have you slept tonight?" Liz asked.

Katarina raised an eyebrow.

"Not really," Katarina said.

"I don't need sleep," Liz said. "But I'm pretty sure you do."

"Is that worry I hear in your voice?" Katarina asked with a vague smirk on her lips.

Liz face hardened.

"Whatever," Liz said. "It's your life, do whatever you want."

"I appreciate the concern," Katarina said, ignoring Liz's latest comment. "But I am fine."

Liz sighed and looked away. Liz's eyes glanced over to the book shelf and she was reminded of their discussion from before. *"If you need something done with magic, just ask."* Perhaps… Could she ask without revealing too much? That's what had stopped her before.

"Are you okay?" Katarina asked.

Liz snapped out of her thoughts and looked back at Katarina.

"I'm fine," Liz said quickly.

Katarina didn't say anything but didn't take her eyes off Liz as she took another sip of her tea.

"Just…" Liz continued slowly, feeling that it got harder and harder to speak. "I know you've done a lot for me but…"

Katarina tilted her head in curiosity. Liz closed her eyes and swallowed and told herself over and over to get it together and just say it.

"I asked about your spell book before for a reason," Liz finally managed to say.

"I guessed as much," Katarina said calmly.

Liz bit her lower lip and as she opened her eyes and looked over at Katarina, she saw no rush or irritation in her eyes over how slow Liz was speaking. Just curiosity.

"Is there… Anything about breaking curses in that book?" Liz said low.

Katarina frowned lightly and put down her cup.

"There is no spell to break your vampire curse," Katarina said slowly.

"I know that," Liz said, her voice thick. "That's not the curse I'm talking about."

If Liz had had a heartbeat it would have been beating so hard it hurt, but instead there was nothing and yet her whole chest felt as if it was going to implode.

Katarina said nothing, just waited for Liz to continue.

"Well, is there?" Liz said with a hoarse voice.

Katarina was silent for a moment.

"I'd have to know what type of curse it is," Katarina said.

Liz clenched her jaw.

"First," Liz started. "Tell me… Is there *anything* at all about breaking curses in that book?"

"Yes," Katarina said, not hesitating in the slightest.

Silence.

"But I need to know what curse it is," Katarina said. "Otherwise I'm stumbling in the dark."

Liz wasn't listening anymore, everything after Katarina had confirmed that there were spells in that book to break curses just went in one ear and out the other. All Liz could think about was the fact that this young and inexperienced girl might be able to help her with something that no one else had been able to do. Just because she had this book of hers. Liz had met witches before and asked for help, at this point it felt as if she'd exhausted any viable option through her long life but something about this felt different. Katarina felt different.

"Liz," Katarina said.

Liz snapped out of it and looked at her.

"What curse is it?" Katarina asked once again, though very calmly.

Liz opened her mouth to speak but nothing came out. *"Just say it, just spit it out, it's just words,"* Liz told herself over and over.

"It's a…" Liz said almost inaudible. "It's an eternity curse."

"You can't die?" Katarina asked with a pinch of surprise in her voice.

"That about sums it up yeah," Liz said and tried to speak with a lighter toned voice.

Katarina frowned and she looked away slightly as if she was thinking about something. Liz was afraid that meant there was nothing she could do about it.

"I'm going to have to look through my book," Katarina said. "I don't know it by memory and sometimes there seems to be new content. But I'll tell you if I find something."

Liz was just staring at Katarina with large and shocked eyes. She didn't blink and she barely moved, she'd thought she'd be happy but she told herself that it was just the shock making her feel this empty. Liz had looked for a way to break her eternity curse for hundreds of years and she'd jumped at the opportunity when Lady Morgana had offered to search for a way to break it. After all they had all the money and resources and Liz had none inside the Sanctuary but it had come with a price, which Liz had paid and now Katarina offered to help her without asking for anything in return. Liz didn't know if she wanted to cry or laugh at the whole situation.

It felt unreal and Liz was afraid she was dreaming, but she was also afraid it wasn't a dream because if Katarina found a way to break her curse, that meant that what she'd done for Lady Morgana was for nothing and that almost made Liz sick to her stomach.

Liz rose from her seat and cleared her throat, feeling once again like it was getting hard to breathe. Why didn't her body or head realize that she had no need for air? She was dead and yet this phenomenon had happened way too many times in her long dead life, not to mention the last week.

"Thanks," Liz said, trying to keep her voice from shaking. "I'm just... I just need..."

"To clear your head?" Katarina said, filling in Liz's words.

"Yeah," Liz said low.

Katarina glanced out the window and so did Liz. It was faintly raining and it was cloudy, not a ray of sun as far as they could see. Liz looked at Katarina for a short time before she reached for the door but was stopped by Katarina speaking.

"You don't have to be ashamed of your curse Liz," Katarina said. "Neither of them. They're not your fault."

Liz swallowed and licked her lips before she answered.

"I'm not ashamed, and the vampire curse I could do nothing about," Liz said low.

Liz quickly glanced back at Katarina.

"But let's just say," Liz said, her voice thick. "The eternity curse, I had that one coming. I'm not ashamed of it, I'm ashamed of what I did to get cursed."

Katarina opened her mouth but before any sound could escape, Liz opened the door and exited.

Chapter 26

Liz walked around the streets for about ten minutes, getting her skin and clothes damp from the light rain before she got restless. There was an itch in her body, probably coming from the fact that she was so anxious that Katarina might or might not find something to help her and she'd said she needed to clear her head but walking around with only her own thoughts didn't help. It just made everything worse, she needed to do something, something to distract her from these thoughts that haunted her.

Before she'd even realized it, she was standing in front of the Bar.

"Damn it," Liz muttered to herself.

Liz knocked and after a little while Vendela opened the door and raised an eyebrow as she saw the slightly wet Liz standing there.

"I told you I'd come ge-…" Vendela started.

"Let's just go," Liz snapped. "Let's meet his rebel leader of yours and get this over with."

Vendela frowned slightly.

"Are you alr-…" Vendela started.

"I'm fine," Liz said, interrupting her. "Can we just go?"

"Stop interrupting me," Vendela said seriously. "What's wrong with you?"

Liz turned away her gaze.

"I'm fine," Liz said, her voice filled with annoyance. "Can everyone stop asking me that? I'm fine."

"Yeah, clearly," Vendela said sarcastically.

Liz rubbed her eyes.

"You wanted me to meet this person," Liz said. "So can we just get this over with?"

"Not until you tell me what the hell is wrong with you," Vendela said. "You're shaking like a leaf."

"I'm fine!" Liz said. "I'm just…"

Liz bit her lower lip.

"Ami hasn't woken up yet and that's making me… A little on edge," Liz lied.

It wasn't a complete lie but it certainly wasn't the cause of her irritation and her nerves going haywire. Vendela stared at Liz as if she contemplated whether she was telling the truth or not.

"Okay," Vendela finally said slowly. "But you need to calm down, don't take out your irritation on Josefine. Or me."

"I'm not gonna bow to her if that's what you want," Liz said. "I'll treat her like everyone else."

"No, you will not treat her like everyone else," Vendela said. "Because she isn't everyone else. In here, for a lot of people, she is the embodiment of hope."

"More like embodiment of foolishness," Liz muttered.

Vendela shot her a gaze of warning.

"You agreed to meet with her," Vendela said. "But I won't take you to her if all you're going to do is pick a fight."

Liz sighed low.

"I'm no-…" Liz started.

"Do you promise?" Vendela asked. "Do you promise not to start a fight?"

Liz was silent for a moment before she finally spoke.

"I… I promise not to pick a fight," Liz said slowly. "Unless I am provoked."

Vendela sighed.

"Liz-…" Vendela started.

"Do you want me to lie?" Liz asked. "Cause I can do that."

"No," Vendela said tiredly. "I don't want you to lie. I just… I know you don't like the idea of this rebellion but please don't say that outright. Josefine is the leader for a reason, she takes this seriously and without her there wouldn't be a resistance."

"What is she?" Liz asked.

"Shapeshifter," Vendela said. "And a damn good one. You should be careful how you act around her."

"Why?" Liz asked.

"Because like Katarina, Josefine can read emotions and feel your energy," Vendela said. "And she takes advantage of that."

"Great," Liz said. "I already don't like her."

Being able to read emotions and feel someone's energy wasn't an uncommon ability with shapeshifters, it was the closest to mind reading as far as Liz knew. If a shapeshifter was powerful enough, some were even able to see others' desires and fears written on their faces and then be able to take advantage of that. Liz had only met one like that before and it had been hell. Especially since that shapeshifter had not been a nice one, he had liked to mentally torture his victims, showing them their deepest love and desire just to turn it into a nightmare. Then killing them and eating their brains. A shiver went down Liz's spine as she was reminded of that and she hoped that Josefine wasn't like that.

If she and Josefine got on the wrong foot and she took advantage of her powers and turned into someone Liz had loved just to mess with her, Liz could not assure that she wouldn't rip Josefine's head off.

"Let's go," Liz said. "Show the way."

"Alright," Vendela said. "But please, behave."

"Don't treat me like a child," Liz muttered.

"Then don't behave like one," Vendela replied and opened the door and exited the Bar.

It had started to rain more heavily which meant not a lot of creatures were out on the streets, not that Liz had actually seen many of them out on the streets at all since she'd come back. Maybe creatures stayed inside and hid more nowadays, and only came out to go to the Town or the Bar. Neither Liz nor Vendela were bothered by the rain and Vendela was scanning their surroundings as if she was thinking they were being followed.

"So where are we going then?" Liz asked.

"To the headquarters," Vendela said low.

"You have a headquarters?" Liz asked. "Fancy. Where is it?"

"You'll see in a minute," Vendela said. "Have some patience."

"You should know by now that I don't have much patience," Liz said.

"I do know that," Vendela said low.

They finally stopped in front of the old burned down Bar and Liz just looked around. There was nothing here except ashes. Liz glanced over at Vendela who was making sure no one else was around them.

"This is it," Vendela said.

Liz just stared at the ashes of the old Bar.

"Ehm, alright," Liz said. "I only see the old Bar in ashes."

Vendela took a few steps forward until she suddenly disappeared as she entered the area where the Bar had been. Liz frowned in confusion and looked around.

"Vendela?" Liz said low.

"Just walk," Vendela said.

Her voice came from in the middle of where the building had been but Liz couldn't see her, it was like she had vanished into thin air. Liz slightly shook her head, this didn't feel good at all. But she trusted Vendela and took a few steps forward. As she entered the area of the burned down Bar it felt as if she walked through a wall of running water and when she came out on the other side she saw Vendela standing in the middle of the ashes. Liz blinked fervently for a few seconds and then looked behind her but it looked completely normal.

"What-...?" Liz started.

"Magic," Vendela said. "To keep this place as hidden as possible."

The hair on Liz's arms stood up and she almost felt violated by the fact that she'd just walked through a magical barrier.

"You could have warned me first," Liz hissed.

"I was afraid you wouldn't have come if you knew," Vendela said. "So I didn't tell you."

"Did Katarina fix this for you?" Liz asked bitterly and looked around.

"No, she's… She's not involved in this," Vendela said.

"Why not?" Liz asked. "I mean, I think that's good but still, she's pretty powerful."

"Because I'm not sure we could trust her," Vendela said uncertainly. "She's got parents in Town and-…"

"Yeah, I get it," Liz said. "I've thought the same."

Vendela looked slightly surprised at those words.

"Then who did it?" Liz asked.

"Mona," Vendela said.

Liz didn't say anything else and Vendela then looked down at the floor. There was a large, metal hatch on the floor, Liz recognized it as the way down into the large cellar which had existed at the old Bar.

"It's down there? Really?" Liz asked.

Vendela shrugged.

"No one comes here," Vendela said. "It's just ashes."

Vendela reached down and knocked four times on the hatch and then they waited. Liz looked behind her and then the sound of the hatch quickly opening was heard, it was a squeaky and rusty sound and from the dark beneath the hatch bright red hair emerged. It was the girl Tess who Liz had met briefly before.

Tess smiled when she saw Vendela but it disappeared slightly when she saw Liz.

"Is that-…?" Tess said slowly.

"Yeah," Vendela said.

Tess just nodded and then disappeared into the dark again, Liz knew that there was quite a long stair down into the cellar, she'd been there before.

"I feel like a celebrity," Liz said as a joke.

"After you," Vendela said, ignoring Liz's comment.

Liz glanced into the dark once again before she started to climb down the steep stairs. She'd never liked this cellar and especially not the climb down. Liz didn't exactly have fear of small places but she didn't like when there wasn't an immediate exit close to hand. When there wasn't, she often started to feel like a trapped animal wanting to get out. As she looked up she could see Vendela above her but when she glanced down she only saw vague contours and a weak light.

The light coming from the bottom became brighter and within another few seconds, her feet hit solid ground. The cellar had been a large one, five rooms built to hold everything from food to wine to anything else really. The first room was the largest and Liz was quite surprised to see over two dozen people down there. What surprised her more was that she recognized some of them. There was of course Tess who'd opened the hatch and who she'd met at the Bar some time ago, she was looking at Liz with cautious eyes, but there was also Mona who wouldn't meet Liz gaze. In the corner Liz saw the shape of a person with bandages on both of their forearms and Liz recognized them as Gray, the person she'd met the day she'd come back. The rest were foreign faces to her but they were all staring at Liz as she entered, they probably didn't like people they didn't know in here. They all knew the risk they took.

Finally Vendela came down the long stairs and some of the creature's eyes lit up in friendly recognition when they saw her. Tess walked up to Vendela and smiled lightly.

"She's in there," Tess said and pointed towards a door to the left.

"Is she expecting us?" Vendela asked.

"I mean, she expected you to come around at some point," Tess said. "But she's free right now."

"Thank you," Vendela said before turning back to look at Liz but her eyes lingered on Gray's form in the corner. They were sitting perfectly still, only seemingly staring into the floor. Liz glanced over at them as well and they looked horrible, it looked like they'd lost weight, their face was ashy and their eyes looked uncomfortably empty. Not to speak about the bandages around their wrist who had stains of blood on them.

"How are they?" Vendela asked and leaned in close to Tess.

Liz didn't have a problem hearing what they were saying, even though everyone else in the room had gone back to talking among themselves. Tess turned and looked at Gray and when she turned back she just shook her head.

"Alright," Vendela said and put a hand on Tess's shoulder. "We probably shouldn't let Josefine wait."

"Probably not," Tess said.

"Is she in a good mood?" Vendela asked.

"Well…" Tess said slowly. "She's in her normal mood, if that tells you anything."

Vendela just nodded and then grabbed Liz by the arm and dragged her towards the door. They stopped in front of it but Liz quickly glanced back.

"What happened to Gray?" Liz asked.

Vendela had a look of surprise on her face as she also glanced back towards Gray sitting in the corner.

"You mean Tryphon?" Vendela asked.

Liz looked over at the person sitting in the corner, as if checking to see that they were talking about the same person.

"Their last name is Gray," Vendela explained. "Their first name is Tryphon."

"Well, they presented themself as Gray to me," Liz said.

"How do you know them?" Vendela asked in confusion.

"I don't," Liz said. "I met them once but they didn't look like that then."

Vendela sighed, a flash of melancholy in her eyes before she spoke again.

"We can talk about them later," Vendela said evadingly.

"Fine," Liz said. "Let's meet this amazing leader of yours."

Vendela sighed deeply before she opened the door.

Chapter 27

The door opened and they entered a much smaller room without much in it, there were only some rickety old looking chairs and paper with drawings and scribbles put up on the walls. Though the first thing Liz noticed wasn't any of that, what she noticed was a tall and broad shouldered young man with an undercut, his light blond framing his cold blue eyes. Before anyone could react, Liz ran up to the boy, who was well over a head taller than her and slammed him into the wall. Something close to a laugh escaped his lips as he crashed into the wall. Liz's hands were shaking violently but she had a firm grip of his shirt. Liz's eyes were large dark, burning orbs, completely focused on the boy.

"Liz!" Vendela yelled in outrage. "What the hell are you doing?"

"Hi Elizabeth," the blond boy said with a smirk on his lips. "Long time no see."

Liz couldn't speak, the anger felt as if it was burning her up from the inside and her whole body was shaking. A part of her wanted to beat the boy into a bloody pulp on the floor, yet another part of her barely dared to move as she held him in an iron grip. Liz had tuned out everything else except herself and the blond boy and the smirk on his lips, the smile she was so familiar with which made her want to slam his head into the wall repeatedly until it cracked open.

So many emotions were running through Liz at this moment, rage, shock, fear. Her head was swimming with thoughts and she was practically paralyzed from the surprise of seeing the boy. Liz wanted to hit him badly, she wanted to take out her anger on someone who really deserved it yet she wasn't sure if she could do it. The boy wasn't struggling, he mostly looked amused. Liz felt a strong and cold hand on her shoulder, squeezing hard and she turned around to see Vendela's cold eyes piercing into her. Liz blinked fervently for a few seconds, like she had forgotten where she was and that other people were in this room except her and the boy.

"Let go of me," Liz said, her voice shaking from anger.

"Let go of him," Vendela said coldly.

"You have no ide-…" Liz started.

"Would you kindly let go of him?"

Liz's eyes darted towards the only other figure in the room, the one Liz had completely ignored as she'd entered. It was a girl with short straw blond hair and a round and soft face. She wasn't especially tall and she had an athletic build but what made Liz freeze in place was her eyes. The girl's eyes were gray but they weren't just any gray eyes, they were Vendela's eyes. Liz's gaze darted between Vendela and the girl and there was no difference.

Liz would recognize those eyes anywhere.

As Liz was frozen in confusion the boy took the opportunity and slipped out from Liz's grip and quickly moved across the room and stood behind the girl who Liz assumed was Josefine. Vendela was staring at Liz as if she thought she'd lost her mind but Liz couldn't stop staring at those gray eyes.

"Are you alright?" Josefine asked without turning to look at the blond boy.

"Of course," the boy said, still with that smirk on his lips. "She's all bark and no bite."

Liz took a step forward as the boy spoke but Vendela squeezed her shoulder harder and held her back. Josefine had her hands behind her back and was looking at Liz with a scrutinizing gaze.

"What the hell is he doing here?" Liz yelled towards Josefine and the boy.

"How do you know him?" Vendela asked low.

"Yes, Elizabeth, how do you know me?" The boy asked, the smirk only growing on his face.

"Albin, could you please leave us for now?" Josefine asked calmly. "We'll speak later."

Albin did a little bow and started walking towards the door but shot Liz a gaze with his cold blue eyes and if Vendela hadn't still been holding Liz, she would have tried to jump at him again. He left the room and closed the door behind him and Liz could feel herself relax a little.

"Let go of me," Liz said and pushed Vendela away.

"What the hell was that about?" Vendela whispered angrily.

Liz walked up straight to Josefine, who looked young but Liz knew that shapeshifters could slow down the aging process, they just had to eat human brains every other week, if they didn't, they started to age again. They couldn't live forever, but longer than humans. So this Josefine might look like she was twenty, but she might as well be fifty.

Josefine didn't flinch as Liz walked up to her with burning eyes.

"You have him in this rebellion of yours?" Liz asked. "You're even stupider than I thought."

Liz could feel Vendela's piercing eyes in the back of her neck, she'd done exactly what Vendela had told her not to do, though that seemed to be her talent. Josefine just looked at Liz for a moment before her gaze drifted to Vendela behind Liz.

"Could you leave us as well?" Josefine asked. "I want to talk with her in private."

"I'm not-..." Vendela said with caution.

"She won't hurt me," Josefine said and her gaze returned and met Liz. "Right?"

Liz didn't answer, just stared at Josefine with anger burning in her eyes. Josefine gave Vendela a nod to leave and with a deep sigh, Vendela left. Now it was just Liz and Josefine left in this relatively small room.

Josefine sat down in one of the chairs in the room and crossed her legs.

"Sit, please," Josefine said.

Liz couldn't tear her eyes from Josefine's. She'd heard about shapeshifters who took after features of people near to them or people they felt were important but she hadn't actually seen it before. Or Josefine could just have taken Vendela's eyes to see Liz's reaction to it. Either way it made Liz uncomfortable because the rest of the face and body didn't match those eyes she knew so well.

"Are my eyes making you uncomfortable?" Josefine asked.

Liz said nothing, just swallowed. Josefine blinked and when she opened them they were a bright green color.

"Better?" Josefine asked.

"What do you want?" Liz spat out.

"I want to talk with you," Josefine simply said. "You sure you don't want to sit down? I've heard you've had quite the week."

Liz glanced back at the door before she sat down in the chair furthest away from Josefine. Josefine smiled vaguely.

"Who told you that?" Liz asked.

"Well, Vendela for starters," Josefine said. "I know how much you mean to her-…"

Liz rose so hard and fast that the chair she'd been sitting on fell over.

"Don't," Liz said as a warning.

Josefine almost looked pleased by this reaction.

"I know you can read emotions and feel energy," Liz said. "And I've met shapeshifters like you before, so I'm warning you."

Josefine raised an eyebrow.

"Have you?" She asked with an amused expression. "That's interesting. And what exactly are you warning me about?"

"To tread carefully," Liz said low. "Because I don't have the best temperament."

"Please sit down again," Josefine said and gestured towards the chair. "We're not enemies here Liz."

Liz slowly pulled up the chair from the ground and sat down on it again.

"You wanted to talk, so let's talk," Liz said. "Let me start. Why the hell is Albin here? Do you have any idea what he's do-…"

"Albin has given us valuable information," Josefine said, interrupting her. "He was transferred from another Sanctuary two months ago and he's been able to send messages between our two Sanctuaries."

"Bullshit," Liz said.

"You can call it whatever you want," Josefine said and put her hands in her lap. "But it is a fact that we've received a lot of information we would never have heard about if it wasn't for Albin. But you are right, I don't know what he's done for you to feel such wrath towards him and frankly I don't really care. That is a personal problem, and we cannot afford to let feelings get in the way here."

Liz leaned forward.

"He'd sell you all out for a can of soda," Liz said. "I don't believe for a second he's helping you out of the goodness of his heart. He has no heart."

"He wants to get out as much as the rest of us," Josefine said. "That is quite the motivator."

Liz shook her head.

"No," Liz said. "Not for him. Getting out isn't enough for him."

Josefine just stared at Liz for a moment before she sighed.

"You're not entirely what I was expecting," Josefine said honestly.

"What, you were expecting someone willing to jump at the chance to get killed in the most stupid way ever?" Liz said. "Or start a war without even realizing it?"

Josefine shot Liz a burning gaze and her eye color had become bright red for a split second. Josefine's face then relaxed a little and the eyes softly faded into the same cold gray color as Vendela's eyes.

"You saved that girl," Josefine said. "What was her name?"

"Ami," Liz said coldly.

"So let me get this right," Josefine said. "You saved her life but you don't want to be a part of a revolution to save all our lives?"

"Because that's not what you will do," Liz said. "You'll start a war."

Josefine shrugged.

"Yes, that is very likely what will happen," she said, honesty filling her voice. "But nothing great was achieved without sacrifices. If blood has to be spilled for us to be free then I'm willing to pay it."

"As long as it's not your blood that gets spilled right?" Liz said with spite.

Josefine frowned deeply and almost looked offended.

"I'm not afraid to die," Josefine said. "Believe me when I say that I will stand on the front line of this rebellion at every step. I'm not going to stand in the back and use others as meat shields. I am more than willing to die for this cause."

Liz looked into her eyes and she saw the absolute resolution and determination, there was no doubt that Josefine was believing her own words.

"What do you want with me exactly?" Liz asked carefully.

"When I heard what you did for that shapeshifter," Josefine said. "You defied the Fun House and Mr. Greenlund, I thought, here is someone who wants to fight for justice and freedom. Because why else would they risk everything?"

"Because she's my friend," Liz said.

"Ah," Josefine said as if she understood. "So your friends are the only people that matter? The rest are just disposable?"

"I didn't s-..." Liz started.

"We are standing on the brink of something that could change the course of history," Josefine said seriously. "That could change it for the better. I could use someone like you Liz, someone ruthless and who does what needs to be done."

Liz shot her a gaze, she wasn't sure if she said those things because she'd read her emotions and drawn those conclusions or if she was talking about the reputation Liz had.

"I'm not interested," Liz said.

Josefine didn't look very surprised.

"You won't even do it for Vendela?" Josefine asked. "Outside these walls you could start anew and be-..."

Liz had moved too fast for Josefine to track and she found herself knocked into a wall with Liz hand around her throat. Liz wasn't applying much pressure yet, just enough to make it slightly uncomfortable but Liz's hand was shaking something awfully.

"I said-..." Liz started.

"To tread lightly," Josefine filled in. "But you are a minefield aren't you? Is there anything that won't upset you?"

"You don't know anything about me," Liz hissed.

Josefine smiled.

"Oh I do," Josefine said. "I can feel everything that's going on inside of you Liz. Someone needs to learn to keep their emotions in check. There is just a war of conflict inside of you isn't there?"

Liz hit the wall just right of Josefine's head and she actually flinched at the sudden movement.

"We're done here," Liz said low.

Liz released Josefine and then turned around.

"You'd rather stand by the side and see us get slaughtered than help us?" Josefine said. "You'd rather watch Vendela be killed than-…"

"You have no idea what you are talking about!" Liz screamed with fury. "You are a child playing dictator! You have no idea the consequences this little rebellion of yours might have!"

"I am not a child," Josefine said seriously. "And I am certainly not playing. We're fighting for our survival here and I can see it clear in your face that you'd rather stay away, I just cannot fathom why."

Liz walked back so they were close to each other again.

"Because I have been in countless rebellions," Liz hissed. "I have been in more wars than you have in lived years. War is always hell. I have seen the consequences of rebellions led by people like you. You might succeed and free us from here but you know what? I will still live to see the next Sanctuary, the next war, the next hatred. I have been in places like this before and what I do know is that history *always* repeats itself. I am tired of trying to make a goddamn difference when in the long run, nothing makes a difference!"

Josefine took a small step backwards.

"Perhaps you are right to some extent," Josefine said calmly. "It must be frustrating, to see humanity repeat its mistakes over and over again without the possibility to change it but creatures like myself who aren't immortal, we'll most likely not see it repeat itself. We'll live in the short bliss and freedom that might come from a rebellion and war. Isn't that worth fighting for? Isn't every second of freedom and safety worth fighting for?"

"It's easy for you to say that," Liz said low. "Because as you said, you won't see it repeat itself. You'll live, you'll die and that will be the end but there is no end for me. Only a never ending cycle. So I'm staying out of it and this discussion is over."

Liz started to walk towards the door when Josefine spoke again.

"I'll be here when you change your mind," Josefine said.

Liz let out a low laugh.

"And why the hell would I change my mind?" Liz asked.

"Because you love Vendela," Josefine said as a matter of fact. "And I think that when push comes to shove, you will do whatever is necessary to keep her safe and believe me when I say that she will be in this rebellion, you can't stop her. So your only way to protect her, will be to join. So I'll be waiting."

Liz opened the door and slammed it shut behind her without saying another word.

Chapter 28

As Liz exited, Vendela rushed over to her and Liz could see her mouth move but could hear no sound or words. Liz pushed past everyone in the room and went straight for the stairs up to the surface. It wasn't until she was at the top that she realized someone was screaming at her. Liz's head was pounding and she couldn't get Josefine's words out of her head no matter how hard she tried. It filled her with even more rage as she knew that was what Josefine wanted, she wanted to get inside her head and mess with her, but Liz had lived long enough to not fall for such tricks again. At least that's what she told herself.

"Liz! Liz, talk to me!"

Liz turned around as she finally heard the shouting behind her and saw Vendela. They were standing among the ruins of the old Bar. Vendela looked confused but the worry in her eyes was overwhelming.

"What happened?" Vendela asked when she finally saw that she'd made contact with Liz. "Are you okay?"

Liz closed her eyes and rubbed her eyes.

"We talked," Liz snapped. "As you wanted me to do. Now it's over and I'm fine."

Liz turned to walk away but stopped herself and walked closer to Vendela.

"She's a real charmer that Josefine," Liz said low. "You told me to behave, maybe you should have told her that as well!"

"You attacked Albin the moment you entered the door!" Vendela said.

"Without hesitating!"

"For a good reason," Liz said and glanced towards the hatch. "You cannot trust him."

"Why?" Vendela asked. "Thanks to him we can organize a rebellion with at least two Sanctuaries at the same time! Thanks to him we know we're not alone in this fight!"

"And what does he want in return?" Liz asked.

"Nothing," Vendela said. "Except for freedom."

Liz shook her head violently.

"No, no, I don't believe it," Liz said bitterly. "Why was he sent here from another Sanctuary?"

"He doesn't know," Vendela said. "One day they just decided to move him."

"That is bullshit!" Liz yelled. "Mark my word, you were afraid I was a spy for the Town, Albin is definitely that, if not worse!"

"Liz!" Vendela said, clearly upset.

"There is no way what he's told you is true!" Liz said angrily. "It's all lies to push you to go through with this rebellion!"

"And what would he get out of that?" Vendela asked.

"I don't know!" Liz yelled. "I can never tell with him! But if Josefine doesn't get you killed, he will. He will betray you and hang you out as terrorists."

Vendela stared at Liz.

"How do you know him?" Vendela asked. "What the hell happened between you two?"

Silence.

"It's a long story," Liz muttered. "It seems like no matter what I do I can't escape him."

"Does it look like I'm in a rush?" Vendela asked.

Liz had to bite her lower lip to stop herself from talking.

"It's a *really* long story," Liz said low.

"So just another thing from your past that you refuse to talk to me about?" Vendela said bitterly. "I can just go ask him, you know."

If Liz had some color left in her face, it disappeared and there was a flash of fear in her eyes that quickly vanished.

"You do whatever you want," Liz said. "He's a liar, so don't expect to get the truth."

Vendela frowned slightly and Liz knew she'd seen right through her.

"You're afraid of him," Vendela said slowly.

Liz scoffed in an attempt to draw away the attention from the fact that she was completely right.

"That's ridiculous," Liz said. "I hate him, I'm not afraid of him."

Vendela shook her head and there was an eerie silence filling the air.

"You're not going to help are you?" Vendela asked with a frown. "That's what I'm getting when I'm reading between the lines here."

Liz cleared her throat.

"I told you-…" Liz started.

"Yeah," Vendela said with a thick voice. "That you're gonna stay out of it. I just… thought you'd change your mind. I really thought you'd change your mind."

Liz closed her eyes and frowned deeply.

"Please don't go through with this Vendela," Liz pleaded. "Please."

"I was going to say the same thing to you," Vendela said with sorrow in her voice.

Liz opened her eyes again.

"Liz," Vendela said more softly. "I know you want to help. I know you do."

Liz bit her lower lip until she could taste blood.

"Wouldn't it be nice to actually look back and say, at least I tried?" Vendela said and a melancholy smile spread on her face. "At least I did something to try and make things better? Isn't that preferable than to look back and say, I stood by the side line and did nothing?"

Liz turned her back to Vendela, she couldn't look at those gray eyes right now, how pleading they were. Pleading to the person Vendela had known so many years ago, the person she hoped was still inside of Liz somewhere.

"Stand by my side and do this with me," Vendela said with a sharpness in her voice. "Liz please."

Liz's face was hard as stone as she started to walk away from Vendela, not saying another word.

Chapter 29

Liz walked, her step both determined and uncertain at the same time. She hadn't blinked since she'd left Vendela. Liz wasn't filled with her usual rage, she was strangely calm. Or perhaps a better word would be empty. It was like her inside was threatening to implode on itself and Liz felt conflicted in a way she hadn't done in a very, very long time and she didn't know how to handle it. Both her hands were shaking and she'd turned them into fists in a try to stop them shaking but it didn't help. She could feel her nails piercing the skin on her palm and cold, thick blood drip from her hands, but she couldn't feel the pain from it so she didn't bother to stop.

Liz had walked as if she was in a tunnel, she couldn't see or hear anything except what was right in front of her. Then she felt a sudden warm hand on her shoulder and she turned around, her eyes dark and empty. Her bloody hand had taken an iron grip of the person's throat that had sneaked up on her and she could hear a choking sound before she actually saw who it was.

It was a young boy with shabby looking clothes, uncut long black hair and his light brown eyes were starting to tear up as they were staring at her filled with fear. Liz could see him struggle from her iron grip and he was trying to speak but neither sound nor air could escape his lips. He was carrying something in his right hand which he held onto as if his life depended on it. For a few seconds Liz just stared at him with empty eyes, not caring that she was choking the life out of this boy; that she was literally killing him.

It was only when the tears started to stream down the boy's face that Liz snapped out of it and released her grip. The boy fell to the ground, coughing and crying loudly and did everything he could to get air into his lungs. Liz could see the mark of her hand around his throat, it had left a bloody hand print.

"I almost killed you," Liz muttered too low for him to hear and stared at her blood stained hands.

She felt equally empty and horrified at how she was acting. Liz wasn't sure what it had been, but something had stopped her from killing that boy; because she was sure she would have killed him. Perhaps it was the fear in his eyes or the tears streaming down his face pleading to the flicker of humanity inside of Liz but she truly did not know.

He was crying violently and she could see him shaking in fear. There was a split second where Liz had the impulse to kneel and comfort the boy, but it was gone before she'd barely realized it had existed. The boy wasn't running away, or even trying to crawl away, it looked like he was trying to compose himself to say something. Liz frowned lightly but waited for the boy to speak.

"A-Are you Liz?" He said between sobs, his voice hoarse and dry.

He looked up at her, his light brown eyes were filled with dread that Liz had seen so many times before. Seeing that fear, fear of her, in the eyes of someone so young, made her soften slightly in shame, but only slightly.

There was no tattoo around his neck, he was just a human boy.

"Who wants to know?" Liz asked, her voice low and thick.

He reached over the package he'd been holding in a firm grip and Liz snatched it from his hand and she could see him recoil, thinking she would hurt him further. Liz turned the quite large package over but there was no note or indication what it was or who it was from.

"What is it?" Liz asked. "From who?"

"B-Blood," he said and dried his nose. "From Lad-…"

"I get it," Liz said. "You were supposed to deliver this to the Bar."

"Y-Yeah but I-I saw you and I-I thought I could give it to you directly," he sniffled. "I'm sorry…"

Liz sighed low.

"Thanks," Liz muttered.

She turned around to leave but stopped.

"Next time, deliver it to that place instead," Liz said and pointed towards Katarina's house.

The boy just eagerly nodded.

"And deliver a message for Lady Morgana will you?" Liz said after a short while. "Or her people or whatever. Tell them I want to meet them. And I can't wait a week so they'll have to come here tomorrow. Tell them to go to the same place as the blood, okay?"

The boy swallowed painfully but then slowly nodded. Liz said nothing else and turned around to leave but she hadn't taken more than three steps before she sighed, shook her head and turned back. The boy was still sobbing softly and as he saw that she was coming back towards him, he started to crawl away from her in a slight panic.

"What's your name?" Liz asked, a bitter expression on her face.

There was a look of absolute shock and caution in his eyes.

"Drago," he finally whispered.

"You're an orphan right?" Liz asked. "And you work for Lady Morgana?"

Drago nodded carefully. Liz took off the bag from her shoulder and opened it, her eyes quickly glanced over her box and she sighed heavily; what was wrong with her? Liz put down the package with the blood and then took up the satchel of money she'd gotten from Lady Morgana as payment for her work.

Liz threw the satchel of money in front of Drago and first he looked at it and then at Liz with large eyes. Liz couldn't even bring herself to smile or to reassure this child, so she just left without saying another word. Telling herself that she did not give this boy the money because she felt bad for him, but simply because she had no need of it. She repeated that in her head until she reached Katarina's door.

Liz opened the door and she didn't even look for Katarina, she went straight towards the door down to the cellar. As she knew it was there it had become visible to her and Liz stopped in front of the door and dropped her bag gently to the floor. She hadn't said a single word and neither had

Katarina who was watching Liz carefully from the table.

"Lock the door after me," Liz said with a monotone voice. "And don't open the door until I tell you to."

Katarina said nothing in response and Liz just opened the heavy metal door and closed it behind herself. After a few seconds she heard it lock behind her and with slow steps Liz stepped down the stairs.

Liz saw the chair she'd been sitting in when she'd been starving, it was the only thing in the small and cold room. Liz was staring into the wall, letting her hand rest on the wooden chair. The blood on her hands had dried and felt crusty.

She stood completely still for quite a while, her head feeling both empty and like it was about to explode with thoughts at the same time. The hand that had rested on the chair gripped it hard and she grabbed it with both of her hands and started smashing it into the concrete wall while she screamed at the top of her lungs.

The chair broke into multiple pieces after two hits but Liz continued to punch the wall, with her knuckles, with her feet, she even rushed into it at full speed with her shoulders first. As she screamed, punched and felt bones break and heal, blood started to cover the walls and splattering lightly on her face, she wasn't even entirely sure of what she was feeling. If she was angry and in that case, who was she angry at? If she was sad or desperate? If she felt guilty for feeling too much or for feeling too little.

Liz couldn't tell and that confusion made her into a ticking time bomb.

The one thing she was happy about was that she had known that this place existed. After the fact that she'd almost killed Drago she knew she was a danger to others out on the street at the moment and she could definitely not be upstairs with Katarina right now. So she would confide herself down here for a short period of time, until either she blacked out from exhaustion, it took a lot of her energy to heal her body this quickly and often, or she calmed down.

Liz wasn't sure what was more likely to happen first.

It felt like hours passed and yet she was not out of breath and her muscles didn't ache, though she felt pain in the areas she'd broken and then healed multiple times. She'd screamed herself hoarse and she finally stopped, leaned against one of the walls, putting her forehead against the cold concrete and closed her eyes. The image of Vendela's desperate and almost betrayed gray eyes popped up in her head and Liz swallowed hard as she opened her eyes, leaned her back against the wall and slid down until she finally sat down on the ground.

A few minutes later she heard the heavy metal door being unlocked and slowly open. Liz didn't react, didn't even look up at the sudden bright light streaming into the dark cellar or the fact that she heard low footsteps making their way down the stairs. Liz stared at a piece of wood from the chair she'd destroyed that laid on the floor.

"Are you okay?" Katarina asked low.

Liz wasn't sure she could have answered her if she'd wanted, she'd screamed for so long it wasn't impossible that she might have lost her voice. So Liz said nothing and continued to stare at the piece of wood.

"Perhaps a bad question," Katarina said slowly.

After a few seconds of silence Liz answered.

"I don't know," Liz said almost inaudibly.

"What?" Katarina said, confused.

Liz carefully shook her head, her eyes looked so empty.

"I don't know if I'm okay," Liz said with a thick voice. "I don't know."

"What happened?" Katarina asked carefully.

Liz just shook her head, she couldn't say it. Liz licked her lips and slowly drew her hand over the stubble on her head.

"I don't know what to do," Liz said low and put her face in her hands.

She heard Katarina walking up closer to her and Liz finally managed to look at her. Katarina was wearing gloves and for the first seconds Liz didn't realize what she was holding in her hands. It was Liz box. In any other case, Liz would have raged, screamed, but now she barely reacted. Katarina knelt down in front of Liz and carefully placed the box in her lap. Liz glanced down at it and let her hand glide over the front and the crevices and cracks, leaving traces of blood on it. Something close to safety seeped into Liz, but it was fleeting.

"I don't know what to do," Liz repeated and looked at Katarina. "I feel…"

"Conflicted?" Katarina said, helping her.

Liz closed her eyes and nodded.

"I-I… I can either go against hundreds of years old rules I've set for myself," Liz said, barely able to get out the words. "And… And do something that every fiber of my body tells me not to do… Or… Or I follow my rules and I lose everything. How do you choose between something like that?"

Liz opened her eyes, there was something desperate and childlike in her eyes, like they were pleading for an easy answer in a complicated world.

"A-And I'm afraid," Liz muttered almost inaudibly, more like she was speaking to herself than Katarina. "That if I do nothing… I'll lose the last part of my humanity. The last part of compassion. But another part so badly wants that to happen… Because if I didn't care… If I just… I wouldn't be here."

Liz looked straight at Katarina.

"I can't live forever and also care," Liz said as a fact. "I just… I just can't."

Liz looked down at her box, a flash of shame and rage overwhelming her and she then threw it away from her, it tumbled and its content spilled out on the hard floor.

"Liz," Katarina said low.

Liz looked back at Katarina as if she just now realized she was standing there, even though she'd looked directly at her and spoken to her.

"You care," Katarina said as a statement. "And you cannot shut it off. You can't kill it. So perhaps instead of fighting it, you should embrace it."

"Embrace it…" Liz said bitterly. "Embracing it is what has led me here."

Liz looked into Katarina's eyes.

"I wasn't always…" Liz muttered. "I cared once. In the beginning. Thought I could make a difference. It was when I realized that I couldn't that I stopped… Tried to stop caring. Because trying to fix something that so desperately doesn't want to be fixed, will leave you bloody, bruised and broken."

Katarina didn't say anything else but walked up to the box and carefully collected all the things that had spilled out and put them back before she exited the cellar, leaving the door open for Liz when she was ready.

Liz put her face in her hands.

"I don't know," Liz muttered over and over again to herself. "I don't know what to do. I don't know."

Perhaps it was better for everyone if Katarina just locked the cellar door and threw away the key, leaving Liz down here so she couldn't ruin anything else; or worse, anyone else.

Chapter 30

Liz looked down at her hands and she saw the dark, sticky and cold blood that had seeped through the wounds from when she'd been assaulting the wall.

"I don't know what to do," Liz whispered to herself. "I just don't know."

A short and very abrupt scream escaped Liz's lips, she barely realized it had happened. There was so much pent up anger, frustration and bitterness inside her and it felt like those feelings were forcing themselves out of her through every crack, scar and wound that had ever existed on her. They manifested themselves in screams, punches and poisonous words which Liz often felt like she had no control over. They happened before she'd even realized it.

Liz couldn't help feeling this way, but she hated how she reacted because of them. She couldn't control her feelings, but she could control her actions. Liz knew this yet she found it indescribably hard to control and it made her dangerous to others. When hurting, sometimes that made it a lot easier to hurt others; but she knew it was cowardly and selfish to spread pain, just because she felt it. But sometimes it felt good in the strangest way to know she wasn't alone in her suffering, even if she'd caused it and she despised herself for feeling that way.

As soon as Liz stopped screaming, she glanced up towards the open door and saw the light streaming in and there was suddenly a vague smell of ginseng in the air. Liz closed her eyes but all she could see were those gray eyes staring back at her.

Those eyes Liz knew all too well, those eyes that had looked at her with desperation way too many times. Those eyes Liz would give anything to see shine with happiness, anything, yet she struggled to give herself to make that happen.

Liz had to decide whether she liked it or not, this time she couldn't do nothing. She had to make an active choice to stay away or join. Staying away might mean that she had to watch Vendela and everyone else in the resistance be executed for treason, or watch them die as they started a war against the humans. There was also the chance that she might lose some of the parts of herself that still belonged to the person she was before she died, the few parts that were left and not tainted by her undead touch.

Joining the rebellion could also mean she had to watch them die around her, because people would die in this rebellion. There was no way around it and even if Josefine didn't seem to be bothered by the idea, it did bother Liz. Perhaps because her friends were in the line of fire.

Liz bit her lower lip and opened her eyes again and resisted the impulse to scream again. Liz stared at her blood stained hands and she clenched her jaw. If she'd had a reflection she'd have been disgusted with what she would have seen, what was she doing? Why was she reacting like this?

Like she was alive with a pulse and feelings. Sitting in a dark cellar having a pity party with herself as the only attendee. It was pathetic.

Liz looked up towards the light at the end of the stairs and it was almost like it was calling to her. She hadn't come to any conclusion, she was still as conflicted as before but sitting down here with her face in her hands wouldn't help at all.

At some point she had to stop running, perhaps this was that day.

It almost pained Liz to rise from where she was sitting, like half of her just wanted to stay in the darkness, like an ostrich with its head in the sand, but still she put one foot in front of the other and climbed the stairs. She wasn't even sure what was pulling her, what her motivation was, but there was something pushing her forward, even when she didn't want to take another step.

As Liz came upstairs again she quickly looked over to Katarina's bedroom door but it was closed and no sound came from it, Ami must still be unconscious. Liz then saw Katarina sitting at the table, fervently flipping through the spell book but with a newly made cup of tea sitting close by.

Liz sat down at the table, opposite Katarina and roughly picked on the skin around her nails, making them bleed.

"So you decided to come out of the darkness," Katarina said, still with her eyes on the seemingly blank pages.

"Oh no, the darkness and I are best friends," Liz said, trying to sound lighthearted, even though she felt everything except that. "I just decided to come out of your basement."

Katarina smiled lightly.

"You seem a little better," Katarina said.

"I... Liz stammered low. "Better is an overstatement."

Katarina finally looked up and stared at Liz, but Liz couldn't hold her gaze for long before she looked away.

"You're still conflicted?" Katarina said calmly. "About more than one thing?"

Liz resisted the urge to yell at her, to tell her to stop reading her, to stop asking questions. Liz bit her lip.

"Have you found anything?" Liz asked instead but without much hope. "About breaking the curse I mean.

"No," Katarina said. "But I'm still looking."

Liz nodded slightly.

"Just out of curiosity," Katarina said. "Why were you cursed?"

Liz's eyes shot back to Katarina and her gaze was both furious and frightened at the same time, but Katarina didn't seem fazed by it. Liz opened her mouth to say one thing but another came out.

"I..." Liz said low. "I killed my husband."

Liz was surprised by the words that had left her mouth. She hadn't told anyone that in hundreds of years, she couldn't even remember the last time she'd said it out loud. She hadn't even told Vendela, yet one question from Katarina now and she'd folded. Liz was sure Katarina was going to have a reaction but none came. No horrifying glance, no show of fear, she looked just the way she had done moments before.

However there was something in her eyes that made Liz frown, she recognized that look. Liz leaned forward.

"But you already knew that didn't you?" Liz hissed low.

Katarina raised an eyebrow and closed the spell book.

"How?" Liz asked without blinking.

Katarina finally decided to answer.

"When you collapsed after being hurt by my magic," Katarina said. "I touched you as I caught you from falling. I didn't mean to."

Liz leaned back and she felt strangely empty, she'd thought she'd be angry but she wasn't. Liz almost had to stop herself from laughing, of course the one time Katarina touched her she saw one of the things Liz was most ashamed about.

"I know you killed him," Katarina said. "And I know you didn't mean to. I know how it eats at yo-..."

"Okay," Liz snapped. "You think you know, but you weren't there. You have no idea how it felt to have just been turned, disoriented and frightened and going to the only place you can think of. Of finding your husband and instead of seeing him, you only see a meal."

Katarina sighed and just nodded in response.

"Though, I don't see the connection of you killing your husband and you being cursed." Katarina said after a brief pause.

Liz closed her eyes, a lump had formed in her throat making it hard to speak. Liz cleared her throat and hoped she could speak with enough strength to stop her voice from shaking.

"He... He had a sister," Liz said slowly, the words tasting of bitter acid but she forced herself to continue speaking. "An older sister who he was very close with. She was over every weekend and stayed with us... She was lovely."

Liz took a break to collect her thoughts which suddenly seemed to be spinning around in her head, making it hard to find the right words. Making it hard to remember everything correctly, she hadn't thought about these things in such a long time and now all the memories came rushing back. It was hard to keep track of them, they seemed to rush by at high speed. Liz only had glimpses of some of them, yet others seemed to bump into her, making her lose her footing and making her head spin. Memories were such a strange thing, events that had happened so long ago could still feel as if they'd happened yesterday. Meaning, that the pain that was felt came back as fresh and strong as it once had happened. She had figured it out a long time ago, the longer memories were ignored, the sharper their edges became. Until the mere thought of them bled her dry.

Though that had never seemed to stop Liz from ignoring them, perhaps she was hoping that at some point it would just stop hurting. A childish and foolish dream. Things didn't disappear of themselves, no matter how badly she wanted them to.

Katarina sat patiently and waited for Liz to continue her story.

"She was lovely," Liz continued as her head finally stopped feeling like it was spinning around in circles. "Until I killed her brother. She possessed magic which I didn't know about, I don't know if my husband did or not. She found me over his dead body, drenched in his blood and I think… I think she lost it. They only had each other, their parents had died when they were young so she had practically raised him. To see her little brother killed in such a brutal way by someone he loved. Someone she trusted. I don't blame her for what she did."

Pause.

"After that I disappeared for a short time, still very confused and lost and weak and then she found me… And cursed me," Liz said.

"I don't know anything about the eternity spell," Katarina said. "But I suspect it's not an easy spell."

"No, it's not easy and it requires a tremendous sacrifice," Liz said seriously.

Katarina rose an eyebrow.

"It requires the person doing the curse to… To put it bluntly, kill themselves," Liz said. "It's the last part of the ritual."

"She… She killed herself to make you live forever?" Katarina said with a vague frown.

"So I'd have to live with what I'd done with no hope of rest," Liz said. "To walk this earth with no hope of ever finding peace. To be cursed to see everything be born and everything to end. To not only live forever but live forever as a monster. She knew that was worse than dying. "

Katarina said nothing, she was just looking at Liz with a neutral and somewhat pitying expression on her face.

"Why aren't you horrified?" Liz asked suddenly with an edge in her voice.

"What do you mean?" Katarina asked.

Liz shook her head as if she couldn't believe her.

"I just told you-…" Liz said.

"That you killed your husband," Katarina said. "Yes, but it wasn't your fault. You had just been turned, you had no idea what was going on, you-…"

Liz rose, where this anger had come from she wasn't sure. It seemed like she always had anger stored up somewhere, like it was a part of her that she couldn't escape, no matter how much she tried.

"Then whose goddamn fault was it then? Hmm?" Liz said loudly. "Was it his fault? His sisters? Our neighbors? It was my hands that ended his life, it was I who drained him of blood and to this day it feels like I am covered in it!"

"Things can happen without it being anyone's fault," Katarina said.

"No," Liz said, her voice so fired up she was practically screaming at this point. "Someone is always at fault! It doesn't matter if they didn't mean it, it doesn't matter if it was an accident! The intention doesn't matter if the outcome is horrible!"

"But you don't always know if something is going to turn out bad," Katarina said. "Sometimes good intentions are everything."

"Well, my intentions weren't good," Liz said, her eyes large and dark.

"Your intentions weren't bad either, you weren't in control," Katarina said calmly.

Liz slumped back down again, feeling drained.

"You're either stupid, or too kind," Liz said low. "You should be scared of me, if you had any common sense you'd be scared of me."

"I sure know that I am afraid of myself at times," Liz thought bitterly.

"Do you want me to be scared of you?" Katarina asked.

Liz blinked in confusion for a few seconds, she hadn't expected that question.

"No, but-…" Liz stammered.

"So why are you trying to convince me to be afraid of you?" Katarina asked.

Liz licked her lips.

"Because-…" Liz started.

"You want me to be scared of you," Katarina filled in.

"That doesn't make any sense," Liz hissed. "That's a paradox."

"A bit like you then?" Katarina said. "I think a part of you doesn't want me to be afraid of you because you are a decent person. Another part of you desperately wants me to be afraid of you because you see yourself as a monster. Because you're afraid that you're not always in control of yourself and that you're going to hurt me, even when you don't want to."

Liz swallowed hard.

"You talk as if you know me, but you don't," Liz said, a hint of sadness in her voice. "You really don't know me."

"Correct me then," Katarina simply said. "I say what I feel from others but I am not afraid to be wrong. Correct me if I'm wrong but know that I will probably know if you are lying or not."

Liz was silent for a moment, her jaw clenched but she finally scoffed before she spoke.

"Should I lie down on the sofa?" Liz asked sarcastically. "You know, so we can properly continue this therapy session."

Katarina smiled vaguely.

"Always with the sarcasm," Katarina said calmly. "It's a good defense mechanism."

Liz rose from her seat.

"Whatever," Liz muttered. "Tell me if you find something."

"Are you going somewhere?" Katarina asked.

Liz glanced back at the door and she realized she had nowhere to go, sure she could wander the streets for a while but there was no point to it. Her thoughts drifted to Vendela but all she could see was her betrayed face from the last time they'd spoken.

"No," Liz said low and sat down again. "I'm not."

"You're not going to see Vendela?" Katarina asked.

Liz shot Katarina a quick glance. Was it really that obvious that Vendela was the only thing on Liz's mind right now? Or was it just a good guess on Katarina's part?

"At this point… That's not possible," Liz said bitterly.

"Why not?" Katarina asked, slightly confused.

"I have to decide first," Liz muttered and glanced out of the window.

"Decide what?" Katarina asked.

Silence.

"Whose side I'm on," Liz said with a sigh.

Chapter 31

"I don't understand," Katarina said slowly.

Liz stared at her for a moment, before she said anything else.

"Tell me," Liz said and leaned forward slightly. "If a war breaks out, which side will you be on?"

Katarina frowned lightly.

"I…" Katarina started then abruptly stopped herself. "A war between who?"

Liz stared at her, Katarina knew what Liz meant but for some reason she wanted her to say it out loud. Liz didn't know why, but there were a lot of things about Katarina that Liz didn't understand.

"Between creatures and humans," Liz said seriously. "Whose side will you be on?"

Katarina looked down into her almost empty and now cold cup of tea, her gaze was blank and Liz had no idea what she was thinking.

"My parents-…" Katarina finally said.

"I know," Liz interrupted. "But they are two people, then there are millions of humans who think capturing, killing and doing whatever they want to creatures is okay and justified. Will you stand with millions of humans because of two people?"

"You sound like you have chosen a side already," Katarina said coldly.

Liz went silent.

"No," Liz said finally after a short pause. "But my decision isn't between humans or creatures."

"What is it then?" Katarina asked, slightly confused.

Liz sighed and closed her eyes for a second.

"It's between joining in the fight or simply… Walk away," Liz said and opened her eyes. "Stay out of it."

Katarina was silent for a few seconds, with a growing frown on her face. Their eyes met and there was something in Katarina's eyes, something Liz hadn't seen before. Was it a touch of disappointment?

"I know you don't understand-…" Liz started in a try to explain herself.

"You're right, I don't," Katarina said harshly. "But it is your decision to make. No one else."

"Thanks, that helps a lot," Liz said sarcastically.

Silence.

"I don't know which side I'll be on," Katarina said truthfully and sighed. "I don't think I will know until it happens."

"Or you can choose to stay out of it as well," Liz said. "Save your parents and then get as far away as possible."

"And go where?" Katarina asked. "If a war breaks out between creatures and humans it will happen world wide, there won't be anywhere to go. I am only sure of one thing if a war happens."

"Which is?" Liz asked.

"I'm not going to avoid it," Katarina said.

"You're basically still a child," Liz said and something close to a laugh escaped her lips. "You're mortal and you've spent your entire life in one room. You don't understand what war brings. You don't understand what it means to be in a situation when it's kill or be killed."

"I-…" Katarina said.

"You're a child," Liz said, probably more harshly than she'd intended. "You're not a warrior or a fighter. If you join, you *will* die."

"I can protect myself," Katarina said with a slightly raised voice.

Liz shook her head slightly.

"You don't understand the gravity of the situation," Liz said.

"I do," Katarina said with some force. "But you're right, I've never been to war, not even in a proper fight. And I don't know what war is like or what it does to you. But I know that I can't just choose to do nothing. I can't just choose to pretend that nothing is happening. There is nothing worse in this world than people staring down at injustice and doing nothing to stop it."

Liz stared at Katarina with a stone face. Liz knew those words were directed towards her and they hit her like a smack in the face. Liz told herself that Katarina didn't understand, that it wasn't always that easy but she wasn't sure she believed it herself.

"You-…" Liz started.

"First you ask which side I'll be on," Katarina said. "Then you ask me to stay away completely. Were you really asking *me* those questions or were you asking yourself?"

"That doesn't make any se-…" Liz started.

"You're conflicted because you want to join in the fight," Katarina said. "But you're afraid."

"Afraid?" Liz said almost like a joke. "What do I have to be afraid of? I can't die."

"Afraid to watch everyone around you get slaughtered," Katarina said, her voice steady and sure, as if what she was saying were well known facts. "That's why you're asking me to stay away. You're afraid that when the battle is done you will be the only one left standing."

Liz slammed her fist onto the table so hard it left a mark in the wood. Katarina had jumped slightly at the sudden bang but there was no fear in her eyes, just a split second of surprise.

"I don't ca-…" Liz started, her voice shaking.

"You don't care," Katarina said interrupting, her voice strong. "You keep saying that but you don't even believe it. You do care. I can feel it."

Liz closed her eyes and there was a defeated look on her face, a heavy silence filled the room before Liz spoke again.

"I… I think I've done something really bad," Liz said low, changing the subject slightly. "And if I am right, then there is no way that I can stand and fight with the creatures even if I'd want to. If I am right, no amount of caring can redeem me."

"What have you done?" Katarina asked with caution.

Liz looked into Katarina's eyes but all she could hear in her head was Vendela's voice. *"And you've been away so maybe you haven't heard, but three of the biggest adversaries for creature rights were recently killed in 'accidents.'"*

"We'll see soon," Liz muttered low. "I need you to leave the house for a while tomorrow."

"Why?" Katarina asked, suspicion clear in her eyes.

"Because… Some people are coming here," Liz said. "To talk to me. And I don't want you to be here when that happens, it might turn ugly."

"Liz-…" Katarina said.

"Can you do that for me?" Liz asked with a sudden softness in her voice. "Do this last thing for me. And I promise… I'll tell you what I've done when you get back. But you might not want to hear it."

Silence.

"Okay," Katarina said. "You get an hour."

"That'll be plenty enough time," Liz said. "I only have one question for them."

Katarina frowned lightly but didn't ask what that question was because she knew she wouldn't get an answer. Everything would be revealed tomorrow.

Chapter 32

The morning came and not much else had been said during the night, Katarina had dived back into her spell book and Liz had put herself in the trance state in a try to calm down and find a solution to her problems. When the women working for Lady Morgana came Liz wasn't sure what would happen if they told her what she was expecting to hear. She wasn't sure on how she would react, which was why she wanted Katarina out of the house. Liz hadn't lied when she'd said that things might turn ugly; but what she really meant was that it wasn't impossible that Liz would lose it. Losing control was horrendous in any other situation to Liz but having people she cared about watching it happen; it made it ten times worse. Liz hoped she was wrong about all of this, she hoped so badly that she was wrong.

Liz opened her eyes and saw the sun rise and she was guessing that the women would be coming soon, she guessed they'd want to get it over with as quickly as possible and the safest time of day in the Sanctuary was when the sun was shining. Liz heard Katarina yawn and she turned her head to look at her, she looked tired with dark bags beneath her eyes.

"You should have slept a few hours during the night," Liz said.

"The faster I find if there is something to help you in this book, the better," Katarina said. "I can sleep later."

"I don't think that's how sleep works," Liz said sarcastically. "You'll collapse if you don't sleep."

"Liz," Katarina said and looked up from the book. "We've had this conversation before. I will sleep when necessary."

"Fine," Liz muttered.

Silence.

"When they come," Liz added slowly. "Don't tell anyone."

"Don't tell anyone what?" Katarina asked.

"Don't tell anyone why you left your home, don't tell them about my curse," Liz said. "And when you find out what I've done, don't tell anyone. And if you by any chance meet Vendela... Especially don't tell her any of this alright?"

"Doesn't she deserve to know?" Katarina asked.

"No, she doesn't," Liz snapped. "And the only reason I'm telling you is because you are still practically a stranger to me and if you-..."

Liz trailed off, stopping herself mid sentence. There was a flash of hurt in Katarina's eyes but it was gone in the blink of an eye.

"If I hate you it's not much of a loss?" Katarina filled in with a melancholy voice. "Then if you tell Vendela, someone you love."

"Katarina..." Liz said in a try to save the situation.

"It's fair enough," Katarina said, interrupting her. "I understand."

Liz sighed.

"I'm also telling you," Liz said with a thick voice. "Because even as a stranger you've helped me more than most without asking for anything in return. So... So I feel I owe you that honesty."

"But you don't owe it to Vendela?" Katarina asked.

"Don't push it," Liz said low.

Silence.

"So... What happens if you tell me and I do hate you?" Katarina asked.

Liz frowned slightly, as she didn't completely understand the question.

"I... I'll leave you alone," Liz said uncertainly. "You won't have to see me again."

"And what if I don't hate you?" Katarina asked instead.

Liz opened her mouth but closed it slowly before she spoke.

"Then I'd probably call you a fool," Liz said low.

Katarina was just about to speak again when there was a knock on the door. Both their eyes shot towards the door.

"Open it," Liz said. "Let them in, go into your bedroom and after we've gone down into the cellar, leave."

"Alright," Katarina said.

Katarina made her way towards the door but Liz stopped her.

"Wait, is there a way to lock the cellar door from the inside?" Liz asked.

Katarina nodded slowly and reached into her pocket and pulled out a key.

"It can be locked and unlocked from both sides with this key," Katarina said. "Why?"

"Can I borrow it?" Liz asked.

"What are you going to do?" Katarina asked with caution.

Liz was silent for a moment.

"Make sure they don't leave before I've gotten an answer," Liz said seriously.

Katarina stared into Liz's eyes and Liz tried with all her might to hold her gaze but Katarina's eyes felt as if they were penetrating her mind, revealing every secret in her head. It felt as if Katarina knew how this would end yet she slowly put the key into Liz hand, though with hesitation. Liz let go of Katarina and she walked up to the door.

Katarina opened the door and the two women Liz was well acquainted with stood outside, both looking fairly grim and unamused. When they saw Katarina they frowned lightly before they saw Liz further into the apartment. Katarina simply walked aside and let the two women inside, giving Liz a quick look before she entered her own bedroom.

"This is… Cozy," one of them said and looked around.

Liz pointed at the open cellar door.

"We'll talk down there," Liz said. "So we're private."

The two women exchanged looks before they did as Liz said. Liz let the two women go down first then quickly glanced behind her at Katarina's bedroom door and it was still closed. She could hear the two women walk down the stairs with caution and Liz finally closed the door behind her and as soundlessly as possible she locked it and slipped the key into her bra for safe keeping.

"Is there a light?" One of the women asked. "We can't see anything."

Liz knew that, but she could see them perfectly clear in the dark and she was circling them as a lion circling their prey.

"No," Liz said. "But you'll get used to the dark soon enough. And if you don't, don't worry, we won't be here long enough for the darkness to matter."

Liz heard annoyed sighing and she could see them both looking around the room trying to see anything at all.

"Why did you want to meet us?" One of them said. "We're very busy and entering the Sanctuary-…"

"I wanted to talk to you," Liz said, interrupting them.

"Yes, the orphan said as much," the other one said.

"Drago," Liz said low.

"Excuse me?" She said.

"His name is Drago," Liz said a little louder.

"His name is irrelevant," the other one said, annoyed. "Why did you want to speak with us?"

"Has it anything to do with the rebellion?" The first one asked.

"In a way," Liz said. "But mostly not."

"Then what is it? We don't have all day," the other one said. "Unlike you, we have important things to do."

Liz was silent for a moment, her eyes fixed on the two women who had just started to adjust their eyes to the darkness. Liz guessed they could see the shape of her moving around the cellar at this point.

"Who did I kill for you?" Liz asked, trying to keep her voice from shaking. Silence.

"You said you didn't want to know," the first one finally said. "You didn't want to know anything."

"Well, I've changed my mind," Liz hissed. "Who did I kill for you?"

"Does it matter?" The other one asked. "It's already done-…"

"It matters!" Liz almost yelled. "Now tell me before I lose my patience completely."

Liz could see the two women twitch by her sudden outburst, she guessed they were regretting coming alone without back-up right about now.

"Anna Carmelia, Tony-…" the first one started.

"I don't care about their names," Liz spat out.

"Then what do you want to know?" The second one asked with slight confusion.

"Why did you want them killed?" Liz asked.

Liz could see them both shifting slightly towards where they thought the door was. But Liz didn't let them go with her eyes.

In here, they didn't stand a chance against Liz. If she wanted to, they'd be dead before they'd even realized that she'd moved.

"It's not us," the first one said. "We only wor-…"

"For Lady Morgana," Liz said. "I know. Now answer the damn question." Once again silence.

"Were… Were they creature rights activists?" Liz asked, her voice almost shaking with anger. "Were they?"

A short silence was heard and Liz could hear their irregular heartbeat and their quickened breathing.

"Yes," the second one said.

Liz took a step back, those words feeling like a slap in the face. It was what she had expected to hear and yet it felt way worse once it was said out loud and was confirmed. She'd killed three of the few people who were on their side, who tried to give them some real justice. Liz stared into the void above the two women's heads and she closed her eyes for a moment.

"You said you didn't want to know," the first one said. "You said you'd do anything for our help."

"Why should this change anything?" The second one asked.

Liz opened her eyes and they were dark and furious. She moved quickly and before the two women had blinked, Liz had gripped one of them by the throat. She let out a low gasp of surprise before she started to fight back. Liz heard bullets being fired from behind her by the other woman, the sound echoed uncomfortably in the small space. One of the bullets hit Liz in the side of her back but she barely felt it and the wound had healed within seconds. Liz closed her hand around the woman's throat and stared into her eyes. They were filled with panic and they had started to tear up but she felt none of the compassion she'd felt for Drago.

This was the Liz she was afraid of, the one driven by such a fury that she had no control. Liz knew what would happen next and she knew even before it happened that she would regret it later; but those thoughts were far back in her head. At this exact moment, Liz wanted revenge. She wanted blood.

Liz let go of her throat and the woman tried to catch her breath and cough but before she'd even taken one whole breath, Liz sunk her sharp teeth into her neck. Blood gushed into Liz's mouth, fresh, warm human blood. She hadn't tasted anything this fresh in a long time. The woman screamed both in fear and in pain and Liz could feel her struggling in her grip, but her punches against Liz were as if she was hitting a concrete wall; it did absolutely nothing.

Liz almost disappeared in the sensation of the blood, all she could hear was the heartbeat of the woman beating like a drum in her ears. Then she realized she was hearing another kind of drumming. It was the other woman who'd managed to find the stairs and was banging with all her might on the door and screaming for help. The woman in her grip had gone limp and the heartbeat was next to gone. She'd be dead within a minute or so.

Liz dropped the body to the floor and it made a distasteful sound as it hit the cold concrete. The other woman must have heard it and she'd gone quiet but Liz could hear her irregular breathing and low sobbing.

"P-Please," she stammered. "We're… We're only messengers. We're only doing our job. Please!"

Liz walked up to the other woman and she could feel her whole face dripping with blood which was quickly becoming cold and she knew blood had stained her dress but she didn't care. Liz stopped right in front of the woman, so close that she must have been able to smell the blood on Liz's face.

"P-Please," she cried. "I-I don't wanna… I don't want to die…"

If there had been any amount of light in the room, the woman would probably have been even more frightened, because in the dark she couldn't see Liz's bloody body and her almost black eyes.

"Listen closely," Liz said with a hoarse voice.

The woman tried to breathe but only a sob came out and she nodded slowly.

"I don't work for you anymore," Liz said, her voice so cold it would have sent a shiver down anyone's spine. "Tell that to your boss. But as long as this place exists I will get my blood supply. And you will deliver on what was promised to me."

Liz licked her lips and tasted copper.

"If I don't get the blood," Liz said. "Or if you fail to give me what I want. I will find you and I will kill you all. Just like your friend. Are we clear?"

The woman nodded, her eyes were closed but Liz could see her shaking from fear. Liz reached into her bra and pulled out the key and slowly unlocked the door. As soon as the door opened the woman stumbled out into the light and without looking back she rushed as fast as she could out of the apartment, and Liz could see how she almost tripped twice but managed to recover. The woman was crying but wasn't screaming or making any sound at all and when she slammed the outer door close behind her, Liz was left in the apartment, all bloody and with a body down in the cellar.

Then a second later, a symphony of a dozen eerie screams echoed through The Sanctuary.

Chapter 33

Liz had walked up to the sink and started to wash her face and hands, she could feel the blood get colder and stickier by the second. She saw how the clear water turned light red as it went down the drain and she felt empty. She just stared at the water for a while, she'd gotten her answer but had it improved anything? No. All it had done was make matters worse. Now there was a corpse down in the cellar and Liz had broken all ties with Lady Morgana.

Liz had killed someone; again. Yet she continued to lie to herself and others that it got easier with time, that taking a life wasn't that big of a deal after hundreds of years of horrible actions. It was a lie; every time Liz killed she was washed over with shame and self hatred. In a way, every time Liz took a life; she lost a bit of her humanity with that life.

"I wouldn't have done it if I knew..." Liz muttered to herself. "I wouldn't... I wouldn't have done it..."

But Liz wasn't sure, she'd said she didn't want to know anything so she'd been able to kill those people, because if she'd known their names, age, where they worked, they'd become real with families and lives of their own; which would have made it increasingly harder for Liz to do the job. If she had known who her targets were would she have turned down the offer? Even though the offer was to break her curse?

The thing she desired most in the entire world had been dangled in front of her and she had leapt blindly into the darkness without hesitation or questions.

Liz splashed some water in her face and before she could stop herself a sob escaped her lips.

"What have I done?" Liz whispered to herself.

Liz grabbed one of the glasses by the sink and threw it into the wall opposite herself.

"What have I done?" Liz yelled and felt how her knees failed her and she fell to the floor.

As her knees hit the floor, the front door opened and the first thing she heard was a short gasp then silence. Katarina was staring at Liz who wasn't even glancing in her direction.

"Who's blood is that?" Katarina asked after a few horrible minutes of silence.

Liz glanced over to the cellar door and Katarina followed her gaze. Katarina lost some color in her face but remained calm, at least on the surface; what went on inside of Katarina's mind was a mystery.

"I killed one of them," Liz said, almost chillingly calm. "I let the other one go."

"Why?" Katarina asked, confused.

Liz swallowed.

"So she could leave a message," Liz said.

"No, why did you kill her?" Katarina asked.

Liz looked straight at Katarina.

"To send a message," Liz said plainly. "To know that I am done with them."

"You could be execu-..." Katarina started before she remembered the curse.

Liz almost laughed but managed to stop herself.

"Who were they?" Katarina asked.

Liz stared at Katarina for a moment.

"It doesn't matter," Liz said low and shook her head.

Silence.

"Why aren't you horrified?" Liz asked low. "I killed someone, and their body is down in your cellar."

Katarina's face was calm and still but Liz could sense a storm behind the facade.

"You wouldn't kill someone for nothing," Katarina said with a hint of hesitation, like she wasn't entirely convinced of what she was saying.

"You don't know me," Liz said and shook her head. "You don't know what I would do or what I wouldn't do. You have no idea of the things I've done in my past."

Silence once again.

"You're not your past Liz," Katarina said.

Liz laughed.

"Then who am I? If I'm not the mistakes I've made? The choices I've made?" Liz asked. "Everything I've done has made me, me."

"People change," Katarina said. "People can grow. Mistakes you've made don't have to define you for your entire life."

"I don't know if I'm capable of changing," Liz said coldly. "The dead body in your basement seems like quite the evidence of that."

Katarina sighed.

"Did you kill her without a reason then?" Katarina asked. "Just to send a message?"

Liz was silent for a moment.

"I was angry," she said and stared into the wall with empty eyes. "I needed… No. She didn't deserve to die. Not like that at least."

Silence.

"Alright," Katarina said. "Tell me."

Liz frowned slightly in confusion, that was not what she had expected to hear right now.

"Tell me, what did you do?" Katarina said calmly. "You said you would tell me."

But Liz could see the fear behind Katarina's calm facade, the fear Katarina had of hearing the answer because once it was said; that was it, there would be no turning back. Once the truth is let free, there is no power on earth that can stop it.

Liz sighed.

"They hired me to kill people," Liz said. "They'd learned about my… Little problem-…"

"How?" Katarina asked.

Liz frowned slightly and shook her head, she didn't care about that. She'd never cared about how they found out about her curse, maybe because she didn't really want to know the answer to that question either.

Liz realized how blind she had been, she hadn't known anything really about what she'd been doing and she hadn't even bothered to ask any questions. The truth was perhaps that if Liz had known everything, she might have turned down the offer; so she had chosen to look the other way rather than face the truth. Liz wanted her curse broken more than anything else on this Earth, yet that desire had cost her more than she was ever willing to admit.

That desire might cost her everything in the end.

"I-I don't know," Liz said low. "It's not important."

"So they hired you to kill people," Katarina said slowly. "And in exchange they would break your curse?"

Liz nodded.

"Okay," Katarina said with caution. "It's bad-…"

"That's not the worst part," Liz said low.

Katarina was silent.

"I… I asked to not know anything about them," Liz said. "I didn't want to know anything about what I was doing. So it wasn't until… I realized who they might have been and… And I was right…"

"Who were they?" Katarina asked slowly.

Liz looked up at Katarina, her eyes were blank and Liz tried to keep her face neutral, but she could feel the walls cracking and sadness was leaking through.

"People… People with power that… That wanted to help us," Liz muttered. "Creature right activists."

An eerie silence filled the room and the tension was so thick someone could have cut it with a knife. Liz had averted her gaze from Katarina, she didn't want to see what her expression was; but the long silence was killing her, she preferred if Katarina would just scream at her.

"Say something," Liz said low. "Anything."

Silence.

"You said you didn't know," Katarina said slowly. "Is that true?"

"Yes," Liz said.

"If you'd known, would you have done it anyway?" Katarina asked coldly.

Liz swallowed hard and looked back at Katarina, her face was hard as stone. Why did Liz suddenly feel so helpless?

"I… I don't know," Liz stuttered. "I'd like to think… That I wouldn't have but… I don't know."

"Do you regret it?" Katarina asked a little more softly.

"Yes, but that doesn't change anything," Liz said. "It doesn't change a goddamn thing."

"If you regret it then you should do something to try and fix it," Katarina said.

Liz closed her eyes and she bit her lower lip.

"It's not that easy-…" Liz started.

"It is," Katarina said. "Redeem yourself."

"How can I redeem myself from this?" Liz asked with a raised voice. "I not only killed three people but I undermined any work being made for us to get out of here in a peaceful way! Now there will be a rebellion and a war and it's… it's my fault. Tell me, how do I redeem myself from that? Huh? Because really, if you have any ideas, I'm all ears!"

Katarina bit her lower lip.

"Fight," Katarina said. "Be a part of the rebellion."

"And cause more death?" Liz asked, almost with a manic laugh. "That's redeeming myself?"

Katarina took a step towards Liz but then stopped.

"Liz," Katarina said.

"Tell me you hate me," Liz said. "Yell at me. Throw spells at me, get it over with. I deserve it."

"No," Katarina said.

Liz almost burst into tears at those words and she wasn't entirely sure on why.

"You can't possibly still want to be my fri-…" Liz said with a shaking voice.

"You did something bad," Katarina said. "But you regret it."

"Regretting changes nothing!" Liz yelled. "And I did not just do something 'bad'. I didn't steal money or food, or even punch someone. Those things are bad. What I've done is… Monstrous. I could be the reason you die, don't you see that?"

"There was no certainty that those people working for creature rights would have succeeded," Katarina said. "There would still have been a risk for a rebellion and a war. It's not your fault if that happens."

"I still killed innocent people," Liz said, almost as low as a whisper. "You cannot ignore that, not just because you find me 'interesting'."

Liz shook her head violently and spoke again before Katarina could say anything.

"There isn't just a risk for a rebellion or a war anymore," Liz said, raising her voice. "It's a certainty, and it will happen soon."

"You've met with the resistance?" Katarina asked carefully.

"Yes and they're not backing down," Liz said. "It will happen and people will die."

"But it won't be your fault," Katarina said.

"Don't defend me," Liz hissed. "Don't you dare defend me."

"If you want to fix what you've done then join them," Katarina said. "Help to get creatures out of here. That's how you redeem yourself."

"How can I look them in the eye knowing that I've been working against them?" Liz asked. "How can I look Vende-…"

Liz looked down and bit her lower lip until she could taste blood.

"If you do nothing," Katarina said coldly. "I will not help you with your curse."

Liz's mouth fell open and she stared at Katarina with large eyes.

"I draw the line there," Katarina said. "So if you want my help, you do something."

"Katarina-…" Liz stammered.

"It's your decision," Katarina said, interrupting her. "You have until sundown to decide."

"Are you serious?" Liz asked with a shaking voice.

"I am," Katarina said.

Liz looked away and swallowed hard.

"I want to help you, I think that is quite evident by now," Katarina said. "But at some point you have to help yourself as well. Others can't do all the work for you."

"This is practically black mailing," Liz said low.

"Call it whatever you want," Katarina said. "But I've helped you a lot for nothing in return. But I don't want you to do this for me. Do it for yourself."

"You're starting to sound like Vendela," Liz whispered. "Or like a preacher."

"What good can come from you doing nothing?" Katarina asked. "You'll just feel more ashamed, more guilty-…"

"You don't…" Liz said, feeling her voice shaking. "You don't understand how hard it is."

"You said you can't live forever and also care," Katarina said. "But you can."

"You don't understand!" Liz roared with a sudden flash of anger.

Liz sighed deeply and all the anger just washed away, leaving her feeling horrible for her sudden outburst.

"I-I can't…" Liz whispered low, trying to hold back tears, she was afraid that if she started crying that she might not be able to stop. "If I care… If I care about people I'll have to watch them all die and that'll… Break me. When I look at you, all I see is how fleeting your lives are. How can I care for hundreds of years, live through heartbreak after heartbreak without it driving me mad?"

"You can't just focus on the end of things," Katarina said. "Because everything must end, it is inevitable."

"Except me…" Liz said low. "Everything must end except me."

"I'm going to die," Katarina said. "And it scares me. And I know my parents will die and I will with all likelihood outlive them. But if I lived only with those thoughts it would drive me and anyone else mad. Focus on what you have now, not what might happen in the future. Tomorrow is never certain, it is not promised to anyone."

Liz looked over at Katarina, there were tears in her eyes and she felt like an open wound, as if all of her walls had come crumbling down. Katarina's words had hit her hard and all she could think about was everything she'd ruined because she was scared of the future. Of how she'd ruined her own and Vendela's happiness by leaving her. Of how she kept ruining her own happiness at every turn because at least that was her choice, at least then it couldn't be ruined later.

Liz clenched her jaw and closed her eyes in an attempt not to cry.

"So…" Liz said, her voice still shaking. "So if I help in this rebellion… If I try to fix what I've done. You'll help me try and break my curse?"

"I'll help you search," Katarina said. "Even if we don't find anything in this spell book."

"Why?" Liz almost whispered.

"What?" Katarina asked with a slight frown.

"Why are you showing me kindness? Why are you showing me mercy? I clearly don't deserve either," Liz said. "Nor do I deserve forgiveness."

"Because," Katarina said slowly. "I think you have denied yourself of those things for so long that it has made you harsh and bitter. Without love, without kindness, we lose our way and become someone else entirely."

"I killed people," Liz said low. "And that is barely the worst thing I've done…"

"Yes you did," Katarina said plainly.

"And you forgive me for that?" Liz asked, confused.

"No," Katarina said.

Liz slowly nodded, she wouldn't have forgiven her either.

"But I am giving you the chance to be forgiven," Katarina said. "Which is something I think everyone deserves."

Liz looked straight at Katarina as if she was staring straight into the sun, tears starting to well up in the corner of her eyes before she spoke again after a brief pause.

"I have one condition in that case," Liz said low. "If I am to help in this rebellion."

Katarina frowned slightly.

"A condition?" Katarina asked.

"If I play my part and help in this rebellion," Liz said. "You stay out of it."

"Liz-…" Katarina started.

"I know what you said," Liz said seriously. "But if I'm going to do this, I need to know that you'll survive. You're of no use to me dead and then I'll have joined this rebellion for nothing."

"It's not for noth-…" Katarina said.

"Do we have a deal?" Liz said, interrupting her.

"I can be of use," Katarina said, raising her voice slightly. "I'm not some defenseless child-…"

"You are very much mortal," Liz said harshly. "And your magic won't save you if you get a blow to the head or even worse, a bullet. You don't understand what this rebellion will bring. I'm not sure the people in the rebellion do either. I suspect they think they'll storm the wall, fight some guards and then it will be over and they'll be able to live their lives in peace. But this will start a war that can last for years, involving everyone."

Katarina looked at Liz with a grim look.

"So I will help," Liz said. "I can't die, I am quite the asset. But in exchange, you stay out of it. So if you really want what's best for everyone you'll agree to this. You survive at all costs. Do we have a deal?"

The look in Katarina's eyes was terrifying, even for Liz. It was unlike any look Liz had seen in Katarina before, there was an unnatural glow in her eyes which told Liz that she was far from happy with how this conversation had turned out and was now holding back her magic spurting out with all her might.

"Alright," Katarina said with a grim expression. "I agree."

Liz nodded slowly as Katarina agreed, not entirely sure on what had just happened or what she'd promised.

"I'll go talk with Vendela as soon as the sun sets," Liz said.

Silence.

"I want you to promise me something Liz," Katarina said seriously.

Liz bit her lower lip and glanced away.

"What?" Liz said uncertain.

"If I'm going to stay out of this rebellion," Katarina said. "Promise me that you find my parents and keep them safe."

Liz frowned slightly.

"If the walls are breached and creatures stream into the Town, you want me in the middle of the chaos to find your parents?" Liz asked. "Me, a vampire. They'll run from me."

"Tell them you know me, that I sent you," Katarina said.

"Yeah, I'm sure to do that while they run away from me screaming for the guards," Liz said sarcastically.

"Liz," Katarina said very seriously. "You said I could ask anything of you before."

Silence.

"I said almo-…" Liz started low.

"I'm asking this of you," Katarina said. "If I am to do this, I need to know my parents will be safe."

Liz sighed and looked over at Katarina. Liz was silent for a moment, contemplating what to say. It would have been so easy to lie and stop the conversation, but the lies had to end at some point.

"I can't promise that," Liz said slowly. "I can't promise they'll be safe."

There was a twitch of shock in Katarina's face.

"But I can promise that I'll try," Liz said low. "Alright? That's the best I can do."

Katarina frowned slightly and leaned back in her chair, Liz had no idea what was going through her head at this point.

"Okay," Katarina said. "I trust you."

Liz stared at Katarina and those words were so uncommon for her to hear. Especially from human-like creatures and Katarina was practically a human. She wasn't a monster or cursed, she was blessed with powers to help and all she wanted to do was help others. But she had been denied that chance her entire life, and even now Liz was denying her that.

And as those words left Katarina's mouth there were two thoughts rushing through Liz's head. *"Goddammit"* and *"I don't want to disappoint her."*

"Don't put too much faith in me," Liz said and tried to chuckle. "You'll be disappointed."

Katarina just stared at Liz and she felt her looking right through her facade. Liz swallowed and sat down in the chair opposite Katarina again before she glanced out the window. It was now late afternoon but the sun was still up, another hour or two and Liz could leave.

Liz's eyes moved towards the cellar door that was opened slightly and all she could see was flashes of the woman's dead body laying in the dark down there and she felt a lump in her throat. She'd been down there for a while now and Liz hadn't thought about what to do with the body. The right thing would be to return it to Town and her family, if she had any. But that would direct all the guards' attention right at her and that was the last thing she needed right now. As a lot of other things, she hadn't thought this one through to the end. Liz was all heart and impulses, the consequences came afterwards.

"I'll deal with the body," Liz said low. "Don't worry about it."

Liz said that but she still had absolutely no plan on what to do with it, but she'd figure something out. Katarina's face lost some color and her eyes glanced over to the door but she quickly turned away, swallowing hard.

"Don't go down there until I've fixed it okay?" Liz said.

"If you say so," Katarina said.

Silence.

"Can I be honest?" Liz asked low.

"If you want to," Katarina said.

"I'm not sure what I'm going to say to Vendela and… And to the resistance," Liz said. "And I'm not sure they'll want my help, especially if I tell them the truth."

"Perhaps…" Katarina said carefully. "Wait to tell the truth."

Liz glanced over at Katarina.

"I should lie?" Liz asked, almost amused.

"You can't lie forever," Katarina said. "But you're right. They might not react in the s-…"

"Same way you did?" Liz asked.

Katarina didn't say anything but held Liz's gaze.

"I don't understand you," Liz said slowly. "I don't understand your motivations or why you react in certain ways. I don't understand how you can still look at me like the moment you met me, before you knew about some of the things I've done. Anyone else would have looked at me like the monster I am and run away."

Katarina raised an eyebrow.

"Vendela hasn't run away, Ami hasn-…" Katarina started.

"Ami doesn't know anything about me," Liz said. "She's sweet and kind and she would hate me if she knew the things I've done."

Pause.

"And Vendela," Liz continued. "If she knew about the creature rights activists I fear that she-…"

Liz couldn't finish the sentence. *I fear that she would truly hate me as well and that would break me.* The mere thought frightened her and those words would never slip past Liz's lips.

"You are a stranger," Liz said. "How can you not hate me?"

Katarina was silent for a moment.

"I don't hate you Liz," Katarina said. "And honestly, I don't think there is anyone who hates you more than you do."

Something close to a laugh came from Liz.

"But I also do think that if I did not possess this power," Katarina said. "I would *not* react this way. Because I would not know if your feelings were honest or not; all your words about remorse could as much be lies as the truth. I wouldn't know that you felt regret or shame. That's why I think you should wait to tell the others. They won't know with the same certainty, not even Vendela, as I do; the desire you have to do better."

Both went silent and for a short second, Liz thought that perhaps, just perhaps things could somewhat work out. She was still in a rebellion she didn't want to have any part of and she'd agreed to join a war that would have casualties. She might be breaking her rules but this way, perhaps Vendela could start to forgive her or at least get to a place where Liz wasn't constantly hurting her. Perhaps Liz could try… Try to care, try not to think about the inevitable future and just try to enjoy the moment. It wouldn't be easy, hundreds of years of old habits wouldn't die without a fight.

The person Liz had become wouldn't die without a fight, she knew that. It would not be easy to become someone she was centuries ago.

The only thing Liz knew with any certainty at this point was that she couldn't leave Vendela without a word or warning again. She deserved better than that and Liz had hurt her enough.

Chapter 34

Liz was staring out the window, waiting for the sun to set so she could go to the Bar and see Vendela. The sun seemed to be setting extraordinarily slowly, it was almost excruciating and Liz legs itched from her nerves going haywire. As many times before, Liz didn't really have a plan or any thoughts of what she was going to say, she just hoped that when the time came, she would at least be able to say something. She couldn't freeze up like she'd done before, she would have to speak, have to make Vendela listen to her no matter the cost, even if it felt like it was killing her.

There was one concern, in the back of Liz's head, if Vendela did indeed refuse to hear her out or if she did listen and reject Liz's offer to help; what would she do? Liz couldn't force her to accept her help, or force her to listen even. If Vendela rejected Liz's help, there would be nothing for Liz to do about it.

Liz really wondered how badly she had screwed up, if she had gone too far for even Vendela to give her another chance. There had to come a point when Vendela had to be done with her, Liz had known that from the start; she just hoped it wasn't right now.

Liz turned her head back to Katarina, as she had been unusually silent for a few moments, and found that she'd fallen asleep. Her head was laying face down in the spell book and her hand was reaching out for the cold cup of tea. Liz wondered how many hours Katarina had been awake before she'd practically collapsed out of fatigue? Liz touched the dark mark on her chest and it tingled as her fingers brushed over it, the pain had subsided and it wasn't really bothering her anymore, yet it didn't seem to go away. Maybe it would never completely leave her? It was magic that had caused it after all and magic could leave marks worse than scars. Liz still wasn't completely restored but she hadn't felt the need to faint in a while so that was something.

Liz rose from where she'd been sitting and walked up to Katarina and in one swift move she picked up her small frame and carried her over to the couch in the corner. Katarina was sleeping heavily and she seemed to be free from her nightmares which was good, Liz didn't want to battle with them again. Liz laid Katarina down carefully on the couch and covered her in the blanket that was thrown over the side of it. As Liz was doing it, she wasn't sure on why she was doing it. Perhaps, she was trying to actively care but it felt foreign to her, or rather it felt foreign to her to not fight it.

Liz sat down in the chair again and picked up her bag and opened the package sent from Lady Morgana with the blood. It had the same markings as all the other bottles had and Liz wondered for a brief moment if they'd gotten it from Mr. Greenlund? But she dismissed it, by the tone of the two women who worked for Lady Morgana, it didn't seem like her and him got on so well.

She took a chug of the blood even though she knew it might not be the best idea because it could make her more emotional but perhaps at this point, being emotional was better than being defensive and aggressive that she could be otherwise. All her thoughts were on Vendela and she was honestly nervous, because after their last conversation she wasn't even sure that Vendela would listen to her at all. And Liz wouldn't really blame her if she didn't.

The sun finally set and Liz left the apartment, still with Katarina sleeping on the couch, a corpse in the basement and an unconscious Ami in the bedroom.

Liz walked with unusually slow steps towards the Bar. She passed the old bar and glanced over at the ashes and wondered if someone was standing there now, watching her, maybe even Vendela? But she continued past it and finally stopped in front of the new Bar. It was open and Liz just stood outside it for a few moments. Two creatures exited the Bar and almost walked right into Liz but she moved out of the way just in time, she could hear them muttering something beneath their breath but she didn't care about them. She wasn't sure on what was going to happen once she entered, there would be other creatures in there so perhaps Vendela would hold back on some of her anger but there was no certainty.

"Just rip it off like a band aid," Liz muttered to herself right before she entered the Bar. "You are an ancient monster, don't act like such a baby."

The Bar was filled to the brim with creatures and she saw Vendela standing behind the bar as usual. She was smiling lightly but Liz could see past the smile and there was no happiness in her eyes, they were as cold as ice. She was talking to someone with bright red hair, Liz could only see her from behind but she guessed it was Tess.

Vendela glanced over towards the door and when their eyes met it was like everything stopped, all the noises went silent and there were just the two of them in there. But it was over in a split second. Vendela's face was unnaturally neutral and Liz could see it was masking a storm and the girl Tess turned around to see what Vendela was looking at with such an intense gaze and her smile was wiped off her face as well.

"Everyone get out," Vendela said with a cold voice.

At first no one seemed to pay attention to her, pretending they hadn't heard her.

"Everyone get the fuck out!" Vendela yelled and slammed her hand onto the table.

The whole bar fell silent and no one moved for a few seconds before they all realized the seriousness of the situation and quickly moved towards the door. Liz had just stepped aside without saying anything, letting them all pass and leave. She could see Tess exchange glances with Vendela before she also left, without looking once at Liz. Tess was the last one out of the Bar and then there was just Vendela and Liz left.

Vendela hadn't said another word but she was staring at Liz and she saw how her eyes drifted towards her bloody dress. The still quite fresh and new blood from the woman Liz had killed.

"Who's blood is that?" Vendela asked, her voice alarmingly calm.

Liz looked down at her dress and the deep red stains and for a few seconds she stayed quiet, not sure on what to say. Not sure if she should tell the truth or lie.

"No, you know what," Vendela said before Liz could answer her. "I don't care about the answer."

"I'm sorry," Liz finally said low as those were the only words spinning around in her head.

Vendela didn't move a muscle, she was still as a statue, her eyes piercing Liz like spears.

"What do you want?" Vendela said coldly. "Because I assume you want something, seems to be the only reason you come here."

Liz clenched her jaw at Vendela's harsh words and a few days ago, those words would have made her blood boil and she would have gone into a rant or thrown sarcastic comments back at her. Now all Liz felt was shame with a hint of sadness, she wasn't delusional, she couldn't even lie to herself anymore. She deserved everything that would come, be it either harsh words or physical punishment and she would not raise a finger to defend herself of her actions.

"I changed my mind," Liz finally said.

Vendela was silent but there was a twitch in her eye, almost like she was surprised at those words.

"I'll join you," Liz said, almost as low as a whisper. "I'll fight with you."

"Why?" Vendela asked, her voice thick.

"Does it matter?" Liz asked.

"It does," Vendela said harshly.

Liz sighed.

"Because… I want to redeem myself," Liz said, she was speaking so low it was almost like she was whispering at this point.

It wasn't a complete lie, but not a complete truth either, like most things that came out of Liz's mouth these days.

"Bullshit," Vendela said.

Liz walked closer to Vendela, but made sure to keep a certain distance the entire time; she knew Vendela was upset with her and Liz was not about to push her luck by invading her personal space without permission. Liz looked straight into Vendela's eyes and sighed before she spoke again.

"You want to know the truth?" Liz asked.

"I don't know if I care enough anymore to want to know the truth," Vendela said coldly.

Those words hit Liz like a punch in the stomach but it barely showed on her face.

"Fair enough," Liz said, trying to smile and sound a little more cheerful. "You want to hit me? You get one punch for free."

"No," Vendela said seriously.

"You sure? It's a one time deal," Liz said with a vague smile. "I'll give you a free kick as well if that makes it better?"

Vendela didn't look in the least amused.

"I'm not going to hit you," Vendela said abruptly.

Silence. The first thought crossing Liz's mind was *"I wish you would."*.

"I've been conflicted," Liz said, the smile wiped off her face. "You know that."

Vendela didn't say anything.

"And I won't pretend to believe or care about this rebellion," Liz said a little more harshly. "Because that would be a lie. And you seem to be very done with my lies."

Vendela's face hardened.

"But I care about you," Liz continued. "And about Ami, and about Katarina. And…"

Liz closed her eyes as she wasn't sure on how to continue, she didn't know where to end the lie and start the truth. In some ways, she barely knew what was a lie or truth anymore.

"So I'll help you," Liz continued. "If you still want my help."

"You changed your mind because you care about us?" Vendela asked skeptically. "Don't you usually say that you don't care, that you *can't* care."

"Alright, I know how this soun-…" Liz started.

"Do you?" Vendela said. "Because it sounds shifty as hell to me."

Liz stared down into the floor.

"I am doing this because I care abou-…"Liz started.

"There has to be something else," Vendela said. "Something else that changed your mind."

Liz bit her lower lip and then looked up at Vendela. Liz saw the utter distrust and coldness in her eyes and for some reason, instead of it making her put up her walls, it made her lower them even more.

"You're right," Liz said with a sigh.

Liz was just so tired, she almost felt the urge to tell Vendela everything. Every horrific thing she'd done, just come clean and take the punishments, but she had to keep some secrets to herself. At least for now, at some other time perhaps then Liz would dare to open up more. Liz hadn't realized it but there were few things she feared more at this point than Vendela hating her. It had always been a fear in the back of her mind but now, if Liz saw pure hate in Vendela's eyes as she looked at her; it would ruin her.

Vendela almost looked a little shocked at the honesty in Liz's words, but only for a moment.

"I made a deal with Katarina," Liz said.

"A deal?" Vendela asked.

"I… I have a problem…" Liz said uncertainly. "That she… Perhaps can help me with…"

Vendela frowned slightly.

"But her condition for helping me was that I had to join the rebellion," Liz said honestly. "That I had to do something."

"That sounds like the truth," Vendela said with a monotone voice. "That you are doing something for yourself. Not because you care ab-…"

"Vendela," Liz said uncharacteristically soft. "I know you're mad with me and that's fine, be mad with me all you want. Scream at me, hit me, whatever makes you feel better. I deserve it okay? But I was already contemplating on joining the rebellion because I didn't want to lose you. This deal with Katarina just pushed me to make a decision. A push I desperately needed. I do… I do care about you."

"You have a funny way of showing it," Vendela said coldly.

"Yeah," Liz said sadly. "I know. And I don't expect you to instantly or ever really forgive me for everything I've done-…"

"Good," Vendela said.

"I've disappointed you enough times," Liz said. "It's time I'd do something to make you proud of me."

Even as all of these words spilled out of her, the thoughts about what she'd done was in the back of her head. The corpse in Katarina's basement, the three creature right activists she'd killed. Every truth she told, it felt as if they were tainted by the horrors she'd done. That even her good thoughts and actions became black and corrupted.

"What was the deal about?" Vendela asked.

Liz fell silent.

"What was the deal about Liz?" Vendela asked again with some force.

"Is it-…?" Liz started.

"It is," Vendela said, interrupting her. "You want me to trust you? You want me to believe you? You're gonna have to earn it."

"Fine," Liz muttered.

Liz sat down on one of the chairs before she spoke again.

"She's helping me with… With a curse," Liz said low and put her face in her hands.

"A curse?" Vendela asked and frowned in confusion. "What are y-…"

"I'm cursed," Liz said, trying not to sound irritated. "And I want it gone."

"There is no cure for being a vam-…" Vendela started.

"Not the curse I'm talking about," Liz said bitterly.

Vendela was silent.

"I have an eternity curse," Liz said, honesty flooding her voice. "I can't die. No matter what."

Silence.

"I want it gone, so Katarina might be able to help me with that," Liz continued.

"You're going to join a rebellion so you… So you can die?" Vendela asked, there was a tinge of surprise and confusion in her voice.

There was a short moment of silence, where Liz was just staring at Vendela.

Liz didn't have the heart to tell her the truth, because even in this situation, Liz knew that the truth would hurt Vendela and it was an unnecessary hurt.

Because yes, Liz wanted to die, there was barely anything she wanted more in life; to just have some peace.

"I want the option," Liz finally said. "I want to know that there is an end and not just-…"

Liz closed her eyes for a moment.

"You said you understood how caring about mortals is scary because their time is so limited," Liz continued. "But even your time is limited compared to me. As it is now, there is a certainty that I will watch you and everyone else on this earth die. And that… That's terrifying."

There was a short moment of silence, but it felt like an eternity.

"Alright," Vendela said.

Liz slowly opened her eyes and looked at Vendela, her face was still hard as stone but there was something softer in her gaze, but it was barely noticeable. But Liz knew Vendela's face without fault, she knew every mannerism Vendela had, every expression she made, no matter how microscopical.

"Alright?" Liz asked low in slight confusion. "You believe me?"

Vendela didn't move and was just staring directly at her and Liz could see how badly she wanted to trust her, even though years of experience told her that it was perhaps not the best idea.

"I…" Vendela started. "I'm tired of trusting and believing in you, and being disappointed."

Liz looked away and swallowed hard, but she knew there were no lies in Vendela's words.

"But I can't turn you away if you really want to help," Vendela finally added with a sigh. "When that's all I've been asking of you."

Liz was silent for a moment.

"I want to help," Liz said. "For my sake and for yours. This rebellion will be a bloodbath-…"

"I can take care of myself," Vendela said.

"I know that," Liz said. "You've taken care of both of us and protected me plenty of times. As I can't die and you can, let me repay you."

"I don't need a bodyguard," Vendela said.

There was a moment of silence and Liz stared right into Vendela's gray eyes before she spoke again with the utmost seriousness.

"I won't just stand aside and watch you die," Liz said coldly. "Not in a stupid rebellion."

"There are others who need protection more than me," Vendela said. "Tess, Mona and Josefine for starters."

Liz clenched her jaw.

"If you really care about me," Vendela said. "You'll protect those that can't protect themselves as well as others. The mortals."

Liz rose from where she'd been sitting.

"I should let your rebel leader know that I'll help," Liz said, changing the subject. "Even though it will be insufferable to admit it."

Vendela walked over to Liz with a slight frown on her face.

"Why is it going to be insufferable?" Vendela asked.

Liz glanced over at Vendela and her face had melted like ice in the spring, it was softer but Liz could still see an edge in her eyes as she stared at her.

"Because she told me she knew I'd come back and join you," Liz said, barely realizing she was speaking.

"Why?" Vendela asked, slightly confused.

Liz didn't answer first, just took in all of Vendela's face as if it was the first time she saw her. The way she wrinkled her nose when she was confused or the way her eyes narrowed when she was suspicious. Or the best part, when she showed one of her, nowadays, unusual smiles. As Liz stared at Vendela she couldn't bring herself to say the words, she couldn't even repeat what Josefine had said to her. *Because she knows I love you* was Liz's thoughts. Finally Liz just shrugged.

"I don't know," Liz lied. "She didn't tell me."

Liz had said she would try to care, which meant that the escaping and the lies had to end as well and yet she didn't seem to be able to stop, no matter how hard she tried.

Chapter 35

"I can go and meet with Josefine myself if you want to re-open the Bar," Liz said. "I wouldn't want you to get into trouble with Mr. Greenlund because of me."

"I haven't heard a single word from him since you went into The Fun House," Vendela said plainly.

He must have known Vendela was a close friend to Liz, it seemed like everyone knew that. If he was terrified of Liz, he would be terrified to mess with the people she loved.

"I can still go alone," Liz said. "You don't have to babysit me."

"No, I'll go with you," Vendela said with a low sigh. "I need to speak with some of them as well."

"Alright," Liz said.

They started walking towards the old burned down bar with quick steps, it was a quiet and uneventful journey and Liz had things she wanted to say but couldn't find the words for them and she wondered exactly how mad Vendela was with her at this moment. Liz glanced over at Vendela from time to time but Vendela wasn't looking at Liz at all. Liz was used to being quiet with Vendela but this silence was unnatural and stiff and Liz hated it. She wanted to say something jokingly, make Vendela smile or at least get her talking a little.

"So," Liz tried to say with a little jokeful attitude. "Exactly how mad are you at me?"

Silence, it was clear that Vendela did not find it amusing in the slightest.

"I'm glad you changed your mind," Vendela said. "I really am. But you have walked away and just disappeared without a word too many times these last years for me to think that it won't happen this time as well."

"It won't," Liz said.

"Right," Vendela said with an edge in her voice. "Because if you don't help, Katarina won't help you with your curse."

"Yeah, I'm selfish," Liz said, her voice turning slightly bitter. "Water is wet. What else is new?"

Vendela didn't say anything else and they reached the magical barrier and Liz took a deep breath before she went through and an involuntary shiver went down her spine as she could feel herself being enveloped in the magic for a brief moment. Vendela had already reached the hatch and probably knocked because she was just standing there and waiting. The hatch opened with the same squeaky sound as before and Liz saw Tess red hair come up from the hole. Her gaze went between Liz and Vendela with a slightly confused expression on her face before she started to climb down the stairs again without saying a word.

"She's a real talker," Liz said as a joke.

Vendela didn't even react to that and just started to climb down as well. Liz was last and closed the hatch over her and the only thing she could think of was that she was making a grave mistake, but she tried to push that thought away. There was no other option if she didn't want to lose everything. This way, she might be able to regain some of Vendela's trust and maybe keep her safe during the rebellion and Katarina would help her with her curse. She might also be able to regain some of the humanity she'd lost, some of that compassion and to dare to dream of a better life. Liz couldn't remember the last time she'd dared to dream without it terrifying her.

All it could end up costing her in the long run was her sanity.

As Liz came down into the largest room in the cellar she noticed that there were even more people down here than last time, most faces she still didn't recognize but there was some she had seen out and about in The

Sanctuary and then there was of course, Mona, Tess and Gray who was still sitting in the exact same spot in the corner. Vendela walked straight up to Tess and Liz followed her close behind.

"Is she free?" Vendela asked.

Tess looked behind her at Liz before turning her gaze back to Vendela.

"Didn't you say that she wasn't going to come back?" Tess said low.

Vendela was silent for a few seconds.

"I was wrong," she said almost inaudibly. "Is Josefine free or should we wait?"

Tess glanced over at the door to the right quickly.

"Give her ten minutes I'd say," Tess said. "Then you can talk to her."

"Alright," Vendela said.

"Can you trust her?" Tess whispered and quickly looked over at Liz who could hear her perfectly.

"Trust me," Vendela simply said.

Tess nodded faintly and Vendela turned back to Liz.

"You'll have to wait a little," Vendela said.

"I heard that," Liz said. "So what do we do in the meanwhile?"

Vendela looked around the quite large room.

"Mingle?" She said with the trace of a smile on her lips.

Liz smiled vaguely and a low chuckle escaped her lips.

"Yeah, you know me, I'm a real people's person," Liz said sarcastically.

Vendela looked around the room and Liz could see her eyes settling on Gray in the corner for a short moment before she sighed softly and turned back to Liz.

"What happened to them?" Liz asked. "You said you'd tell me."

Vendela looked like she was contemplating on whether she should answer Liz or not but finally she seemed to decide and she led Liz into a corner, away from the big crowd in the middle of the room.

"When did you meet them?" Vendela asked.

Liz shrugged slightly.

"On the night I returned," Liz said. "Why?"

"The full moon night right?" Vendela said.

Liz nodded.

"Did you talk a lot?" Vendela asked.

"No," Liz said. "They just said their name, that the Bar had been rebuilt and gave me some vague directions to it. That was about it. But I remember they looked a lot better than they do now."

Both Liz and Vendela glanced back at Gray again, who was staring into the floor with empty eyes and dark bags beneath their eyes. When Liz had met them the first time, they'd looked like a large muscular person but now they looked closer to a skeleton. There were still bandages on their forearms but there was no blood on them this time.

"They're new here," Vendela said. "And that full moon night was their first one in here. In fact it was their first full moon night as a creature at all."

Liz was silent for a moment.

"They're a werewolf?" Liz asked.

Vendela nodded.

"They were bit and the one who found them turned them in to the authorities," Vendela said. "They were here about two weeks before the full moon night."

"Alright," Liz said. "That su-…"

"They killed people that night Liz," Vendela whispered seriously. "Those convicts. They disappeared after that for a while, which was why Tess was looking for me when you opened the door. And when we found them…"

Vendela swallowed and clenched her jaw.

"They're not well," Vendela said instead. "Refuses to eat and barely moves at all."

Liz was silent, just carefully watching Gray's unmoving form in the corner. She had nothing to say, she understood them perhaps a little more than she wanted to admit.

"If you're not too harsh, feel free to see if you can talk to them and get a reaction," Vendela said. "At least get them to eat something."

"Not really my area," Liz said. "Harshness and sarcasm is all I've got to offer."

Vendela just shook her head slightly.

"Elizabeth, what a lovely surprise."

Liz tensed up like someone had sent an electric shock through her body as she heard that silky smooth voice and she could almost see the smirk on his lips in front of her.

Liz turned around and just as she had imagined, Albin had a smirk on his lips as he was looking at her. His eyes were lit up with excitement, he obviously hadn't expected to see Liz here again so soon but he seemed delighted by it.

"Vendela," he said politely and turned his gaze towards her instead. "I didn't expect to see you back so soon."

"I wasn't planning on being back so soon either," Vendela said. "But-…"

"But you met our dear Elizabeth on the way?" Albin said and turned back to Liz. "I'd heard you weren't coming back. What made you change your mind?"

Liz's eyes were filled with rage as she stared at Albin, her hands had formed into fists and she was shaking ever so slightly. The anger, the hatred of seeing Albin made her almost incapable of speaking. Liz wanted to scream at him, run away from him, fight him, all at the same time so all those conflicting feelings made her do nothing instead; she was literally petrified by the sight of him.

"Come now Elizabeth," Albin said. "Are you not going to answer me?"

"How do you know each other?" Vendela asked.

There was a spark in Albin's eyes and he looked amused at the question.

"I was going to ask you the same thing," Albin said. "But I almost feel a little hurt that she never mentioned me, after all I am her longest living friend."

Liz managed to scoff at that remark but Albin barely seemed to notice it.

"Friend?" Vendela said and glanced over at Liz's rage filled face.

"Of course," Albin said with a smirk. "We have a long history together."

"We're not friends," Liz managed to spit out.

"That's hurtful Elizabeth," Albin said with mock hurt in his voice. "After everything we've been through? After everything I've done for you?"

Albin turned his attention back to Vendela.

"But let me guess how you know our dear Elizabeth," Albin said and scanned Vendela's face. "You were lovers? She always had a type."

Vendela frowned slightly and glanced over at Liz who was now positively fuming with anger.

"Not that any relationship lasted long," Albin said and chuckled low. "I mean if you can even call them relationships when the longest lasted a night. How long did yours last? Because I assume she screwed it up as usual."

"Fifty years," Vendela answered coldly.

"My my," Albin said with fake surprise. "You must have been special. And here you are now together, what a sweet reunion."

"Shut up," Liz said, low and threateningly.

"But we have so much to talk about," Albin said, his smile becoming bigger by the second. "So much to catch up on. For example, I've heard you were outside the Sanctuary for five months, whatever can you have been up to in that time?"

That comment was the one to push Liz over the edge and she gripped Albin by his shirt and slammed him into the wall. The whole room went silent as everyone's eyes were turned towards them; the only sound heard was a low laugh escape from Albin as he was slammed into the wall.

"Are you going to hurt me?" Albin asked, almost amused. "Go ahead. Do it in front of all of these creatures. Show them what you truly are."

"Liz, let him go," Vendela said low.

It almost hurt but Liz managed to release Albin from her grip. Albin had a smug look on his face which made Liz feel sick to her stomach.

"That's a good girl," Albin said, his voice sounding like he was speaking to a dog, not a person.

Liz growled low and showed her teeth, if Vendela hadn't been standing right behind her, there would have been no stopping her. She would have assaulted Albin and it would have started a bloody fight. It had happened many times before, Liz had lost count on exactly how many.

"What are you doing here?" Liz hissed, trying to keep the burning rage inside her in check.

"Me?" Albin said. "I'm helping of course."

"Bullshit," Liz spat out.

"I like to help people," Albin said.

"You like to help yourself," Liz said low. "And hurt anyone around you at the same time."

"We have that in common, don't we?" Albin said with a smirk. "Now the more interesting question is of course, why are you here?"

Liz didn't answer.

"Go to hell," Liz hissed.

"Is it nice this time of year?" Albin asked sarcastically. "You, if anyone, should know."

"Vendela!" Tess said. "Josefine is free now."

Vendela nodded.

"You should go see her," Vendela said to Liz. "She doesn't like to be kept waiting."

Liz didn't take her eyes off Albin.

"Yes and in the meanwhile Vendela and I can get better acquainted," Albin said. "We haven't had much time to speak one on one."

Liz moved really close to Albin and spoke almost too low for it to be heard.

"I might not be able to kill you," Liz hissed. "But I will hurt you so bad that you wish you could if you do anything to Vendela."

Albin looked extremely pleased by her words.

"Oh, I'm just going to speak with her," Albin said. "Cross my heart and hope to die. She is such a nice person, I wonder how she managed to put up with you for so long."

Liz gave him a gaze of warning but it just made him smile even bigger. Liz turned back to Vendela before she left.

"He's a manipulative bastard," Liz said. "Don't trust him."

Liz then left and moved quickly towards the door leading to Josefine.

"Takes one to know one!" Albin shouted after her.

Liz almost tore open the door and slammed it shut behind her with a loud bang.

Chapter 36

As Liz entered the room she found Josefine sitting in the middle of the floor with her eyes closed and the confusion of that settled Liz's anger a little but she couldn't shake the feeling of dread that Vendela was speaking with Albin at this moment.

Albin always left her feeling horrible in some sort of way. Either physical or mentally, he knew exactly what buttons to push to bring Liz to her knees. Even if she didn't want to admit it, even if she lied to herself; he still scared the hell out of her.

The one thing calming her down a little was that Vendela and Albin were in a room filled with other people but who knew what they were talking about. Probably about her, which was far from reassuring.

"Hello again Liz," Josefine said without opening her eyes. "Please take a seat."

"I'd rather stand," Liz muttered.

"As you wish," Josefine said calmly. "Why are you here?"

Silence.

"You know why I'm here," Liz said reluctantly.

Josefine opened her eyes and Liz had almost forgotten that she had the same eyes as Vendela and she twitched in shock when she saw them before she regained her composure.

"Do you have a problem with me being right?" Josefine asked. "Or do you just hate to be wrong?"

"Oh, I'm wrong a lot," Liz said. "I know that. I'm probably wrong more times than I'm right."

Josefine slowly rose from where she'd been sitting.

"So you just have a problem with me being right?" Josefine asked.

Liz slowly shook her head.

"What the hell were you doing anyway?" Liz asked. "Sleeping on the job?"

Josefine smiled weakly.

"Constantly being around a lot of people when you can sense their emotions and read their auras can get a little overwhelming, especially as I can't really control it," Josefine said. "So I need a few minutes each day to just clear my mind. The more people, the more intense the emotion, the worse it gets. It can get paralyzing at times."

"Do you ever leave this place?" Liz asked.

"Not really," Josefine said. "If I need something done on the surface I send someone, usually my second in command."

"Let me guess, Tess?" Liz said.

Josefine nodded. Liz was silent for a moment and she glanced back at the door and her thoughts lingered on Vendela and Albin, she had said what she wanted and now she wasn't entirely sure on what would happen next.

"I have to say that I thought it would take a little longer for you to change your mind," Josefine said.

"Just shows how little you know about me," Liz said. "I am extremely impulsive."

"I've heard that," Josefine said, slightly amused.

Liz shot her a sharp gaze.

"So what now?" Liz asked.

"What do you mean?" Josefine asked.

"What happens next?" Liz asked, slightly irritated. "I'll join your stupid rebellion, so what am I supposed to do?"

Josefine's face hardened at the words 'stupid rebellion' but quickly softened again. Even Liz could feel the storm behind this polite facade.

"You're going to do what you're told," Josefine said bluntly. "And I'll find something for you to do soon enough."

"That's it?" Liz asked, confused. "You don't have any plans at all to escape?"

"Oh, of course I do," Josefine said. "You just don't need to know about them yet."

"You think I'm going to do your bidding without knowing anything about what I'm doing?" Liz asked.

"Yes," Josefine simply said.

Liz shook her head but there was the shadow of a smile on her lips. She had learned her lesson from working with Lady Morgana, doing things for someone without knowing exactly what they were was always a bad decision. One Liz wouldn't repeat.

"No," Liz said. "Not going to happen."

"You're a soldier," Josefine said. "A good one I assume from the reputation you have. But I don't need your advice on tactics or plans. And you'll have to excuse me that I don't entirely trust you either."

"What?" Liz asked.

"Well as you put it yourself, you're extremely impulsive," Josefine said. "I don't know you very well except from whispers, rumors and what I can feel from you and what I feel is not very reassuring. You're like a bomb ready to explode at any time, taking everyone out with you."

Liz scoffed.

"So until I know that I can trust you completely," Josefine said. "You will only get minimal information."

"If I was going to betray you don't you think I'd already done that?" Liz asked.

Josefine shrugged.

"Perhaps," Josefine said. "Perhaps not."

Liz was silent for a moment.

"Alright," Liz said. "Here's the deal, I won't do anything for you until I know exactly what it is I'm doing. So when you feel like telling me about your plans to escape, tell me and I'll help you, until then screw you."

"It's your choice," Josefine said calmly. "But don't get things wrong, I don't intend to use you as a messenger or a spy, that would be a waste. You are a soldier so that is what you'll be. You'll fight, you'll kill if necessary. When the day comes for the break out to happen, you will know and I hope I can trust you to join us at that point?"

Liz took a few seconds before she answered.

"As long as I'm not fumbling in the dark," Liz said. "Or being deceived about what I'm doing, then I'll fight for you."

Liz took some steps closer to Josefine and stared into her eyes.

"But if you give me false information or leave anything important out I will not take that well," Liz said seriously. "I've done the bidding of people without knowing anything about the mission and I won't repeat that same mistake again."

Josefine raised an eyebrow slightly.

"Don't make me regret changing my mind," Liz said.

Liz had started to walk towards the door when Josefine spoke again.

"I assume that if I need to speak with you that I'll find you at Vendela's place?" Josefine said.

Liz stopped in her tracks, still with her back turned to Josefine. Liz swallowed, there were fewer things she wanted more than patch up things with Vendela but in a way she felt guilty about trying to gain her confidence and trust. Because she knew it would all crumble when Vendela learned what Liz had done outside the Sanctuary. It was crueler to make her let her guard down and make her trust her and then crush it, as she'd done before. And yet she couldn't help it in a way, because Liz truly didn't want Vendela to hate her and she definitely didn't want to hurt her. She wanted to make her smile and laugh and even sigh out of frustration when Liz made a bad joke.

Liz wanted to spare Vendela but it seemed like at this point, whatever she did she would hurt her some way or another. Perhaps the best thing she could do was try to redeem herself in some small way, so that when Liz finally told Vendela about what she'd done it wouldn't be as bad. No, what she'd done would always be bad and monstrous, nothing could change that. Doing something good didn't cancel out the bad, but doing something bad didn't need to tarnish the good either. Liz wasn't kidding herself, she knew that nothing she did from this point forward could make up for the things she'd done, there were no excuses for the horrors she'd committed in her past. It was in the past and it was out of her control but if she did something good, if she tried to change for the better, perhaps with time Vendela could in some way forgive her.

Perhaps she could even forgive herself at some point.

If Vendela couldn't forgive her, Liz would accept that and leave her alone without any protests. Whatever happened, at this point, it was out of Liz's hands and she just had to see how it all played out. Which Liz didn't like, she didn't like being this much out of control. Just sitting and waiting wasn't something she was the best at.

"I don't know," Liz muttered. "I'll probably be around the Sanctuary. But if you need me just talk to Vendela and I'm sure she'll forward the message to me."

"Does she know?" Josefine asked.

Liz tensed up at those words.

"Know what?" Liz asked carefully.

"Know how much you love her?" Josefine said.

Liz shot her a fiery gaze.

"You don't show it, so I also assume you don't say anything," Josefine said. "But I can feel it. You can lie to her, to me, to yourself. But your feelings don't lie."

"It's none of your business," Liz hissed. "My feelings are not something for you to play with and my mind is not for you to dig around in to find weak spots, I warned you once, I won't warn you again."

"I can't help it," Josefine said.

"Well you can keep your goddamn thoughts to yourself then," Liz said bitterly.

"So you'd rather I know what you feel and not tell you about it?" Josefine asked.

"Yes," Liz said.

"Interesting," Josefine said. "But fair enough I suppose."

"Anything else or can I leave now?" Liz asked with an edge in her voice.

"You can leave," Josefine said.

Liz opened the door and walked out into the large room, immediately looking around trying to see where Vendela and Albin had gone but as she scanned the room, she couldn't see them. Liz quickly walked up to Tess and she could see the caution in her eyes as Liz got closer.

"Where's Vendela?" Liz asked.

Tess frowned slightly.

"She went up not long ago," Tess asked.

"Was she alone?" Liz asked.

"No, Albin was with her," Tess said.

Liz gripped Tess by the arm.

"They left?" Liz asked, now with a hint of panic in her voice.

"Yes?" Tess said slowly and looked down at where Liz was holding her. "And could you let me go?"

Liz let her go immediately.

"What's wrong with you?" Tess asked.

"Nothing," Liz said quickly. "I'll leave."

Tess nodded slightly and there was a look of slight confusion on her face, as if she didn't really understood what had just happened. Liz started moving towards the stairs when she heard an ear piercing, inhuman scream echo through the room. Liz quickly covered her ears and looked behind her, she saw everyone had cowered away from the source of the sound and most of them had a pained expression from the loud scream. The only one who stood up straight was Tess who had entirely white eyes, her mouth was opened unnaturally wide and she looked like a statue but the unnatural scream was clearly coming from her.

It lasted what felt like forever but in reality it was over in a few seconds. Tess's whole body relaxed and her bright blue eyes returned and it looked like she was going to fall over but she regained her balance at the last minute. Liz slowly lowered her hands from her ears, her eyes staring piercingly at Tess, waiting for her to speak. As did everyone else. Tess was pale and she was out of breath but she finally regained enough of her composure to speak. Josefine had opened her door as well and was waiting to see what had happened.

"Something terrible just happened," Tess mumbled. "So sudden..."

People had started to speak with Tess again, about how she should sit down and take it easy but Liz was already halfway up the stairs at that point, panic spreading through her body like a disease. She had no other thoughts in her head other than that Vendela had been left alone with Albin and suddenly there had been a banshee scream, which only meant one thing.

Someone had died.

Chapter 37

Liz felt as if the climb up the stairs went on forever and yet if someone had been watching her, it would have seemed like she was almost flying up them because of how fast she was moving. As she came out and saw the dark night sky she quickly looked around to see any sign of either Albin or Vendela but there was nothing, no signs of blood on the ground and no sounds of any voices in the distance. By the look of the sky, there were still some hours until the sun would rise which would give Liz time to find them. *"Where could they have gone?"* was Liz's only thought as she was spinning around.

Finally, she started running, she couldn't just stand there and think. As she ran, her mind was blank and all she could concentrate on was her surroundings. Could she hear anything? Could she see shapes in the alleys? Her senses were heightened and it kept her thoughts at bay for the moment.

The Sanctuary wasn't that big and if she was quick, she could search most of it in a short time. Especially as she knew most of it without fault, the perk of having been in there for so long. Without really knowing it, she'd started running towards the new Bar and halfway there she heard something from inside an alley. Liz stopped dead in her tracks and looked down the dark alley, at first she saw no one then there was a silhouette coming closer to her and within seconds Liz could see who it was.

It was Albin.

"Elizabeth, out for a midnight stroll are we?" Albin asked amused.

Liz didn't answer him, she just saw red and within a split second she was in front of him and had grabbed him by his shirt. A few seconds later Albin was laying on the hard ground as Liz had thrown him over her shoulder with all her force. His body had hit the ground with a crack but the only sound that escaped his lips was a low laughter. As Albin's body hit the ground, cracks spread like spider web in the concrete beneath him. Albin quickly rose and moved his shoulders and neck a little before he stared at Liz who'd walked closer to him.

"That wasn't very nice," Albin said with a smirk. "Didn't your mother ever teach you any manners?"

Liz swung a fist towards him but he dodged it easily which only made Liz even angrier and what perhaps the worst thing was, he wasn't even trying to hit her back. It was like he was made out of water, he moved so effortlessly and with such grace. Albin knew Liz's fighting style without fault, he knew every move she'd make even before she'd made them. Liz growled and showed her sharp teeth but he just smiled back at her, his equally sharp teeth poking through.

"You really want to fight me?" Albin asked with a smile, almost like he'd been waiting for this moment. "Because that can be arranged."

"Where's Vendela?" Liz hissed.

"Vendela?" Albin said with a hint of surprise. "Is that what this is about?"

"There was a banshee scream," Liz said, her voice shaking from anger.

"I heard that," Albin said calmly. "What, you think I killed her?"

Liz once again swung her fist towards Albin and this time it found its mark. The punch hit him so hard it spun him out of balance and he fell face first to the ground.

For a few seconds, Liz herself was even a little surprised at the fact that she'd actually struck him.

There was total silence for a moment; Albin wasn't laughing anymore. Albin jumped onto his feet and when he looked at Liz again, his face was stone cold.

If there was anything worse than that smirk on Albin's face, it was when it was wiped off his face. For a split second, Liz had the instinct to just run away. That look on his face, that killer look, Liz had seen it so many times before. It meant he would no longer hold anything back, and Liz had seen what he could do, what he could destroy when he wanted to.

After all, he'd destroyed her more than once.

But the anger inside of Liz at this moment outweighed any fear she had of him. He couldn't do anything to her anymore, she'd learned and grown, at least that was what Liz told herself over and over.

"I didn't kill her," he said with a cold monotone voice. "I left her at the new Bar."

"So who was the banshee scream for?" Liz asked angrily.

Albin shrugged.

"People die in here all the time," Albin said. "I'm sure a corpse will show up sooner or later."

Liz walked up close to Albin so they could almost touch.

"I gave you a free hit," Albin said coldly but the shadow of a smirk on his face. "I suggest you leave before I repay the favor."

"You could try," Liz said low.

The smile spread across his face once more.

"Try? Do you just have a bad memory or are you so deep in denial?" Albin asked amused. "I tore you to shreds last time, but if you insist I'd be happy to do it again."

Liz didn't break eye contact with Albin, but she swallowed hard at his comment; she remembered.

"If I go to the Bar and Vendela isn't there I will-..." Liz started, ignoring Albin's comment.

"Yes, you'll find me, you'll hurt me, yadda yadda," Albin said. "You're so predictable Elizabeth. You always were. It's really starting to get boring, you know."

Liz clenched her jaw and held Albin's cold blue gaze for a short while. Liz turned around to go towards the Bar when Albin spoke again.

"She's very lovely," Albin said. "Lovely company."

"Stop!" Liz roared. "I am not letting you inside my head again to screw me up!"

"Elizabeth," Albin said softly.

Liz glanced over at him and the smile on his face had only widened.

"I never left," he added.

Liz shot him a sharp gaze and violently shook her head.

"I'm not doing this," Liz said, she'd intended for her voice to be strong and confident but instead she almost whispered. "I'm not doing this."

Albin laughed.

"Vendela is strong, driven, intelligent," Albin said, ignoring Liz comment. "And most importantly, she's *good*."

Liz said nothing, not trusting her own voice at this point.

"So what lies did you tell her to get together with you?" Albin asked with a malicious tone. "She can't possibly know the real you, if she did-…"

"The real me?" Liz asked, her voice shaking. "The real me died centuries ago."

"*I'm no longer a person, I'm rage bottled up inside of a walking corpse,*" Liz thought.

"No, you were reborn centuries ago," Albin said with a smirk. "The real you, Liz."

"Shut up," Liz snapped. "Shut up."

"Why would Vendela fall in love with someone like you, unless every word that has come out of your mouth has been lies?" Albin asked almost with a laugh.

Liz was deadly silent for a few seconds, his words had hit it's mark and Albin knew it.

"I never lied to her, not when we were together," Liz said coldly. "Now this discussion is over."

Liz turned to leave once again.

"Don't you want to know what we talked about?" Albin asked.

Liz quickly stopped.

"No," Liz muttered.

"Come now Elizabeth, at least a part of you has to be a little curious," Albin said.

Liz sighed deeply, she wanted to leave; to end this discussion but this was how it always went. It was like no matter what she couldn't get away from him, she told herself that he had no power over her anymore, that she'd learned. It was obvious she hadn't, or his words wouldn't affect her the way they did.

It was like Albin's words were like a rope, tying her and making it impossible for her to leave no matter how much she wanted to. Liz could struggle all she wanted, but once his rope was around her, she was stuck.

"About me I guess," Liz finally said.

"Not exactly," Albin answered. "We talked about her mostly and just a little about me. But oh the things I could have told her about you."

Liz didn't say anything in response but she could hear his footsteps coming closer.

"What would she say if she knew what you tried to do to me the last time we met? Or the time before that?" Albin asked with a smirk. "Or maybe some of the things we've done together? We've had such great times together, I'm sure Vendela's dying to hear about it."

Liz was silent for a few seconds and even though she was actively trying not to look at him, she could hear how he was circling her. She could feel his gaze burn on her skin.

"She would hate me," Liz said, trying not to sound too emotional. "But she would perhaps understand a little if I told her about the things you've done to me."

"What I've done to you?" Albin asked innocently. "You make it sound like something bad."

Liz finally looked up at him in disbelief.

"You think the things you've done to me have been good?" Liz asked, her voice shaking.

"Good? No. Necessary? Yes," Albin said. "Nothing great was ever accomplished by doing it the 'good' way. You have to break a few eggs to make an omelet."

"None of the things you did were for my sake," Liz spat out. "Don't you *dare* try and put that on me. You did it because you like to see people suffer, to make them suffer."

Albin chuckled.

"You always were so dramatic, " Albin said and rolled his eyes. "If what I've done to you is so horrendous, if I am such a villain and you are such a victim, why haven't you told Vendela about us? Why haven't you told her about what I've done to you?"

Liz opened her mouth, closed it and then opened it again before answering.

"I'm not a victim *anymore*," Liz said, putting all the emphasis on the last word.

"*You destroyed me but I let you do it. And I haven't told Vendela because I am ashamed; ashamed of the person you made me. If I'd been stronger, I would have resisted you. If I'd been stronger I would have been a survivor, now instead I'm just a villain like you.*" Liz thought bitterly.

"And I'm not telling Vendela," Liz lied. "Because I'm not dragging her into this mess, I want to keep her as far away from you as possible."

"Or as far away from the truth about you as possible," Albin said with a smirk as he stopped right in front of her, tilting his head to the side.

Liz clenched her jaw and her hands formed into fists, she had nothing to say to his comment. Because perhaps he was right to a certain extent, Liz wanted to keep Vendela away from Albin but she was afraid; as always. Afraid people would learn the truth, afraid Vendela would learn the truth. With quick steps, before Albin could say anything else, Liz pushed past him. Albin was obviously done with her, Liz knew that he could have easily roped her back if he'd wanted to but he stayed silent. It felt as if there was a stone sitting on her chest as she walked with heavy steps.

Liz didn't trust Albin but she hoped that he for once was telling the truth and that Vendela was fine. Liz wasn't sure on how she'd react if she wasn't.

Chapter 38

Liz didn't run towards the Bar but she walked faster than she usually did. A part of her dreaded coming to the Bar because she was so afraid that Albin was lying to her and she didn't want to see Vendela's dead body. The mere thought of that terrified Liz and she wasn't even sure what seeing that would unleash inside her.

Albin had lied to Liz more times than she could count, she wasn't even sure if he was capable of telling the truth.

Finally Liz stopped outside of the Bar, it was closed and she couldn't hear anything from inside or around her. With a lump in her stomach and with a shakier hand than she would have liked, she knocked on the door and waited. The silence seemed to stretch on forever and it felt as if Liz was standing outside the door for hours.

Finally it opened and Vendela stood inside with a slightly confused expression. Before Liz could stop herself she had thrown herself at Vendela and was holding her in a tight hug.

"You're not dead," Liz whispered.

"Ehm, no," Vendela said slowly. "Liz, what's wrong with you?"

Liz finally let go of Vendela and stared into her eyes, almost regretting having hugged her so out of the blue. It must have been strange and maybe even uncomfortable for Vendela but the relief of seeing her alive had just made Liz lose control slightly. She couldn't hide the relief and the care in her eyes.

"I-I… I thought you were dead," Liz said slowly.

"What?" Vendela asked, frowning slightly.

"The banshee scream," Liz said.

"Oh yeah, Albin and I heard that," Vendela said. "But why did you think it was me who'd died?"

"Because you were with Albin," Liz said low.

"What, you don't think I can handle myself?" Vendela asked.

"What?" Liz asked, confused.

"Why did you assume he'd killed me and not the other way around?" Vendela asked.

Liz frowned, this wasn't how she'd expected the conversation to go.

"Because… You wouldn't just kill him," Liz said.

"In self defense then," Vendela said. "Do you think because I've spent a lot of time behind the bar counter that I can't defend myself?"

"That's not what I'm saying at all," Liz said. "I know you can handle yourself. I know you can fight. But that's not what this is about. This is about Albin taking advantage of your weaknesses, of him tricking you into feeling safe and then stabbing you in the back. Albin isn't that strong but he's resourceful and cunning."

"Have you lost against him?" Vendela asked a lot calmer.

Liz was silent for a moment and clenched her jaw.

"Yes," Liz said bitterly. "I have."

There was a short silence before Vendela sighed lightly.

"Okay, I don't know what's between you two," Vendela said. "But he's been nothing but nice. Despite the things you've done and said."

"He likes to keep that act up for a while," Liz muttered. "Sooner or later you'll see the real him. Even if it's only before you all die when he sells out the whole rebellion to the humans."

Vendela shook her head slightly.

"I'm sorry," Liz said. "For barging in here like this. I was just… Worried."

Vendela glanced at Liz and she could see uncertainty in her eyes, almost like she wasn't entirely sure if she'd hear her correctly.

"Just… I know you don't trust me or believe me," Liz said. "But please, believe me when I say that Albin is bad news. I know him. I know the real him and I know that he's willing to do anything to get what he wants."

"Like you?" Vendela said. "Like you barging in to get Ami without thinking about the consequences? Or like you watching people die so you can say to yourself that you followed your rules?"

Liz was silent for a moment.

"We're similar in more than one way, for a reason," Liz said low. "I know that. But… If I'm bad, he's worse. He doesn't care about anyone or anything except himself."

"And I do" Liz thought to herself. *"Even though I've tried for so long not to care."*

"Just be careful around him alright?" Liz said. "I'm not saying you should beat him up or even throw him out of your rebellion. Just keep an eye on him."

Vendela stared at Liz and she detected no lies or dishonesty and she sighed lightly.

"Okay," Vendela said. "I'll take your warning."

"Thank you," Liz said with relief.

Silence.

"So what did Josefine say?" Vendela asked.

Liz shrugged.

"She'll contact me when she has something for me to do," Liz said. "But I said I wouldn't do anything without knowing exactly what I'm doing. She doesn't trust me."

Vendela frowned slightly.

"But that's fair enough I suppose," Liz said and tried to smile. "I don't seem to have anyone's trust anymore."

"Liz," Vendela said low.

Liz looked up and into Vendela's gray eyes.

"I am really glad you changed your mind," Vendela said with honesty in her voice. "Even if you partially did it for yourself it shows tha-…"

"I'm not an entirely lost cause?" Liz said with a lighthearted voice but she swallowed hard.

Vendela didn't say anything but only nodded ever so slightly.

Liz picked at the skin around her nails and cleared her throat.

"I'll go," Liz said. "I'll leave you alone."

Before Liz moved Vendela had leaned down and gently kissed her on her forehead. As Liz felt Vendela's cold lips on her skin, she closed her eyes and sighed. For just a second it felt as if her chest had been ridden of some of its burdens.

"Tell me how Ami is doing later alright?" Vendela said.

Liz nodded slightly.

"I hope she wakes up soon," Vendela said.

"Me too," Liz said. "Or I'm going to have to visit Mr. Greenlund again."

"Don't do anything drastic," Vendela said. "Promise you won't do anything rash."

"If I promised that it would be a lie," Liz said half jokingly. "But I'll try to restrain myself."

Liz smiled weakly towards Vendela but she saw something in her eyes. They knew each other too well and Liz knew when Vendela was thinking about something. There was something bothering her and Liz wasn't sure if she was in any state to talk about whatever was on Vendela's mind right now. Whatever it was, Liz bet it had something to do with her and if that was the case. It couldn't be anything good. Liz turned around to leave but she didn't get far.

"Why didn't you tell me about your curse before?" Vendela asked.

Liz sighed deeply and was silent for what felt like an eternity. She kept her back towards Vendela as she started to speak.

"I was… I was afraid you'd hate me." Liz said. "Afraid you'd look at me with disgust and horror. It's not something you just tell over dinner."

"We were together for fifty years," Vendela said. "You never trusted me enough to tell me?"

"It's not about trust!" Liz said, her voice slightly raised.

Liz swallowed hard and it felt as if she had a lump the size of a baseball in her throat, making it hard to breathe.

"If you didn't know," Liz started again, her voice slightly shaking. "If you didn't know what I'd done I could pretend… I could pretend for a short while that I was better… That I was a person you deserved… Not this monster."

"You're not a monster," Vendela said as a fact.

Liz closed her eyes and as she heard those words leave Vendela's mouth all she could see was all the awful things she'd done flash before her eyes, all the things Vendela didn't know about but perhaps most astonishing, all the things Vendela did know about. Liz couldn't fathom how Vendela didn't see her as a monster or as evil, it was beyond Liz.

How many times had she heard people tell her that she wasn't a monster? She'd heard she was a monster a lot more, that was for sure. And she'd heard it mostly from herself. Liz wondered if she could ever believe Vendela? She wondered if she could ever think of herself not as a monster? If she could ever earn that privilege.

Liz knew a lot of creatures who were called monsters and who were far from it, and many humans who were the real monsters but were never called it just because they were human.

"I am sorry that I deceived you, lied to you, kept you in the dark," Liz said. "I'm sorry about it all. Not that that changes anything."

"Liz," Vendela said softly.

"You're too kind, Liz said low. "I know you can't help it."

"Kindness isn't a weakness," Vendela said.

"No," Liz said slowly. "Maybe it isn't."

Liz flashed her a sad smile before she left the Bar.

Chapter 39

Liz exited the Bar and as she saw the sky she knew there was only an hour or two before the sun would be up so she made her way back towards Katarina's house, still with that lump in her throat that didn't seem to want to go away. There was such a big part of her that hated trying to be nice and caring and sharing, that part hated it so much that it was physically painful at times. And afterwards it always left her anxious that others now knew the truth about her, even if it was just one truth in a bigger scheme. Telling people one thing about herself felt as if she was baring herself naked in front of them.

And those feelings made it hard for her to be really kind, harder than it should be. If she was excessively kind she often retreated into sarcasm quickly or said something nasty, it was like she couldn't help it. But the other part of her, wanted to change so badly, wanted to be good so badly and Liz thought that that part of herself was why she'd come out of the cellar before, why she'd agreed to meet with the rebel leader. The reason she did things she perhaps did not entirely want to do, like breaking her rules.

There was a war in Liz's head and she wasn't sure on which side was winning.

As Liz came out to the main street again, the first thing she saw was that Katarina's door was wide open once again. Liz didn't think anything of it, Katarina must have woken up and opened the door for Liz to enter, like she'd done before. It wasn't until she came closer that she realized that something was very wrong. She saw a blood trail coming from Katarina's apartment and leading towards the gate and from the look of it, it was fairly fresh. Liz had stopped dead in her tracks at the sight of the blood, all her other thoughts and concerns were blown away in the wind.

"No," Liz whispered low to herself but still she didn't move towards the open door.

Liz was just staring at the blood trail, she didn't want to look through the door or approach it because she knew what she would see and by not looking at it meant she could escape it just a little longer; she could pretend that everything was fine.

It felt as if she was standing out there for hours until she finally moved her stiff body towards the apartment. The room was destroyed with what looked like bullet holes in the walls and dark burn marks on the floor and door. There had been a battle here and it wasn't hard to figure out what had happened. Townies must have come and taken her and Katarina had put up a fight and Liz sincerely hoped that the blood trail was from one of the townies and not from Katarina. *"People have disappeared but so few and far apart that no one noticed at first."* Katarina's words echoed in her head.

Liz remembered the banshee scream, someone had died and it had to be someone from this fight but Liz refused to believe that it was Katarina who had died. It would have been pointless for them to come here just to kill her and take her dead body, they must have wanted her alive.

As Liz had entered the apartment and looked around her mind shifted gear, what about Ami? Liz rushed through the mess and tore open the closed bedroom door and to Liz surprise yet relief, Ami was laying on the bed, sleeping as if nothing had happened. Liz sighed slightly, the townies must have come for Katarina and when she put up a fight they must have just taken her and left without looking around.

As Liz was staring at Ami she wasn't sure on what to do, she didn't know if Katarina was hurt or where they'd taken her. And with her ties cut with Lady Morgana, she had no one outside to ask for information. At this point there was nothing Liz could do and it made her feel useless.

Liz gave Ami a last glance before she exited the bedroom and closed the door behind her, when she saw the destroyed room again it filled her with rage. The room was already trashed, it wouldn't matter if Liz took out her anger and frustration on it as well. Liz lifted one of the chairs from the ground and threw it into the opposite wall before she then picked up the table which was almost torn in half and slammed it in the ground.

"You're ruled by your heart and impulses" Vendela's voice popped up inside her head and it strangely calmed her down and she sank down in the one chair that wasn't broken. There was no point in destroying things, it wouldn't solve anything except make Liz look like a lunatic who couldn't think because she was so riddled with emotions. Emotions she hated having, were ashamed of having.

Liz rubbed her eyes and tried to think but her head was muddled and when she finally opened her eyes again, they caught a glimpse of something on the ground. Carefully Liz picked up the piece of paper, it had bloodstained finger prints on it and there wasn't much written on the note.

"If you want the witch returned, give us you in exchange. You have until tomorrow's sunrise. Knock three times on the gate."

Liz just stared at the words but it was like she didn't understand, like she was trying to read a foreign language until it finally sunk in. It wasn't just any townies who'd taken Katarina, it must have been Lady Morgana's forces. The woman she'd let go was the only one who knew what Katarina looked like properly and Liz had told them to leave the blood here. It was revenge for what Liz had done, for breaking all ties and for killing that other woman, and she knew they didn't really want Katarina or hurt her. They just wanted Liz and they must have thought it easier to capture one young girl and exchange her for Liz, than actually go out and hunt her down themselves. They must have met more resistance than they'd thought.

Liz scrunched the paper in her hand and she felt strangely empty. This stupid human girl who'd help Liz with everything she'd asked. Liz had told her she would hurt her, that she was bad luck and would get her killed. If only at least one of them had listened to her. Liz stared out the open door, the sun would rise in about half an hour and Liz knew what she had to do.

She didn't like it, it went against every instinct in her body and she would have to force herself to do it. But there was no escaping it, not if she wanted to try and redeem herself. Not if she really wanted to try and change.

Liz just had to do one thing first.

Chapter 40

With quick steps and with more confidence than she'd had in years, Liz walked back towards the new Bar. There were only minutes left until the sun rose but she didn't concern herself with that right now, it wouldn't kill her after all. In a way, Liz was more sure of what she was about to do than most things, and in another way she knew that she was making one of the biggest mistakes of her life. Which said a lot.

Liz knocked hard on the Bar door and Vendela quickly opened the door and without saying anything Liz slid in between the door crack. Vendela frowned slightly but said nothing as she closed the door behind her.

"Why are you ba-…?" Vendela asked.

"They've taken Katarina," Liz said with a matter of fact voice and reached over the crumpled together piece of paper.

With shock more than anything else on Vendela's face, she took the piece of paper and the confusion seemed to grow in her eyes.

"Why do they want you?" Vendela asked with a pinch of panic in her eyes.

Liz opened her mouth to speak but she couldn't say it, she couldn't tell Vendela about Lady Morgana and what she'd done. Not when this might be the last time she would ever see Vendela. If Liz gave herself over to Lady Morgana it meant that she couldn't be here for the rebellion which meant that she couldn't look out for Vendela and she might die. And even if the rebellion failed, Vendela would likely be executed for treason and Liz would be away because she had made some horrendous mistakes.

If not telling Vendela the truth made her a monster, she would gladly accept it this time around.

Liz wanted to spare Vendela's feelings and Liz promised herself that if she by some miracle would see Vendela again, she would tell her everything. No more secrets, no lies. Only the pure, horrible and bloody truth.

"I don't know," Liz finally said with a thick voice. "Maybe it's Mr. Greenlund for what I did in the Funhouse?"

"But why would they take Katarina?" Vendela asked.

"They must have thought it was easier to take a teenager than me," Liz said.

"But do they really think you're gon-…" Vendela started but her voice faded as her eyes met Liz golden.

There was an eerie silence in the air.

"You didn't come here to tell me about this did you?" Vendela said, her voice sounding uncharacteristically fragile. "You came to say goodbye."

"Yeah," Liz said, almost inaudible.

"You can't do this," Vendela said and shook her head.

"I'm the reason they took her-…" Liz started.

"Skip the heroic bullshit," Vendela said. "You're doing this because you feel guilty and I understand that but you can't-…"

"Damn right I feel guilty!" Liz said with a raised voice. "She's a child, Vendela! And I dragged her into my mess! I don't *want* to do this, believe me I don't. But I *have* to."

"No, you don't," Vendela said.

"I can't die," Liz said. "She can and they will surely kill her if I don't give myself up."

Vendela walked up to Liz and gently grasped her face.

"You can do more good in here for the rebellion than in some prison," Vendela said, her voice thick. "Stay and after the break out we'll find her together I promise-…"

"They don't want her!" Liz said angrily and Vendela let go of Liz's face. "Why would they keep her when they realized I'm not coming? She'll be dead within a day!"

"Liz, please stay," Vendela begged. "Please. Stay."

Stay. That word echoed inside Liz until it was all she could hear for a few seconds. That was the only thing Vendela had ever wanted from Liz. For Liz to stay with her.

"First unselfish thing I'm doing and you're telling me not to do it," Liz said and laughed low. "What has the world come to?"

Vendela shook her head with sorrow in her eyes and bit her lower lip.

"Tell me you understand," Liz said weakly. "Why I have to do this. Why I came to you when it would have been so much easier to leave without a word?"

Vendela had her back turned to Liz and refused to speak.

"Because I owe you the truth about where I'm going," Liz said when she noticed Vendela wasn't going to say anything. "And you deserve a goodbye this time around."

Silence.

"And I can't die," Liz said and tried to laugh. "I'll be fine."

"They're gonna hurt you," Vendela said low. "If they know or find out you can't die they'll-…"

"I know," Liz said. "And honestly… I'm a little scared."

Vendela turned back to Liz and she looked more shocked than anything else at first.

"I've been… At the mercy of men who's only mission was to see how far they could go before," Liz said low. "How much they could hurt me until it drove me insane. Test the boundaries of my immortality. And it scares me to death that I'm possibly going back to that with open arms."

"Liz," Vendela said with a sad frown on her face. "Let me help you."

"You can't," Liz said. "There is nothing you can do for me at this point."

"I'm just supposed to stand aside and watch you give yourself up to the townies?" Vendela asked almost desperately. "Knowing that they will-…"

"Yes," Liz said. "You'll be fine. You're strong, you don't need me."

There was a harsh silence and Liz closed her eyes for a short while before she spoke again.

"Could you do something for me?" Liz asked and she tried to push back the tears.

"What?" Vendela said almost to low to hear.

"If you make it out of here," Liz said and tried to smile. "Find me? If you don't I'll understand-..."

Vendela pulled Liz into a tight hug and Liz bit her lower lip before she hugged back with all her might and Liz buried her face in Vendela's neck and she took in the feel of her cold skin and the way Vendela smelt. Of something sweet and coppery. As they finally let go of each other, Liz picked up her box from her bag and looked at it for a short moment.

"Keep this safe for me would you?" Liz asked.

Vendela looked with disbelief at the box that was reached out towards her.

"Take it," Liz said. "And you can give it back to me once you find me alright?"

As Liz was giving her the box she knew that it might be the last time she saw Vendela and her box and if she lost both of them, she would probably lose herself all together. She would be lost forever. And yet Liz handed it over because she trusted Vendela and even though she had the nagging and terrifying feeling that Vendela might get killed, there was something else as well, belief and hope that she would not, and that she would find her.

These strange feelings of hope, trust and belief which had escaped Liz for so long all came rushing back as she stared into Vendela's gray eyes. There was a shadow of a smile on Liz's face, so this was what it felt like to open yourself up to someone? To lay your life and trust in someone's hands and fully believe they wouldn't betray you. But it also made the thought of leaving Vendela harder.

Vendela took the box in her hands as if she was holding something sacred and fragile and she might as well have been holding Liz's heart.

Liz cleared her throat and glanced back at the door.

"I'll be going, if the weather allows it," Liz said.

Vendela gripped Liz by the arm.

"Please stay a little longer," Vendela said pleadingly. "I've lost you twice before, why must you rush the third? It said you had until the next sunrise, can't you stay until nightfall at least?"

"I thought you were mad at me?" Liz said with a weak smile. "That you hated me."

"Stop," Vendela said. "I am mad, I've been mad for so long that it feels like poison in my veins. But I can't hate you, even if I should. I just can't."

"Perhaps it would be best for everyone if you did," Liz said half as a joke, but there was truth in it as well.

"We don't get to decide who we fall in love with," Vendela said sadly.

Liz was silent for a moment but with the shadow of a smile on her lips yet with a light frown on her forehead.

"You're right that we don't get to decide who we fall in…" Liz said but choked on the word love. "But we do get to decide what to do with that… That care. You shouldn't care for someone that hurts you, you shouldn't forgive someone that hurts you."

"Liz," Vendela said low.

"I am serious," Liz said before Vendela could continue. "Our relationship was never healthy, because of me. I know alright? And I honestly just want the best for you and… And the best for you would probably be to throw away my box and forget about me once I leave."

Silence.

"I shouldn't have asked you to find me," Liz said. "It's selfish of me. I do want to be with you but not at your expense. Whether I want it or not, I destroy everything I touch."

"Stop it," Vendela said with force.

Liz quickly shut her mouth, preparing herself for whatever Vendela was going to say. Preparing herself to hear Vendela agree.

"I'm not a child Liz," Vendela said. "I've known since the moment I met you that you've been troubled, it doesn't take a genius to figure out that something's haunting you. I just never knew what it was but you know what? I don't care, I never cared. Yes, you're angry at times, you're harsh and you push people away. But you know why I stayed for so long?"

Liz couldn't answer.

"It wasn't because I was afraid of you, or even that I thought you might change," Vendela said. "I stayed because I saw that those traits weren't really you. They were a facade, they're symptoms from the horrors you've lived through. Of the ghosts that haunts you."

Pause.

"I stayed because every single time push came to shove, you stood beside me," Vendela said. "You could say no at first but you always changed your mind. I would have left you, no matter how much I loved you, if I thought you were poisonous or if you were hurting me in any real way. And because you never once made me unhappy when we were together, sure irritated, upset even. But not unhappy. And I can take harsh words because I can deal them out as well. I can take anger because I feel it too. I could take anything you threw at me."

"Until I left you," Liz said low.

"Yes," Vendela said. "And I was so angry with you for a long time. Do you know what it's like to see someone and feel both happy and sad at the same time?"

Liz shook her head, she wasn't sure why she was lying; she'd felt it. Every time she looked at Vendela she felt happy to see her face, yet sad because of what she'd done to her.

"It is…" Vendela said, her bottom lip shivered slightly. "Confusing beyond belief. You see them and you see someone that once made you so happy, but also someone who broke your heart. You start to wonder… Why would they do something like that to you? I've been wondering for so long, do I trust the Liz I knew and loved or should I stay away from the Liz that broke my heart and left me?"

Liz opened her mouth to say something but she had nothing to say, so she stayed quiet.

"I wanted to trust you at first, but little by little I started leaning towards staying away," Vendela said. "Because I couldn't see anything of the Liz I loved, I was afraid I'd lost you entirely. That you really had stopped caring. But here you are."

Liz frowned slightly and looked into Vendela's eyes.

"You're giving yourself up for someone else," Vendela said slowly. "Even though you know the consequences. That is an act of kindness, an act of mercy. It's selfless."

"None of those words have ever been used to describe me before," Liz said with a weak smile.

Vendela was silent for a moment and caressed the box slowly with her fingers.

"I'm going to keep your box," Vendela said seriously. "And I'm going to find you."

"You don't owe me that," Liz said. "You've done enough for me."

"You're right," Vendela said. "I don't owe you."

Liz didn't say anything in response.

"But I'm still going to do it," Vendela said. "I gave you information to help you save Ami because I care about you. Because I don't want you to give up on your humanity, to give up on yourself. If you're saving Katarina for selfless reasons, I'm going to give you some hope to hold on to. I don't want to lose you."

"I still can't die," Liz said slowly.

"That's not what I meant by losing you," Vendela said seriously.

Liz glanced down onto the floor but quickly looked up again with a smile masking pain.

"I'll stay," Liz said. "For a couple of hours."

Liz saw the shadow of a smile on Vendela's lips. The reason why Liz wanted to leave as soon as possible was because she wasn't sure that she could force herself to leave if she stayed with Vendela for to long, it was hard enough as it was. Liz was afraid she'd change her mind and that wouldn't be good for anyone. But she'd agreed because she knew that Vendela understood that she had to do this. None of them liked it, but there was no other option.

Love. The word kept echoing in Liz's head. Vendela had said that word so many times and Liz had never uttered it because the word got stuck in her throat, it wasn't just a word for her, it was an unclimbable mountain. And after everything they'd been through, Liz couldn't understand that Vendela still perhaps in some way loved her. Despite everything she'd done, everything she said and perhaps the biggest obstacle.

Vendela had loved Liz even when she'd hated herself. And to love someone who doesn't feel like they deserve to be loved is something special.

Chapter 41

During the entire day they never spoke a word, they didn't need to. The silence was comforting and calming and the only thing they'd been doing was laying down in Vendela's small bed embracing each other, barely moving. Every time Liz glanced over at Vendela there was a stabbing pain in her chest but she tried to ignore it. How had she gotten to this point? The past week, no, the past months were like a haze to her and five months ago she would have laughed if anyone had said this would have happened. Because Liz wasn't supposed to care. And yet, by the smallest changes and words, it had led her here. Exchanging her own life for someone else. It felt strange for her to even think about it. And what amazed her more was that the spell book or her curse had nothing to do with the fact that she wanted to help Katarina. It hadn't even popped into her head until much later.

Liz hoped that Katarina would try to keep her end of the bargain, even if Liz couldn't complete her deal. Maybe saving Katarina's life would make up for not helping the rebellion as she had promised.

The hours flew by and before anyone of them realized it, the sun had set and Liz had to leave. Liz rose from the bed but her body felt stiff and it was fighting her, all her body wanted to do was to lie down next to Vendela again but she couldn't. If she didn't do this she would never forgive herself, if she didn't do this, there would be no chance of redemption.

Ultimately, in a strange way, she did it for herself. To save herself.

"Do you really have to go?" Vendela asked low.

Liz closed her eyes and tried to concentrate on remembering what Vendela's voice sounded like. Liz couldn't even answer Vendela or look back at her.

"Maybe they just want to talk with you?" Vendela said in a pathetic attempt to lighten the mood.

"Yeah, because kidnapping a child and keeping them hostage in exchange for yourself, sounds just like they just want to talk," Liz said bitterly.

Silence.

"I'm sorry," Liz muttered. "I'm gonna go now."

"Do you want me to go with you?" Vendela asked.

"No," Liz said quickly. "I'm not getting you involved in this mess as well. And… And I don't want you to see it. I don't want you to remember me being taken away, I want you to remember me walking out the Bar door of my free will, like I will walk back at any moment."

Short pause.

"Take care of Ami for me, okay?" Liz said, changing the subject. "She's still in Katarina's apartment, unconscious. Take her here, take her to the rebel base. Just… Take care of her okay?"

"Okay," Vendela said low.

Liz started to move towards the door when Vendela spoke again.

"Thank you," Vendela said softly.

Liz stopped abruptly.

"For what?" Liz said uncertainly.

"For saying goodbye," Vendela said. "And I will find you. I promise."

Liz couldn't help but to laugh low but there were tears in her eyes and she was glad she had her back turned to Vendela. Even though it was Liz who had asked Vendela to find her, she found it unbelievable that she promised she would do it as well. It was like Liz had said it as a last act of trust but with no real hope of it happening.

"I've left you twice," Liz said. "Now a third time. Why would you want to find someone who just leaves you?"

Short silence.

"Because at one point you might stop running," Vendela said. "I don't want you to change Liz, I just want you to see yourself in a different light. You don't think you deserve to be saved, you don't think you deserve happiness. But you do. And so do I. Our happiness might not be with each other, but we still deserve it."

Pause.

"I don't think I'll ever stop being angry or upset with you for leaving," Vendela said honestly. "But that doesn't mean I can't forgive you, if you earn it. And for you to have a chance to earn that, we have to see each other again."

Liz flashed Vendela a weak sad smile before she spoke with a low voice.

"Thank you," Liz said sincerely.

"For what?" Vendela asked, slightly confused.

"For every time you've forgiven me," Liz said. "And for every time you haven't."

Vendela slowly moved up to Liz, she carefully placed her hand on Liz's cheek and the touch alone almost made her legs betray her.

"Can I kiss you?" Vendela asked low, her voice sounded so fragile and uncertain, it broke Liz's heart.

Silence.

"If you do, I don't think I could ever make myself leave your side again," Liz said, her voice thick.

Vendela opened her mouth to say something, there was a weak frown on her face but in the end she just closed her mouth without another sound escaping her lips and her hand fell from Liz's face.

Liz licked her lips and there was a twitch in the corner of her mouth but she couldn't bring herself to smile sincerely, she quickly exited the Bar without saying another word.

Liz couldn't get Vendela's voice out of her head and for once she didn't want to get it out either. She wanted to remember her voice, how it sounded when she was sad, mad, happy. Liz wanted to remember the tone in her voice as she said her name. Voices were the one thing Liz struggled to remember and they faded faster than she'd liked. She could see faces in front of her but there was no voice attached to them and that was the worst part of losing someone.

As Liz walked towards the large gate she didn't see another soul out on the street and as she passed the burnt down Bar she wondered what Josefine and Albin would say when they heard the news. Because Liz was sure that Vendela would tell them what happened. Josefine would probably be upset that Liz prioritized one creature over the greater good, Liz didn't think she'd understand the way Vendela did. Albin would probably say minimal about it but she knew it brought him pleasure to see her suffer.

After saying goodbye to Vendela and leaving the box with her it felt as if she had left a large piece of herself there. Which for once felt like a good thing, because whatever happened to her from now on, no matter what they did to her, there would be a piece of her still with good intentions waiting for her.

So Liz walked without much fear, Vendela's words fueled her forward even when her legs wanted to stop.

Vendela's voice filled her up, bringing a heat only ever matched by her rage; except now, there was no shame, only determination. It was as if Vendela was holding her hand in a tight grip, leading her forward.

Liz was afraid that if Vendela's voice slipped from her mind, even for a second; she would stumble and not go through with it. That Liz would retreat, run away as the coward she really was. Out of all the things Liz had ever done in her life, this was probably the bravest she'd ever been. She was scared, but she did not act on that fear as she usually did. Liz tried to face her fears, which made her brave.

Even if she couldn't really grasp that herself just yet.

Liz was afraid to relive some of her most horrible days but she would not give them the satisfaction to see her frightened. Liz would swallow her fear and she would get through this. And then she would kill anyone who had laid a finger on her or Katarina. Liz might be trying to redeem herself and become a better person, but that didn't mean that she would grow soft or weak.

Liz would destroy the ones who hurt her and the ones she loved, she would just stop destroying herself and the ones she loved.

The large gate loomed over Liz's short body and she knocked with three hard knocks and waited. As she heard that the gate was about to open Liz put up her hands and put them on top of her head.

Everything happened so fast, Liz had no thought of resisting but they had apparently not taken any chances. A dozen soundless shots were fired and hit Liz's body and she could feel the bullets like acid in her body.

Holy water bullets.

If just one or two had hit her she could have shaken it off quickly, but a dozen bullets sent her to her knees and she could see that her wounds weren't immediately healing and black blood was dripping onto the ground.

Then Liz heard shouting and footsteps all around her and a flashlight was shone in her face, making her squint and there were suddenly four pairs of arms gripping Liz and pulling her up from the ground. During all of this, Liz didn't move at all to resist or fight them, she just let it happen. There was a sharp pain in her neck and her eyes rolled back into her head and her sharp teeth came out.

The euphoria only lasted for a few seconds before the pain set in. The vampire blood coursed through her veins as she started to shake uncontrollably. The pain shoot from her neck down through her whole body, like someone had injected poison into her bloodstream and after another few seconds, Liz lost consciousness.

About the Author

L.A Egerbladh is a Swedish genderfluid queer author who has been writing their entire life. Born in 1995 in Sweden they spent most of their childhood lost in imaginative worlds of their own and always with a book in hand. They are also an avid cosplayer and does anything to chase the high of creativity.

Also by L.A Egerbladh

Feed the Fire

Feel The Pull. Answer The Call.

Anya, a young woman who keeps to the shadows, is drawn out into the light and learns the hard way that magic can never really die. Her days of thieving turns into a fight for survival.

James, an older man with a bad leg, passes the time tending to the sick and wounded. Some people see him as a saint, others whisper about darker secrets he holds.

Runa is haunted by her past with Anya. One choice Runa made drove them apart. She now works for one of the gangs in the Capitol, just trying to keep one step ahead of the Capitol guard.

Inara is a bright and upcoming guard; she is driven by a deep sense of right and wrong. But is it possible to hold on to morality in the face of destiny?

The Capitol is divided, the west side is filled with the rich and privileged. The east side is filled with the poor and forgotten. The Castle with the King stands in its middle.

Magic will come at a price... one they might not be willing to pay